L. BALLEW

His Ringsend Rose

Love on Tap Series

Second edition

ISBN (paperback): 979-8-9928281-0-8
ISBN (hardcover): 979-8-9928281-1-5

Editing by Nova Nox
Cover art by Aida Linnea

This book was professionally typeset on Reedsy.
Find out more at reedsy.com

For Mel, who loves Irish men and soccer as much as I do.

"Don't forget - no one else sees the world the way you do, so no one else can tell the stories that you have to tell."

CHARLES DE LINT

Contents

Regarding Irish Lingo   iii

Chapter One   1

Chapter Two   11

Chapter Three   20

Chapter Four   25

Chapter Five   32

Chapter Six   37

Chapter Seven   49

Chapter Eight   55

Chapter Nine   62

Chapter Ten   67

Chapter Eleven   76

Chapter Twelve   83

Chapter Thirteen   90

Chapter Fourteen   98

Chapter Fifteen   107

Chapter Sixteen   111

Chapter Seventeen   118

Chapter Eighteen   125

Chapter Nineteen   133

Chapter Twenty   141

Chapter Twenty-One   148

Chapter Twenty-Two   155

Chapter Twenty-Three   166

Chapter Twenty-Four   175

Chapter Twenty-Five   184

Chapter Twenty-Six   192
Chapter Twenty-Seven   201
Chapter Twenty-Eight   210
Chapter Twenty-Nine   223
Chapter Thirty   229
Chapter Thirty-One   239
Chapter Thirty-Two   247
Chapter Thirty-Three   259
Chapter Thirty-Four   267
Chapter Thirty-Five   274
Chapter Thirty-Six   283
Chapter Thirty-Seven   290
Chapter Thirty-Eight   300
Chapter Thirty-Nine   308
Chapter Forty   315
Epilogue   325
Bonus Content   331
What happens next?   332
Acknowledgments   339

Regarding Irish Lingo

First and foremost, I am *not* Irish. I have visited Ireland and spent countless hours researching, but I do not claim to be an expert by any means. My goal has always been to represent the lingo, people, places, and culture in my books as accurately and respectfully as possible. If anything written within these pages is considered offensive, please know it was unintentional. Much of the lingo used in His Ringsend Rose was learned from my short time in Ireland or https://www.theirishroadtrip.com/irish-slang-words/.

Chapter One

Norah

"Get up! Get dressed! We're going out!"

I stare, wide-eyed, at the dark-haired woman in my doorway. "I'm sorry, what?"

"You heard me," Myra says, her big brown eyes full of mischief as she plants her hands on her hips. "We're going out. You haven't gone out with us in *forever,* and I refuse to let you sit here on a Friday night like some kind of old lady."

"It hasn't been that long." I roll my eyes at her. "And besides, I have costumes to make tomorrow. The play is in two months, and I really need to focus on the gowns for the ballroom scene."

"Oh please," she says, flipping her hair over a shoulder. "You know as well as I do that you have them mostly completed. Do them next Saturday. *Please!*"

She's not wrong, but she doesn't need to know that.

Myra is the life of the party and the reason our group never lacks amusing stories. She always wants to go out, always enjoys a drink - or five - and always has guys falling all over her. We are polar opposites. I'm the quiet and reserved friend who keeps to myself and avoids large crowds as much as possible. Being surrounded by strangers makes me more anxious than normal. To keep my day-to-day anxiety in check, I design and create costumes. There's just something magical about being able to sketch something on paper, and then bring it to life. If my hands are busy, my mind is calm. My love for costume designing started as a little girl and evolved throughout the years until I decided that I wanted to make a career out of it. Now moms all over the city flock to me for their kids' dance recitals and Halloween costumes, and the local community theater requests my services regularly. On top of that, I'm currently working for the Department of Theatre at the University of North Carolina Wilmington as their Costume Designer.

At the age of twenty-one, I moved away from the Midwest town I called home and enrolled at UNCW. Before that, I spent the two years following high school caring for my ailing mother. When she passed away, I took another year off to settle her estate, travel, and heal. I wasn't just healing from losing my Mom, but from *the incident* too. I've always loved North Carolina, but being close to the ocean brings me peace. I can almost feel my Mom beside me each time I inhale the salty air.

"Myra, I really don't—" My front door flies open again, revealing a gorgeous blonde knockout. Amelia.

For fucks sake.

"Did she say no? I knew she would," Amelia says arrogantly like I'm not sitting *right here*.

"I'm not done convincing her yet!" Myra barks. "I told you to give me ten minutes!"

"There's no way you can convince her to go out with us in ten minutes!

2

You know you have to ease her into this stuff gradually," Amelia counters.

"Girls, please," I beg. "I really don't feel like it and I'm already in my sweats. I just poured a glass of wine and I'm getting ready to start the next episode of Outlander. Why don't you stay and watch it with me? You know, girl time!"

Please say yes. Please say yes.

The two intruders look at each other before facing me again. "No," they say together and reach for me.

Twenty minutes later, I'm donning dark blue skinny jeans and my favorite Kelly green V-neck t-shirt with my auburn curls hanging loosely around my face. I'm in the backseat of Amelia's car, watching out the window and listening to them argue over whether we're going to the pub or the dance club downtown. If it were up to me, I'd choose the pub in a heartbeat.

"You know," I hedge, "tonight *is* open mic night at O'Nelly's. I'm pretty certain the soccer team is going to be there."

"But we can't dance at the pub. I wore this outfit with the whole purpose of finding a hot guy and dancing," Myra huffs, pulling the visor down to check her reflection in the mirror.

"You can dance at O'Nelly's." I roll my eyes at her.

"Ugh. No thanks." She wrinkles her nose. "But maybe I can convince one of them to take me out tomorrow night!"

Amelia catches my gaze in the rear-view mirror and winks. "You know, I think Norah's right. Let's go to the pub tonight and the club tomorrow! They usually have ladies' night on Saturdays anyway."

Bingo.

"So it's decided," I announce gleefully, pulling my phone from my purse. "O'Nelly's it is. I'll text the others to see if they want to meet us!"

When these two get together, things tend to get a little crazy, so I'm going to need a buffer. Pulling up our group chat, I text Charlie and Layla.

Norah: *Hey, girls! Myra and Amelia kidnapped me and are taking me to O'Nelly's. Please come rescue me!*

Layla: *Ugh. Those jerks. Don't they know you're watching Outlander tonight??? Sorry, I'm in for the night. I work a double tomorrow. Lunch later this week?*

Norah: *Boo. Sorry about the double. Yes to lunch! xoxo*

Charlie will be my best bet. I love all of my friends with a passion, but Charlie has always been there for me. We grew up together in the Midwest. After everything happened, she tied up loose ends and moved to Wilmington six months after I did. I'll forever be in her debt for that.

Charlie: *Hey, girl! I'll meet you there! Just got off work, so I'm going to go change! Did you hear it's open mic night?!*

My lips curve into a smile. Like I said, she's always there for me.

Norah: *Yay! God knows I'll need a backup with these two! They wanted to go clubbing. I'm just thankful I talked them out of that!*

Charlie: *I got you, girl!*

Layla: *Do they even know you?*

Norah: *Right? When have I ever gone clubbing? No thanks.*

Layla: *Good luck! ;)*

Layla is one of those dark beauties with curves in all the right places, her Hispanic heritage shining through her dark hair, eyes, and tawny skin flawlessly. She somehow manages to rock every shade of lipstick known to man and is a wizard at eye makeup. I've been begging her to work in the Theatre Department with me as one of the makeup artists, but she keeps turning me down.

"Charlie is going to meet us there," I tell my traitorous friends up front.

"Scared to be alone with us?" Myra turns around in her seat and waggles her eyebrows.

"Absolutely," I deadpan.

Amelia laughs loudly. "Oh, Norie, you're cute. But I'm glad Charlie's coming too! I haven't seen her in ages."

We all have such crazy schedules. Myra, Amelia, and Charlie work full-time, while Layla and I work *and* go to school full-time. Finding a night where we're all free is nothing short of miraculous.

"Layla works a double tomorrow, so she can't come," I tell them.

"She needs to get out of there and find something else," Myra adds, still admiring her reflection. "I don't know how she manages that schedule with school."

I nod, even though I know she can't see me. "I know. She works so hard all the time. And her degree isn't even something she really enjoys."

"Then why is she doing it?" Amelia asks.

"She says it's because there are better job opportunities."

Of course there are better job opportunities in the IT field, but I have to question if it's worth it if she's miserable.

Myra lifts her phone to snap a selfie. "If she didn't have anything holding her back, what would she *want* to do?"

"Honestly, I don't know," I admit. "She's insanely talented with makeup application. She'd probably make a killing being a professional makeup artist or esthetician. I've begged her to apply for a position in my department, but she shrugs it off. I don't think she feels confident enough in herself."

"That's really sad," Amelia says, peeking over her shoulder before switching lanes.

"I agree," Myra replies, catching my eyes in the mirror. "Maybe she just needs more exposure to people who need her services. If she sees there's a market for that, it might encourage her to seek it out."

I grin in response. "That's a great idea! I'll talk to our department head about having her help with stage makeup for the play. If I can convince her we need the extra help, it won't be just a job to her."

"Agreed," Amelia says while swinging the car into a surprisingly vacant parking spot just outside of the pub.

We clamber out of the car and make our way toward the gilded pane-glass doors of O'Nelly's.

* * *

"Hello? Earth to Norah. Are you even paying attention to me?" Myra whines, waving a hand in front of my face.

"No, your majesty, I was not," I quip. "Were you saying something important?"

Amelia bursts out laughing. We're sitting in a corner booth near the stage, Myra complaining about the lack of mixed drinks while Amelia and I discuss getting a flight of the local craft brews. The place is packed, but the pub owner, Pat, is on stage plucking at a guitar and singing an old Irish jig. Being here always makes me think of my trip to Ireland. It was overwhelming going by myself, but I fell in love with the country and soon learned that I could manage just fine as long as I had a Guinness in hand and could find my way back to Temple Bar. I can't wait to go back.

"You bitches are so rude!" Myra glares at us before glancing around the room. "When do those soccer players go on stage? I call dibs on the hot one."

"The hot one? And which one would that be, My?" Amelia laughs.

"Whichever one I decide! You can have whoever is left over." She turns her nose into the air and waves a dismissive hand towards the stage.

"I hear you kidnapped poor Norie here!" Charlie says, appearing out of seemingly thin air and plopping herself down next to me. "You know Friday nights are for Outlander."

Both Myra and Amelia roll their eyes. They're clearly *very* remorseful.

"Charlie, she can't just stay sitting in that house every weekend. She's never going to meet anyone," Myra says.

"Well, maybe she doesn't want to meet anyone. Maybe she's satisfied with me. Ever think about that?" Charlie asks, leveling them with a playful scowl.

"Guys, I'm literally right here. I can hear you, ya know. And yeah, maybe Charlie is all I need in life. She understands me and doesn't make me do things that I *clearly* don't want to," I say with a pointed look in their direction.

The girls tease me relentlessly about not dating anyone, even knowing my history. I've gone out a time or two since being in North Carolina, but nothing ever lasted more than a single date. Myra opens her mouth to say something, probably highly inappropriate when the lights dim and Pat O'Nelly taps on the mic.

"Good evenin', friends! I'm so glad to be seein' ya in O'Nelly's tonight! We have a special surprise for ya! As some of you know, our very own UNCW

6

football team—no, not that rubbish American pigskin game, but the *real* football we play in my homeland—is here tonight…"

Cheers erupt all over the pub. Over in a corner closest to the stage, I can finally see where the team sits—half of them in their jerseys and the other half in t-shirts. Most of them whoop and holler and high-five each other while only a few remain silent. My eyes snag on one in particular. There is nothing *not* attractive about a soccer player, but this one has something extra. His hair is inky black, cut close on the sides but long enough on top to drape across his forehead. His sharp jawline is lightly stubbled and has me wondering what it would feel like if he nuzzled my neck…wait, what the hell? I shake my head to dislodge that line of thinking and turn back to the stage.

"Now, calm down!" Pat barks, his Irish brogue thickening the more agitated he gets. "As I was sayin', our boys here have agreed to perform a little ditty from the Green Isle to start Open Mic Night! Isn't that wonderful? Let's give them all a big welcome to O'Nelly's stage!"

Cheers explode once more as the team rises from their chairs and walks toward the stage. It's a small platform, so anyone not playing an instrument has to stand in front of it, much to the ladies' delight on the first row. The three players who had been silent at the table take to the stage, moving toward the instruments. The dark-haired mystery man grabs a guitar and sits on the bar stool at stage left while the other two—a tall guy with thick, wavy copper hair and matching beard, and a shorter guy with tousled brown hair—grab a violin and a harmonica.

"This should be interesting," Amelia whispers in my ear, making me snort in amusement.

"Look at that blond in the front!" Myra blurts out, eyes wide. "Look how ripped he is!"

She's not wrong. He's extremely handsome with the body of a Greek god, smiling like he knows exactly how good he looks too, and the girls closest to him aren't helping his ego any. As handsome as he is, my eyes keep getting drawn back to the guitarist. I try not to ogle random men, but *damn*, he's beautiful.

7

"Stupid," I mutter.

"What's stupid?" Charlie asks, brow raised.

"Oh, nothing. Just all these girls acting like these guys are superstars or something." I fold my arms on top of the table.

"Well, they kind of are. They did win Nationals last year," Amelia reminds me. She would know since she grew up playing sports and is a walking ESPN channel.

"True. But they're just people, like the rest of us," I say with a shrug,

"Oh, yeah? Is that why you can't take your eyes off the guitarist?" Myra asks loudly.

My face flushes as I shoot daggers at her. It's my biggest tell. I blush over literally everything. "Shut up! I was not staring. I was just trying to figure out how all of those guys are going to do any justice to Pat's song. That guy probably doesn't even know how to play the guitar."

Nice save, me.

Then the music starts, with the guitar no less, and it turns out I'm wrong. Very wrong. Tall, dark, and handsome strums gently at first but then picks up the pace. Somehow he manages to transport me right back to the streets of Dublin—music spilling out of the pubs, people laughing and singing loudly along. I'm completely mesmerized. It feels like a lifetime of music, but it's only a handful of seconds. The harmonica and fiddle join in, and I'm officially a goner.

Until the singing begins.

It's *horrible*. They're loud and off-key. Pat O'Nelly stands offstage with his fingers in his ears, grinning. Nothing makes Pat happier than bringing his homeland to this pub. That's why it's my favorite. There are pubs all over the Wilmington area, and each one boasts its authenticity, but Pat's is the real deal.

When he lived in Renvyle, Ireland, he owned a small pub with his wife, Ellie. He came to America after she passed away. His oldest son was getting his medical degree at UNCW at the time, so he moved over to be close to him and open up O'Nelly's. Above the polished mahogany bar, there's a black-and-white picture of Pat and Ellie when they were in their late twenties or early thirties. You can tell in the picture that Ellie was a redhead and full of the fire that accompanies it—I'm more than a little aware of that stereotype. Having been born towheaded and then progressing naturally to a shade somewhere between copper and auburn, I've heard every remark under the sun. Some playful, others downright perverted.

As the horrible rendition of "All For Me Grog" ends, everyone stands to applaud and cheer. Myra puts her fingers in her mouth and lets out a shrill whistle, quickly attracting the attention of the blond Neanderthal she set her sights on earlier. Amelia and I give each other a knowing look. She won't be leaving the pub with us tonight.

"I'm going to get another drink while the hordes are distracted. Want anything?" I ask, leaning into Charlie.

"Nah, I'm good! Mark has a bottle of wine waiting for me at home." She wags her eyebrows.

Charlie started dating Mark shortly after she moved to Wilmington. They met while volunteering at a local children's home, and it was love at first sight. They moved in together a few months later. I adore Mark; he's perfect for my quirky best friend. He encourages her free spirit while also keeping her grounded. It's a match made in Heaven.

I weave my way through the crowds toward the bar. My favorite bartender, Alicia, is pouring drinks tonight. Alicia is a no-nonsense kind of girl who never lets anyone hassle her but is always quick with a laugh. We've hung out a time or two away from the bar and always have a great time, but our schedules only seem to line up a couple of times a year. Unless I just happen to catch her behind the bar, like tonight.

"Norah!" Alicia shouts. "What did you think of that circus up there?"

Chuckling, I slide onto the stool in front of her. "The music was lovely. Not so sure about the singing!"

"Understatement of the year!" She laughs, her long black ponytail swinging behind her as she turns to grab a bottle of coconut rum. "What'll you have, dear?"

I glance at the tap. The flight with Amelia was good, but after hearing that Irish ditty, I need a Guinness in a bad way. And Alicia is an expert pourer. She learned from the best, after all.

"Guinness, if you please!"

"Coming right up!" She grins at me.

"A Guinness girl, I see," says a smooth voice behind me.

Chapter Two

Norah

I whirl around to see the blond Neanderthal from the soccer team looming
behind me.

"Um…yeah," I say nervously, looking down at the floor. God, please let
one of my friends come to the bar. It's not that I'm terrified of all men, just
the entitled ones who don't take no for an answer. Blondie is giving off
those vibes right now.

"Do you really like Guinness, or do you drink it just to attract attention?"
he asks, grinning wickedly.

My head whips up, and I gape at him. What the fuck? Did he really just
ask me that?

Myra appears suddenly, sidling up next to me.

"Hi, handsome. Norah here really does like that nasty tar. I'd be the one looking for attention. Now, why don't you buy me a drink?" She winks at me before looping her arm through his and leading him to the other end of the bar. *My hero.* I turn back to the bar to find Alicia holding my beer with a worried look on her face.

"You good? Was Mac giving you a hard time?"

"Oh. No, I don't think so. Just looking for some action." I roll my eyes.

"Well, don't let him scare ya. He acts intimidating but is all talk. He likes to think that because his name is Mac Flanagan it makes him Irish. The jackass is as far from Irish as they come!"

I laugh and sip the foam off the top of my drink.

"Now, Eamon, Rowan, and Teagan are another story. They truly are Irish." Alicia looks pointedly over my shoulder. I turn my head to peek, not so subtly. Coming up behind me are the three that played so beautifully on stage. And tall, dark, and handsome is even better up close. *Holy shit.* I might be drooling.

"Alright, Alicia?" asks the ginger-haired one in a lilting voice.

"Yeah, Ro. You? Good job up there tonight," she replies, cheeks turning pink. Can't say that I blame her.

"Thanks." He winks. "How about a pint of the black stuff, love?"

"You got it!" she replies quickly, whirling to the tap.

"Dammit, Ro! You did it again!" The shorter, brown-haired one curses. "You always make her so flustered that she forgets to ask Eamon and me what we want. It's absolute bollocks!"

My eyes immediately dart to the dark-haired guy. *Eamon.* I take a drink of my Guinness, trying to study him covertly. He's standing with his sinewy forearms resting on the bar, fingers intertwined and lips tipped up in a smirk as he listens to his two friends bicker back and forth. He's breathtaking. Taller than Teagan, but not quite as tall as Ro. Broad, muscular shoulders connect to biceps that look like they're about to bust out of the sleeves of his black t-shirt. The fabric stretches across the expanse of what I can only imagine is a sculpted chest and tapered waist. I'm taking a huge gulp of Guinness when his gaze lands on me. His brilliant blue eyes instantly lock with mine, and I stop breathing—then immediately start choking on my beer. *Fuck*. Nothing is worse than being caught ogling and then making a spectacle of yourself. All three men are now staring at me with wide eyes. Ro chuckles while Teagan continues to look at me with concern. To my absolute horror, Eamon reaches over and starts thumping me on the back like I'm a child.

I am completely mortified.

"Hey!" Alicia snaps as she sets Rowan's beer in front of him. "What are you doing to poor Norah?"

"I'm okay," I cough out. I'm pretty sure my face is actually on fire.

"No worries, Alicia. Just trying to keep your friend here from choking to death," Eamon says in what would be the most beautiful voice I've ever heard if not for the words that come out of his mouth next. "Looks like the Guinness is a little strong for her. Maybe you should give her something a bit watered down next time."

Bristling at the insinuation that I can't hold my drink, I turn to tell him exactly what I think of that comment when Alicia cuts in.

"You've never seen our girl drink, then. I reckon she could give you a run for your money, Eam."

The Irishmen swing their attention back to me, doubt marring their faces. *Assholes*. Trying to regain some of my dignity, I turn back to the bar and say something really stupid.

"Line 'em up, Alicia."

She stares at me for a moment before raising her arm in the air to beckon my friends. All of them rush over immediately.

"What's happening? Are we doing shots?" Myra asks hopefully.

"Looks like Eamon here has slighted Norah's honor and she feels inclined to demonstrate just how capable she is," Alicia informs them, one side of her mouth quirking into a smirk.

"Nor, are you sure you want to do this? You did say that you have to work tomorrow," Charlie says, her eyes begging me not to do this.

"Shut up, Charles!" Amelia says, calling her by the nickname she knows Charlie hates. "This is the most exciting she's been in months! Alicia put

13

her drinks on my tab!"

What the hell am I thinking? I haven't done this since I came back from Ireland, and it was not my finest moment.

"Uh, my apologies, lass, for questioning your drinking ability. I was only slagging you. Please don't feel like you need to prove yourself," the gorgeous Eamon drawls.

I glare at him. "Let's see if you can keep up, Irishman."

Three shots of Jameson and three Guinness draughts later, Eamon and I are surrounded by everyone in the pub. The supporters are divided equally with the women cheering for me, while naturally, the men are encouraging Eamon. So far, we're evenly matched in terms of drink consumption. I'm definitely feeling it, but I'm determined to show this cocky Irish bastard that I'm no prissy girl. My head is swimming, and Myra is making all sorts of remarks that have me laughing so hard my sides hurt. Alicia is pouring round four when Pat walks up and grabs the beer glasses from her.

"Now, listen here, you two," he says, looking at us disapprovingly. "I don't know what the feck is going on, but this isn't like either of you. You know I'm all for a lively drinking game or two, but when my two most sober customers are up here drinking like fish, it's time for me to step in. Now, go sit down and drink some water. Alicia, grab them some chips to soak up the alcohol. You eejits." He walks away shaking his head, and I suddenly feel like a child being scolded for tracking mud through the house.

While the crowd groans in disappointment, I'm thanking my lucky stars. Glancing over at Eamon, he doesn't even appear tipsy.

Damn Irish.

"Do you really feel that way, then?" he asks, eyes wide in amusement.

Shit. Did I just say that out loud?

"Yes, lass. You did," he chuckles.

Awesome.

"Uh, sorry. Must be the booze talking." I flush and look down at my feet.

He laughs loudly. "Eamon Kennedy."

I raise my head to see his hand outstretched in front of me. I gingerly take it and give it a quick shake. His grip is warm and firm, and I'm immediately imagining those hands on me in a less formal way. What is wrong with me? I clear my throat and introduce myself.

"Norah Grady."

"Sounds Irish to me," he says with a shrug. "No wonder you're able to keep up with me."

I snort a laugh and roll my eyes.

"Come on, Nor. I think it's time to head out," Charlie says, putting an arm around my waist and turning us toward the door. Amelia slaps some cash on the bar and gives Eamon a quick once over.

"She really would have kicked your ass, you know." Tossing her straight blonde hair over her shoulder, she turns and walks away.

I really do have the best friends.

* * *

The alley is dark and cold, and it reeks of piss and garbage. I'm sprawled on the pavement, eyes shut tightly. My face hurts, and I can't move my arms. Something's pressing me down. No. Not again. I start struggling, determined to get out of this with as little damage as possible. I manage to roll to my back and will my eyes open only to discover three large forms towering over me.

"What do you think, Eamon? Keep her or toss her?"

I scream.

"Norah! Norah! Wake up!" I hear a voice yelling and feel my body being shaken. "Nor!" I bolt upright and find Charlie sitting next to me, her hazel eyes filled with concern.

"You were having a nightmare. Are you okay?" she asks while shoving a cup of coffee into my hands. Bless her.

"Ugh. I feel like I've been hit by a truck." I groan, rubbing my forehead in an attempt to soothe the alcohol-induced ache.

"Well, considering you drank the equivalent of a keg of Guinness and downed a few shots of whiskey, you *should* be feeling pretty awful."

I cringe at the reminder. "What the hell was I thinking?"

"Methinks your pride and a pretty Irishman are to blame." Charlie grins at me.

"Well fuck. I was hoping that part wasn't real. I'm *such* an idiot. He probably thought I was crazy." I sigh, then quickly add, "Not that it matters what he thinks."

She gives me a curious look while twisting her brown hair into a topknot on the crown of her head.

Just then, a knock sounds at the door before it opens. Layla walks in with a bottle of aspirin and a brown paper bag that smells very much like a cheeseburger. These two girls know me so well. Nothing cures a hangover better than a steaming mug of coffee and a greasy cheeseburger.

"Good morning, sunshine. Or rather, almost afternoon. I heard you might need these today," Layla says, setting everything down on the kitchen island.

"Why are you girls so good to me? You always know exactly what I need."

I start to ease myself off of…the couch? Odd. My house is small, and my bedroom is just a few feet down the hallway.

"Why am I on the couch?"

"Oh, about that…" Charlie grimaces.

The bedroom door opens and out creeps Myra, her hair disheveled, in just a t-shirt and panties. My jaw hits the floor.

"Please tell me you're alone in *my* bedroom…"

"Um…yes?" she says sheepishly.

"Who the hell is in there? It's not that Neanderthal is it?" I rage at her.

"Neanderthal? What are you talking about?"

I quirk an eyebrow at her. "You know exactly who I'm talking about. That big blond jerk, Mac, from the pub last night. You brought him back to my house and took him to my bed?"

"Slow your roll, Nor. Sheesh." Myra rolls her eyes. "I'm just messing with you. Amelia and I shared your room last night since we both couldn't fit on the couch. You were too passed out to know the difference."

Amelia walks out of my room, grinning like a Cheshire cat.

"You two are jerks." I glare at them. "I'm only in this state because of you two to begin with."

16

"Aw, Norie, you know you had fun. You certainly made an impression on that dark and sexy Irishman! What was his name? Evan? Ethan?" Amelia asks as she saunters into the kitchen and grabs a mug out of the cabinet.

"Eamon," I answer too quickly and immediately regret it. All four of my friends are giving me looks with varying degrees of mirth.

"Stop," I order, holding up a hand. "I know what you're thinking. He insulted my drinking abilities, and I had to prove him wrong—no matter how much I may be questioning my sanity now."

"Tell me more about this mystery man," Layla demands, curling up on the other side of the couch. "I missed all the fun and now I need the details. Did you really drink him under the table?"

"You should have seen her!" Amelia exclaims while pouring herself a cup of coffee. "She had already shared a flight with me, and then she challenged this guy, who is gorgeous by the way, to the Whiskey Guinness chasers! I've never been so proud! But then old man O'Nelly put a stop to it before they could get to round four."

"Round four? *Dios mio*, you really were trying to impress him!" Layla laughs.

"No." I shake my head and then wince from the movement. "No, I was not trying to impress him. I was proving a point. Proving that just because I'm a woman does not mean I can't enjoy a good beer or hold my own against said man."

"Oh, Norah. Whatever you say," Myra retorts from where she's perched at my kitchen island. "It's been too long since you've set your eyes on a man. I'm happy for you".

"I have *not* set my eyes on anyone. I don't even know him, and I'll probably never see him again. It was just a moment of pride. Now," I say, rising from the couch. "I need a shower."

I march to the bathroom to wash off the humiliation of last night and take a moment to myself. As much as I love these girls, sometimes I just need peace and quiet to process. Last night was a mistake. Thrilling, but a mistake.

My mind flashes back to my last mistake almost four years ago. Having just returned from Ireland I headed straight for the nearest Irish pub needing to feel that magic again. Normally a sunshine and warm weather-loving girl, I missed the overcast skies and constant greenery. I walked into the pub and looked around slowly. It was exactly like the numerous pubs I had visited around Temple Bar. The shining wooden bars had stained glass on the front faces of them, and Irish ditties were playing overhead. At the bar, wiping the water drops from clear glasses, stood Pat O'Nelly. With a tweed cap on his head, round glasses sitting on his nose, and a friendly face covered with a white beard, he was just what I needed. I walked up and sat on the stool in front of him.

"Good evenin', lass. What can I do for you on this warm summer's eve?" he asked in a thick brogue.

"Guinness, please. A proper Guinness," I told him quickly. "I just got back from Ireland, and since I can't jump on a plane and head back, this is the next best thing."

"Ah! The Green Isle! And how did my homeland treat you?" he asked jovially.

"It was…a dream come true. So magical. Everything was perfect. I've never been to a more wonderful place," I prattled.

"Aye. It is a land of magic, lass. Did you go for holiday or studies?"

"Holiday. One day, I'll go back," I promised, "and find my husband!"

"Ach! There's not a better place to find a husband if I do say so myself! If only you could talk to my dear Ellie. She'd confirm it."

"Does she not work in the pub with you?" I asked, looking around.

With a hint of sadness in his eyes, Pat told me the story of his voyage to America after the passing of his wife. The love they shared seemed to be genuine and everything I wanted in a partner. Someone full of affection and a little bit of mischief, to hold and protect me and make me laugh. I sat there for an hour, listening to his stories until the pub started to get busy. People were filing in and crowding around me. Everyone was anxious to get their drink and visit with Pat. Before I knew it, I had downed a couple of Guinness and a shot of whiskey. Towards the end of the night, I found myself surrounded by a group of guys cheering me on as I downed more alcohol. One in particular stuck close to my side throughout the night, and against my better judgment, I welcomed the attention. With my inhibitions lowered, I ignored not just the warning bells ingrained from past trauma, but also the looks Pat was giving me and let myself be reckless for just one night. I like to think that I had handled my Mom's death in a healthy way, but sometimes the pain of losing her hit hard and I just wanted to be someone else for a while.

When I finally decided to call it quits, my new friend, whose name I will never remember, offered to walk me home. As we cut through the park close to the pub, he put his arm around me and I didn't object. When we rounded a corner that put us in a more secluded part of the park, he stopped abruptly and turned me toward him before kissing me harshly and groping me. Terror flooded my veins and I froze. When he realized I wasn't responding the way he wanted, he got angry and accused me of being a tease. Tearing myself from his grip, I began backing away. He attempted to grab me, and I screamed loud enough that he stopped his advances, spat some ugly words at me, and left. By then, the panic attack had begun. I felt completely helpless as I stood there gasping for air and shaking violently. It was several minutes before I was able to calm myself enough to call Charlie.

My thoughts drift back to the present as I finish showering. The hot water soothes away the memories from that night leaving me feeling only slightly better than when I woke up. The cheeseburger waiting for me in the kitchen should help with the rest before I go apologize to Pat for last night's debacle. I hate the idea of him being disappointed in me.

Chapter Three

Eamon

Groaning, I roll over and hit the snooze button on my blaring alarm. It's been a while since I drank that much, but it's a relief to know that I'm not in tatters after last night. Why did I drink so much again? *Oh, that's right.* I'd *offended* that lass. Norah. That was her name. She was a fine thing, with a head of red hair and stormy blue eyes. The way she glared and then challenged *me* to a drinking contest brings a smile to my face. While she had given her demand to Alicia, I had taken the time to check her out. With curves like that, how could I not? Her hourglass figure was perfectly encased in her green V-neck shirt and dark jeans. I deserve sainthood for not staring at the moderately plunging neckline that showed off the swell of her breasts. Not that I noticed.

I amble out of my room and into the kitchen, where I pour a glass of water and grab an aspirin to clear my head. I have practice in a couple of hours. That should give me enough time to shower and apologize to Paddy. I never drink that much, and he was not happy about it. For an Irish pub owner, he's pretty strict on his consumers. Cranky old codger. Either way, I'm not about to get on Pat's bad side.

After showering and getting ready, I lock up my flat and head to my car. I'm just sliding into the driver's seat when I feel my phone buzz in my pocket. I pull it out and groan when I see who's calling. My younger sister, Caity. She only ever calls when she wants money.

"Hiya, Caity," I greet her as cheerfully as possible. "How are ya?"

"Hey. What are you doing?" she asks absently.

I can't stop my eyes from rolling. Leave it to Caity to forgo civilities.

"It's nice to hear from you too, wee sister. I'm doing great; thanks for asking," I reply sarcastically.

She sighs heavily before saying, "Sorry, Eam. How are you, big brother?"

"I've got a bit of the fear in me, but nothing unmanageable."

"You get wankered last night, then?" Caity asks with a laugh.

"Ach. Just having the craic. Some fire sprite challenged me to a drinking contest of the black stuff. It would have been ungentlemanly of me to decline."

"Naturally," she says with a snort before continuing nervously. "Hey, listen. I don't have a lot of time to talk, but I was wondering if you could lend me a few quid to get me through the week? I'm strapped, and I don't want to bother Mam."

My heart sinks, but I'm not surprised. Caity's been hanging with a bad crowd for the better part of her life. I've always suspected she's doing drugs, and I don't want to enable her, but better me than Mam. I feel guilty enough having left Ireland, so I make it a point to keep Caity from worrying our mother. And my wee sister knows this.

"Fucks sake, Caity," I say with a sigh.

"I know," she groans. "Listen, I'm sorry. It's okay. I'll figure something else out."

Raking a hand through my hair in frustration, I take a deep breath before

21

asking, "How much do you need, Caity?"

Norah

"Well, well. Good mornin' to ya, Miss Grady," Paddy O'Nelly drawls as he wipes the bar down with a cloth, eyeing me over the rim of his glasses.

He only calls me Miss Grady when I'm in trouble, so this should be fun.

"Pat, I'm so sorry for last night. I don't know what came over me. I didn't even want to go out." I explain. "Will you please forgive me? I'll come wash dishes for you this week if I need to!"

"Ach. I'll tell ya what came over ya, Miss Grady. That Irish temper of yours, and don't be tellin' me you don't have Irish blood in ya." He pauses to glance up at me before continuing, "It doesn't help matters that Eamon Kennedy was egging you on. I'll have words with him too before the day is up. Just you wait."

My heart beats wildly at Eamon's name. Of course, he's close with Pat. They're both Irish. Nobody claiming to be from Ireland would even think of going to any other "Irish" pub in Wilmington. They'd be crazy.

"I'd never met him before last night, Pat. I just couldn't stand him accusing me of being a wimp and unable to hold my Guinness."

Pat chuckles at first but then turns serious. "Acushla. Just be careful. The last time you let yourself go in my pub like that, you came in the next day looking like you'd seen a ghost. I never want to see that look in your lovely blue eyes again. You're practically family."

I smile warmly at him. "Don't worry, Pat. I've learned my lesson, and I feel awful today. Thanks for letting me off the hook."

"Now hold on there, lass. Who said I was letting you off the hook? You said you'd do dishes, and I mean to see that you do. I'll have you back tomorrow night if you don't mind."

Damn.

"Of course!" I quickly agree, "I'll be in tomorrow at seven."

"Alright, then. I'll see you at seven. Now let me get back to my work, you wee sprite!" he teases.

I giggle and bounce out of the pub with a wave goodbye.

Eamon

I'm getting out of my car, fuming over the conversation with Caity, when I notice someone coming out of Paddy's. I freeze when I see that it's the lass from last night. Norah bounds out of the pub, looking pleased as punch. She certainly doesn't look like she's hungover. In fact, she looks bloody gorgeous with that radiant smile on her face. And do all of her jeans fit her like that? I stand there gawking after her like some sort of creeper before snapping out of it and making my way inside.

Paddy's taking stock of the liquor bottles when I saunter in. I love this pub. It's the closest thing to home I'll allow myself to enjoy. I love Ireland, truly, but I vowed I'd never go back, not after everything that happened.

"Oy! Eamon! Why are you dallying in my doorway like some lost pup? I do believe you and I have a score to settle, young man," Paddy yells, pulling me from my thoughts.

"Aye, I'd say we do, Paddy." I make my way to the bar, sliding onto a stool. "Don't suppose you'd overlook last night's incident would ya?"

"For such a bright lad, you're a wee dumb in the head, aren't ya? 'Course I'm not going to overlook your offenses! After what you did to that wee lass last night. You ought to be ashamed of yourself!"

"Now just a minute," I counter, pointing a finger at him. "I do believe the blame falls squarely on said *wee lass*. She provoked me. I swear it." I can't help the grin that spreads over my face.

"See here, young man. I've known Norah as long as I've known you, and she's as innocent as they come. I've only seen her do that once before, and I never wanted to see it again, you hear?" the older man protests.

"How was I to know? I've never seen her before in my life. I won't deny it was a bit of fun dueling it out with her, though. She's got spunk, that one. Are you sure she's not Irish?"

"Ach. She may be Irish a little bit. But either way, shame on you for behaving that way towards a lass. I've a mind to ban you from this pub," he threatens.

That won't do. I mindlessly grab a coaster and spin it between my fingers.

"Ah, Paddy. Come on! It was just a bit of craic. You're not going to ban me. How can I make it up to you?"

"Well, now that you mention it, you can come back tomorrow night at seven and wash dishes."

"What? You're not serious," I say in shock, the coaster drops to the bar. I didn't think he'd actually make me work off my transgressions.

"I am serious. As serious as Christ on the Cross, and you know I don't take that lightly, lad. This is a respectable place. I can't have it turning into one of those sports bars or whatever they are. Come and have a good time, yes, but taunting young girls into drinking until they fall over gives the wrong impression. Now, get out of here. I'll see you tomorrow night." And with that, he turns his back and continues counting bottles.

What the bleedin' hell? Looks like I've been properly dismissed. He'll change his mind. He's just slagging me. Has to be.

Chapter Four

Norah

"So, tell me more about your night out," Layla demands. "Charlie gave me the Cliffs Notes, but I want your version."

News certainly travels fast in this group. I'm rarely the source of excitement, so all this extra attention is putting me on edge. *Hello, anxiety.* I take a sip of my coffee in an attempt to stall the conversation. God, I love coffee. It's always there for me when I need it.

"I know you're stalling, Norah. Spill." Layla levels me with a look I know she inherited from her mama.

"Ugh, Layla. I don't know what came over me. Honestly, I'm just ready to forget about it and never do it again," I confess.

"So don't. Move on. It was just one mistake. You never do anything fun or adventurous, so consider this your rebellion era and shake it off." Sage advice. She's probably the most levelheaded in our entire group.

"You're right," I say, then backtrack. "But I *do* have fun, thank you very much! I'm not an old maid. I'll be twenty-five in a month. I'd like to think I still have *some* life in me. Even if I'm not like Myra and Amie."

"You know what I mean. You have your own definition of fun, and it usually includes a bottle of wine, sweatpants, and Netflix."

I glare at her.

"Now, don't give me that look. You know as well as I do that I'm all for that kind of night, but sometimes we need to let our hair down, you know?"

"I guess," I concede with a shrug.

"Now, what I really want to know is who the guy is. You can blame this on My and Amie all you want, but you wouldn't have done that without proper provocation. Out with it."

This is exactly what I didn't want to talk about.

"There's nothing to tell," I hedge. "He accused me of not being able to hold my own, and it just triggered something in me. An Irish guy thought I was just another stupid girl at a bar trying to look cool. I couldn't stand it. Next thing I know, I'm three sheets to the wind."

"That red hair of yours certainly doesn't help, Norie. The girls told me he was good-looking…" Layla wags her eyebrows.

If she only knew. As stupid as my actions were, I can't say I regretted staring at his face all night.

"For the sake of honesty, yes. Yes, he was. He was tragically handsome. Built just right and had eyes that could suck out my soul." I tell her dreamily.

Layla cocks her head to the side. "You know, it probably wouldn't hurt to go out with a good-looking guy every now and then. Now, before you get up in arms," she holds up her hands in defense as I bristle. "Just hear me out. You have a bad history with men, I know. I'm not saying go out and have a one-night stand or find the man you'll marry. I'm not even saying to date. But maybe, just maybe, get to know a guy on a friend level."

"Pot, meet kettle," I say. Layla is almost as shy around guys as I am.

"Rude. I have male friends." She scoffs.

"Your brothers?"

"Shush. They're not my only male friends. Plus, they're my brothers, so they don't count anyway. But we're not talking about me!" she says hurriedly.

I know she's right, but I have no idea how to be friends with a guy. I'm polite to the ones in my classes and the drama department. I tolerate the guys at the pub, but I can't say that I've ever actually taken the time to befriend one of them. I don't see the point, honestly. With my history, there's no way I will ever be relationship material. That requires trust with your heart and your body, and I don't trust any guy with either.

"I don't know if I can do it. Where would I even begin?"

"Well, we all know how much you love Pat O'Nelly. Start there. Maybe he can give you some tips or something. You trust him, right?" Layla asks.

"Absolutely, I do. But he's older, like a grandfather. Nothing is threatening about him—though he did scold me pretty good today and put me on dish duty." I shrug.

"Are you serious? For how long?" She laughs.

"I don't know. He told me to come in tomorrow night at seven. I hope it's just one night!"

* * *

Sunday night has arrived, and I'm running late. It shouldn't be a big deal, though. Sunday nights are usually pretty slow, so there can't be that many dishes, right? And surely Pat was just messing with me. He'll probably pour me a pint as we gab the night away. It's ten after seven when I walk through the door and come to a screeching stop. The place is absolutely packed. With senior citizens. *What the hell?* I glance at the bulletin board to my left, where various groups and organizations post their fliers. Sure enough, tonight is Seniors' Night. When did Pat start that? I shake my head and walk up to the bar, catching Paddy's eye.

"It's about time, lass! You're late! I'll have to make you work a second night now," he says, winking at me.

I laugh and hop onto the bar stool across from him.

27

"Oh no, you don't, Miss Grady. You promised dishwashing, and that's exactly what you're going to do tonight. I didn't expect so many people to turn up, and they all drink like fish. We need glasses. Now, get back there!" he orders me.

I'm stunned. He was serious! I hesitantly walk back behind the bar and through the swinging door. To my right is the kitchen, complete with an industrial-type stove and fridge against the far wall and a stainless steel island in the center of the room with a pot rack hanging overhead. Pat doesn't offer much in the way of food, but he always has stew and fish and chips. The dishes are piled high in the sink, the large dishwasher already running a load. I don't even know where to begin.

"Norah! Glad to see ya! Grab that apron over there and get to washing! Pat said I wasn't supposed to let you two do any slacking tonight!" Alicia yells through the door.

"Two of us?" I start to say, just as the door from the pantry opens and Eamon Kennedy walks through carrying an armload of fresh vegetables. He looks just as good as I remember.

He slams to a stop with a baffled look on his face. "If you've come for round two, forget it. I won't be doing dishes for Paddy again after this," he says as he walks around me to the island and begins sorting the veggies into piles.

"What? I thought I was doing the dishes. What are you doing here?" I ask stupidly.

Eamon lifts his blue eyes to mine and smirks. "Looks like he's punishing us both for bad behavior the other night. I blame you, you know. Now, if you really are here to wash, then hop to it. I've been put on stew duty until Paddy gets things calmed down out there."

Seething, I say, "Me? You're the one that started the whole damn conversation! If anyone should be washing dishes, it's you!"

"Easy, lass. That temper of yours will get you into trouble again." He chuckles darkly. "And, like I said, I won't be doing any more dishes."

Pat chooses that moment to walk through the door. "What's the raucous back here? Why aren't those tubers chopped, Eamon? You should have been halfway through them by now."

"Sorry, Paddy. Ginger over here is arguing over who's supposed to be doing the dishes. Looks like you forgot to mention you had us both on duty," Eamon says accusingly.

"My name is *not* Ginger," I snap at him. He's infuriating.

"Norah, darling, would you be so kind as to start on those dishes? I'll be serving stew from my boot before the night's over. I'll be holding you to your promise now." Pat says mischievously.

I look back at the sink. It's going to be a long night.

An hour into dish duty, Pat comes back to relieve Eamon of making stew. It smells heavenly, but I'm not going to admit it to him. The B&B I stayed in at Clifden was run by an older lady who made the best stew I have ever had. I still have vivid dreams about it on rainy nights. This stew smells similar.

I'm completely lost in memories of Ireland when Eamon's deep voice says, "I'll rinse now".

"Shit!" I screech, jumping sky-high while the dish I was washing falls from my hands.

Eamon's hand darts forward, catching it before it hits the ground. "Sorry, lass. I didn't mean to frighten you again."

"Again?"

"Aye. The other night I had you choking on your beer, if I remember correctly," he teases, eyes wrinkling at the corners in amusement.

I narrow my own eyes at him, "From what I recall, *lad*, I was choking because I *couldn't handle a pint of Guinness*. I'm not sure which accusation is more insulting."

I turn back to the dishes and start scrubbing furiously at a bowl. He chuckles softly and begins rinsing the plates I've already washed. I try to keep my eyes from darting over to look at his strong hands and forearms, but I fail miserably. Our elbows brush every so often as we go about our duty, and my heart beats wildly at every point of contact. But it's not the typical fear of a man's touch that has my nerves frayed and thoughts muddled.

Several quiet minutes pass as we continue to wash and rinse the dishes. I choose to remain silent because I honestly have no idea what to say, but

Layla's words keep coming back to me. *Make friends with a guy. Learn that they aren't all dangerous.* I know nothing about Eamon Kennedy other than the fact that he's the forward for the UNCW Seahawks, one hundred percent Irish, and gorgeous.

Steeling myself, I clear my throat and ask nervously, "So. Have you known Pat long?"

Eamon pauses and looks over at me. "Aye. He's the first fellow Irishman I met when I came over. It's been about four years now."

I mull this over. "I also met him about four years ago. He was the first person I actually talked to when I got here."

"Where are you from, then?" he asks politely.

"Just a horrible small town in the Midwest. But I had just gotten back from Ireland when I met him," I tell him.

"Oh yeah? On holiday?"

"Yeah. After my Mom died, I decided to just pack up and go. I stayed for a month, and it was the best time of my life," I say sadly, thinking back to how broken I was before that trip.

"I'm sorry about your mam," he says quietly. "Who went with you on your trip?"

"No one. I don't have any close family. Mom and I had always talked about going, so I booked my ticket and a couple of AirBnBs across the country and just left. I didn't have a plan, but I knew I was going. I wouldn't have left if I could have helped it," I confess, and when he doesn't respond, I ask, "Why did you leave Ireland? Scholarship?"

"Yeah, that's part of it," he replies.

"What's the other part?" I ask boldly.

"I just needed to get away. The scholarship was as good of an excuse as any."

"You're nuts," I scoff. "Why on earth would you want to escape Ireland? It's magical and vibrant and peaceful."

"It's beautiful alright, but it's not all rainbows and leprechauns, lass," Eamon says sarcastically.

Feeling embarrassed at my sudden outburst about a country I've never lived in, I mumble an apology and go back to washing dishes.

I hear him sigh next to me before he says, "Tell me more about your trip. Where did you visit?"

"No, it's okay," I tell him. "Let's talk about something else. How long have you played soccer?"

After a brief pause, he says, "I've played all of my life. As a kid, I played in the streets and the fields with my mates and cousins. But in school, I joined a team and have always been a part of one. I thought someday I'd play professionally, but that's unlikely."

"Why?" I ask incredulously.

It's been a while since I've been to a game, but I might have done some internet stalking in the last twenty-four hours.

Eamon laughs. "I enjoy the game, but I'd like more from life than traveling all over and kicking around a ball with a group of sweaty guys."

I'm immediately imagining said group of sweaty guys on the UNCW field...shirtless. Is there such a thing as an overweight soccer player? With all that running and sweating...

"Do you play?" he asks, pulling me from my very inappropriate thoughts.

I snort out a laugh. "No. Does it look like I play soccer? Does it look like I play any sport?" I gesture to myself, slinging water everywhere.

He looks me up and down appreciatively. "I'm not sure what you mean by that, but I'd appreciate it if you'd hold off on the showers."

"Oh my god!" I squeal, flailing my wet hands around. "I'm so sorry! Here, take my towel!" I mindlessly start trying to wipe the water off of his jeans with my towel, wishing the floor would open up and swallow me whole.

Eamon begins chuckling just as Paddy and Alicia walk through the door. I bolt upright, my face flaming in embarrassment.

"What exactly is happening back here, you two?" Pat asks, laughing. "I think I asked you to wash dishes, Miss Grady, not Mr. Kennedy's pants."

"No," I splutter, "I accidentally splashed water on him. I was just..."

God, this is humiliating. Eamon grins wickedly and goes back to rinsing the dishes. *Jackass.*

Chapter Five

Eamon

Pat closes the pub early on Sundays. Last call is at ten o'clock and the doors are locked by eleven. Every other night of the week, the lights are off by one a.m. It's half past ten when Norah and I finally toss our aprons in the hamper by the back door. Norah groans as she stretches her arms over her head and arches her back, causing her shirt to lift slightly, exposing the skin of her stomach. She's completely unaware of the effect she has on me. I watch her surreptitiously as I dry my hands, then hang the towel back up on its hook. She lowers her arms and straightens her shirt. I'm still staring when she looks back up, but I don't bother hiding my interest. She looks away quickly, a small smile playing on her lips.

"If I would have known that dishes put a smile on your face, I would have asked you to do them a long time ago, lass," Pat says as he walks through the door.

She chuckles and says, "I can honestly say that dishes are the last thing to make me smile. I was thinking about one of the costumes I made last year and the girl that wore it."

"You make costumes?" I ask, leaning back against the counter and folding my arms over my chest.

Norah's eyes light up with pride, "Yes, I'm the Costume Designer for the Theatre Department on campus. I also do the costumes for some local dance studios."

"That's impressive," I tell her honestly. "Do you sew them yourself or just design them?"

"I do both. I have a team, of course, for the theater, but the dance studios and personal orders I do myself."

I raise my brows in surprise. "Are you a student too?"

"I am," she nods. "I'm in my senior year of business. Nothing special, just learning what I need to do to open my own design studio someday."

Pat interjects, "Did you see the performance they put on a couple of years ago? The one about Sleeping Beauty? She actually created the color-changing dress!"

Norah shakes her head, cheeks turning pink. "It wasn't actually color-changing. I just chose a reflective material for the skirt, and the lighting crew did the rest."

"I'm sad I missed that one," I say truthfully. "Guess I'll have to catch the next one to see just how amazing these costumes are."

I don't normally go to the plays the university puts on unless it's for class credit, but I might start making an exception.

"They're putting on a modern rendition of Beauty and The Beast in November. It's definitely been a stretch of the imagination, but I think it will be pretty great," she replies shyly, twisting her fingers together in front of her.

"Alright, you two," Pat starts. "I think you've spent enough time here. Go home and get some rest before classes tomorrow. Norah, I'll give you a lift, love, if you don't mind riding with me while I drop this deposit off at the bank."

"Oh, really, Pat. It's okay. I can just walk. It's not that far." She shrugs.

"I can take you," I say quickly. The thought of her walking alone at this time of night sets my teeth on edge. "I don't live too far away either, but I had practice today, so I took my car. It's parked out front."

"Now, there's an idea!" Pat exclaims with a little too much enthusiasm. "You won't have to wait on me, then! Eamon, you're a good lad. Norah, thank you again for your dishwashing services tonight. We'd be lost without you!"

"I suppose you'd have managed well enough without me, then, Paddy," I say begrudgingly.

He laughs and says, "Ach, Mr. Kennedy. I do thank you for your excellent cooking skills. From what I heard, those snowbirds all thought I changed my recipe and, believe it or not, like it better than the old one! I'm not sure I should really be thanking ya for that, though. You might put me out of business."

"I highly doubt that." I grin at him. "I can cook, but I'm not Paddy O'Nelly."

He beams at me and bids us farewell with the order to set the alarm on the way out. The trust this man places in us is something else.

I turn to Norah and gesture towards the door.

"Shall we?" I pause, taking in the nervous expression on her face. "Er, are you alright, lass?"

She blinks rapidly. "Uh, yeah. I just—um…well, if I'm being honest, it's that I don't really know you, and I don't make it a habit to accept rides from someone I don't know."

Nodding in understanding, I offer, "Well, I'll tell you what. I'll give you the keys to my car, and you can drive yourself home, and I'll walk. Easy as that."

"No!" she practically yells. "I couldn't possibly do that. It's really not that far. Just a fifteen-minute walk through the park. I can manage."

"I admire your bravery, Norah, but I won't be letting you walk through the dark alone. What kind of man would I be if I sent a pretty lass like yourself off on her own at night?" Honestly, my Mam would have my balls for that.

"I—" she starts, but I cut her off.

"No. I won't hear of it. I respect your decision completely to not ride in a car with someone you don't know, and I won't press that, but you will be driving my car home. You can bring it back to Paddy's tomorrow. I'll give you my number so you can let me know when it's here."

I hold my keys out in the palm of my hand. She cautiously takes them and meets my eyes. "Thank you, Eamon."

God, I love the sound of my name coming from her mouth. I glance at her perfect lips and am suddenly imagining what it would be like to place a soft kiss on them. She clears her throat, breaking the spell I'm under.

"Sorry, what?" I quickly ask, dragging my gaze back to her eyes.

"I asked which car is yours," she replies, an eyebrow cocked in question.

"Ah, I'll show you."

We exit through the back door, setting the alarm as Pat requested, and walk around the north side of the building to the parking lot out front. The pub is on the corner of an outdoor shopping center. There are parking spaces in front of the building, all the way down the street, and a small parking lot around the back. Most people show up early or pay for parking in the city lot a couple of blocks away. Thankfully, I had the good sense to show up early tonight. Why, I don't know. Maybe I was hoping to talk Paddy out of doing the dishes. I point to my black SUV sitting a few spaces down from the entrance to the pub. It's the only vehicle on the block.

"Sorry, there aren't heated seats or remote start," I say, grinning at her.

"Not a problem at all. At least you have a car! I sold mine once I got here. I figured I'd just walk everywhere or use public transportation," she explains.

"I'm sure you fit right in when you were in Ireland, then. That's all I did growing up."

"It just seems so simple. But I felt safer there than I do here." Norah shrugs.

I grimace. Being alone on the Luas at night can be a pretty scary place.

"I hope you never took public transportation at this time of night there.

35

It's not always the safest either".

"No. When I stayed in Dublin, my room was right in Temple Bar, so I just walked everywhere. There were always people around."

I can picture her there—walking around Temple Bar, neck craning to take in all of the sights. I can see her sitting in a pub like Auld Dubliner, drinking a Guinness—or three—and laughing at the cheeky Irish ditties. The thought makes me wish we were there right now.

"Do you miss it there at all?" she asks quietly as we approach my car.

"Sometimes," I tell her. "I miss Temple Bar. There's nothing quite like it. I miss the way you can look up at the sky in the country and see the stars. You can't find that kind of solitude in Wilmington."

"That's true. In my hometown, you could easily find a field outside of city limits that would let you stargaze. There would always be a group of us that would get together on the weekends, and…" she stops and shivers.

"Here, get in. You're getting cold, and it's late," I order her.

She obeys and slides into the driver's seat, inhaling deeply.

"Sorry, about the smell," I apologize. "We football players aren't known for our lack of sweat." I wish I would have cleaned my car out before letting her get in.

Laughing, she shakes her head and glances up at me. "It doesn't stink. I promise."

"Is it okay if I give you my number so you can let me know when you've dropped the car off?"

She nods and hands me her phone. I type it in quickly and give it back to her.

"Just give me a call or text me when you drop it off here tomorrow."

"I will. Thanks again, Eamon." She smiles sweetly at me.

I wait until she closes the door and buckles her seat belt before moving to the sidewalk. I watch as she cautiously backs out of the parking spot and drives away. I think back on the night as I head towards home, and I can't be entirely upset with Paddy. Who would complain about spending hours with a beautiful girl like Norah? Even if it was doing dishes.

Chapter Six

Norah

My alarm rouses me from a delightful dream I'm having about walking around Temple Bar with Eamon. The thought makes those pesky butterflies come to life. Groaning, I roll over to shut off the offending alarm and check my phone. There are four missed calls and a ridiculous amount of text messages. All from my friends. Groaning again, I open up my inbox.

Layla: *Whose SUV is that??? Do you have someone in there with you??*

The next message is a group text with all of the girls. Oh lord, here we go.

Layla: *Norie, please tell us whose black SUV is in your driveway!*

Amelia: *WHAT?! NORIE, WHAT IS GOING ON?!*

Charlie: *WHAT DID YOU DO LAST NIGHT?!*

Myra: *OMG! NO WAY! I NEEEEEEEED DETAILS!!*

With bleary eyes, I text the group.

Norah: *Calm down. There's not a man in my house. I'm here alone. Someone let me borrow it last night so I didn't have to walk home by myself.*

Amelia: *WHO??????*

Charlie: *WHY DIDN'T YOU CALL ME?!*

Myra: *WHERE WERE YOU?!*

A separate message from Layla pops up.

Layla: *I'm coming over!*

Sometimes having a best friend for a neighbor is annoying. I roll out of bed and head towards the bathroom. Layla will be here in about two seconds. Sure enough, just as I finish brushing my teeth, I hear the front door open. I regret giving out copies of my house keys to all of the girls now.

"Good morning," I call from the bathroom. "Start the coffee pot, will ya?"

"Psh. You think you can just order me around before telling me who owns that SUV?" Layla has the audacity to sound offended.

"Yes. Yes, I do. You won't get anything from me until coffee hits my veins."

They all know that I don't function without coffee. I will never turn down a cup, no matter what time of day it is. I shuffle to the kitchen to find Layla sitting at the island with an expectant look on her face, fingers tapping on the bar.

"Can I help you?" I ask, brow raised.

"You're damn right you can, chica. Start talking."

Rolling my eyes, I tell her, "You're so pushy. Can't I just explain it to all of you at once? I really don't want to repeat it a million different times."

"Fine. Get your laptop. We're going to FaceTime them all," she replies. *Damn it.*

Ten minutes later, miraculously, all of them are available. With the screen split into four different sections, I can see that Myra is still in bed, Amelia is driving, and Charlie is applying her makeup in the bathroom.

"Good morning, Norie!" Charlie chirps. She's an early riser and almost always cheerful.

"Yeah, yeah, yeah," Myra grumbles from under a pink comforter. "Good morning and all that. Now spill!"

"Sheesh," I complain, taking a sip of my coffee. "You don't see me questioning all of you when a vehicle shows up in your driveway. Nosy Nancies."

"Yes, that's because it's not uncommon for us to have strange cars in our driveways! You don't even drive!" Amelia yells at me.

"Maybe if you all would just shut up, she'd actually tell us what happened," Layla barks.

I choke on a laugh. She's usually pretty mild-tempered, but when she's feeling spunky, it's very entertaining.

"Fine," I begin. "On Saturday, I went in to apologize to Pat for my *despicable behavior*. I jokingly told him I'd wash dishes to make up for it. He thought that sounded like a great idea and told me to be back at seven on Sunday. So I went, still expecting to *not* do dishes." I pause to take another drink of coffee. "I was very wrong. Apparently, he does Senior Night every other Sunday or something. He was slammed and immediately sent me back to the kitchen, but I wasn't the only one. Good old Pat took it upon himself to have Eamon Kennedy do dishes too."

There's a collective gasp at this point. Myra starts to say something, but I pointedly cut her off. Once she gets started, it's almost impossible to get her to stop.

"Before you start getting any ideas, there was nothing *remotely* romantic about it. At the end of the night, Pat asked Eamon to drive me home so I wouldn't be walking alone—I guess he lives close to Pat's as well. Anyway, I told him I wasn't comfortable riding in a car with someone I didn't know. Much to my surprise, he demanded that I take his car keys and he would walk."

"Aw!" they all coo at once. I roll my eyes.

"I tried to tell him no, but he wouldn't have it. He told me to drop the car off at Pat's today and call him when it was there. That's all. Nothing exciting."

"You're joking, right?" Amelia asks in disbelief, eyes darting back and forth between her phone and the road. "This is the *epitome* of exciting! He cares about your safety, trusts you with his car, and gives you his number!

He *wants* you to call him!"

Myra adds from the cocoon of blankets, "Why not just call him over to your house? Thank him *properly!*"

I cringe. "Ugh. No. You're all wrong. He was just being nice. That's all."

"Whatever. You guys are totally going to hook up!" Myra sing-songs.

"I mean, it wouldn't really be a bad thing! He's super hot!" Charlie says while she coats her lashes in mascara.

Rolling my eyes yet again, I look at Layla. "Please talk some sense into these crazies."

"I don't know, Norie. It kind of sounds like he's interested," she says carefully, head tilted to the side as she observes me. "Guys, maybe Norah isn't interested in *him*," Layla finally says. "He may be hot, and he may be nice, but maybe—just maybe—Norah has no desire to be with him."

Well, let's not get carried away.

"If Eamon Kennedy doesn't stoke your fires, who does?" Amelia asks curiously. "Unless you're not into men anymore. Which is understandable."

I glare at her. "Did you really just ask me that? Do I really have to explain my hesitancy to get involved with someone?"

I'm on the verge of tears now. It's all too much. Yes, I'm physically attracted to Eamon, but given my past, I don't think that there's any way I'll ever be able to make a relationship with a man work. Those scars run too deeply.

"Okay, Norie. Take a deep breath," Charlie says softly, sensing my rising anxiety. "We all know why you haven't been in a relationship. We know it's hard for you, but we all just want to see you happy and to find someone that truly brings you joy. That's all. We love you."

They all murmur their agreement as I sniffle and wipe the corner of my eye. I know they have my best interests at heart, but I'm still terrified.

"Thanks, girls. I love you too. It's just overwhelming. I will freely admit that Eamon is very attractive and the fact that he's Irish doesn't hurt." I pause for a moment to breathe slowly before continuing, "But I just can't bring myself to consider a relationship with anyone, let alone him. That's if he's even interested, which isn't likely."

"Stop that. You obviously don't know just how gorgeous you are," Layla says sternly. "Before you roll your eyes at me, hear me out. You're stunning! You have flawless skin, and your eyes sparkle when you talk about something you love, *and* you're a ginger. What's not to love? No, we can't all be like the other skinny bitches in the group—sorry, ladies, we still love you—but your curves are in *all the right places*. I don't want to hear that talk out of your mouth again."

I sniffle again, but a smile plays on my lips. "Now that I've been put in my place…"

They all laugh, and I reassure them that I'm okay. We chat for a few more minutes until I realize that I really need to head to class. I end our little conference and hug Layla goodbye before racing to my room to throw on some clean clothes. I'm going to be so late.

* * *

I pull into the same parking spot that I left from last night and sit there trying to convince myself to call Eamon. When was the last time I called a guy? Just as I'm about to dial his number, there's a knock on the driver's side window. I shriek, tossing my phone into the air. The man in question is standing there peering in at me with a wicked grin on his face. I glare at him, and he holds his hands up in surrender.

I open the door and climb out of his SUV. "Oh my god, Eamon, you scared the shit out of me!"

We're standing mere inches apart, and I have to tip my head back to look at him. The sun is behind him, encasing him in a soft morning glow. At certain angles, you can see hints of red in his dark hair and beard. And he smells so good.

"Sorry, love," he smirks. "I won't lie and say it wasn't funny, but I truly am sorry for scaring you. Thought I'd save you the trouble of deciding if you were actually going to call or not."

I take a deep breath in an attempt to steady my pounding heart. "I was going to call. That's what I was actually getting ready to do before you

41

scared the daylights out of me."

His perfect mouth lifts on one side before he says, "Allow me to make it up to you? Let me buy you a coffee and breakfast this morning,"

My eyes widen in surprise.

"I have class at nine…" I say hesitantly.

He pulls his phone from his pocket and checks the time. "I don't think you'd make it even if you left right now, I'm sorry to say. When's your next class?"

He's got me there. If I'm being honest, I don't hate the idea of spending some one-on-one time with him.

"Not until one," I tell him. "I don't even really like my nine o'clock class."

"What is it?"

"History with Evans." I shudder. "I've put it off as long as possible. Now that I'm headed towards graduation, I figured I should probably take it."

Eamon chuckles. "I'll admit, Evans is truly awful, but the subject isn't so bad, is it?"

"Yes," I deadpan. "I hate history—at least in a classroom setting—it bores me to tears."

"Maybe you just need a tutor," he shrugs.

"Ha!" I laugh. "If you know of one, send them my way. Anything to help me get this class over with."

"As it happens," he says, "you've found one."

I look at him blankly.

"I'm a history major with a secondary degree in education," Eamon shares.

"Shut up. No, you're not."

A history teacher? He's going to be a history teacher, and for some reason, I suddenly find the subject far more interesting.

"Aye. I swear it on my life." He places a hand over his heart.

"Well, I'll keep that in mind, then," I say sheepishly.

I wouldn't learn a damn thing with him as my tutor, other than how perfect his face is.

"Do. But, in the meantime, how about that coffee?" He gestures towards the coffee shop across the street.

I take a deep breath and blow it out.

Am I accepting a coffee date, and possibly tutoring, from Eamon Kennedy? I go from ogling him from across the pub to now spending more time with him in forty-eight hours than I could have ever imagined. What universe am I living in?

"Okay," I agree, pushing my glasses up my nose. I was in such a rush this morning that I forgot my contacts.

He eyes me curiously. "Have you always worn glasses?"

I blush, because *of course I do.* "Yes and no. I've always needed them, but I only wear them when I plan on straining my eyes, like in History class. Or while working on a costume. Or reading." I prattle nervously as we walk towards the cafe.

"How do you even have time to read with your costumes and heavy drinking on the weekends?" he teases me. He holds the door open to the coffee shop and ushers me in.

I glare at him playfully. "Fair question. I've considered listening to audiobooks while I drink, but I'd probably end up challenging them to a drinking contest."

Eamon laughs as we approach the bar. Looking at me expectantly, he asks, "What will you have this morning?"

"You really don't have to get mine. Actually, I should be getting yours for letting me borrow your car," I reply quickly, but he's shaking his head.

"I don't think so. I was happy to do it, and I needed the exercise anyway," he says with a shrug.

I pointedly look him over from head to toe and scoff at him. "Right."

I turn back to the cafe employee patiently waiting for us to order. "I'll have a large coffee with room for cream, please."

"Is that all?" Eamon asks. "Anything to eat? Their scones are phenomenal. Especially the cranberry."

"Ooooh. I love cranberry scones. Okay. I'll have one since you insist."

I don't shy away from food, especially good scones. Life is too short to not enjoy delicious food.

Eamon orders a large black coffee and a scone for himself, then pays.

While he's finding us a table, I take my cup over to the condiment bar and add some cream and sugar to my coffee, gauging the color carefully. Once I'm satisfied, I find him sitting at a table near the door and slide into the chair opposite him. I hold my coffee under my nose and inhale, smiling at the comforting scent.

"I take it you enjoy your coffee," he says, watching me closely.

"Very much so. It runs in my veins," I confess, taking a sip.

"It's a wonder you don't have Guinness running through those veins." He winks at me, and my heart stutters.

I lean forward and rest my elbows on the table. "Ah, but now you know why I can handle my Guinness. I've built up a tolerance for all things dark and delicious."

Eamon's brows shoot up, and he shifts in his chair, clearing his throat roughly.

Oh. My. God. I can't believe I just said that. How mortifying! He's still staring at me with wide eyes.

"Uh, right," I say, quickly changing the subject. "So, how long have you been playing?"

"Playing football?" he asks like I've lost my mind.

"No, the guitar! You played wonderfully at open mic night. In fact, that was the only enjoyable sound coming from that stage." I shudder at the memory of the rest of the team singing loudly and off-key.

He laughs before saying, "Aye, they butchered it, didn't they? My Da was a musical genius; he could play anything. I grew up listening to him play and my Mam sing."

I smile, envisioning a young dark-haired boy sitting next to his father and learning to pluck a guitar while his Mom sings in the background.

"It sounds like you have a wonderful family. Do you miss them?" I ask.

Eamon's eyes shut, and he takes a deep breath. "My Da passed away when I was young. My ma is still alive. I miss her terribly."

My heart breaks. I know all too well the pain of losing a parent. "I'm sorry about your father. Losing a parent is crushing," I tell him. "When was the last time you visited home?"

He leans back in his chair and looks out the window of the coffee shop. "I haven't been back since I arrived in the States." The finality in his tone keeps me from asking about it again.

We talk for hours, mostly about our degrees and plans for after graduation. Eamon teasingly tells me that he hopes to teach high school and make history lessons enjoyable so the students don't turn out like me—I roll my eyes at him. We talk about the current costumes for the Beauty and The Beast production and how there are talks of a drag show replacing the spring play.

"That's amazing," Eamon says. "The LGBTQ community needs more spotlight."

Sexy *and* inclusive. Could he be any more perfect?

I smile warmly at him. "Agreed. I would be absolutely honored to design their costumes."

A buzzing sound wrenches me from the little bubble we've cocooned ourselves in. Reaching into my bag, I grab my phone.

"Oh no," I groan. "It's almost noon. I really need to get going."

I don't want to leave. I could sit here talking to Eamon all day. "Don't you have classes today?"

He shakes his head. "Not on Mondays or Wednesdays. I usually spend the mornings catching up on assignments before heading off to Paddy's."

"Ah, so he's a day drinker," I tease him.

"Hardly." He says the word with a scoff. "I'm a pretty handy carpenter, and Paddy won't tell you this, but he's shite with a hammer and nails. He hired me early on as his repair man. You'd be surprised at how often he breaks things."

I can't help but laugh at the picture he's painted of Pat. "He must be pretty clumsy if he can afford to keep you on."

Eamon nods. "That he is. But I also repair for a couple of other businesses in town. It's not constant work, what with school and soccer, but it pays the bills."

The bell above the coffee shop door chimes, and a voice calls out loudly, "Oi! Eamon! There you are! I've been trying to get a hold of you all morning!"

We both sit upright, having leaned closer to each other across the table at some point during our conversation.

Rowan saunters up to us and stops suddenly, smiling mischievously at us. I quickly gather my things and start to stand up.

"Don't leave on my account, lass. I didn't realize that Eam here was on a date," he says with a wink.

"No, it wasn't…" I start to say.

"Aye, I don't have to tell you where I'm going, Ro," Eamon snaps at his friend. "You're not my Mam."

"I really do need to go," I tell them. "Thank you again, Eamon. This was nice."

Eamon stands as I sling my bag over my shoulder. "It was a pleasure, Norah."

I give them both an awkward wave and head towards the door.

Eamon

I watch Norah from the window until I can't see her anymore. Then I turn to glare at Ro. *Fecking eejit.*

"What?" he asks stupidly. "Don't look at me that way! Maybe if you bothered to tell us that you and Ginger were an item…"

"Norah. Her name is Norah, and we're not an item. It was just coffee." I shrug.

Ro looks at me doubtfully. "Oh, so you won't mind if I ask her out, then? She is a pretty little thing, and that hair of hers means she'll be fun to…"

I instantly see red.

"Don't even think about it," I snarl.

Ro laughs and claps a hand on my shoulder. "No worries, mate. I'm thinking about asking Alicia out anyway. Think she'd mind going to Paddy's on her night off?"

I roll my eyes. "Only you would take a bartender to her place of employment on a date. That's if she'll even say yes."

"Ach! You know she will! Why do you think she always gets my drink and ignores you and Teag?" he brags, wagging his eyebrows.

"You're a louse, Ro," I tell him, shaking my head. "Anyway, I really should get to Paddy's. I'll tell Alicia to be on the lookout for you, mate."

"Don't you dare, Eamon Kennedy! You'll ruin the surprise!" Ro calls out as I walk towards the door.

* * *

I finally finish putting the shelves back up in Paddy's office and notice that I've been here for two hours already. How the old man managed to get his boxes of papers to stay on those cockeyed shelves is beyond me. It's a miracle this pub stays standing at all.

I put my tools back in the toolbox and walk out into the hall where Paddy is staring at a calendar on the wall, rubbing his forehead. "Alright there, Paddy?" I ask.

"Aye, lad. Just trying to fill in some gaps on the schedule. Not sure how I'm going to be in two places at once," he mutters.

"Anything I can help with? I can run some errands for you if that's what you need."

"If only it were that easy, my boy. I'd happily let you have my doctor's appointment if I could. Lord knows I'd much rather be at the pub," Paddy says with a laugh.

I'm automatically worried. "Doctor's appointment? Are you talking about a golfing appointment with your son or an actual appointment?"

"No." He chuckles. "I'm overdue for a checkup, is all. Nothing wrong. Just been putting it off long enough."

Relief fills me. I'm not sure I'd survive if anything happened to this old codger.

"Doesn't Alicia run the place while you're away?" I ask.

"Aye, but we're short-handed in the back. She can't tend the bar, do the cooking, and do the washing. Well, she probably could, but I'd never ask that of the lass. She'd have my hide!"

I think it over for a minute, an idea forming in my mind. It's not exactly selfless though. "I owe you another day of kitchen duty, don't I?"

Paddy turns to eye me skeptically. "Aye…"

"I suppose I could come in on that night and make the stew. Your customers do seem to prefer it, anyway," I say with a smirk. "And we could always see if fire sprite could come back for dish duty," I say nonchalantly like I'm not looking for an excuse to see Norah again.

Paddy grins and bursts out laughing. "Ach! Eamon, lad! You'll never be able to play poker. You know that, don't ya? But aye, it's a solid idea. I'll let you call Norah with the good news. Her number is in my office." He walks off, still chuckling to himself.

I'm not as sly as I think I am, apparently.

Chapter Seven

Norah

I made it to the campus early. My theater class is from one to three o'clock, and it's my favorite class, for obvious reasons. But I also love the hustle and bustle of everyone during rehearsal season, the whole team working so hard to put on an amazing production.

We typically do two bigger programs, one in the fall or winter and one in the spring. When the department head, Dr. Andrews, approached me with his idea for a modernized Beauty and The Beast, I wasn't sure I'd be able to pull off designing the costumes he wanted. We spent countless hours pouring over Google searches, books, and catalogs until we finally found something that fit his vision. I went home that same night, locked myself in my house, turned on some music, and started sketching. I sketched until four in the morning. Naturally, I started with Belle. Beauty and the Beast was my favorite Disney movie as a child, but I've always loved fantasy and anything magical. There's just something about falling in love with a beast, someone filled with hatred and so much rage, and changing their heart. I sketched the opening scene—a cobbled French street with cafes lining the sidewalks, a car or two parked along the side, and bikes leaning up against bike racks. Belle is walking next to a flower vendor in a soft light blue sweater that hangs loosely off of one shoulder and light denim, artfully distressed jeans tucked into knee-high boots. Her long brown hair falls over her shoulder in a loose braid, and she's reading a book, naturally.

I'm so lost in my thoughts while sitting in the courtyard, that I don't even hear Layla come up beside me. "What are you daydreaming about, Norie?" she asks.

I start and let out a squeak. "Layla! Sorry, I was thinking about the production."

"What else is new?" she teases and sits down on the bench next to me.

"Ha!" I laugh. "Well, if you must ask, I skipped history this morning and had coffee with Eamon Kennedy,"

I hadn't planned on sharing that with anyone just yet, but I know that I can trust Layla to keep my secret for a little longer.

Her dark brows shoot up in shock. "What? Are you serious? Tell me more!"

I shrug and tell her about how Eamon scared the living daylights out of me, then offered to make it up to me with coffee. I even told her about how I made a complete fool of myself with the coffee and Guinness comment.

Layla laughed loudly at that. "You're kidding me! Wow, this guy must really be something for you to lose all of your inhibitions like that!"

"I have no idea what came over me!" I exclaim, rubbing my hands down my face.

"I do!" Layla says. "It sounds like our Norie has finally found someone who piques her interest."

I scowl at her.

"Don't say anything to the girls yet," I beg her. "I'm not ready for the onslaught of comments and questions. No doubt Myra will already have me sleeping with him."

"You know that's true. Myra has only one thing on her mind," Layla agrees with a laugh.

We chat for a few more minutes before heading our separate ways. When I walk into the empty theater, I head towards the stage, pulling my sketch pad from my bag and flipping to an empty page. I've found that the best way to clear my mind when I'm feeling overwhelmed is to pour it onto paper. This time, I start sketching a dress that's long and flowing with a small train on the back. It has a sweetheart neckline with a tight-fitting bodice covered in delicate lace. The skirt is a soft A-line, and I'm imagining a lightweight fabric that shifts easily with the wearer. It's simple and beautiful.

"That looks an awful lot like a wedding dress, Norah." I hear from behind me.

I turn quickly to see Macie standing there. "Sheesh, Macie. You scared me!"

Pathetic. That's the third time today someone has snuck up on me and made me jump.

"Sorry! I wanted to see what you were sketching. It's beautiful. Are you making wedding gowns now?" Macie asks.

I pause to think about that. I'd never considered making wedding gowns before, but the thought intrigues me. I always said I would make my own wedding dress someday—not that I'm even entertaining the idea of getting married. Dr. Andrews walks in and I realize the room filled up while I was sketching away, completely oblivious to my surroundings.

"Attention, everyone! Attention!" he calls, hands cupped around his mouth. "Today, we are going to work on Act Two, Scene One. Where are my villains?"

This scene always makes me uncomfortable, so I usually sneak back to the costume room and work on the outfits for whatever scene is next. Creating costumes for the villains was easy enough; they're donned in black hoodies and black pants. It wasn't hard to create this scene: Belle walking through Central Park at night alone. She had just stormed out on the Beast after a quarrel and needed some air, unexpectedly finding herself surrounded by men with ill intentions. Knowing it could be a trigger, Dr. Andrews changed the villains to muggers instead.

I wander over to the rack of costumes for the next scene when Belle and Beast start to realize their feelings for each other. I let the colors from the Disney film influence these designs. Belle will be wearing a light pink hooded sweater with leggings. Her hair will be half up with soft curls framing her face. Beast will be in a white shirt with a denim jacket, complete with a bruised eye gallantly acquired while protecting Belle from her attackers. This was always my favorite part of any story, when the couple escapes from a dangerous situation and realizes that life is too short to not love each other.

I'm confident the costumes are all set for this scene, as most of the items were found in the actors' own closets. The attire for the ballroom scene will be the most time-consuming to make, but thankfully, my team is amazing, and we've never missed a deadline. However, Dr. Andrews is demanding so much more with this production. He wants it to dazzle and stay in the minds of the viewers forever. I spent over a week sketching ideas for this scene and none of them dazzled. Eventually, I approached Andrews about an entirely new idea for that scene. Rather than keeping the traditional ballroom scene, we could change it to a garden party that included not just Belle and Beast dancing together, but other couples as well. The women would be wearing dresses resembling different types of flowers. He loved it immediately. My sketches began to flow like water after that. Roses, calla lilies, peonies, hydrangeas. Each one came naturally to me, which wasn't surprising as I was raised by a mother who was an avid gardener. She had some of the most beautiful flower beds in the whole Midwest, and I easily brought Mom's garden to life on paper. Andrews raved over each one, stating it was some of my best work. Creating it on the department's budget would be the difficult part.

* * *

I'm walking back across campus when I feel my phone buzz in my pocket.

Fully expecting it to be one of the girls, I don't even look at the caller ID and just answer with, "Yes, my love?" Then wait for one of my friends to start prattling.

"Well then, lass. I hadn't realized we were declaring ourselves today, or I might have planned a better speech."

I gasp, nearly dropping the phone, as my heart starts galloping in my chest. "Eamon?"

"The one and only. I hope I'm not interrupting anything?" he inquires.

Why is he calling me? How did he get my number? Why are my hands so sweaty?

"Uh, no. I'm just on my way home. How did you get my number?" I ask, surprised that I'm not outraged that he has it.

"Ah, you can thank Paddy O'Nelly for that," he explains.

I should have known. Who else would have my number that knows Eamon as well?

"I see. What can I do for you, then? Is Pat okay?" I ask, suddenly worried.

"Aye, fit as a fiddle," he says, his deep brogue doing more than just reassuring me that my favorite pub owner is okay. His warm voice reverberates down my spine. "But it is because of him I'm calling. Would you be interested in coming back in for dish duty on Wednesday night? Our dear Paddy has an out-of-town appointment and needs the extra coverage. I offered to make stew and wondered if you wouldn't mind helping out?"

Dare I say he sounds...hopeful?

"I don't see why I couldn't. What time should I be there?" I ask, feeling as giddy as a schoolgirl.

"He said the dinner rush starts around seven. Can you be there then?"

"Absolutely!" I nearly shout, then take a deep breath before adding, "I mean, yeah, of course. Seven is great."

There's a low chuckle in response. "Great. Thanks a million, Norah. You're a gem."

"Sure, anytime. Can't wait!" I say a little too enthusiastically.

"To wash dishes?" he asks, clearly amused.

"Uh, well, no. Just...uh...happy to help out. That's all."

Real smooth, Norah. I slap my hand to my forehead.

"Right," he says, seemingly unconvinced. "I'll see you then. Have a good day, love."

My brain short circuits. *Love. He called me love.* I know that's a common phrase in Ireland, but damn. I like the way it sounds rolling off of his tongue.

"You too," I choke out.

Chapter Eight

Eamon

Tuesday morning comes too soon. I roll over, slam a hand down on my alarm, and groan, cursing our sadistic coach. Practice is way too fecking early on Tuesdays and Thursdays. If it were up to him, he'd have us practice at this time every day, all week long. We start drills at four in the morning and keep it up for two hours. Monday, Wednesday, and Friday are easier to manage, and the weekends are usually free unless we have a game.

I pull on my practice kit, brush my teeth, and head for the door. It's going to be a long day. My first class isn't until eight, so blessedly, I'll have time to shower and grab breakfast before hitting the books. I have three classes today, though, and each one lasts around two hours. Education degrees are no joke.

When I arrive at the field and step out of my car, a bleary-eyed Teagan approaches from a few spaces down and grunts out greeting as he pulls his hood over his head. He's not much of a morning person, so we walk in silence for a few moments before he speaks.

"Ro said you were out with Ginger yesterday. When did that start?" he asks, voice gruff with sleep.

I roll my eyes. *Fucking Rowan.* "If Ro had half a brain in his head, he'd keep his mouth shut."

"So it *is* true. I thought he was full of shite. Guess I was wrong. So, found a new flame did ya?" he asks, a hint of longing in his voice. It's only been a handful of months since his long-term girlfriend ended their relationship to run off to Dallas with another guy.

"No, Teag," I tell him. "Paddy had us come in for dish duty to atone for our behavior on Friday night. I let her drive my car to her house so she wasn't walking home alone. We had coffee when she returned it. That's all."

"No plans to see her again, then?" Teagan hedges.

I shrug. "We're working at Paddy's again tomorrow night."

"Watch out for Ro. You know how he is."

Do I ever? "Aye," I say. "He already brought it up. He has his eyes on Alicia at the moment though"

"Ach! He better not fuck things up. I'm not finding another pub because he screwed over the bartender. Plus, she's a good lass. I'd hate to see Ro hurt her," Teagan says indignantly.

"I don't think we have to worry about that. If anyone can set him straight, it'll be Alicia."

We're on the field at this point, so we set our bags down and begin stretching. Coach likes to start practice off with a long run because apparently, we don't run enough on the field. While warming up, my thoughts keep turning to Norah. I like the idea of spending more time with her and it doesn't hurt that she's absolutely gorgeous. I'm entertaining the idea of asking her out but haven't *really* dated anyone since moving to the States—a night out here and there, but nothing serious. Norah doesn't strike me as a hookup kind of girl and if I'm being honest, I'm not sure I want just a hookup with her.

* * *

I'm sitting at a table by the window of the cafe, drinking coffee and eating a protein bar I grabbed from home, as I study for a quiz in my first class. Giving my eyes a break, I look out the window. It's lovely out today and it reminds me of home. I'm about to turn back to my book when a glint of red hair catches my attention. It's Norah. She's walking across the street, heading for this very cafe. Her hands are stuffed into the pocket of a weathered hoodie with IRELAND sprawled across the front in faded lettering. Suddenly the clouds part and a ray of sunlight hits her hair and my breath hitches in my throat. She truly looks like a fire sprite with her auburn waves burning like a bright flame. I can't believe I've never noticed her at Paddy's before. My heart pounds as she walks through the door, the little bell tinkling above her head. She moves to the back of the line and glances around as if she's looking for someone. It's when her eyes meet mine and she smiles that I think she might have been looking for me.

Norah

I wake up early on Tuesday and drink a cup of coffee while I get ready for my eight o'clock class. It doesn't take me long to get dressed, fix my hair, and put on a little bit of makeup, and after scrounging around my fridge and pantry for a moment, I discover that I am in desperate need of some groceries. There's not a single thing in my house that will pass as a decent breakfast. What I really want is another one of those cranberry scones.

I glance at the clock and realize that I actually have enough time to stop and get one on my way to class. Grabbing my bag and locking the door behind me, I step into a perfect September morning. The sun is shining and the air is crisp, perfect for the heather-green hoodie I have on. I got it in Ireland and it's my favorite article of clothing. I'm surprised that it isn't completely threadbare with how much I wear it.

It doesn't take me long to reach the coffee shop. The extra pep in my step is strictly about the scone and has nothing to do with the possibility of seeing Eamon there. When I walk through the door, I immediately go to the back of the line before looking around the cafe. It's quaint and cheery with light wood furniture and pops of pastel colors scattered throughout. I look towards the corner by the window and see Eamon sitting at a table, books open in front of him. Our eyes lock immediately and his lips spread into a slow grin. God, he looks good enough to eat in a black button-up shirt with the sleeves rolled to his elbows, the color making his blue eyes pop. I smile brightly at him in return.

I'm not sure how much time has passed but apparently, it's enough that the person behind me coughs to signal that I need to move forward and order. *Rude.* I quickly give my order to the cashier and pay, then wait at the end of the bar for my coffee and breakfast. It's an exercise in self-control to not keep glancing over my shoulder at Eamon. Once my order is in hand, I wander towards his table.

"Mind if I join you?" I ask cheerfully.

"Please do," he answers quickly, gesturing to the seat across from him. "Fancy meeting you here. No coffee at home?"

I scoff as I sit. "Are you kidding? It's the only thing in my house right now. This is cup number two. Plus, I'm currently addicted to these cranberry scones. All thanks to you, I might add."

His mouth curves into a lopsided grin that makes me want to cry a little. It's *the smile.* The one every romance novel describes. That heart-stopping grin that makes you fall in love with the one wearing it. I look away before I do something really stupid, like confess my love for dark and delicious things again.

"Do you have class this morning?" Eamon asks, snapping me back into reality.

"Yes, at eight; I'm afraid I can't stay long," I tell him regretfully. Stupid classes. Who needs college anyway?

"I do as well. Want a lift?" he offers, and my heart flip flops.

"Oh, I usually take the bus…"

"I see." He nods slowly. "I understand if you're still uncomfortable riding with me. Just thought I'd offer."

I don't miss how his shoulders droop, almost as if he's disappointed. Truth be told, I *want* to ride with him, and the fear I normally feel around men is nowhere to be found.

"Actually," I start, "I think I will take you up on that ride. The bus is so crowded at this time of day."

I peek up at him through my lashes and see that lopsided grin plastered on his perfect face again. *Swoon.*

"Alright, then," he says, closing his book. "Let me pack up and we'll go."

I take that time to pinch off a piece of the scone and pop it into my mouth. I chew slowly as I watch him methodically gather his books and place them in his backpack. Once everything is packed away, he stands and slips his arms through the straps. The movement causes his shirt to stretch across his broad chest, and I'm momentarily transfixed—and jealous of those straps that get to cling to him like that. *What I wouldn't give to be a backpack strap right now.*

We walk out of the coffee shop to his SUV, and I'm surprised when he reaches around me and opens the passenger side door. He's so close that whatever manly scent he possesses envelopes me completely. I inhale deeply.

"Sorry for the mess," Eamon says sheepishly after I climb into the seat. "I had practice early this morning. I usually just toss everything in the car and go."

I smile at him. It's not a mess at all, but the scent is more concentrated here. He shuts my door and rounds the front of the car to the driver's side. He slides in and starts the engine before making sure I'm buckled up. Once we're on our way, he asks me about the play's progress.

"It's coming along," I tell him. "I have all of the costumes designed and half of them are already in physical form. I'm struggling to figure out a way to create the costumes for the dance scene while staying within Dr. Andrew's budget though. I swear, the man thinks this is Broadway!"

"I can't honestly say I know what scene you're referring to," he admits, shocking me.

"What?" I gape at him. "You've never seen Beauty and The Beast? How is that even possible?"

Eamon rubs his jaw and chuckles. "No, I haven't. I didn't watch many movies growing up. By the time I came to America, cartoons weren't exactly on my watch list."

"We're going to have to remedy that immediately," I say decidedly.

"Are we?" he asks hopefully.

I pause, realizing what I just said, and laugh nervously. "I mean, I suppose *we* don't have to remedy that. You could always watch it with the soccer team..."

Eamon laughs heartily, the corners of his eyes crinkling. "I'd much rather watch anything with you than the team."

My cheeks heat, and the butterflies in my stomach start fluttering like crazy at the thought of being curled up on my couch with him, lights low, watching Beauty and the Beast.

"If that's what you want, of course. I don't want to force you into anything," he adds quickly.

I'm touched by his thoughtfulness. He has no idea how much it means to me that he's giving me the choice. I consider making it a group thing but decide against it. The more I think about it, the less I want to expose him to my group of friends. At least right now.

"Actually, it's more like I'm forcing you into watching a Disney movie. You can say no," I offer.

"Hardly, lass. I need to be up to date when I go see your work on stage," he says, turning his gaze on me briefly.

"You're going to come to the play?" I ask incredulously.

"I hadn't planned on it, but the more you talk about it, the more I want to," he says with a shrug.

I beam at him in response.

"Now," he says, "when should we plan our movie date?"

I giggle nervously. He said it was a date. Does he mean an actual date? Or just a date on the calendar? Am I overthinking this? I'm still pondering this when we pull into the student parking lot near the Economics building. The car sits idling as he turns and looks at me expectantly.

"Tomorrow night is out obviously, but maybe Thursday?" I suggest. "Or if this week doesn't work, we can do next?"

"I hate to say it," he says with a frown, "but it will have to be next week. We have an away game Thursday night and Friday is open mic night. Paddy said it gave the customers a good laugh last time, and he wants us back."

"Ah. I'm not sure I can endure that again." I grimace. "I'd suggest Saturday, but I'm working on costumes all weekend. What about Monday?"

"Monday is free for me." He smiles softly at me. "I have practice until six. I can head over after a quick shower, so let's say a quarter to seven?"

"That sounds great," I breathe. "I'll have the popcorn, so just bring yourself."

I'm simultaneously shocked at and proud of myself. I just made a date with a man. A really, really hot man. Just the two of us. Together. At my house. I keep my face calm, but inside, my poor little anxiety-ridden introverted soul is screaming at me.

"Grand," he says, opening his car door. "Looking forward to it."

We step out of the car and meet on the sidewalk.

"Thanks for the ride," I say, looking up at him

"Anytime, lass."

We part ways and head in opposite directions, casting the occasional look over our shoulders at each other as we go.

Chapter Nine

Norah

I float through my day, barely paying any attention to my professors. My mind keeps drifting to the upcoming movie date with Eamon. Why did he agree to that? He can't honestly want to watch an animated movie with me. He's probably just one of those really nice guys who agreed because he didn't want to hurt my feelings. I'm suddenly second-guessing everything and feeling all sorts of stupid. Ugh. Why am I like this? No. I am *not* going to think like that. Layla's words come back to me and boost my confidence. Even if nothing romantic happens between us, maybe I'll at least make a new friend.

Arriving at Dr. Andrews' office, I knock twice before entering.

"Good afternoon, Dr. Andrews!" I greet him cheerfully.

"Hello, Miss Grady," he replies, looking at me curiously. "You're in an exceptionally good mood today."

"Yes, I am." I smile widely at him. "I was hoping to talk to you about the costumes for the garden scene."

"Oh no." His face falls and his eyes fill with concern. "Please tell me there's not a problem. I can't give up your idea. It's too perfect."

"Well…" I start. "It depends on how you look at it. The costumes can be done by dress rehearsal, but they aren't going to be done within the budget. I've scoured every source I can find for discounted fabric that will have the effect we're looking for, but I'm coming up empty-handed. I can cut corners in some areas, but for the overlays on the skirts, I can't."

He frowns, steeping his fingers together in front of his face, "I see. That is a predicament." He pauses to think for a moment before continuing, "I could talk to the Dean about a special allowance, but I'm not sure he'd be so keen. For now, just focus on finding the materials you need for Belle's dress. If we need to cut people from the scene or dim their attire, we will. But let me see what I can come up with in the meantime."

"Okay, I can do that," I tell him. "I'm spending this weekend doing nothing but working on costumes. Thank you, Dr. Andrews."

I stand to leave when he says, "Miss Grady, you really are one of a kind. You could do this for the big screens, you know."

I blush at the compliment. "I'm flattered that you think so."

* * *

On my way home, I stop by the fabric store in search of the perfect material for Belle's dress. The skirt will resemble an upside-down yellow rose, falling in soft layers that lightly brush the ground. The bodice will be modest with a scalloped off-shoulder neckline. Of course, she'll be wearing long gloves, but they'll be made of lace. As for the fullness of the skirt, that's still up in the air. A full ball gown will be a lot of work, but it needs to at least be an A-line.

I walk through row after row of fabrics before I find myself in front of white silk. I run my fingers over the soft material, immediately envisioning my newest design. Maybe wedding dresses should be in my future. Each one would be unique to the bride that wears it. Now my fingers are itching to sketch, but that will have to wait at least until I finish the costumes for Beauty and the Beast. But for now, I leave the store with samples of chiffon, crepe, and organza.

The sun is just starting to set when I get home. I unlock the door and step inside, flipping on the light. I love my house. It's a small, open-concept bungalow with one bedroom and one bathroom. There's a laundry room off of the kitchen that leads to the sunroom; it's my favorite part of the entire house. The natural lighting from the three walls of windows makes it the perfect sewing room

I set the fabric samples on the kitchen island and open the fridge to see what my dinner options are: an almost empty bag of cheese and a green pepper. I need to go grocery shopping, but maybe I can talk Layla into taking me tomorrow before I go back to Pat's for dish duty. My heart flutters at the thought of seeing Eamon again. I really need to get myself under control. This is ridiculous.

My phone buzzes, alerting me to a text message from Charlie.

Charlie: *You home?*

Me: *Yeah, what's up?*

Charlie: *Missing you. Can I come over?*

Me: *Sure. No food here. Just a warning.*

Charlie: *I'll bring the wine. ;)*

Charlie knows me so well, and guilt floods me when I realize that I haven't told her about the last couple of days with Eamon. I'll tell her tonight.

Twenty minutes later, Charlie walks through the door carrying a large brown paper bag.

"How much wine do you think we need, Charlie?" I laugh.

"After the day I've had, all of it. But I also brought dinner. Hope you're okay with Chinese!" she says brightly after setting the bag on the island and begins pulling out cartons from our favorite Chinese restaurant. My mouth immediately starts watering as the smell of General Tso's chicken fills the kitchen.

I give her a quick hug and say, "I'll grab the bowls and glasses while you tell me about your day. What has you so willing to destroy your liver?"

Charlie groans, positioning the corkscrew over the top of the first bottle of wine. "Today was just awful. For starters, we were short-staffed and then we had the worst afternoon rush in the history of afternoon rushes. It's like the whole world decided that at two o'clock this afternoon they all needed to come to *my* store. It was insane. I didn't even get to take a pee break until after my shift. And why are old people so damn cranky?"

I snort in amusement while I fill our bowls with rice. "You sound like Layla. There's not a day that goes by that she's not insulting the elderly."

Charlie has been the store manager for Starbucks for years. When she transferred from our hometown to Wilmington, they were glad to have her since the store back home had the highest ratings in the area. Nobody works harder than Charlie, so for her to even complain about a busy day is a big deal.

"Go sit down," I tell her, handing her a bowl. "Put your feet up. I'll pour your drink."

It's not often that I get to take care of Charlie. It makes me feel useful. I pour a glass of wine for each of us and move to the couch. Her bowl sits on the coffee table as she rests her head on the back of the sofa and sighs heavily.

She rolls her head in my direction. "What's new with you, Norie? I feel like we haven't had a chance to just talk in a while," she says, reaching a hand over to squeeze my arm.

Here we go.

"Well, it's funny that you ask. There have been some new developments with the costumes for the play, and I have a date with Eamon Kennedy next week," I say quickly before taking a sip of my wine.

Charlie bolts upright, eyes comically wide. "What? Why was that not the first thing out of your mouth when I came through the door?"

"You're having a bad day. I wanted to hear about it." I shrug, stuffing a fork full of chicken in my mouth.

"Oh, please. This trumps my shitty day at work, and you know it! Tell me how this happened! Have you told the others?" She's bouncing up and down in her seat, her wine sloshing around the glass precariously.

I carefully take the glass from her hand, setting it on the coffee table before replacing it with her bowl of food.

"You eat. I'll talk."

Charlie hastily scoops some rice into her mouth and I take a deep breath before telling her everything that's happened since Monday morning. She's a great listener, interjecting with the proper reactions at just the right time.

"Oh my god, Norah!" she squeals. "I'm so happy for you! You deserve this. I mean, I don't really know him, so of course, I'll have to approve. But if he passes all my tests, he sounds like a dream come true."

"Let's not get too excited. There's no guarantee this is going anywhere. He could just end up being a friend." Charlie starts to say something, but I cut her off. "I'm not trying to downgrade myself, but he is beyond gorgeous. And I'm still not sure if I can completely let myself do this. I feel safe when I'm with him, but what happens if things do progress and he tries to kiss me? What if I have a panic attack on him?"

The idea of Eamon kissing me makes my blood thump heavily through my veins.

"Just take it one day at a time. If he's worth it, he'll understand and walk this road with you. And if he doesn't understand, then he's not worth your time," Charlie says.

We talk for a couple more hours until Charlie can't hide her yawning anymore. She stands up and stretches.

"I've gotta go, Norie. I'll be dead on my feet if I don't go home and go to bed," she says, hugging me.

I squeeze her back. "Go. You need the rest. Love you."

"Love you. Keep me posted on the Eamon situation. Oh, and you know you're going to have to tell the others soon. Myra has some sort of radar, so beware," she says, shutting the door behind her.

Chapter Ten

Eamon

I walk into Paddy's at half past six to find Alicia pulling a few beers behind the bar and a handful of people scattered throughout the pub. The dreary skies are reminiscent of Ireland, and for a moment, I actually miss it. Ireland will always be the most beautiful country in the world to me.

I should probably call my Mam soon since it's been a while since we've spoken. I know it broke her heart when I left for the States, but I just couldn't bear being there anymore. After everything went to shite, I was desperate for an escape, so when the Coach of the UNCW Seahawks called and asked me to come play for them, I said yes without question. I told Mam it was the chance of a lifetime, and a week later, I was boarding a plane for America.

"Hey, Eamon," Alicia greets me as I saunter up to the bar. "Thanks for filling in tonight. I have a feeling this weather will bring us a fair bit of business. Something about stew and beer on a rainy day…"

"Aye." I nod in agreement. "Anything for Paddy. Have you heard from him?"

"No. Why he doesn't see a doctor in town, I'll never know. Surely his son can find someone for him." She shrugs, her long black ponytail swinging behind her.

"Who knows? Shall I start on stew, then?" I ask, knocking my knuckles on the bar.

"Paddy set up a batch before he left. It's already on the stove warming up. Might go ahead and start the next batch," she suggests. "When will our Norah be here?"

I smile at the reminder. "I told her seven. Hope that's okay."

"Perfect. Now off to it, Chef," she says cheekily.

I'm in the middle of chopping carrots when a pleasant laugh sounds through the swinging doors. I look up as Norah walks in, laughter still evident on her face.

"Hi!" She beams at me, and I damn near cut my finger off with how radiant that smile is.

"Hello there, lass. You're certainly in a good mood this evening," I tell her, carefully navigating the knife away from my fingers and back to the carrots.

She ducks into Paddy's office to put her purse away before responding, "Everyone keeps telling me that today. Makes me wonder if I'm normally grumpy."

"No. At least not that I've seen. Other than Friday night…" I wink at her, unable to keep myself from teasing her. It's too easy and entirely way too much fun.

She narrows her eyes at me and says pointedly, "That was a completely different situation. My honor was being challenged. *Anyone* would be cranky."

"Fair point," I concede, holding my hands—and knife—up in surrender.

She grabs an apron from the hook and ties it quickly around her waist.

I watch her as she twists those auburn curls into a knot on the top of her head. Once she's satisfied with its position, she puts her hands on her hips and looks at me expectantly.

"Alright. Where do you want me?" she asks.

I can think of a few places I want her, but not one of them is appropriate. Stopping those thoughts in their tracks, I cough roughly and look around the kitchen. There aren't any dishes to be washed yet, but I do have a pile of veggies still needing to be peeled and chopped.

I nod towards the pile and ask, "Do you cook, Norah?"

"I do," she says. "Baking is my forte, but I'm pretty good with a peeler and knife."

She grabs the peeler and a large potato and gets to work. We stand next to each other in companionable silence for a few minutes, lost in our own thoughts.

"How was practice?" Norah asks, breaking the silence.

I glance sideways at her. She's not looking at me; she's still focused on her work.

"Wet," I tell her, "and grueling. Coach has been in a foul mood this week."

"You have to practice in the rain?" she asks, scrunching her nose at the idea.

I chuckle. "We play in the rain, so why not?"

"Good point," she says with a shrug.

"Have you never been to a game when it rains?"

The stands are usually pretty empty on rainy games, which is understandable. None of us enjoy playing in the rain, so I imagine sitting in it isn't much fun either.

"I can't say that I have, to be honest. I've been to a few games, but always under optimal conditions," Norah says brightly.

I stop dicing carrots and turn to her. "Well, we'll have to remedy that, then. Won't we, Miss Grady?"

I hear her suck in a short breath and see her cheeks turning pink as she looks up at me. Her skin is already flawless, but when she blushes? I can't get enough of it.

"Um…" she hesitates.

"It's only fair," I tell her, lightly nudging her arm with my elbow. "I've never seen your Beauty and the Beast, and you've never been to a rainy game. Don't you think we should settle both scores?"

Laughing, she says, "You're not wrong, but it's different. You'll be playing, while I sit in the stands alone—no one to explain things to me. Whereas, with Beauty and the Beast, I'll be there to help you navigate."

"It's a Disney movie. How much navigation do I need?" I grin at her, and she rolls her eyes before going back to peeling.

"And when exactly is the next rainy game going to be? Weather this time of year is pretty temperamental, so there's really no telling when that will be."

"I guess you'll just have to come to all of them, then," I tell her. "I think I'd enjoy seeing you in the cheering section on a regular basis."

She stares up at me with those wide blue eyes, and I'm a goner.

"Hey!" Alicia barks, coming through the doors from the pub.

We both startle at her intrusion. I don't remember moving closer to Norah, but somehow, there's little to no space between our sides and arms. She must realize it the same time I do, because her face flames again and she takes a large step away.

"Love birds, the dishes are starting to pile up, and we're gonna need that stew tonight!" Alicia continues, smirking at us knowingly.

"Sorry, Alicia. I'll go grab those dishes now," Norah says quickly. She puts down the peeler and wipes her hands on the closest towel. Grabbing a bussing tote, she scurries out of the door before Alicia can say another word.

Alicia turns to me with a severe expression. "Don't do her wrong, Kennedy. She's one in a million. If you're just looking for a fuck buddy, you won't find it with her. Not with what she's been through."

And with that, she turns and exits the kitchen, leaving me completely stunned and mildly insulted that she thinks so little of me. Sure, I've had a fling or two, but I'm not Mac. I don't chase girls, and I'm certainly not looking for a *fuck buddy*. I won't say that I haven't had some less-than-proper thoughts about Norah, but I have absolutely zero intention of pursuing those thoughts. I know she's one in a million. It's what drew me to her to begin with.

But what did Alicia mean when she said *what she's been through?* Obviously some wanker did something to break her heart, but then, I think back to our earlier interactions. My blood freezes in my veins when I recall how hesitant she was to be alone with me at first. I figured she was just being cautious, but now I'm wondering if that caution goes beyond *stranger danger.* The thought of someone hurting her enrages me so much that I grip the edge of the counter to steady myself and calm my breathing. I have the sudden urge to be her avenger and destroy anyone who's ever done anything to harm her or make her fearful.

Norah

I bustle through the door with a tub full of glasses, bowls, and silverware and make my way to the dishwasher. Setting the tub on the counter, I begin unloading it. I'm about to make some sort of smart-ass comment about Eamon's slow chopping skills, but stop short when I see the expression on his face. His strong jaw is clenched tightly, and he looks anything but amused. In fact, he looks angry. He scoops up the chopped veggies in both hands and drops them into the pot, then goes back to chopping more carrots with more force than necessary.

What could possibly have angered him in the mere minutes I was out of the kitchen? Is it what Alicia called us? *Love birds.* Maybe I've been reading him all wrong and he just wants to be friends. My heart sinks as the realization hits. Feeling foolish, I pour my focus into washing dishes, moving loads through the dishwasher, and then heading back out to the dining room to collect more. Eamon and I don't say another word to each other until Alicia comes back to tell us the kitchen is officially closed.

Sighing with relief, I lean against the dishwasher to catch my breath. When I look up, Eamon is standing in front of me holding two pints of

Guinness with a wary expression on his face.

"Here," he says softly, "you earned it."

Taking one of the pints, I attempt to lighten the mood by raising an eyebrow at him and asking, "Are you sure they aren't both for me? You know how much of a lush I am."

He smirks and I feel the tension crack. I take a long drink, staring at him the whole time, then lick the foam off my lips. He tracks the movement with those vivid blue eyes.

"Something bothering you, Eamon?"

His brows furrow in confusion. "Why do you ask?"

I shrug then nod towards the stove. "You seemed pretty mad at that pot of stew earlier. You were staring daggers at it."

I may be quiet and shy, but I'll always try to add laughter to unpleasant moments.

He hesitates, rubbing the stubble on his jaw. "It's just that…that batch of stew wasn't as good as I had hoped."

Eyeing him dubiously, I take another swallow of Guinness. "Whatever you say, Kennedy."

"It's nothing. Don't worry yourself about it," he says, moving his hand to rub the back of his neck. The movement raises the bottom of his t-shirt, revealing his well-defined stomach and the start of his happy trail. I gulp down another drink, trying not to ogle him *too much* but failing miserably. He's too beautiful *not* to look at. The longer I stare, the more my skin heats.

"You alright, love? You're looking a bit flushed," he asks with concern.

Thoroughly embarrassed, I clear my throat. "Yeah, sorry. It's warm in here; that's all."

Good lord, Norah. Pull yourself together.

"Aye, it is," he agrees with a nod. "Thanks again for coming to help out tonight. Alicia and I would have drowned without you here."

"Sure, no problem. It was actually kind of fun. And I'd do anything for Pat."

"He's a good aul fella, to be sure." Eamon smiles softly.

I smile in return. "Well, if we're done for the night, I better head home.

Another early morning awaits me."

"How are you getting home?" he asks, pushing off of the kitchen island and taking a couple of steps towards me.

"I was going to call Charlie and have her pick me up."

Taking my now-empty glass, he reaches past me to put it in the dishwasher tray with his own. My spine straightens at his proximity. Why does he always smell so good? I resist the urge to bury my nose in his shirt. After setting the glasses down, he pulls back, leaving just a few inches between us. I should be filled with anxiety right now with how close he is, but that's not what I'm feeling at all.

"I'll take you home, lass," he says simply. "No need to have her get out when I'm already here."

"N-no, it's okay," I stutter, looking up at his face. "I can't ask that of you."

"You didn't ask, love. I offered. And it's not any trouble." He smiles warmly.

"Are you sure?" I ask, twisting my hands together nervously. I don't want him to feel obligated.

"Absolutely. I don't say things I don't mean, so you can be sure that if I'm offering, it's because I *want* to."

"Oh," I breathe out. "Well, okay, then. Thank you, Eamon."

"You're welcome." He gestures towards the doors leading to the bar. "Let me just check with Alicia to see if she needs us for anything else, then we can go."

I duck into Pat's office to grab my purse from the bottom drawer of the filing cabinet. When I come back out, Eamon holds the door open, letting me go before him. Glancing up at him as I pass I give him a small smile. His eyes soften, and one side of his mouth lifts in return. We find Alicia closing out the cash register and completing the nightly deposit.

"Hey, Alicia, we're done in the back. What can we help with out here?" I ask.

She holds up a finger to signal us to let her finish her current task before putting down her ink pen and turning our way.

"Okay, sorry." She grins. "When I'm closing out the cash till, I'm laser-focused."

"Aye, seems like a good thing to be focused on," Eamon responds. "Pat appreciates it, I'm sure."

Alicia rolls her eyes. "Only because he hates doing it. I don't know how he manages on my nights off, to be honest. Anyway, no, we're done for tonight, guys. Thanks so much for coming in. Seriously, you saved my ass."

"No problem. Happy to help," I tell her honestly.

"Need a ride home, Norie?" she asks as she stuffs the cash and deposit slip into a blue bank bag.

"I've got her," Eamon says quickly from behind me.

My eyes go wide, and Alicia raises her dark brows, a coy smile playing on her lips. "Norah, you good with that?"

"Yep!" I respond a little too cheerfully.

She chuckles before saying, "Alright, you two. Behave. Thanks again."

Waving our farewell, Eamon and I leave the pub and walk straight to his SUV. He opens the passenger door for me before rounding the front and climbing into the driver's seat.

"Where to?" he asks as he starts the car.

"I'm on the other side of Marstella Park. Just head North on Third Street and turn left onto Meares," I direct him.

"Right. You are close, then. My flat's halfway between here and campus," Eamon says.

"That must be nice. I probably should have found a place a little closer to campus, but as soon as I saw my house, I knew it was where I wanted to be."

"Do you live by yourself?" he asks, glancing over at me.

"I do. Charlie and I were going to get a place together, but she didn't know when she was going to be moving to North Carolina, so she told me not to pick a place based on that." I shrug. "It worked out well. She met Mark shortly after moving here, and it was basically love at first sight."

"You don't get nervous living alone in Wilmington?"

"Nah. It's a quiet neighborhood, and Layla lives next door, so I'm not really that alone. We usually have dinner together a few times a week if she's not working," I tell him, angling my body to see his face better. "What about you? Do you and Rowan and Teagan live together?"

Eamon huffs a laugh. "No, thank Christ. Teagan and I would probably do alright together, but I think I'd murder Ro after a day or two. If you couldn't tell, he's a bit...much."

I snort a quiet laugh. "Yeah, I gathered that. Oh, I'm the second house on the right."

I point at my house, and he pulls into my driveway. It's already a short drive, but it seemed to go quicker while talking with Eamon.

"Thanks again for the ride, Eamon. I appreciate it."

He turns towards me, running his eyes over my face and tipping the corner of his mouth up in a warm smile. "Anytime, lass. It was my pleasure."

I throw up a silent prayer of thanks that it's dark in the car so he can't see my traitorous face blushing.

"Good luck at practice tomorrow," I tell him.

"Aye, I'll need it," he says.

We stare at each other for a handful of seconds, but it feels like a lifetime. Finally, he blows out a breath and says, "Goodnight, Norah."

His deep voice feels like a warm caress that I can feel trail down my entire body.

"Goodnight, Eamon," I whisper and clumsily exit the vehicle.

When I make it to my front door, I turn to wave, fully expecting him to be backing out of the driveway, but he's sitting there watching to make sure I get inside safely.

Chapter Eleven

Norah

Thursday passes in a blur. I've downed four cups of coffee by the time my second class rolls around, so I'm jittery but no more awake than I was at seven this morning. When I got home last night, I was absolutely exhausted, but I jumped in the shower anyway just to rinse off the smell of dishwater and beer. Knowing my hair would be an absolute disaster if I went to bed with it wet, I put some gel in it and braided it. After brushing my teeth, I fell into bed and didn't budge until my alarm went off a handful of hours later.

On my way out of the Economics building after class, I pull my phone out and call Layla.

"Hey, what are you doing?" I ask when she answers.

"Not a lot. I work a late shift tonight, so I'm just taking it easy until then. What's up?"

"I was wondering if you maybe wanted to give your car-less friend a lift to the store? My cabinets are completely empty. I'm working on costumes all weekend, so I don't want to starve," I confess.

Layla laughs. "Yeah, we can do that. Come on over when you're ready."

"You're the best! Have I told you how much I love you?" I ask her.

"Not today! See you in a little bit!" she says, then hangs up.

My phone buzzes immediately with a group text.

Myra: *Girls night tomorrow night? Please say yes!*

I wince at the thought. Our last Friday night out together did not end well; with the exception of meeting Eamon, of course.

Amelia: *You know I'm in! I vote for the pub again! Open mic night turned out well for us! ;)*

Charlie: *LOL. I'm game.*

Layla: *I'm actually off on Friday! Where and what time?*

I'm surprised by that. Normally, Layla stays home when she's off work, claiming that she's *peopled out* and wants to hide from social interaction.

Norah: *Here's the deal. I HAVE to work on costumes this weekend, so I will have one drink, then head home. Got it?*

Myra and Amelia both send a laughing face and I just roll my eyes.

* * *

Two hours later, Layla and I are walking into the grocery store—one that Layla doesn't work at. We chat idly, placing necessary and random items in our cart. Layla has been picking up some overtime shifts to save money to go back home for the holidays, and even though it's not technically a vacation, I envy her. I haven't left the state of North Carolina in four years. While I love it here, I miss traveling somewhere unknown. I daydream about Ireland constantly. If time allows, I search for the best flights and lodging in all of the places I didn't get to experience last time. Maybe that will be my graduation gift to myself.

When we're both satisfied that we've spent way too much money on things we really don't need, we load up and head home. It's so convenient having a best friend who lives next door. I offer to make Layla dinner before she goes to work as payment for taking me shopping. Spaghetti is a quick and easy option. While I wait for the water to come to a boil, I tell her a little bit about dish duty with Eamon last night. I don't mention our date—or whatever it is. I'd like to avoid an onslaught of questions, but it's nice to talk to one of my girlfriends about a guy in a positive light.

Layla looks at me knowingly. "Norie, I think something is brewing here. He seems really into you, and you're definitely into him!"

I can't help the grin that spreads across my face. "I hope it's not that obvious to him. I already feel like an idiot most of the time."

"Why? You're gorgeous, smart, and funny," she admonishes me.

I roll my eyes at her and drain the pasta, adding it to the pot of sauce I've been simmering.

"When will you see him again?"

So much for not mentioning our date.

"About that..." I grimace, glancing her way. "We kind of have a date on Monday?" It sounds more like a question than a fact.

"WHAT?" Layla screeches. "I can't believe you didn't mention it before now! Who else knows?"

"Just Charlie. I didn't want to just send out a text to you all, but now I wish that I would have so I could answer all of the questions at once. In fact, how about I just text you all in the group later? Like tomorrow?" I offer hopefully.

Layla snorts. "Nice try, Norie. Out with it."

So once again, I repeat the story of our agreement to watch Beauty and the Beast and how we were discussing rainy soccer games when Alicia interrupted us. By the time I finish, Layla is so giddy that she's bouncing in her chair.

"Norah Grady! You're dating Eamon Kennedy! This is the best thing to happen since... Well, I don't know, but it's the best!" she exclaims.

Exasperated, I say, "Stop! I'm not dating him. I just have *a* date with him. That's all."

"Technically, it sounds like you have two—or more, considering he wants you at all of his games. That sounds pretty serious to me," she teases.

"I don't think me sitting in the stands by myself, watching him play soccer, counts as a date. Sitting and watching a movie, I'll concede. Maybe if we were watching two other teams play together…" I trail off.

"Whatever you say, Nor," she quips, standing to take her dishes to the sink. "Now, I have to go. Work waits for no man. Or woman. No matter who she's dating! Thanks for dinner. I owe you."

I clean up the dishes after she leaves, then sit down on the couch with my laptop to work on the history assignments I've been neglecting. They're due on Monday, and I know I won't have time to do it this weekend. I've never seriously considered cheating before, but sometimes I think I'd happily pay someone to take this class for me. This, of course, makes me think of Eamon's offer to tutor me, which I could never accept because the only thing I'd be studying is his face. I have a hard enough time focusing with him not around, let alone having him sitting in close proximity.

Eamon

It's after midnight by the time the Seahawks make it back to Wilmington. We won the game with a two-point lead, and I scored one of those goals, but I don't feel like I played my best. Even though I skipped classes to catch up on sleep before the game, I still felt groggy and off-kilter all day. I was more surly than usual on the way home, avoiding conversations with anyone. Ro talked incessantly during the trip home and I eventually had to put in my earbuds and pretend to be asleep just so he'd shut up.

Once we're finally back on campus, I don't waste any time grabbing my gear and tossing it in the backseat. I'm climbing into the front when I hear Mac call out my name. God above, he irritates the piss out of me. I'm hoping if I don't respond he'll think I didn't hear him, but no such luck. He's jogging my way, not stopping until he's leaning on the door frame.

"Don't forget about open mic night tomorrow! I have it on good authority that a pretty little redhead is going to be there," Mac reminds me with a knowing smirk.

My eyes narrow. I'm going to kill Ro. "I don't know what Ro told you, but…"

"Who said anything about Ro?" He winks. "I might have made a friend of my own last week."

Thinking back to when I first saw Norah, I remember walking up to the bar with Ro and Teagan just as Mac was walking away with a dark-haired lass hanging on his arm. It's hard to picture Norah being her friend when they seem so opposite from each other.

"Good for you, Mac," I say blandly, reaching to pull my door shut.

Shrugging, Mac heads back towards the bus. We've never had an easy relationship. As seniors, we've played together for UNCW since our freshman year. From the first day of practice, I knew Mac would never be my favorite person. He's a great defender, always showing up on the pitch and doing what needs to be done, but aside from that, he's a complete wanker.

That first year, I was a raging mess and never backed away from a fight. Even though Mac is about fifty pounds heavier and three inches taller than me, we were evenly matched in a brawl. It wasn't until the end of the season that Coach stepped in and set us straight. In the middle of our ugliest fight yet, Coach walked up and dumped a cooler of ice water on us. I'd never received a tongue-lashing like the one we got that day. I felt like a child. Not to mention that Coach swore to kick us both off of the team if we stepped out of line like that again. The fighting has since stopped, but neither of us goes out of our way to be nice. Mac still makes smart arse comments here and there trying to get a rise out of me, but I've learned not to engage if I can help it.

I'm brooding over the situation all the way home. I don't like Mac referring to Norah as a *pretty little redhead*. She is that, and more, but when Mac says it, it sounds all sorts of slimy. I'll be damned if I let that tosser anywhere near her. At the same time, I hope he's right and that she is at Paddy's tomorrow night. I'd like to see her with her friends. See what her life is like outside of costume-making and dishwashing.

A buzzing in my pocket effectively pulls me from my thoughts. Who would even be calling this late? I slide it from my pocket to see it's my Mam and my first reaction is to panic until I remember there's a five-hour time difference between North Carolina and Ireland.

"Mornin', Ma," I greet her.

"Hiya, love. I know it's late there, but I saw you won your game and wanted to congratulate you."

Rosie Kennedy is a pure angel. I don't know what I did to deserve her as my mother, but I thank my lucky stars every day for her.

"Thanks a million. We just got back to campus, and I'm on my way home. Keep me awake as I drive, yeah?" I ask.

"'Course I will," she says warmly. "What's new there? It feels like we haven't talked in ages."

"Ach, I know. Sorry, Mam," I apologize, the guilt eating me alive. "I've been going ninety to nothing lately. Classes are good; football is grand. Been picking up some extra work at Paddy's. How are you? Caity behaving?"

Mam makes a disgusted noise. "That girl. When she bothers to come home at all, she's surly as can be. Otherwise, all is well here. Nothing new or exciting."

"Do I need to have a word with her?" I ask. She still owes me for the money she borrowed. Not that I'll ever call in her debt, but it would be nice to know that my sister isn't taking advantage of me.

"No, leave her be. She'll come round." She sighs. "I miss you, my boy. Would love to see you for the holidays."

My heart sinks. I know she's not trying to guilt me into coming home, but I still feel like absolute shite. I miss her—so much—but the thought of stepping back onto Irish soil makes me break into a cold sweat.

"Yeah, I know, Ma. I miss you too. I don't know about the holidays, but I'll look into it, yeah?"

"That would be grand!" she says, her voice full of hope that I know I'm going to crush. "But I understand if you can't. I know you've a lot on your plate."

We visit for the rest of the drive to my flat about nothing in particular.

She tells me about her days at work, and I fill her in on my classes. When she asks if I've been seeing anyone, I immediately think of Norah. I tell her there's nothing new to report on that front, but secretly, I am hoping to change that soon.

Chapter Twelve

Norah

I've spent all of Friday in the Theatre Department working on costumes. I had a meeting scheduled with my team at ten this morning, where I relayed the information Dr. Andrews gave me about possibly pulling actors from the ballroom scene. No one loves that idea, but they all understand the budget. Each person is brilliant on their own, but as a team, we run like a well-oiled machine. Just as I'm about to move on, Dr. Andrews walks through the door, smiling broadly.

"Good news, everyone!" he calls out, clapping his hands together. "I just spoke with the Dean about our budget, and he's agreed to give us an allowance!"

Cheers ring out and I heave a sigh of relief. Having a higher budget makes the creative process more enjoyable.

"However," Dr. Andrews continues, "We have to pull that amount from the spring show's costume budget."

I share a look with a few of my team members. Other than rumors of a drag show, we haven't even been told what the spring program is yet. If we're doing something grand, like Beauty and the Beast, how would we make it work?

"Maybe you could tell us what production we're doing this spring and how much our budget is now. That way we can get a head start on researching less expensive materials?" I prompt him.

"I had really hoped to hold off until after Beauty and the Beast was finished, but you make a good point, Miss Grady," he says, nodding at me. "I know you received the email this week about my idea for a drag show. With today's culture, I thought it might be a good idea to expand our views and embrace something new. That being said, I haven't mapped out the details yet, but I welcome your suggestions."

"Are you wanting it to be an all-male cast, Dr. Andrews?" asks Michelle from the makeup team.

"That's a great question, Michelle. No, it wouldn't be fair to exclude the actresses in the department. I was considering making auditions campus-wide so that anyone who regularly performs in drag shows can try out." he answers her.

A thought pops into my head, and I have to take a deep breath to suppress the sudden giggles bubbling up my throat. I flip to a blank page in my sketchbook and begin drawing a male form, starting with strong, muscular legs that lead to a tapered waist. Next is a broad chest and shoulders followed by powerful arms. I draw the neck and a stubbled jawline, adding smirking lips, mischievous eyes, and dark hair that drapes across his forehead. I cover the figure in a black leather bodysuit complete with a long black tail and cat ears. Finally, I add some black platform boots, and I'm looking at Eamon Kennedy as the sexiest black cat ever.

* * *

I walk into O'Nelly's with my friends at seven-thirty that night, and it's already getting crowded. Surprisingly, we're able to grab our favorite corner booth. Myra and Amelia are talking excitedly about their plans for the weekend while Charlie, Layla, and I listen halfheartedly. The late nights washing dishes for Pat have taken a toll on me this week. I'm more than ready to go to bed, but I promised I'd stay for one drink, and that's what I'm going to do. And if I happen to see Eamon here tonight, then it's an added bonus.

One of the newer waitresses saunters up to our table to get our orders and I decide to skip Guinness tonight, requesting a glass of the house red wine instead. Pat always carries some great local wines, so I'm not picky about which one I get. My phone chimes in my purse alerting me to a text message.

Eamon: *Fancy seeing you here.*

My head snaps up, and I quickly look around the pub, searching. Finally, I spot him sitting at the end of the bar, nursing what looks like a glass of whiskey. Our eyes lock, and a grin spreads across my face. Eamon gives me a crooked smile in return before sipping from his glass. I quickly text him back.

Norah: *They made me do it.*

Eamon: *I'm wounded, lass. I thought you wanted to see us perform again.*

I snort and look up at him with a raised eyebrow. He's still looking at his phone.

Norah: *Hardly. I'm still trying to block out the sound of Mac's voice. ;)*

Eamon: *I can't argue with you there.*

Norah: *How'd the game go?*

Eamon: *Grand. We won.*

Norah: *Congrats! How will you be celebrating?*

His response takes longer. The little bubble pops up, then disappears a few times before he finally replies.

Eamon: *Hopefully by having a drink with you tonight.*

I look up at him again with wide eyes. He's taking a drink, peering at me over the glass.

"Norah! Are you sexting?" Amelia suddenly asks, her voice much too loud.

I turn, glaring at her and simultaneously flipping her off. This, naturally, has all of the other girls looking at me, demanding that I answer the question.

"You wouldn't be talking to tall, dark, and handsome at the end of the bar, would you?" Myra asks, batting her fake lashes at me.

I think about lying, but honestly, I'm too tired to try to come up with a ruse that they'll inevitably see through, so I inhale deeply before saying, "Actually...I am."

This spurs a round of gasps, squeals, and mock outrage. They all want details, but I'm not about to spill them here, especially with the subject of such details sitting just across the way.

My phone chimes again.

Eamon: *Did you need to consult your friends before answering?*

My face heats in embarrassment, but I reply to his text quickly.

Norah: *No. I can make my own decisions, thank you very much.*

Eamon: *So what decision have you made?*

Norah: *Hmm. I'll make up my mind after the team's performance.*

Eamon: *That's not fair, lass!*

I reply with a winky face then pointedly drop my phone into my purse. My friends are relentless though eventually weasel the short version out of me.

"Yes, we've been talking. Yes, we have plans to hang out on Monday. No, nothing is official. No, nothing has *happened*."

Myra and Amelia groan their disappointment, while Layla grins from ear to ear and Charlie sits there silently.

Amelia notices her lack of response and narrows her eyes. "Why aren't you more excited?"

Charlie, coming to the rescue, shrugs and says, "It was inevitable. You honestly thought that nothing would come out of their drinking contest? Norie doesn't even talk to guys, let alone drink with them."

"I talk to guys!" I exclaim indignantly. "The Theatre Department is full of them."

86

"Those don't count. They all wear more makeup than you." Charlie laughs.

"That's not fair. They still count as men—if that's how they identify," I tell her. "Actually, on that note, I have to tell you about this idea I had for the spring play."

I lean forward to share my idea with the girls when Pat steps onto the stage to start open mic night. Tonight, he's wearing a tweed flat cap and a brown cable knit Aran sweater. If his accent didn't give him away, his attire definitely would.

"Good evenin', lads and lassies! Welcome to open mic night at O'Nelly's! We have a very special surprise for you tonight! Not only are our beloved Seahawks back to start us out with a rollicking rendition of 'Come In,' but our very own Irish trio will be performing 'Ringsend Rose'! Now, let's give our boys a warm welcome!"

Everyone cheers wildly, clearly forgetting how horrible the Seahawks performed last time, musicians withstanding. Pat walks off the stage and heads behind the bar.

Suddenly finding myself in need of another drink, I excuse myself from the table, weaving through the crowds of people until I reach the bar. Pat grins broadly when he sees me.

"Hello, lass! Good to see you!" he greets me.

"Hi, Pat! How'd your appointment go?"

"Ach. It was grand. Nothing but a checkup is all. I'm extremely grateful to you and Eamon for helping an old man out. Your drinks are on the house tonight. As long as we don't have a repeat of last week!" he says with a wink.

"It was my pleasure, really. I'm just glad you're okay. And there will not be a repeat of last week. I promised you that already," I remind him.

"Aye, that you did. Now, what can I get for you?"

"How about a whiskey to get me through the opening song?" I scrunch my face up.

Pat laughs as he pours me two fingers' worth of his best whiskey and slides it over to me. I thank him and begin to make my way back to the table. The Seahawks have arranged themselves in front of the platform, but my eyes are on the guitarist standing center stage, tuning his guitar. He's wearing an army green polo, stretched tight over his chest, and slightly distressed jeans. He gives Teagan and Ro a nod, and they begin playing a lively song that the crowd immediately starts clapping along to. Again, the singing is atrocious with Mac being the loudest of them all. Myra lets out a shrill whistle that only encourages him. I thought for sure that flame had already died out, but I guess I was wrong.

When the song finally ends and the cheers die down, I'm suddenly feeling nervous. The team heads back to their seats, leaving the Irish trio on stage. Eamon walks to the microphone, clears his throat, looks directly at me, and says, "This one goes out to a wee fire sprite who knows how to hold her Guinness."

Laughter floats through the crowd, and my cheeks begin to burn as I slide down in my seat, attempting to hide from the faces looking in my direction. The girls don't help matters by whipping their heads my way and gasping loudly. *Oh god, please let the floor open up and swallow me whole.* I breathe a sigh of relief when the song begins with Ro drawing a long note on the violin and everyone looks to the stage. Eamon begins strumming on the guitar, and Teagan, who abandoned the harmonica for a banjo, begins plucking the chords. The introduction is short, and then Eamon closes his eyes and he begins singing in a warm, clear voice.

"In Dublin Town there lived a girl,
Fairer than the flower I'm wearin'
Rose Donoghue - all fresh and new
And I love her past all carin'"

The rest of the pub and the people in it fade into the background as I focus on the lyrics. It's not the first time I've heard him sing but knowing that he chose this song with me in mind has a lump forming in my throat. With his comment about holding my Guinness, I was expecting a drinking song, not a *love song.*

"Sweet seventeen, my seamstress queen
She's no bigger than a thimble

Soft satin skin, street Arab's grin
Sure she makes the work looks simple"

I feel Charlie reach over and gently squeeze my arm, but I don't dare take my eyes off him. I couldn't even if I wanted to. Apart from the fact that he's singing a love song about a seamstress to a seamstress, he's just so beautiful.

"And there she goes my Ringsend Rose
In God's Garden there's none rarer
And there she goes my Ringsend Rose
Dublin Town has seen none fairer."

Eamon

I sing with my eyes closed, looking calm and collected on the outside, but on the inside, I'm a nervous wreck. I have no problem singing with a group or leading a pub song, but to get on stage and serenade a lass that I've only just met? I've lost my mind. At least Teagan and Ro agreed to play along. No one else would know "Ringsend Rose" except for Paddy.

When the song ends, I open my eyes, immediately seeking out Norah, but she's no longer sitting at her table. I start to panic, thinking maybe it was too much and I scared her away. My eyes dart frantically over the crowd until I finally spot her leaning against the bar, holding two pints and smiling softly at me. It feels as if my heart has grown wings and is trying to fly out of my chest. Grinning, I mutter a thank you to the crowd, place my guitar on its stand, and jump off the stage. Every eye in the room follows me as I make my way to Norah. When I'm a foot away from her, I stop and she hands me a glass.

Christ, she's gorgeous with her flushed cheeks and bright blue eyes looking up at me. Then she takes a step forward and asks, "How about that celebratory drink?"

Chapter Thirteen

Norah

In front of the main bay of windows at Paddy's, there's a small patio with bistro-style tables and chairs. Finding one directly beneath a light post, we sit, facing each other. I just stare at Eamon, for a moment, unable to put my thoughts into words.

He leans forward, placing his elbows on the table and lacing his fingers together before saying "I'm sorry if I embarrassed you."

I laugh softly. "It doesn't take much to do that, but no apology is necessary. That was…amazing, Eamon. Is there anything you can't do?"

"Stop thinking about you," he blurts out.

Both of our eyes go wide as if neither of us can believe he just said that.

"Wow…That just came out, didn't it?" he asks, reclining in his chair and rubbing a hand along the back of his neck. The way his bicep flexes with the movement is more distracting than it ought to be. He takes a deep breath and adds, "It's true though. I'm sorry if that's too forward of me, but I just wanted you to know."

Rendered speechless by his confession, I'm unsure of how to respond. I'm simultaneously thrilled and confused.

Because this doesn't feel real, I blurt out, "How much have you had to drink tonight?"

"What?" he asks, looking perplexed. "What does that have to do with anything?"

"I'm just making sure that the alcohol isn't influencing you right now. People say and do things they'll regret later when they're under the influence. I would know..." I say, pointing a finger at my chest.

He gives me a sardonic look and says, "Lass, I'm perfectly sober. And I'm perfectly serious. I'd like for us to get to know each other better. If you're okay with that, of course."

I look down at my hands which are tracing the condensation on the pint glass in front of me as I contemplate his request. My mind wars back and forth between what my heart *wants* to do and what my past trauma is trying to convince me I *should* do. I've spent the last several years letting my fears dictate my life, and for the first time, that voice isn't the loudest noise in my head. "Yeah, I'm definitely okay with that."

Eamon beams at me, and I can't help but return a smile of my own.

"So how does this work?" I ask nervously.

He tilts his head to the side questioningly, "Surely you've dated before..."

"Um..." I look back down at my hands. "I've gone out a time or two, but it was just for a drink and nothing more."

He's staring at me in disbelief. "You're joking. How is that possible for someone as lovely as you?"

I hesitate, knowing this is where things get tricky. How do I tell him that I've shied away from men because I was raped as a teenager? That's not exactly something you work into casual conversation.

"I, uh, it's kind of a long story..."

"It's okay, Norah," he says gently. "You don't have to tell me anything you don't want to. But to answer your question, why don't we start out just talking and spending more time together? Preferably not while washing dishes for Paddy."

He winks, and I let out a snort of amusement. "Alright. I think I can manage that."

We spend the next hour or so talking about anything and everything. We start simple with favorite colors and bands, followed by birthdays and hometowns. I'm getting ready to ask him about his family when the doors to the pub are thrown open and Myra and Mac come stumbling out, laughing loudly, arms wrapped around each other. They're drunk off their asses but stop short when they see Eamon and I sitting together.

"Oh, there you are, Norie!" Myra shouts. "We thought maybe the two of you disappeared somewhere more...private." She gives me an exaggerated wink.

"Yes, because after all these years of knowing me, that's *totally* my style," I tell her, rolling my eyes.

"I can't keep up with you anymore! You also swore off men after the last *incident*, remember?"

I gape at her in disbelief. Obviously, she's letting the alcohol do the talking for her, but Myra knows how hard it is for me to trust men.

Before I can stop myself, I snap, "Well, better no men than every man within a thirty-mile radius. I'm actually surprised I've found someone you *haven't* slept with."

Myra rears back like I've struck her, then narrows her eyes at me. "No need to be a bitch, Norah. Come on, Mac. Let's get out of here."

Turning their bodies, they stumble down the sidewalk. I hang my head in my hands and groan out, "I should have kept my mouth shut."

Eamon is silent for a beat, then says, "I don't know what incident she's talking about, but it clearly isn't her story to tell. I'd say she deserved that. Besides, anyone that hooks up with Mac can't have much moral fiber."

I lift my head and smile at him. "Good point. I don't even know him, but it's easy to see they have a lot in common. I just can't believe she said that. She's one of my best friends. We've had disagreements before, but we've never purposefully hurt each other."

"You know I'm curious now," he tells me. "But, like I said, you don't have to share anything you don't want to."

"Thank you, Eamon."

He has no idea how much that means to me. I know I'll have to tell him eventually, but not tonight. Checking the time on my phone, I realize it's after eleven and I have a busy day tomorrow. I'd love nothing more than to just sit here and talk to him all night.

"I hate to be a grandma, but I really do need to get home. I'm working on Belle's dress tomorrow and have to get an early start," I tell him regretfully.

"I don't think that makes you a grandma." He chuckles. "Can I drive you home?"

"I was just going to walk since it's so nice. You could walk with me. If you want to, of course."

"Even better," he says with a smile.

Standing, he offers his hand to me. This shouldn't make the butterflies in my stomach flit around so much, but I place my hand in his, and he gently pulls me from the chair. Expecting him to release my hand, I'm surprised when he loops it through the crook of his arm. *Swoon.*

With my free hand, I quickly send a text to the group message thread that I'm headed home and I will talk to them tomorrow. The speed in which they respond, demanding to know where Eamon and I disappeared to, is astounding. I ignore all of them. *Busybodies.*

We walk in silence for a few minutes, enjoying the beautiful night. With autumn just around the corner, the days are still warm and humid from the ocean air, but the evenings are cooler. One of the main things I love about living in North Carolina is the lack of the brutal winters I'm used to back home. The temperature can dip, but very rarely do we get freezing temps or snow. I hate winter. December through February in the Midwest are brutal and feel like they last forever. I always dreamed of living in a warmer climate growing up. I begged Mom for years to move to the coast, but we could never make it work financially, and then she was diagnosed with lung cancer.

As if reading my mind, Eamon says, "So tell me about your family."

"There's not much to tell," I reply. "I never knew my father, so it was just Mom and me. We lived in Missouri until I moved here four years ago. I have extended family, but Mom never wanted me around them, and after her funeral, I understood why."

Eamon squeezes my hand in his arm gently. "Can I ask how she died?"

"She had lung cancer. Smoking was her only downfall. I tried for years to get her to quit, but she kept insisting that she didn't smoke that often and her lungs were fine. I guess, to her at least, smoking two packs a week wasn't *that bad.* Compared to some, I guess it isn't, but it was enough to kill her," I say sadly.

"I'm sorry, Norah. Truly."

"Thanks. I miss her. She was my best friend and constant encouragement." I pause a moment before saying, "Your turn. Tell me about your family."

I feel him tense up, so I stop walking and turn to face him. "You don't have to if you don't want to. I get it. Families can be extremely difficult."

He nods and looks down at his feet. I can see his brow furrowing and have the urge to smooth it out with my fingers before running them through his dark hair.

"Well, you already know that I lost my Da. He was in a car accident on his way home from work one day. We were all devastated, but none more than my Mam. They were soul mates." Eamon smiles softly before continuing. "He was a good man. Always loved his family and worked hard to provide. We were never without."

"I can't even imagine what that was like for your Mom. Losing a parent is awful, but to lose the love of your life?" I shudder at the thought.

"Aye, even though she was completely wrecked she always made sure my sister and I were taken care of and loved."

We start walking again.

"She sounds amazing," I tell him honestly. A quiet moment passes, then I ask, "What part of Ireland are you from?"

"Kilkenny. Born and raised." A group of drunk college guys pour out of a bar and Eamon pulls me back before they can run me over. " When did you go to Ireland?" he asks when the path clears and we resume meandering down the sidewalk.

"After Mom died. I didn't start college until I came here. The year I would have, she got sick. Two years later, she died. I couldn't stand it anymore, so I sold the house and most of everything in it. I bought a ticket to Ireland, and away I went."

"I can't believe you went by yourself," he tells me, shaking his head.

"Yep. It was a little terrifying at first, but I fell in love with that country. I can't wait to go back," I say dreamily.

Eamon smiles in response but doesn't comment, which surprises me some. The few Irish people I've encountered in the States are always quick to tell me how wonderful it is.

"Tell me about your sister?" I prompt him.

He tenses up again and a grimace appears on his handsome face. "She's a few years younger than me, but we aren't as close as we used to be."

"Oh," I mumble, "I'm sorry to hear that. I'm an only child, so I can't really understand what that would be like."

We go back to walking in companionable silence. My pale yellow house comes into view. I love how close it is to O'Nelly's. If I cut through the park, I can be out the door and at the pub in less than fifteen minutes. We stroll up the street to the sidewalk in front of my house.

"Thanks for walking me home."

"Thank you for letting me," Eamon murmurs.

I smile and point to the blue house next to mine. "That's Layla's."

"Was she at Paddy's with you tonight?"

"Yes," I say. "She's the quiet Hispanic beauty."

"Who else was there?" he asks.

"Charlie, Myra, and Amelia. Myra is the one you saw outside." I scowl at the memory of our altercation.

"Myra and Mac. Has a lovely ring to it, eh?" he teases.

I make a gagging sound that makes him chuckle. As we step onto my small porch and stop in front of my door, I look towards the street, at my feet, anywhere but his handsome face.

"What's wrong, lass?" Eamon asks, sensing my discomfort.

"Erm..." I start nervously. "This is the part in the books and movies where the guy usually kisses the girl goodnight. I don't want to sound presumptuous, but I guess I should tell you that I don't think I'm that kind of girl."

"Ah, I see," Eamon says, cheeks flushing slightly. It's quite possibly one of the sexiest things I've ever seen.

"I'm sorry! I can't believe I just said that" I moan in humiliation, covering my face with my hands. "I'm so awkward and have no idea what I'm doing!"

Laughing, he places his hands on my arms. "Norah, look at me."

He waits for me to lift my head, then says, "Don't be sorry. If more women would be as honest as you from the get-go, it would save a lot of men some embarrassment. I promise you that I'm not going to pressure you into anything you don't want. We agreed to get to know each other better first."

My lips turn up in a small smile. Is it possible that I've actually met a man who isn't thinking of how soon he can get me into his bed?

"You're not Myra, and I'm not Mac," Eamon says firmly, hands still lightly gripping my arms.

"That might just be the sweetest thing anyone has ever said to me," I smirk.

He grins at me fully, taking my breath away.

"What are your plans for tomorrow?" he asks.

"Costumes. Specifically Belle's. Her gown will take the longest."

I refrain from giving him all of the details, like how each petal of the rose dress has to be attached at just the right angle or how sewing beads on the bodice is the ultimate test of patience.

"You're doing that all day?" he asks, eyebrows shooting upward. "Will you be working on campus?"

"No. I'll work here at home. I have a sunroom that I use for sewing. On costume weekends, I brew a large pot of coffee, turn on the music, and spend all day putting everything together." I shrug casually.

"And do you refuse company?" he asks, releasing my arms and stuffing his hands into his pockets.

"Oh. Usually," I start to say but then backpedal when I see his shoulders

96

droop and want nothing more than to bring a smile to his face. "But...I make exceptions for anyone that sings to me in front of a crowd."

Eamon's eyes light up, and his lips tip into that devastating smirk I swoon over. I've never had a man in my house. Not even in a group setting. I'm momentarily stunned to realize that the idea of having him here all to myself doesn't scare me like I thought it would.

"Although," I tell him sternly, "I wouldn't appreciate an *unplanned* drop-in."

He nods in mock seriousness. "Understood. That would be rude. What if there were company around, say, lunchtime? You have to stop to eat at some point."

"Oh yes," I agree. "Food is fuel. Can't sew on an empty stomach!"

Eamon grips his chin between his thumb and forefinger as if contemplating how the dilemma should be solved. "I suppose I could possibly procure a meal while I'm out and about. We can't let you starve."

I snicker in response. "Only if it won't put you out. I'd hate to be an inconvenience. And let me give you some money."

"Ach! Don't offend me, love! I wouldn't dream of it," he says, placing a hand over his heart.

I know that *love* is a common term in Ireland and the UK, but hearing it from his lips in reference to me has me all sorts of flustered.

"Now, go to bed. You look completely wrecked after a night of drinking. That won't do at all for a seamstress queen," he says with a wink.

Lord have mercy.

He starts to step off the porch but turns and says, "Goodnight, Norah. Pleasant dreams, lass."

"Goodnight, Eamon," I say quietly before unlocking my door and stepping inside.

Chapter Fourteen

Norah

It's not so bright, but definitely early when my alarm goes off, as is typical for costume weekends. Stretching my arms over my head, I smile thinking back on last night. It took me longer to fall asleep last night due to my mind racing with thoughts of Eamon. He told me to have pleasant dreams, and once I finally did fall asleep—after practicing several breathing exercises—my dreams were indeed pleasant.

My phone starts buzzing incessantly, which effectively keeps me from slipping back into those dreams. Rolling over, I grab the device and scowl at the screen. There are eighteen text messages. Apparently, when my friends didn't get a response in the group chat, they each sent individual messages asking the same questions, as if a private conversation would get them answers quicker. I roll my eyes at their antics. They're relentless. To my surprise, there's even a message from Myra, but I'm not in the mood to even touch that situation yet.

Opening the group message, I skim through them as they become more and more obtrusive. I should probably be annoyed at their lack of respect for my boundaries, but find myself chuckling. I don't respond to any of them. They can wait a bit. But I do finally open the message from Myra.

Myra: *Norie, I'm so sorry about last night. I was drunk and stupid, and that's no excuse. Please forgive me!!! I love you!!!!*

Shocked that she's actually apologizing, I text her back.

Norah: *I love you too, but we will need to hash this out. I'm sorry for my words as well.*

Then, I cave and respond to the group text.

Norah: *Calm your tits, ladies. All is well. Eamon walked me home and dropped me off at my door. Nothing exciting to report. We're getting to know each other.*

With that, I get out of bed and head for the shower. Normally, on sewing weekends, I stick to sweats and my hair in a topknot. It's just me, sequestered in my sewing room all day, so there's no one to impress. Today is different. I'm still comfortable in black yoga pants and a light blue tank top, but I put some mousse in my hair to control the frizz and take the time to put on a touch of makeup.

Padding into the kitchen in bare feet, I head for the coffee pot before making breakfast. I turn on the TV just for background noise, and the meteorologist is saying that today will be cooler than yesterday with the possibility of a thunderstorm in the afternoon. It's currently in the sixties, so I open all of the windows. I love listening to the breeze outside and feeling it cascade throughout the house; it's so peaceful. Satisfied with the weather report, I switch from the TV to Spotify, opening up a recent playlist I put together of European men crooning love songs at me.

With a coffee mug in hand, I walk out to my sunroom. The morning sun is filtering through the windows, casting shadows on the floor and warming the tiles under my feet. Gathering my sketches I begin to map out the layers of Belle's gown. Soon, I'm surrounded by yellow fabric. I've been working diligently and just finished the lining, petticoat, and base layer of the skirt when my body tells me that it's time to stretch. My back is aching from sitting in the same hunched-over position for so long. Once I've worked out all of the kinks, I trek into the kitchen for a glass of water. As I sit the glass down, there's a knock on my door. I glance over at the microwave clock to see that it's already a few minutes past noon. The morning passed by in an absolute blur. I run my fingers through my hair then straighten my shirt as I walk to the door.

With butterflies in my stomach, I open it. And my mouth runs dry. Eamon is standing there in a white t-shirt and faded jeans, his dark hair mussed in the sexiest of ways, and the stubble along his jaw beginning to look thicker than normal.

"Hello, Norah," he drawls, gifting me with that crooked smile.

"Hi there," I say, breathlessly. "Would you like to come in?"

"Please. Unless you'd rather eat on your porch," he teases me.

Shaking my head with a smile, I step back to welcome him inside. I can't believe I'm willingly letting a man into my home. And not just any man, but Eamon Kennedy. I don't think I'll ever be able to wrap my mind around this.

Eamon

Stepping into Norah's small but cozy house, I take in the living room that's painted a warm beige color, and the large window on the same wall as the front door. The navy blue couch is deep set with plush white and yellow throw pillows scattered over it. It's the kind of couch meant for sprawling out and watching TV or reading a book. Or curling up with a significant other. The rectangular coffee table sits on a patterned rug and has a stack of books in the middle of it. To my left is the kitchen, and like the rest of the house, it's small but welcoming. The narrow island separating the kitchen from the living room has three wooden bar stools sitting neatly against it. Directly between the two rooms is a small hallway that leads to what I'm assuming are bedrooms and a bathroom. The house suits her perfectly.

"Can I get you something to drink?" Norah asks, interrupting my observations.

"That'd be grand, thanks," I reply, suddenly feeling nervous for reasons I don't quite understand.

I watch her walk to the fridge, trying not to stare at her backside in those tight-fitting pants, and pull out a pitcher of lemonade. She sets it on the island before turning to a cabinet to pull out two glasses. She fills them carefully and slides one across the island to me.

"Thanks," I tell her, taking a drink. "Did you accomplish as much as you hoped to today?"

"I think so," she answers, taking a sip from her glass. "The base of Belle's dress is finished. I just need to finish the bodice and the petals of the skirt."

"Skirts have petals?" I wonder stupidly.

Norah laughs, and the sound reverberates through my body. She's beautiful, as always, but there's something softer about her today. My eyes travel over her red hair, just begging for my fingers to comb through the curls, and down to the blue tank top that makes her blue eyes shine and accentuates her curves.

"This one does!" she exclaims. "We decided to navigate away from the traditional ball gowns and ballroom scene and make it a garden party, with the dresses resembling flowers. Belle's will look like a yellow rose. Fitting, don't you think? Oh, wait. You don't even know what I'm talking about!"

I smile at her rambling, marveling at how she comes to life when she's passionate about something. "No, I don't, but I'm sure I'll learn soon enough," I tell her. "Now, I'm starved. I brought Chinese. That alright with you?"

"Absolutely!" She grins.

We set into an easy rhythm, unloading the food and dividing it into bowls. I didn't think to ask what she liked, so I got a couple of different dishes. Norah seems pleased with both options and takes a little of each, so I do the same.

"Would you like to sit here, on the couch, or on the patio?" she asks hesitantly, seemingly unsure.

"It's a lovely day out, how about the patio?" I offer.

"Good call. It's just through there," she says, pointing to what appears to be a laundry nook off the kitchen.

Following her through a doorway next to a washer and dryer, I step into the room and have no idea what I'm looking at other than yellow fabric. *Everywhere.*

"Wow... How much fabric do you need to make one yellow rose dress?" I ask, bewildered.

Norah giggles at my stupidity. "A lot. Please don't judge the mess. When you're dealing with this much fabric, there's no containing it."

She leads the way through a storm door to a small patio with a wrought iron table and chairs just off of the sunroom. The yard is quaint with a small flower bed in one corner, and a couple of trees grow nearby, providing just enough shade to keep the grass from scorching in the summers.

"I really like your place, Norah," I tell her as we sit down. "It suits you."

"Thanks. I love it. It's small, but I don't need any more than this."

We eat in silence for a few minutes before Norah asks, "So. What did you do this morning?"

"Honestly? I slept," I confess. "Coach has been relentless at practice this week. I'm not sure how he expects us to play when we're bone-tired from running for three hours straight."

"That sounds horrible. How do you stand it?" She grimaces.

"I love the game. Coach really is a great guy, but he's been extra crotchety. I think he's trying to kill us."

"Well, I hope not," she cuts in. "Surely he can see the merits of keeping his team alive."

I shrug. "One would hope."

We sit quietly, looking into the yard at nothing in particular. The air is warm but not overbearing; a soft breeze makes it almost perfect. Clouds are rolling across the sky, occasionally covering up the sun for moments at a time. They're starting to turn gray, indicating the possibility of rain.

"Any word from your friend Myra?" I ask, breaking the silence.

"Ugh. Yes. She apologized, but we still need to talk about the whole situation. We were both out of line, but she really took it too far," Norah says, her brow furrowing.

"By bringing up *the incident?*" I hedge. I wasn't kidding when I told her she doesn't have to tell me anything she doesn't want to, but I'd be lying if I said that the curiosity isn't driving me mad.

Norah sighs heavily. "Yeah. Her words weren't wrong; it just wasn't her place."

"I don't need to know, Norah," I tell her, lifting my hands in surrender.

"Unfortunately," she starts, glancing over at me, "you probably do. If we're going to be spending more time together, *the incident* will likely affect you too."

Immediately I'm filled with trepidation but determined to lend her whatever strength she needs.

"First," I say, "I'm honored that you want to share this with me, but please don't feel obligated. If you're not ready to talk about it, I respect that. There's no rush. For anything."

Norah looks at me with an unreadable expression before it shifts to absolute trust. "You don't know how much that means to me. Thank you," she says, "but I do want to tell you though. Which is surprising, since I usually avoid this subject at all costs."

I reach across the table and cautiously lace my fingers through hers. "Then, I'm all ears and no judgment."

She looks at our hands and takes a shuddering breath, while I brace myself for what she's about to share with me. I sense that whatever it is, she was traumatized by it.

"When I was in high school," Norah begins, "I was out with a group of friends on a Friday night, and we were being stupid and reckless—as most seventeen-year-olds are. In my hometown, there's not a lot to do on a Friday night—other than get into trouble. As the night progressed, we ended up in an abandoned barn, drinking alcohol smuggled from our parents' liquor cabinets. I had been shamelessly flirting with this guy, Ashton, who was a couple of years older than me. He was known to be a nice guy, and everyone loved him. Super smart and charming. The fact that he even knew my name was flattering. We all started taking shots around midnight. I was young, but I knew better. My Mom had always impressed upon me the importance of not drinking underage and what could happen if I did. But I really thought this time was different. Slowly, couples began disappearing to other parts of the barn or into the field. Before I knew it, Ashton and I were outside, kissing up against the side of the barn. There was no one near us. Teenagers with raging hormones and alcohol...never a good combination. I didn't have any intention of doing anything further than that, but Ashton did. When he started trying to..." She pauses to chew on her lip for a second before continuing, "...unbutton my jeans, I knew it was time to stop."

My blood begins to boil as I see where her story is going and I have to take a calming breath as she continues. "So I pulled away and told him I wasn't ready for that. Thinking that he was a nice guy, I expected him to back off. I was wrong. He got so angry. He shoved me back against the barn and violently kissed me. I kept trying to push him away, but he was so much stronger than me, and when I tried to yell, he put his hand over my mouth and threw me to the ground. He...he raped me and left as soon as he was done." Pausing to swallow, she glances down at her lap before her gaze drifts back to our hands. "I stayed there curled up on the ground for hours after. I was too ashamed to go home."

I'm speechless, and my heart is absolutely shattered in my chest, yet somehow racing out of control. I'm practically shaking with rage and the desire to find the monster that took advantage of this amazing woman and tear him limb from limb with my bare hands. The hand not holding onto Norah's clenches in my lap, and I exhale the breath I've been holding. I squeeze her fingers gently and she glances up at me, having averted her eyes while reliving the hell she experienced.

"And now you know why I was so hesitant to accept a ride from you," she whispers. "And why I need to take things slow."

Inhaling another deep breath, I will myself to calm the fuck down so my anger doesn't scare her.

Leaning closer, I look directly into her eyes and say, "First, thank you for sharing that with me. I can't imagine how hard it was to relive that. Second,

I'm going to need this bastard's information." I'm cradling her hand in both of mine now. "And third, we can take this as slow as you need and want to. I'm happy to just sit here with you and listen to you talk."

Norah blushes and places her other hand on top of mine, fingers trembling slightly. "Thank you," she says, "for all of this. I'm really happy to be here with you. I've avoided guys for so long that I'm actually shocked that any of this is even happening."

My heart stutters. I am humbled and honored to be the one she trusts enough to take this step with. That she finds me worthy of her time and attention is astounding. Being with Norah in any capacity, let alone dating her, is something to be treasured and something I don't take lightly.

"So what happened to that arsehole? Please tell me he went to jail," I demand.

"I wish. But no. I was so ashamed that I never told anyone. Not until years later. I realize now how stupid that was, but what can I do now? A whole lot of nothing," she answers with a shrug.

"You're joking?" I sputter in shock. "This needs to be reported. He can't get away with this."

Norah sighs. "I know. But won't it seem strange coming years later? I don't even know where he is now."

"That should be easy to figure out with today's technology. You can find anyone on the internet. I'll even do the work for you," I volunteer.

I'd love nothing more than to find this fucker and bring him to justice.

"I don't know, Eamon. I'll have to think about it," Norah says uncertainly, looking away.

"Hey," I say, squeezing her hand again until she looks at me. "I understand. I have no idea how difficult it would be for you, but he cannot get away with what he did to you. The States are seriously lacking when it comes to punishment for rapists. In Ireland, if convicted, a rapist will spend life in prison. It's the absolute least they deserve."

"Wow," she breathes, eyes wide. "It's good to hear there are places that actually do more than just slap the offender on the wrist and tell them to be good. Anyway, enough of that. Today is too beautiful to waste on sad stories."

I stand, pulling her up with me, and twine our fingers together on both hands. "Thank you for telling me, Norah. For trusting me with this. I'm honored. I meant what I said about not rushing anything. You're in control here."

Norah's eyes turn glassy and a tear slips through, trailing over her cheek.

"Ach, don't cry, love," I say, releasing one of her hands to wipe the tear away.

"I'm sorry," she sniffs. "I've spent so long avoiding guys and the first one I take a chance on is..." She huffs a little laugh then meets my eyes before saying, "You're one of the good ones Eamon Kennedy."

Chapter Fifteen

Norah

The forecasted weather has arrived. At the first rumble of thunder, we move inside and perch on my couch, listening to the soft drumming of the rain, while we talk about current classes. I still can't believe Eamon is even here, choosing to spend the afternoon with me. We're seated on opposite ends of the sofa, mirroring each other. He has an arm slung over the back of the sofa and an ankle propped on his knee, while my legs are curled underneath me.

"...the next thing I know, I'm covered head to toe in dirty street water."

I throw my head back, laughing at Eamon's recounting of the time he visited London with his family. They had gone on holiday when he was about thirteen, and he wanted to see Big Ben, while his sister, Caity, wanted to see Kensington Gardens. They had each been pulling on the map, and it tore down the middle, causing them both to fall. Caity managed to land on the sidewalk, while Eamon ended up in a puddle.

As I'm walking him to the door a couple of hours later, I realize that I feel lighter than I have in years. Mostly from opening up to Eamon about my past, but also because I could sit and talk with him all day. He's an amazing listener and fascinating storyteller, and I know that he's going to make one hell of a teacher someday.

"Thank you again for lunch and the company," I say, looking up at his handsome face.

"It was my absolute pleasure. Thank you for letting me interrupt your busy day. I feel properly educated on how to assemble a ball gown now," he teases me.

"Careful," I tell him, "or I'll make you stay and sew tiny beads on the bodice. It's the worst part of creating these pieces. Always worth it in the end though."

"As much as I would love to spend the rest of the day with you, I'm confident that I'd ruin it all and you'd never speak to me again."

The thought of spending the rest of the day with him is oh-so-tempting.

"You're probably right," I concede. "However, I happen to enjoy talking to you and am innately selfish. So off you go, Kennedy."

I move towards the door, expecting him to move aside, but he stays still. I freeze as I brush up against his rock-solid body. Knowing he's in decent shape from playing soccer is different than actually feeling those muscles. My heart is racing as I trail my eyes up his torso and over his broad chest and shoulders. I suck in a breath when our eyes meet. His ignited gaze flickers to my mouth, and he inhales a deep breath. Squeezing his eyes shut, he takes a half step back.

"Right." Eamon clears his throat. "I better leave you to it, then." He turns toward the door, taking a step onto the small porch. "I'll see you Monday. Unless..."

"Unless what?" I ask, curiously.

"We have a match tomorrow on home turf. I know you're swamped with costumes, but if you think you might want a break, I'll leave your name at the booth for a couple of VIP seats. Bring a friend if you'd like."

Grinning like an idiot, I nod my head. "I'd love that, thank you. I probably won't bring Myra though. I'm not sure I could sit through the game listening to her talk about all the things she'd like to do with Mac."

Eamon laughs loudly. "Can't say that I blame you, lass. Plus, I'd rather your attention not be on that tosser."

"Oh, I can assure you that I won't be watching Mac."

Realizing what I just admitted, I slap a hand over my mouth, face going up in flames. Eamon's smile transforms from his signature smirk to a full-on grin—with dimples! *Of course* he has dimples. Why not? Everything else about him is perfect.

"I better not botch the game, then." He winks at me, which sends heat straight to my core. "Game's at four. See you tomorrow, Norah."

I stand there, gaping like a fish, as he gets in his car and drives away. Turning to go back inside, I tell myself to focus and finish as much on the costumes as possible so that I can make it to the game tomorrow.

Eamon

Back at my flat, I'm on the couch, laptop balancing on my knees. I'm determined to find the arsehole that attacked Norah, but I need more information. I remember his name and the town she lived in, but I doubt that will get me too far. Like any good detective, I start by stalking her social media account. Her profile picture is of her and who I assume is her mother. They have the same deep blue eyes and smile. Clicking the *About* section, I scroll down to past education. There. Pine Hills High School. Switching to her friends list, I figure someone has to be a mutual friend between the two of them. Before I get too far into my investigation, my phone buzzes in my pocket. Fishing it out of my pocket, I see it's Ro.

"Hiya, Ro," I say absently.

"He actually answered! Figured you'd be busy with your new mot if ya catch my meaning."

"Fuck off," I mutter. Of course, that's where Ro's mind wanders too.

"Ah, c'mon you narky hole. I'm only slagging you. Where are you anyway?"

"My flat. Doing a bit of research on…well, never mind that. What's up?"

I shut the laptop and place it on the coffee table, knowing I'll never be able to focus with Ro gabbing at me. The wanker can talk the hind legs off a donkey.

"Heading to O' Nelly's tonight? Mac's after getting hammered."

I pinch the bridge of my nose between my thumb and index finger, letting out a groan. "Is he mental? We've a match tomorrow. You're not seriously thinking about going, are you, Ro?"

"Yeah, I might. Have one pint with me. Come on, Kennedy. Don't make me deal with Mac on my own," Ro whines.

"You know I don't drink before a match, you eejit. Why doesn't he wait until tomorrow night?"

I knew Mac was stupid, but this is a whole new level.

"He wants to impress that new girl that's been hanging on. She's friends with your Norah. What's her name, again?"

"Myra," I tell him. It's not like Mac to want to impress a girl. Normally he hooks up with them once or twice, then wipes them from his memory. They do seem pretty perfect for each other though from what I can tell.

"That's the one! So are you coming or not?"

"Yeah," I grumble. "I'll make an appearance. I won't stay more than an hour or two though. End of."

"Grand! See you then!" Ro hangs up, and I immediately shoot off a text to Norah.

Chapter Sixteen

Norah

I'm just finishing up the bodice of Belle's gown when I hear my phone chirp from the kitchen. I stand and stretch my cramped muscles before heading inside. I'm pleasantly surprised with all that I've accomplished since Eamon left. Our time together had been more enjoyable than I expected, and I still can't believe how comfortable and safe I feel with him. It's a welcome change to the trepidation I normally feel around men.

Speak of the devil.

A text from the man himself.

Eamon: *Sounds like there's a meet-up at Paddy's tonight. Mac and Myra set it up. Ro's begging me to go. Keep me company?*

My cheeks hurt from the huge smile on my face and the thought of seeing Eamon again so soon makes me giddy. I should spend the evening working on costumes, but maybe I can go out for an hour or two. A girl has to take a break sometime, right? I'm not thrilled about seeing Mac and Myra together, but there's going to be a pretty gorgeous distraction holding my attention. Feeling emboldened, I decide to flirt a little.

Norah: *Missing me already?*

Eamon: *Guilty as charged. I'm only staying an hour or so. And I won't be imbibing.*

Norah: *Someone probably needs to make sure you stick to water. I don't trust Mac to do that.*

Eamon: *Considering how we met, I'm not sure you're the one for the job either, but I'm happy to let you try.*

Norah: *Fine, Kennedy. Just so I can prove to you that I'm a responsible adult, I will come and babysit you. What time should I be there?*

Eamon: *I'll come pick you up if you'd like. Or I can meet you at your place, and we can walk together. Say 8:00?*

Norah: *I'd like that. See you at 8:00!*

It's official. Bantering with Eamon is my new favorite hobby.

Taking my time getting ready, I pair my favorite black skinny jeans with a cream-colored off-the-shoulder sweater and curl my hair just enough to tame my natural waves. I finish applying my make-up and am just putting in my pearl earrings when I hear a car pull into my driveway. Taking one last look in the mirror, I spin and hurry to the front door. When I open it, I nearly gasp out loud. I just saw Eamon a few hours ago, but he still takes my breath away. We stand there, eyeing each other, then burst out laughing. He's wearing black jeans and a cream-colored cable knit sweater.

"Nice outfit," Eamon says, grinning at me.

"Right back at you. Maybe I should change so others don't think we planned this…"

"Don't you dare. You look ravishing," he growls, eyes heating. "I don't give a single fuck what anyone has to say about us."

I shiver in delight at his words. This man is making me feel things I never thought I'd feel again. "In that case, let me just slip on my shoes and we can go," I say with a laugh.

* * *

Fifteen minutes later, Eamon opens the door to O'Nelly's and ushers me in with his hand on the small of my back. I'm hyper-aware of the contact, and it's hard to focus on anything else around me. Saturdays are usually busy, but it's absolute chaos in here tonight. As we make our way through the masses, his hand never leaves me.

"There he is!" Rowan exclaims, jumping from the booth the team normally sits at. He claps a hand on Eamon's shoulder, then turns to me. "With the lovely Norah! What a pleasant surprise. We haven't been properly introduced. I'm Rowan Gallagher, but you can call me Ro!"

"No, we haven't," I reply, smiling at the handsome redhead. "It's nice to meet you, Ro."

"Likewise," he beams. "Come and sit! Mac was just trying to impress your friend, Myra, with some tall tales!"

I hesitate a moment but slide into the booth next to Myra. Eamon drifts in close behind.

"Norie!" Myra squeals, throwing her arms around me and pulling me in for a tight hug. "I'm so, so sorry for the other night. I was being a Grade A bitch and don't deserve to be your friend. Will you please forgive me?"

Pulling out of the hug and looking her in the eyes, I sigh and tell her, "Of course, I forgive you. I'm sorry too. We both said hurtful things. It actually worked out..." I nod my head in Eamon's direction.

She peeks around me, waggling her eyebrows. "We have a lot to catch up on, it looks like. So what's the status? Are you two dating now?"

"Uh..." I'm not sure what we are exactly. We haven't made any sort of declaration, but have agreed that we want to spend more time together, and the physical attraction is there, but are we dating?

"We're whatever Norah wants us to be. She's the one calling the shots," Eamon's deep voice interjects, his warm breath fanning over my exposed shoulder, giving me chills.

I turn towards him and suck in a breath when I realize how close our faces are. His bright blue eyes are boring into mine, and I have the strongest

113

urge to reach up and trace my fingers along his full lips. I duck my head to break eye contact.

"Should I not have said that? I was just trying to take some of the pressure off," he says in a low voice.

I look back up at him and smile softly. "No, it's just that…I appreciate you giving me the choice. I also don't want to label us without coming to a mutual decision."

"You will always have the choice. I wasn't joking when I said we can do this at whatever pace you're comfortable with. As for what we are…"

A loud cheer rings out through the pub, bursting the little bubble we've encased ourselves in. We both look to the stage to see Mac stumbling up the steps, heading straight for the microphone. Myra lets out a cat call, earning her a grin from Mac.

"Oh, Christ…" Eamon starts, pinching the bridge of his nose. "We can leave anytime you want, love. It's only going to get worse from here."

Laughing, I shake my head. "We only just got here!"

"Right, but I hadn't planned on drinking tonight, remember? There's no way I'm going to be able to sit here and listen to Mac howl about up there without a drink in my system."

I raise an eyebrow and look at him for a moment. "Alright, Kennedy. *One drink.*" I hold up a finger. "Just one, and then we can go."

"Deal. What'll you have? Guinness?" Eamon winks at me.

Damn, if that doesn't make my toes curl. "Definitely not. A glass of the house red, please?"

"Good choice. Be right back. Don't listen to anything Ro says while I'm gone." He gives my knee a gentle squeeze and slides out of the booth.

I watch him walk towards the bar, not at all upset at the view.

"Finally! Never thought the bastard would let me have a chance to talk to you," Ro complains, sliding in next to me and throwing an arm around my shoulders.

Tensing slightly, I purse my lips and say studiously, "I'm under strict orders to not listen to a word you say."

He places a hand over his heart, eyes widening. "I'm wounded! He's just

114

worried that I'll snatch his girl away. I'm exceedingly more charming than he is. In fact, he learned all of the best lines and moves from me!"

"Strange," I say, in mock concern. "I can't imagine I'd be here with him if that were true."

A loud laugh and the sound of chair legs scraping on the floor interrupt our banter.

"Sounds like you've met your match, Ro. It seems only another ginger can beat you at your own game," Teagan says while taking a seat and extending his hand across the table, "Norah, I presume? Name's Teagan. Pleasure."

Returning the handshake, I respond, "You presume correctly. Nice to meet you as well."

What is it with these Irishmen? All three of them are beautiful in their own way. A girl could get used to being surrounded by this kind of scenery.

"Now, Teag, don't be getting any ideas. Norah has already told me I'm her next choice when she gets tired of Kennedy, here," Ro says, shaking a finger at Teagan.

"Is that so?" Teagan responds, raising an eyebrow. "I suppose that's alright. I've had my eye on Alicia anyway. She seems like she'd be a fun..."

"Fuck off. Don't you dare go messing about with Alicia. I'll have your bollocks for breakfast," Ro grinds out, fire in his eyes.

Way to show your cards, Ro.

"Now, where were we?" Rowan turns back to me. "Oh, right. You were about to tell me what your intentions are with our fella."

"My intentions? I wasn't aware you were his parent and that I needed to declare myself to you," I quip back.

"Ah, lass, but that's where you're wrong," Teagan chimes in. "While in the States, we all look out for each other. Like the Three Musketeers."

"More like the Three Stooges. Which one is Curly?" I ask, looking between the two of them.

"Did you just refer to me as one of the Three Stooges?" Eamon asks incredulously, coming up to stand behind Teagan. "I leave for a whole five minutes and you eejits have already turned her against me."

"We're just looking out for you, mate. Wanting to make sure the fire sprite has your best interests at heart. Can't have her taking advantage of you just because you're a star footballer," Ro says.

Eamon rolls his eyes then, noticing Ro's arm around my shoulders, glares pointedly at his friend. I go rigid as Ro pulls me tighter to him, running a lock of my hair through his fingers. I know he's not being nefarious, but the unexpected, and unwanted, contact has my breath coming faster and anxiety rising.

"Norah, love. Have I ever told you how gorgeous your hair is? I'm a wee bit biased after all." Ro leans in as if to smell my hair.

My eyes must be begging for help because Eamon says, "Alright, that's enough. Get your dirty paws off of her before I tear them from your limbs. Besides, you're making her uncomfortable, and I know your Mam raised you better than that. Don't make me call her up…"

"Jaysus, Kennedy. Calm your tits. I'm just messing about. If you're going to keep this one around, she might as well get used to the gang. Right, Norah?" Finally looking at me, Ro stops short, noticing the panic in my eyes. "My apologies, lass. I didn't mean a thing by it."

"It's alright. I just have a…thing…with being touched without warning or permission," I hedge.

"Right, I'll just get out of our boy's spot, then! I need a drink anyway!" he says jovially, leaving the booth and heading towards the bar.

Eamon sits a glass of wine down in front of me before resuming his place beside me and turning concerned eyes on me. "Are you alright, love?"

"I'm fine. Really. But I can't tell you how much I appreciate you picking up the cues. Usually, the girls are the ones to save me," I reply, hesitantly sliding my hand into the one he has resting on his thigh.

Eamon looks down at our hands and twists so our fingers are interlocked. Why does something as simple as hand-holding have my heart thumping hard?

"So, Norah, what do you do here in Wilmington?" asks Teagan.

Yet again, I forgot that there were others around us, somehow even managing to drown out Mac's horrible rendition of whatever country song he's singing and Myra's cheering.

I smile apologetically at Teagan and say, "I'm the costume designer for the Department of Theatre at the university and also a business student."

"No kidding? Do you make costumes as well?" he questions.

"I do, with my team of course. I couldn't do it alone."

"You should see her work, Teag," Eamon says proudly. "It's phenomenal. I know nothing about designing or making any type of clothing, but I got to see it firsthand, and I'm seriously impressed."

"Okay, enough about me," I say quickly, my face flaming at the compliments. "How are you feeling about the game tomorrow?"

"We're playing Duke, so it could go either way." Teagan shrugs, taking a drink from the beer bottle in his hand. "I hate to say it, but they've really improved since last season. Wankers."

I can't help but laugh. "Right. They're your rivals. Shows you how much I know."

"You're coming tomorrow right?" he asks curiously.

"Yeah, I think I'm going to ask my friend Layla to come with me. She's been wanting to see a game."

"That's a good idea," Eamon says. "I'll make sure both names are given to the attendant."

"Yeah, definitely bring a friend," Teagan says with a smirk. "The more pretty lasses there, the better!"

Hmmm. Layla *is* single, and from what I can tell, so is Teagan. This could be fun.

Chapter Seventeen

Norah

Two hours later, Eamon, Ro, and Teagan have been persuaded to perform a few pub songs, much to everyone's delight. Except for Mac's. He complained for a few minutes but didn't seem too upset as he let Myra slide her hand up his chest and whisper in his ear. The Irishmen were barely into the second song when the two of them snuck out the side door. I roll my eyes and nurse my third glass of wine while watching Eamon on stage.

The longer I watch him, the more turned on I get. *God, he's sexy.* The muscles in his forearms flex as he strums the guitar, and his low, clear voice sends a shiver down my spine and heat straight to my core. I wonder what it would be like to kiss that mouth and rake my fingers through his dark hair. Or to run my hands up his chest and wrap my arms around his neck.

Taking another sip of wine, I let my eyes roam over his muscular body. When I glance back to his face, I find his eyes watching me ogle him. I'm embarrassed for about half a second until I realize the heated gaze he's returning. Suddenly flushed and dying of thirst, I slip from the booth as the last song finishes and make my way to the bar for a glass of water and to say hello to Paddy and Alicia. It's finally calmed down enough for them to take a breather. They've been running all night.

"Norah, lass! It's about time you came to say hello. I was beginning to think you were too good for us poor bar folk!" Paddy chuckles.

"Never!" I exclaim, sliding onto a bar stool. "It's a packed house tonight. How are you holding up?"

"Aye, right as rain. Isn't that so, Alicia?" the pub owner yells over his shoulder.

Alicia is wiping down the bottles behind the bar and filling the condiment containers. "Sure thing, Pat," she grumbles, rolling her eyes. "I must have been the only one busting my ass."

Laughing loudly, Paddy turns back to me. "So I noticed you sticking close to Eamon tonight. Is there something I should know about?"

Alicia mutters something under her breath that sounds an awful lot like, "As if you didn't plan it."

I tuck my hair behind an ear and start to tell Paddy that we're just friends, but decide to just be honest. This is definitely more than friendship, even if we haven't put a label on it yet. "Well, we have been seeing each other outside of dish duty, so…"

Paddy's grin stretches from ear to ear. "Ach, nothing would make me happier than to see the two of you become an item! You'd be good for the lad. Help him get over his broken…"

"I think we can stop right there. Thanks, Pat," Eamon says cooly, stepping behind me and placing a hand on my waist.

"Right. Sorry, lad. Not my place. Anyway, can I get you two another drink?" Paddy asks quickly.

Pat's round cheeks are stained with color and there's clear remorse in his eyes. It's obvious he was about to share something Eamon didn't want shared and my heart sinks a little at the thought of him keeping secrets, but then I chastise myself. Everyone is entitled to their secrets and isn't obligated to share anything they're not comfortable with. I just lashed out at Myra for the same thing. When, and if, he's ready to tell me, he will.

In the meantime, I'm hyper-aware of his hand on my waist, touch searing through my sweater. I'm tempted to lean back and snuggle into his chest.

"No, I think we're good. I'll just pay my tab, and we'll be off. Is that okay with you, lass?" Eamon asks, his fingers flexing against me.

Nodding, I turn my head to look up at him. His jaw is clenched, and his eyes are ablaze with an emotion I can't place. Wanting to ease some of the tension, I angle my body towards him and place a hand on his broad chest. Watching him is one thing, but touching him is a different experience altogether. The hard muscle beneath his shirt tenses at my touch, but when he glances down at me, his eyes soften and he pulls me closer to him. I don't resist.

Eamon hands some cash to Paddy. "No change, Pat. Thanks."

"Aye. We good, son?" Paddy asks hesitantly, brow furrowed.

Reaching across the bar, he grips Pat's shoulder. "'Course we are. Nothing could change that."

Pat clears his throat and harrumphs before waving a hand at us to go on. I say my goodbyes as Eamon turns us towards the door, his arm still around my waist. Once we're outside, I turn to face him.

"Are you okay?" I ask. "I don't want to poke my nose where it doesn't belong, but someone would have to be deaf and blind to miss that exchange with Pat."

Eamon scrubs his free hand over his face, then runs it down my right arm until he reaches my hand. Intertwining our fingers, his expression changes from uncertainty to determination in a blink.

"There's a reason I left Ireland other than for university," he says slowly. "Can we walk while I tell you?"

"Eamon, you don't have to tell me anything you're not comfortable with. I just want to make sure that *you* are okay," I tell him earnestly. As curious as I am, I don't want him to say or do anything he'll regret later.

He lets go of my hand and tucks a strand of hair behind my ear. "You're a rare gem, Norah Grady. I find myself wanting to tell you everything about me, even the parts I've locked away for the last few years."

"Thank you," I say. "I'm honored you feel that way."

"Come on. I'll tell you on the way to your house."

We set off walking. The air has a slight chill to it, enough to signal that fall is well on its way, but I don't feel cold at all with Eamon's hand gripping mine.

"I left Ireland with no intention of ever going back. I was engaged. To Rhiannan," he pauses, glancing sideways at me.

My heart sinks, and try as I might, I can't wipe the look of shock from my face. I also can't shake the surge of jealousy I'm feeling. He must sense it because he starts rubbing comforting circles on the back of my hand with his thumb.

"We grew up together," he continues. "Our parents always teased that they arranged our marriage at birth, and we had no reason to believe otherwise. Rhi was the life of every party. She thrived on attention and was always close with my mates. It seemed perfect at the time. Who wouldn't want a girl that enjoyed spending time with the fellas? After school, I proposed, and she obviously said yes. We planned on marrying within the year. No reason to delay what everyone already knew was going to happen. About three months before the wedding, I could tell something was going on with her but figured she was just stressed from all the planning. She wouldn't answer when I called or made up reasons not to stay over. We had a planned date that she canceled. Claimed she was sick. I decided to surprise her with soup and a movie. Since she couldn't go out, I'd go to her. As I pulled into her driveway, I noticed a familiar motorcycle parked outside. My mate, Declan, owned this bike. I figured he was looking for me, so I didn't think much of it. I let myself in and headed for her room. She definitely wasn't sick, and Declan wasn't looking for me."

He pauses to inhale deeply before saying, "They had been sleeping together for over a year. My girl and best mate."

"Oh my god, Eamon. How horrible. I'm so sorry," I tell him sincerely

121

while cursing Rhiannon for what she did to him. "Nobody deserves that, least of all you."

"Thanks, lass. I'm not proud of how I reacted," he says sheepishly while rubbing the back of his neck.

"What did you do?"

"I uh…I threw the soup at the wall, and it splattered all over them. Declan jumped off the bed, trying to cover himself, telling me to just calm down. That was the wrong thing to say. I beat the shite out of him that night and never talked to Rhi again. Less than a year later, I was flying to the States," he concludes.

I'm not a violent person, but I can't seem to find an ounce of sympathy for Declan.

"What about your Mom?" I ask.

"I miss her terribly, but I just couldn't stay. Ireland isn't that big, so there was nowhere I could go that was far enough away from them. Especially when I found out she was pregnant with his kid a couple of months after I caught them. My Mam understands, but she keeps hoping I'll come back after graduation."

"You won't even go to visit?" I can't blame him for wanting to leave, but surely, he wants to see his Mom and sister.

"I know I should, but Rhi and Declan are living in her parent's house. Next door to Mam," he explains.

"Ah. Makes sense. I wouldn't be able to handle being that close to… Ashton." I shudder at the thought, and Eamon releases my hand to slide his arm around my shoulders, tucking me in close to him.

"I can assure you that I will never let that fucker near you again. And if I'm ever within range, he'll receive the same attention Declan did."

He sounds like he plans to be around for a while and I think I like the sound of that.

Reaching my house, we walk up the front steps and stop in front of the door. I turn and place my hand on Eamon's chest again before looking into his eyes.

"Thank you for sharing that with me," I tell him. "I imagine that was really

122

difficult to relive, and I hate that the two people you cared for most did something so horrible to you. You deserve so much better."

His brows furrow and his gaze moves to my mouth, then back to my eyes. I feel his hand slowly move up my arm to my neck before cupping my cheek.

"I think I've found it, lass," he breathes, then shocks me by asking, "Can I kiss you, Norah?"

I freeze, not from fear but anticipation. Tingles spread from my head to my toes, lingering in my belly. He feels me tense up, but misinterprets it and starts to take a step back.

"Shite. I'm sorry. Too soon. I should have..."

"Eamon," I whisper, wrapping my hand around his wrist. "Yes. Kiss me."

His eyes widen in surprise but quickly blaze with a heat so strong, I can feel it radiating from him. Threading his fingers through my hair, he slowly lowers his mouth to mine, pausing briefly before his lips brush mine softly, tentatively. Eamon kisses me like I'm something precious. I've never been kissed like this. Every kiss I've ever experienced has been the other person taking what they wanted.

Eamon touches the seam of my lips with his tongue, silently asking permission for more. Without a shred of hesitation, I open for him, granting him access. A small grunt of surprise sounds in his throat that sets me on fire and emboldens me. I press myself into him, deepening the kiss. I explore his mouth with my tongue before it sets into perfect rhythm with his. He untangles the fingers of one hand from my hair and snakes it around my waist, crushing me to him. A moan escapes me as I dig my fingers into his hair. I'm losing my mind; my body is burning with need. I'm about to climb this man like a tree.

All too soon, Eamon slows, kissing me softly—once, twice, a third time— before leaning his forehead against mine. He chuckles. "Easy, lass. As much as I'd love to see where this goes, I told you I'm not rushing anything with you."

I blush violently, realizing just how close I was to rushing things significantly.

"I...wow...I can't believe I just did that! I'm sorry!" I blurt out, averting my eyes.

Gently grasping my chin between his finger and thumb, he lifts my face to his. "Absolutely *do not* apologize for the best kiss of my life."

I blink at him in surprise. "Really?"

"Without a doubt." He nods, and I bite my bottom lip to keep from beaming.

"Not to go digging for compliments," he smirks, "but you seemed to enjoy that yourself."

Letting out a bark of laughter, I say, "Understatement of the year. The century. I've never been kissed like that."

Eamon raises a brow, "Kissed like what, exactly?"

"Like you wanted to give as much as you wanted to take. I didn't feel like an object or a conquest," I confess.

"Ach, Norah love," he says, pressing a kiss to my forehead, "I could murder the bastards that made you feel that way. A kiss should never be one-sided."

He pulls me into him and wraps his strong arms around me. I settle in and rest my head on his chest, the sound of his rapid heartbeat mirroring mine and beginning to heal the broken parts of me I never thought could be mended.

Chapter Eighteen

Eamon

I toss and turn most of the night, replaying my kiss with Norah over and over in my mind. I still can't believe I even asked her, let alone the fact that she consented. I feel like the luckiest bastard alive to have earned her trust like that. And I wasn't exaggerating when I told her that it was the best kiss of my life. Even my more passionate moments with Rhiannan, and other flings, don't compare to kissing Norah. Feeling her lips against mine, her tongue meeting mine stroke for stroke, completely consumed me. When she pressed her body against me and made those needy little noises, it was almost my undoing. I know I need to tread carefully, especially physically, given Norah's history. I don't want to trigger any memories and fears, but Christ Almighty, do I want her—more than I've ever wanted a woman before.

Leaving her had been a cruel form of torture. We had lingered on her porch for half an hour longer, knowing that going inside would be the opposite of taking things slow. I finally forced myself to tell her goodnight. With the match coming up, I was going to need sleep. I stole another gentle kiss from her before walking backward down the sidewalk, grinning.

"I'll see you tomorrow, right? Your tickets will be at the booth."

She had cocked her head to the side, a mischievous smirk on her beautiful face. "I don't know. I'd hate to be a distraction."

"Ach, love, you'll be me lucky charm." I winked at her.

She snorted at my lame joke and said, "I'll be there. Goodnight, Eamon." Then she slipped into her house, shutting the door behind her.

* * *

It's two hours before game time when I arrive at the pitch to get centered. I'm not nervous about playing with Norah in the stands. I'm never nervous when I'm on the pitch, just determined and focused. When I walk into the locker room I find Mac already there. *Lovely.*

"Hey, man," Mac says with a nod.

"Mac," I reply dryly, shoving my gym bag in my assigned locker before sitting on the bench to put my cleats on.

"I can't believe you came out to the pub last night. *Eamon Kennedy doesn't drink before a match.* Isn't that what you've always said?" Mac says mockingly.

"Aye. I don't. I shouldn't have let Ro talk me into going," I say, knotting my laces.

"At least you got some action out of it." Mac waggles his eyebrows.

"What the fuck are you talking about?"

"Oh, come on. We all saw you leave with Norah." He shrugs.

Rolling my eyes, I stand and start to walk out of the room.

"What's she like in the sack? Quiet girl like her, I bet she's a tiger..."

Before I can fully register what I'm doing, I have Mac by the collar of his shirt, slamming him into the wall.

126

"The only reason I'm not knocking you out is because we have a match. But if I ever hear you talk about her that way again, all bets are off. Understand?" My words are quiet but lethal. I shove him into the wall once more for good measure.

"Jesus, man, it was a joke. What the fuck is wrong with you?" Mac stares at me while rubbing the back of his head where it had hit the wall.

I don't say a word as I walk down the hall to the pitch. I shouldn't have lost my temper with Mac, but the fact that he was even *thinking* about Norah like that has me seeing red. For more than one reason. First, Mac is a dirty bastard who views women as his own personal playthings. If I ever catch him so much as looking at Norah, I'll likely beat the hell out of him. Just the thought of him putting his hands on her makes me murderous. Second, given her history, I know that when—if—we become intimate, it will be slow going. She'll have to set the pace.

"Kennedy, get over here!" I hear Coach yell, pulling me from my thoughts.

Breaking into a jog across the field, I can see the scowl forming on Coach's face. *Great.* I stop a couple of feet away, nodding to a few of my teammates.

"Coach," I say in greeting.

"What's this I hear about you going out drinking last night?" the older man says sternly, folding his arms across his chest.

"Aye, I went to Paddy's last night. Had a couple of drinks with my girl, then walked her home." I hold my head up proudly. No, I don't usually drink before a match, but I don't regret any part of last night.

Coach lifts an eyebrow and shoves his hands in his pockets. "You weren't partying with Mac and the other idiots?"

"No, sir. I was there at the same time as them, even spoke with them, but I wasn't *with* them."

"Good," Coach nods. "If we weren't playing Duke today, I'd bench all of their sorry asses. Be prepared for extra laps if we don't pull a win."

I respect Coach's methods of discipline. It sucks, but if a couple of guys do something stupid to blow the game, he makes the whole team run extra laps so that the offending parties will feel the team's wrath as well as Coach's.

"Aye," I nod, stretching an arm across my chest.

"So who's the girl? I wasn't aware you were seeing someone," Coach says casually.

A grin spreads across my face. "It's a recent development, but one I'm hoping lasts. Her name is Norah. She'll be here later."

"As long as she's not a distraction, Kennedy..." Coach cautions.

"No, sir. If anything, I think she'll be a motivator." I grin again.

"Alright, back to your warm-ups. I want you hustling out there today."

Half an hour before game time, the team is in the locker room getting ready for Coach's pep talk. I hear my phone ding from my locker and open the door to turn it off, but I see a text from Norah. Opening it eagerly, my breath catches at the selfie she sent of her in the stands, wearing a Seahawks jersey with my number on it. As proud as that makes me, I can't take my eyes off of her face and those wide, blue eyes. She's so stunningly beautiful. The sun gilds her hair, transforming it into a halo of fire and her smile is shy. It has me wanting to be right there kissing the life out of her. Below the picture, she's sent a message.

Norah: *I'd say 'break a leg,' but I'm not sure if theater well wishes are the same for soccer. Either way, I'm cheering for you! xoxo*

I chuckle quietly as I quickly text her back.

Eamon: *How could I not play well when the most beautiful lass here is cheering for me?*

Powering off my phone, I turn back to the team to see Ro staring at me questioningly.

"You ready, mate?"

I clap a hand on his shoulder, feeling on top of the world. "Oh yeah. Let's do this."

Norah

My heart flips as I read the text Eamon sent back. I was nervous about sending a selfie, but Layla encouraged me. Out of all of my friends, Layla enjoys soccer the most, so it made sense to bring her. Her brothers are both soccer players in Texas. Thankfully, she has the day off.

"What did he say?" Layla asks, peeking over my shoulder.

I angle my phone towards her and giggle, feeling my cheeks turn pink.

"Oh, girl, you've got it bad!" She laughs, bumping my arm with hers. "He's good with his words. Makes you wonder what else he's good with, doesn't it?"

I blush even more and turn my head away from her pointedly.

"*Norah Grady!*" Layla shrieks. "You better spill, and I mean *right now!*"

Covering my face with my hands and still giggling like a schoolgirl, I peek through my fingers. "Shh! I'd rather not tell the whole world, thank you very much. But if you *must* know…he kissed me last night."

I try to control the grin on my face, but it's futile. Eamon makes me happy, and it's really, really nice to feel happiness instead of anxiety.

Layla's eyes bug out of her head, and she grabs me by the shoulders. "Oh my god! Norah, that's amazing! I'm guessing by the big grin on your face that you not only consented but enjoyed it?"

Squealing a little, I nod. "Layla, it was earth-shattering. I know that sounds cheesy, and I don't have much to compare it with, but I didn't have an ounce of fear. He asked, actually *asked*, if he could kiss me, and I didn't want it to end."

"So where *did* it end?" Layla wags her eyebrows.

"Stop it! He was a perfect gentleman. He was the one to end it, actually." I blush again, remembering my response to his kiss.

Layla gasps. "Norah! You were going to…"

"No!" I squeak. "I mean, I don't think so anyway. It was a pretty heated moment, but he said he didn't want to rush anything with me, so we said goodnight."

I can tell that Layla is about to bombard me with more questions, but thankfully, the announcer chooses that moment to bellow through the loudspeaker announcing the teams. Since it's a home game, the Seahawks will be announced last. I know that Eamon is a forward, but other than that, my knowledge of soccer is seriously lacking. If I'm going to be coming to more games, I better start doing my research.

"Introducing the UNCW Seahawks!" the announcer roars over the speakers, bringing my focus to the tunnel where the team will exit.

The crowd goes absolutely wild. Everyone is on their feet, screaming and swinging teal shirts and banners above their heads. As the announcer lists the numbers, positions, and names of the players, I recognize a few of them. Teagan is announced as the goalie, followed by Mac as one of the defenders. Eventually, he announces Rowan Gallagher, and I finally hear the name I've been waiting for. I surprise not only Layla but myself as a loud cheer erupts from my lungs. Eamon runs onto the field, and the butterflies come alive in my stomach. Seeing him in street clothes is one thing, but watching him run out onto the pitch in his uniform is downright sexual. He stops by Ro, his eyes roaming the crowd until he finds me. As soon as he sees me, he grins widely and winks. On a whim, I blow him a kiss.

The game is intense. The Seahawks are playing their rivals from Duke University, and the fans don't hold back on their chants and cheers, sweeping Layla and me into the fray. It's impossible to take my eyes off of Eamon as he moves around the field, completely focused on the task at hand and moving in perfect harmony with Ro—like they're of one mind. When a Duke player fouls Eamon with an elbow to the ribs, hitting him hard enough to send him to his knees, I gasp and grab Layla's arm. It takes him a minute to catch his breath, but he's soon back on his feet. The offending player receives a yellow card, awarding Eamon a penalty shot. He places the ball in position and lines up his shot, pausing to stare down the goalie before he runs forward and kicks the ball. It flies right into the upper left corner of the goal, and I explode out of my seat, arms in the air, screaming along with the rest of the fans. Layla is laughing at me, but I don't care. I haven't had this much fun in ages. Ro charges Eamon and picks him up off the ground, making me laugh. The rest of the team closes in and wraps their arms around him or slaps his butt for a job well done.

There's a renewed energy in the team, and Duke doesn't stand a chance. Not five minutes later, the Seahawks score another goal, sending the crowd into a frenzy, and by the end of the game, the Seahawks are up five to one—with three goals from Eamon. The announcer comes over the speakers to

130

inform the fans that this is Eamon's second career hat trick. I have no idea what that means, but it seems like a good thing, judging by the cheers in the stadium.

"Holy shit, Norah! That game was insane! I'm so glad you invited me." Layla says as we gather our belongings.

"Oh my god, I know!" I agree. "I've never really been into sports, but this was so much fun! We should make this a regular thing!"

"Deal! And, don't hit me, but *damn*! Eamon is on fire! I get why you can't take your eyes off that man," Layla says playfully.

I chuckle. "I won't hit you. Just keep your hands to yourself, and we won't have a problem. You'd have to be blind not to appreciate God's handiwork."

"Speaking of, God's handiwork is headed this way..."

I turn in time to see Eamon jogging in my direction. He jumps over the barrier and the row of seats in front of me, making me grin stupidly. Especially when he cups my cheeks with his hands and kisses me passionately. I stand there shocked for half a second before sliding my hands up his chest and tangling my fingers into his sweaty hair. He trails a hand from my face down to my waist and crushes me to him. I'm completely lost in the moment, vaguely aware of the people around us catcalling and whistling. Much to my dismay, he eventually pulls away and brushes a thumb across my cheek.

"Hi," I pant.

"Hi, love," he chuckles. "I'd apologize for that, but it would be a lie."

"I wouldn't accept your apology anyway. Good game, Kennedy." I beam at him.

"Ahem." Layla clears her throat.

We slowly come back to earth and look over at the voyeurs watching us.

"I didn't think they were going to come up for air, did you, lass?" Teagan asks, peering up at Layla from the sideline. She giggles and shakes her head, her cheeks coloring slightly. I file this away for a later conversation.

Eamon's hand squeezes my hip to get my attention. "I'm not quite through here yet, but I'd like to see you later. Do you have plans?"

"I have some history homework to catch up on, but I'm probably going to need to call a tutor. Know of anyone?" I tease.

He buries his face in my neck and whispers, "I know someone who gives private lessons. He could probably be there in a couple of hours."

I shiver in response and nod.

"Oi! Kennedy! You can snog your girl later! Coach wants us in the locker room like five minutes ago!"

Eamon sighs and I catch a flash of red hair running off the field. Ro. Of course. He pulls me to him again and kisses the top of my head. "See you soon?"

"See you soon," I agree. "I'm sure you're hungry. Want me to make dinner?"

His eyes widen in surprise, lips curving up on one side. "You want to cook for me?"

"I probably can't make an Irish stew like you can, but I'm actually pretty decent in the kitchen. I do more than just sew."

"It's true," Layla chimes in. "She's an amazing baker too! I can blame every single one of these curves on her!"

"You say that like it's a problem," Teagan says, climbing over the barrier to stand by Eamon. He eyes Layla appreciatively, making her blush and look down at her feet. Sticking a hand in her direction, he drawls, "Name's Teagan O'Brien. You are?"

"Uh...um. Layla. Layla Diaz," she answers nervously, placing her hand in his.

"Pleasure, love. Now, excuse me while I take Romeo here before Coach blows a gasket. See you around, Layla." He winks at her before turning back to the field.

Eamon chuckles and kisses my cheek before walking away with Teagan. I watch as he walks away, because who wouldn't want to watch that? Sighing, I turn to Layla to see that she's also watching the guys walk away.

"Earth to Layla! You're drooling."

Layla's dark eyes snap to mine, wide as saucers. "He was... Did he just... I didn't imagine that, did I?"

"No, you definitely did not," I tell her. "If I've learned anything over the last week, these Irishmen don't have a problem expressing themselves."

132

Chapter Nineteen

Norah

I'm just pulling dinner out of the oven when I hear a knock at the door. I'm anxious to see Eamon, but I've never cooked a meal for a guy before, so I'm stupidly nervous. When I throw open the door, my heart sinks. It's not Eamon but a thoroughly pissed-off Myra.

"Myra, what are you…" I start, but she shoves her way through the door and turns on her heel to glare at me.

"What the hell is your man's problem?" she seethes.

I am officially confused. "I have no idea what you're talking about. What happened?"

She scoffs and says, "Apparently, Eamon threw Mac up against a wall before the game, defending your honor or some shit like that."

"He what?" I gasp, completely shocked.

"Mac said that Eamon freaked out on him and told him if he heard Mac say anything about you again, he'd knock him out." Her hands are on her hips, and she's looking at me for support.

"Wait, what did Mac say exactly?" I'm not about to just let her barge in here demanding sympathies without some sort of explanation.

"What does that matter? He pretty much assaulted his teammate," she fumes.

I bristle at her tone. What does it *matter*?

"Myra," I say thickly, feeling the burn of tears in my eyes. "What did Mac say?"

Heaving a sigh, she says, "Ugh. He was *totally* joking around, but he asked Eamon how you were in the sack and implied you were probably pretty wild because you're so prudish with everyone."

I make a disgusted noise as I will myself not to cry.

"Right? Not even a big deal. Eamon has some serious anger..."

"Get out," I interrupt her in a hoarse whisper.

"What?" Myra gapes at me.

"After everything I've been through and the huge step I'm taking just dating Eamon, you think it's okay for Mac to talk about me like that?" I'm so angry I'm shaking.

"Oh my god, Norah," she rolls her eyes. "How long are you going to play that card? It's been how many years now? Time to move on. Maybe if you let him fuck you, you'll get over it."

Before I can respond, a deep voice growls behind me, "Myra, I think it's time for you to leave now."

"Ugh. I'm out of here," she spits as she shoulders her way past Eamon.

Eamon

I don't bother looking at Myra or I might say something I'll regret later. It takes every bit of self-control I have to *not* go off on her for the vile things she said to Norah. Norah, who is standing there with tears rolling down her cheeks.

I walk towards her slowly; taking her elbow, I pull her into my embrace. She starts crying in earnest now. I don't blame her. The conversation I walked in on was brutal. How anyone could say such things, especially to someone they call a friend, is mind-boggling. I'm sure Mac spun the story to make himself look like the victim. Apparently, I need to have another conversation with him. I'm not a violent person by nature, but I want nothing more than to seek vengeance on anyone who has ever caused Norah an ounce of pain.

"Shhh, love. It's okay," I murmur as I run my hand over her hair. "I'm so sorry. You didn't deserve that."

"Is it true?" she asks, looking up at me with watery blue eyes. Christ, even crying she's gorgeous.

"Is what true?"

"Did you really shove Mac against a wall defending me?" She sniffles.

"Aye," I don't hesitate to say. "I did. He had no business talking about you the way he did. He shouldn't be talking about any woman that way."

Norah wraps her arms around my waist and rests her head against my chest. "Thank you," she whispers. "And thank you for coming in when you did."

I hold her tightly and kiss the top of her head. "I only wish I would have gotten here sooner, but I stopped to get you something on the way."

She raises her head again, a small smile forming on her tear-streaked face. "You got me something?"

She's adorable. I grin at her and say, "It's in the car. I'll be right back."

I return carrying a white paper sack. I set it on the kitchen island, motioning her over. "Open it," I order.

She unfolds the top of the bag and peeks inside before squealing,

"Cranberry scones!"

"I know you're a baker, but I couldn't let you do all the work," I tease her. "Which, by the way, it smells incredible in here."

"Thank you. I just pulled it out of the oven before Myra showed up, so we should eat before it gets cold."

"Grand. I'm famished," I tell her.

She made a proper Sunday roast, and I'm all but delighted.

"I'm not all that knowledgeable about soccer, but the game was a lot of fun to watch. You're really in your element on the field, " she compliments me, and I preen a little.

"Aye, I love it. I'm glad you were there. I credit my hat trick to you, you know," I say before taking a bite of food and moaning loudly. I haven't had a roast this good since before leaving Ireland. "Norah, this is amazing. What kind of witchcraft do you use?"

Laughing, she pours us each a glass of wine. "What kind of witch gives up her secret spells? Also, don't laugh, but what exactly is a hat trick? That sounds more witchy than me cooking a roast."

I laugh anyway because she's so fecking cute.

"I said don't laugh!" She glares at me playfully.

"Sorry, love. Truly." I grin at her before continuing. "A hat trick is when a player scores three goals in a single game."

"Oh, okay. The announcer said today was your second hat trick. I take it that's a big deal?" Norah asks curiously.

I nod around a bite of potatoes. I don't want to sound like an arrogant arsehole, but I'm proud of my achievement.

"Well, then congratulations!" she says, tipping her glass in my direction.

We spend the next half hour eating and talking about the game. She's genuinely interested, and I enjoy teaching her. Rhiannan never cared enough to ask. That should have been my first indication that she was messing around on me.

When we finish the meal, I help Norah clean up the dishes and put away the leftovers. Standing beside her at the sink, I'm reminded of washing dishes with her at Paddy's and when she sloshed water on me. Before I can talk myself out of it, I splash her with water, grinning like a fool.

She gasps in shock and stands there looking at me like I've lost my mind. And maybe I have because I didn't consider how the water would make her shirt cling to her body the way it is.

"What was that for?" she screeches.

"Payback." I shrug.

"Payback? Payback for what?" She narrows her eyes at me. My fire sprite is starting to come out to play, and I love it.

"You don't remember dousing me with water when we did dishes at Paddy's? It wasn't that long ago, lass," I tease her.

"Eamon Kennedy, that was an *accident*, and you know it!" She turns back to the sink suddenly, grabs the sprayer, and releases a cascade of water over me.

"Oy! That's cheating!" I yell, reaching for the hand holding the sprayer. My other arm snakes around her torso instinctively, and I pull her into me.

Norah squeals again, squirming to get out of my grasp, but I'm not having that. I wrestle the sprayer from her and set it back in its spot before grabbing her around the waist and hoisting her onto the counter so we're eye to eye. Panting and dripping water, we stare at each other as the tension grows thick around us. I hear the soft sound of her sucking in a breath before she reaches up to brush a strand of wet hair from my forehead. The soft touch of her fingers tracing along my jaw makes me shudder and she smiles faintly. That smile is a magnet, pulling me closer.

"Norah," I whisper before she brushes her lips against mine.

Norah

Eamon's mouth is barely inches from mine. My heart is thundering in my chest, but I don't break eye contact as I close the distance between us. When my lips touch his, I feel his hands tighten on my hips, and I smile against his mouth. Teasing the seam of his lips with my tongue, he grunts in surprise before eagerly joining in. Our kiss is slow and building. My eyes drift closed as I thread my fingers into his hair and draw him closer, my legs parting to wrap around his hips. A warm hand runs up my spine and back down again, causing goosebumps in their wake. But when his fingers begin to wander under the hem of my shirt, I freeze. My brain is betraying what my body clearly wants.

"I'm sorry," Eamon says quickly, taking a step back and shifting uncomfortably.

I am acutely aware of the cause of his discomfort since the countertop I'm sitting on had me perfectly aligned with his...*arousal*.

I heave a sigh, shaking my head. "No, don't be. I just...haven't had anyone touch me like that since..."

"Christ. I'm an eejit. I shouldn't have done that without asking. Or at all. I meant it when I said you're in charge..." The words pour from him as he rubs his hands over his face.

"Eamon, stop," I say, reaching for his hand to pull him closer. "You didn't do anything wrong. I'm not upset; I promise. Things just got carried away, and my brain triggered that response."

He looks at me carefully, trying to discern if I'm telling the truth. Tentatively, he reaches to tuck a lock of my hair behind my ear.

"You're safe with me, Norah," he says earnestly. "I won't let that happen again."

"Well, let's not be hasty..." I tease.

He raises a dark brow at me and purses his lips. "You know what I mean. I don't want to do anything to scare you off."

"Not going to happen, Kennedy. I trust you."

And I do. I know beyond a shadow of a doubt that this man will not willingly hurt me or push me to do something I don't want to do. The problem is, I *want* to do something. I want *him*.

We clean up the evidence of our water fight before I grab the bag of scones and curl up on the far end of the couch. Pulling my feet underneath me, I watch Eamon walk in my direction, eyeing him from head to toe.

"You keep looking at me like that, and I may have to kiss you again," he growls playfully, giving me a wicked grin.

Heat floods my body, and my face flushes in embarrassment. I can't take my eyes off of him though. He sits down next to me, wrapping an arm around my shoulders and drawing me closer to him. When he brushes my cheek with the thumb of his other hand, I lean into his touch because it just feels right. Everything about Eamon feels right.

"That's not really motivating me to stop," I say breathlessly, heat still lingering in me, but it's a slow burn.

Eamon groans and closes his eyes. "Norah, I'm going to be honest with you. I would love to take you right here on this sofa."

And now I'm on fire.

"But I want more than just the physical with you," he says softly. "I want to get to know you. And I want you to know me. I want you to be one hundred percent positive that this"—he gestures between us—"is what you want."

I take a shuddering breath. "I…I want that too, Eamon."

Bringing his hand back to cup my face gently, he slowly presses his lips to mine in a chaste kiss.

"Good," he says then leans back. "Now, what are we going to do for the rest of the evening?"

I hum as an idea forms. "We could watch Beauty and the Beast. I know we said we'd watch it tomorrow, but maybe we can find something else to do."

I don't care what we do just as long as we're together, and I should probably be ashamed to feel like a teenager in the throes of first love, but I'm not. I didn't date in high school, and after the attack, I didn't even consider dating as a possibility. Eamon just does something to me, and I like it.

"Aye, we could. What did you have in mind for tomorrow?" he asks.

"I don't have anything in mind, really, but we could figure that out then. I feel like being spontaneous."

He looks at me dubiously. "I'm intrigued now. You don't strike me as a spontaneous person. No offense."

I huff a laugh. "I'm usually not, but apparently, all things Irish bring out a different side of me. Like a drinking contest."

My mind wanders back to my time in Ireland. I was a different person on that trip; exploring everywhere, trying everything, and talking to everyone. Then I discovered O'Nelly's, which led me to Eamon, who has a way of drawing me out of my comfort zone.

Eamon looks at me in mock outrage. "I see how it is. Blame it all on the Irish bloke! Never mind the fact that I tried to talk you out of said drinking contest."

Laughing loudly, I turn to poke him in the chest, but he catches my hand, bringing my fingers to his lips and kissing them. "I'm really glad you didn't listen."

"Me too," I sigh, resting my head on his chest.

Chapter Twenty

Eamon

It's well past midnight when I wake up to find that, at some point, Norah and I shifted positions. My legs are outstretched with my head resting on the arm of the sofa. Norah is wedged between my body and the back cushions, her slender arm draped over my stomach and her head on my chest. One of my arms is wrapped around her while the other is tucked behind my head. I don't remember how or when we got here, but I'm not upset about it. I watch her for a few minutes, slowly running my fingers over her hair. I'm always aware of how beautiful she is, but seeing her asleep on my chest takes my breath away. Her delicate features soften while she sleeps, the tension melting away and making her appear angelic and peaceful. I shift carefully out from under her so that I don't wake her.

"Eamon?" she murmurs, just as I start scribbling her a note. I turn to see her sitting up, covering a yawn with the back of her hand.

"Right here, love. I was hoping I wouldn't wake you," I reply, stepping back to the couch to sit beside her.

"What time is it? How long have I been out?" she asks, her voice husky with sleep.

"It's just after midnight, and I'm not sure, honestly. I fell asleep as well. The last thing I remember is the Beast showing Belle the library."

"Oh, that's my favorite part! And right before the ballroom scene. I'm sorry we missed it." She tucks a loose strand of hair behind her ear. "I'd offer to go back, but it's so late. I really should go to bed."

Standing, I pull her up to her feet. "Aye. You've a busy day tomorrow, don't you?"

She nods as I wrap my arms around her, gently hugging her to me. I brush a kiss to the top of her head before walking to the door.

"Lock up behind me so I know you're safe," I order before stepping onto the porch.

"Yes, boss." She playfully rolls her eyes.

"Good girl." I grin, ducking to kiss her gently. "Goodnight, Norah. I'll see you tomorrow."

* * *

A loud, blaring noise startles me from my sleep. Groaning, I reach for the alarm, desperately wanting to hit the snooze button, but I have too much to accomplish today. Homework is stacking up, I have a few odd jobs to do at Paddy's, and then there's practice before spending another evening with Norah. The thought of seeing her again perks me up significantly. Stretching, I head for the shower. I have about three hours to devote to homework before going to Paddy's. He wasn't intentionally doing anything to upset me, but I'm not happy with how we left things the other night. I just wasn't prepared for the conversation that would undoubtedly follow. It worked out well enough though, so there's no sense in holding a grudge.

After getting ready, I grab my bag and head to Margie's. Not just because I'm addicted to her scones, but because it's my favorite place to study. It's too easy to be lazy at home, and the library on campus is too quiet. Margie's is perfect because it's busy enough to have a white noise effect, but not so busy that it's chaos. I find my usual spot by the window and set my bag down so no one will snatch it while I order coffee.

I'm just finishing up a paper for one of my education classes when I feel a hand clap down on my shoulder, nearly scaring the life out of me.

"Hey, mate," Teagan greets me as he flops into the opposite chair.

Teagan and I met when we joined the Seahawks, but we had lived only twenty minutes from each other in Ireland. We probably drank at the same pubs without even realizing it.

"Mornin', Teag. Doing alright?"

"Aye," he answers hesitantly.

"You sure, mate? You look stressed. What's going on?" I close my laptop to give him my full attention.

He runs his hands through his hair, tugging on the strands and letting out a frustrated groan before looking at me. "I've been evicted from my flat. I have two weeks to be out."

"What?" I ask, astonished. "You're joking."

I don't believe for one second that Teagan has done anything to warrant an eviction. He's straight-laced, never late with his rent, keeps his place clean, and hasn't hosted one party since living there.

"I wish I was, Eam. The landlord sold the complex to some multimillion-dollar company that wants to completely remodel the place. They want to turn them into executive suites or some shite like that. They're kicking out everyone. We don't even get first dibs on the new ones—not that I could afford it anyway. The monthly rent is three times what I'm paying now."

"Fuck. That's robbery. How can they get away with that?"

"No clue, mate. I'm completely flummoxed. There aren't any other flats available now that the term has started," Teagan says.

I don't hesitate to offer the spare room at my flat. It's not much, but I'm not about to leave the fella homeless.

143

"Why don't you take the second room at my place? It's just sitting there. And if we split the rent and utilities, it will save us both some money," I offer, knowing that Teagan would never ask that of anyone.

"No way, Eam. I'm not going to infiltrate your space. Especially now that you have your new girl. No offense, but I don't want to listen to the two of you go at it all day every day."

I roll my eyes. "Don't be a twat. Norah and I haven't progressed to that place in our relationship. Plus, she has her own place, so if things do head that way, then you're good."

"You two haven't..." Teagan wags his eyebrows. "How? She's smoking, and that kiss you shared the other day was borderline pornographic, man."

"Fuck off, you wanker." I laugh, throwing an ink pen at him. "Seriously. Move into the second room. It solves your problems, and if you decide it's not working, you can move out whenever you want."

Teagan hesitates, rubbing the back of his neck. "I don't know, man. Are you sure it wouldn't be an issue?"

"Not at all. Between classes and practice...and Norah...I probably won't even be there much." I shrug, then grin wickedly. "And maybe I could get Norah to come over and bring her friend Layla. Don't think I didn't notice you flirting with her yesterday."

Teagan visibly brightens at the mention of Layla. "What can I say? She's a fine thing."

"So it's settled, then? I'll get the room sorted, and you can start moving your stuff as soon as today. I'll get you a copy of the key."

"You're a gem, mate. Really, thank you. Can you send me a list of when the bills are due and how much you want me to pay?"

"We'll talk about it later, yeah? I've got to get to Paddy's to fix a few things for him." I stand, hoisting my bag onto my shoulder before clasping a hand with Teagan and pulling him in for a hug.

"Right. See you at practice. Thanks again!"

I wave at him over my shoulder as I leave the cafe. He'll be a good flatmate. He's not wild like Ro and won't give me too hard of a time about Norah. And maybe, just maybe, I can play matchmaker. He hasn't gone out with anyone that I know of since his ex dumped him out of the blue. They'd dated for about a year before she broke it off, and he acted like it didn't bother him much, but I know him better than that. He'd been head over heels for that lass.

It's just past noon when I walk into Paddy's. All of the chairs are turned over on top of the tables, and the main lights are on. There's some clanking coming from the kitchen, so I head towards it. As I walk through the swinging doors, I see Paddy on his hands and knees, looking under the dishwasher. Leaning against the wall, I cross my arms over my chest, and watch the aul fella swear at whatever he's trying to fix.

"Jaysus, Mary, and Joseph! This bleedin' machine can go straight to the fiery pits of hell! Fu…"

"Look at the state of you, Paddy! What did you do to that dishwasher?"

Paddy jerks his head up, hitting it on the bottom of the sink, and I wince knowing what's coming next. "Ow! Son of a… Kennedy! You shitehawk! Give a man some warning would ya? I could have cracked my skull open!"

I stifle a laugh and hold out a hand to help him to his feet. "Sorry, Paddy. Couldn't help it. You looked a right eejit on the ground like that, cursing enough to make a harlot blush."

"Oh, bugger off. I did no such thing. You must have misheard me. Easy to do when your head's up your…"

"Paddy O'Nelly, you watch your mouth around my virgin ears," interrupts Alicia as she waltzes through the employee entrance, a shite-eating grin spread across her face. We love nothing more than to tease Paddy relentlessly.

I snort a laugh as Paddy glares at her. "Virgin ears? Ach, no barkeeper has virgin ears, lass. And I've heard that sailor's mouth of yours, so you're fooling no one."

Alicia throws her head back, laughing loudly, while she ties an apron around her waist. "Alright, you caught me. What's got you in such a fuss today, anyway? Eamon, what did you do to him?"

"What did I do? Nothing at all. Just walked in here to find Paddy under the dishwasher, calling it every name in the book." I hold up my hands up in defense.

"He's conveniently leaving out the part where he snuck up on me and caused me to hit my head on the damned thing," Paddy grumbles.

"What exactly are you trying to fix anyway?" I ask. I've told him time and time again to call me or make a list of what needs to be done, and I'll take a look at it. Paddy is *not* a handyman, and more often than not, he just causes more damage.

His round cheeks turn pink, and he clears his throat. "Well now, there was a small leak, and I was just trying to figure out what was causing it. I'm more than capable of handling it on my own."

Alicia and I glance at each other, both trying to hold in our laughter, but it's no good. When she puts a tattooed hand over her mouth and starts giggling, I laugh along with her.

"Paddy, don't you remember the last time you tried to fix a leak in the bathroom? There was water everywhere!" Alicia says, wiping tears from her eyes. "I thought I was going to have to get a canoe to take care of our lovely patrons!"

"It took me days to get that mess cleaned up!" I remind him.

Paddy crosses his arms over his chest and huffs like a small child who isn't getting their way. "Alright. I'm not paying the two of you to stand around slagging me all day. Go find something useful to do before I replace you!"

"Awe, Paddy. You know we're just having the craic. Besides, you'd be bored to tears if we were any other way, " I throw an arm around his shoulders.

Alicia steps over to him, planting a kiss on his cheek before bouncing towards the bar, "You know we love ya, Pat!"

"Aye. Go on. Get to work, girl." He harrumphs, turning towards the office. "She's a good lass, isn't she?"

"Ro certainly thinks so," I answer. "But yeah, she is. Glad she found her way here."

"Ach. Rowan Gallagher is nothing but trouble. He'll break that girl's heart faster than he can drink a pint." Paddy shakes his head, groaning as he sinks into the chair behind his desk. "Speaking of breaking hearts, Eamon. I hope

I didn't cause a rift with you and a certain fire sprite. You know I'd never—"

"I know, Paddy," I cut him off. "You don't need to explain. You're a good man. I wasn't expecting to have that conversation with Norah so soon, but it ended up being for the best. So, thank you."

"She's good for you, son. And you seem to be good for her. I don't know her full story, but I can tell she's had a rough go of it."

"She has, but she's stronger than I think anyone gives her credit for."

My chest swells with pride thinking about all Norah has accomplished despite the obstacles she's faced. Moving away from your home is scary enough when you have your family alive and supporting you, but to be completely alone? That takes a different level of bravery. I know what it's like to lose a parent, but I still have my Mam, even if we do live an ocean apart. Norah never knew her father and isn't close to her remaining relatives, so losing her Mom would have been like losing a limb.

"Aye. Not many get to see that side of our Norah. It was four years ago when she came wandering into my pub. I remember it clearly. She marched right up to the bar and requested a *proper* Guinness." He chuckles at the memory. "She sat there and talked my ears off. Told me about her trip to the Isle, and how she wanted to live there. Told me she'd go back one day and find her husband…" He pauses to give me a pointed look.

My breath catches in my chest as my mind floods with images of Norah in a white gown—no doubt something she created herself—against a backdrop of the Irish countryside, walking down a path littered with rose petals - straight to me.

"Anyway," Paddy continues, "she lit up talking about Ireland. Reminded me of my Ellie, God rest her. If we'd ever been blessed with a daughter, I imagine she'd have been like Norah. All sugar and spice. Treat her well, lad and you'll never lose her."

We've only just met, but I already know that I don't want to let her go.

Chapter Twenty-One

Norah

I stayed an hour later than normal in my theater class. With the play only weeks away, there's so much to accomplish. I wouldn't trade the time with Eamon for anything, but I need to focus, and I absolutely cannot focus when he's near me.

More than once I've caught myself replaying our heated moment in the kitchen. The way his hands left a trail of fire when they slid over me and how he wedged himself between my legs leaves me feeling tingly in the most delicious ways. I touch my fingertips to my lips and smile. I'm still shocked that I initiated that kiss and even more surprised at how I didn't want to stop. I hate how my past trauma triggered my panic when his fingers crept under the edge of my shirt. Rationally, I know that he would never force himself on me, but I still froze. Maybe it's time to call my therapist.

When I finally leave the theater, it's a little after four in the afternoon. I check my phone as I walk out of the building, delighted to see that I have a text from Eamon. We haven't talked all day.

Eamon: *Looking forward to seeing you tonight, love.*

I grin so wide that my cheeks hurt. How can something so simple make me feel so happy? I start to text him back but remember he has practice, so he likely won't see it until later. Now that I think about it, the field isn't far from where I am, and I don't want to wait another two hours to see my Irishman. I turn in that direction, and my phone buzzes. It's Layla.

"Hey, Lay Lay! What are you doing?" I ask excitedly.

"Lay Lay? Really? Am I five?"

I can just see her rolling her dark brown eyes at me. "What? I thought 'Hey, Lay' sounded too weird. Whatever. It doesn't matter. What's up?"

"I just got off work and was bored. Thought I'd come to see you if you're free," she suggests.

I'm about to tell her that I have plans before I remember her interaction with Teagan at the game the day before.

"Actually, I'm headed to the soccer field to wait for Eamon. They have practice for a couple of hours. Want to join?"

"Oh, uh…" Layla starts.

"Teagan will be there…" I tell her in a sing-song voice.

I can't help it. Anyone would have to be blind to not see the sparks flying between those two, and as far as I'm concerned, everyone can benefit from a hot Irish footballer flirting with them.

"You're the devil. You know that, right?"

"I'd like to think I'm more angelic, bestowing blessings upon my friends. I'll see you soon! Kisses!" I hang up before Layla can say another word.

It's not long before Layla and I are sitting halfway up the stands, watching a group of sweaty, shirtless men run around the field.

"Did you know that soccer players run an average of seven miles every game?" I ask, trailing Eamon. Even from here, I can see the sweat rolling over the dips and grooves of his abs. He hasn't noticed me yet, so I don't feel too bad about gawking at his sculpted body.

"That sounds like literal hell. Why do they subject themselves to this kind of torture?" Layla questions, equally distracted by the players on the field.

"I'm not complaining," I tell her. "God, look at him. It should be illegal to look that good. He makes me have very inappropriate thoughts."

Layla laughs. "Who are you and what have you done with Norah Grady? I don't think I've ever even heard you talk about a man's body before!"

I sigh dramatically. "I can't describe it, but Eamon makes me feel alive in ways I didn't know I could feel. He's not just the sexiest man alive, but he's kind and thoughtful. He hasn't even tried to pressure me into sleeping with him. Listen to me. I sound like a crazy person. We just met, and I already sound like…"

"You're in love!"

My cheeks flame as I shake my head in denial. "No, that's not possible. People don't fall in love that fast in real life. I'm in lust, that's for sure, but every time things start to get heavy, my body locks up in fear. I'm not sure if we'll even be able to have a physical relationship."

"Hey," Layla says, placing a hand on my arm. "You're not always going to feel so scared. This is the first guy you've talked to in years, and if he's half as amazing as you say he is, then I'm sure he understands your hesitations. And if he doesn't, then he can take it up with me and the rest of the girls. You know we've always got your back."

I wrap my arms around her, hugging her tight. "Thanks, Lay. I have the best of friends. Well, maybe not Myra at the moment, but the rest of you are the best."

"What?" Layla snaps her head back in alarm. "What happened with Myra? I haven't talked to her in a while."

"Ugh. It was awful." I groan before recounting the entire story, including Eamon's well-timed arrival.

Layla's mouth hangs open in disbelief. "I can't believe she said that. I expect her to do stuff like that with everyone else, but not her friends! Especially over her newest fuckboy. Do you think she's serious about Mac?"

"God, I hope not. He's so sleazy. She can do so much better."

"You're too good, Norie," Layla says. "After all that Myra's done, you still give her the benefit of the doubt."

Sighing, I prop my legs up on the seat in front of me. "I'm so pissed at her, but she's still my friend, and I love her. We can't all get along all of the time, right? We're bound to have our bad moments. I don't necessarily want to talk to her right now, but I really hope we can work this out."

The shrill blast of a whistle interrupts our conversation and we look to the field to see the team taking a water break. My eyes instantly find Eamon. He's lifting a water bottle to his mouth as he casually scans the bleachers. When his gaze stops on me, I give him a little wave. He grins back at me before reaching over and playfully hitting the arm of the player next to him and murmuring in their ear. Teagan's head pops up, and his eyes land immediately on Layla. Just like Eamon, his face breaks into a huge grin, and he tosses her a wink. Giggles bubble from my mouth as I watch Layla's tawny skin turn crimson.

"Are you going to acknowledge that?" I ask teasingly. "He sure as hell wasn't winking at me!"

"Oh my god. Shut up. I don't even know how to respond!" Layla splutters.

"Well, a wave would be sufficient, but if you really wanted to drive him wild, you could blow him a kiss."

"Stop. I can't do that."

"Are you not attracted to Teagan?" I ask her, knowing full well that she is.

She glares at me. "Of course I am. I'd have to be an idiot to not be attracted to him. But I'm not about to make a fool out of myself in front of him and the entire team. He's probably just a shameless flirt to anyone with tits."

"You're thinking of Ro. *He's* the shameless flirt. Teagan is more reserved, like Eamon. Or so he tells me. Just wave at him, then! Don't leave the poor guy hanging."

Layla rolls her eyes and wiggles her fingers in Teagan's direction. His grin only grows bigger.

After practice, we gather our bags and head towards the exit. Layla keeps trying to make up excuses to leave before Teagan comes out, but I won't let her. I planned on an evening with just Eamon, but now I'm considering a double date, so I send Eamon a discreet text.

Norah: *Bring Teagan along tonight. I'm bringing Layla. ;)*

His reply is instantaneous.

Eamon: *Reading my mind, are ya? I already told him to tag along.*

Norah: *I'm sure it didn't take much convincing. Layla doesn't think he's into her.*

Eamon: *Is she mental? It might as well be written across his face. Heading your way, love.*

Layla clears her throat pointedly. "Norah, what are you doing? You have that look."

"What look?" I ask innocently, batting my lashes at her. "I don't know what you're talking about."

"You know exactly what look I'm talking about."

I start to deny her accusations when we're interrupted by a very loud rendition of *Galway Girl*. Turning, we see Ro skipping, *actually skipping*, towards us.

"You know, she played the fiddle in an Irish band, but she fell in love with an English man! Kissed her on the neck, and then I took her by the hand," Ro sings as he grabs my hand and twirls me under his arm, making me laugh.

"Gallagher! If you place your lips anywhere near her, I will personally rip your bollocks from your body and shove them down your throat!" Eamon bellows at him.

I quickly duck out of Ro's reach and move towards Eamon. Not to be deterred, Ro waltzes up to Layla, grasping her fingers and bowing low to kiss her knuckles. She rolls her eyes but giggles and blushes, not immune to his charm any more than I am.

"And is this the lovely Layla I've heard so much about?" he questions. "O'Brien said you were—"

"Oy! Rowan!" Teagan yells at him. "Shut yer bleedin' hole, you gobshite. I swear to God, you are more trouble than you're worth."

He shakes his head and shoves Ro playfully before stopping in front of Layla. "Sorry about the riff-raff, lass. He was dropped on his head as a wee baby, and he hasn't been right since. We only keep him around because we feel sorry for him."

Eamon laughs loudly and drops his bag before grabbing my hand to pull me into his arms. I sigh blissfully as my head rests on his chest, inhaling deeply. He must have showered before coming out because he smells divine.

"I didn't expect to see you here, love. Not that I'm complaining. It was a nice surprise," he murmurs in my ear and I shiver.

"I stayed late finishing up a few things for the play and decided it would be more fun to watch you practice than to go home. Turns out I was right."

"Lucky me." He smirks. "How'd you get Layla to join?"

"That was a happy accident. She called just as I walked out of the building and wanted to hang out. I convinced her it would be worth her while to meet me here. Again, I think I was right." I nod my head towards Layla and Teagan, who are talking quietly a few yards away.

Eamon chuckles and presses a kiss to my temple. "I think they'll be seeing more of each other. Teagan is my new roommate as of today."

My eyes swing to his. "You're kidding!"

"Not at all. He's been evicted from his flat due to new ownership, and I have an extra room. Couldn't let him end up on the streets. Ro's another story though. Where is that eejit, anyway?" Eamon glances around.

"Probably going to bug Alicia," Teagan says as he walks up, Layla at his side. "He couldn't stay away if he tried."

"Wait," I say. "Alicia? Like, Pat's Alicia?"

"Aye, the one and only," Teagan continues. "He's been pining after her since the moment he met her, but he doesn't have balls enough to ask her out. Which is probably a good thing. If he messes things up with her, which he no doubt will, we'll have to find a new pub."

"Or we could just keep going to Paddy's, and he can find a new pub?" Eamon suggests with a shrug of his shoulders. "I'm not changing pubs just because he fucks up."

"So, are you guys actually friends with him? Because it doesn't sound like it," Layla cuts in.

Teagan laughs. "Ah, we love the eejit, truly. It's just the Irish way. You give a good slagging to the ones you care about. Friends, family, significant others…" He pauses to wink at her. "If you ever come across an Irish couple that's not calling each other names, they're miserable together."

"It's true," Eamon adds. "My Da and Mam were constantly slagging one another. I always knew when they were in a tiff because she'd be doting on him. 'Seamus dear, shall I bring you some more biscuits with your tea?' Normally, he'd ask for some, and she'd tell him that God gave him two legs that work just as well as hers. He'd laugh and slap her on the arse on his way to the kitchen, muttering about how she's always harping on him."

I can't help but laugh at his impersonation of his parents. It's obvious he grew up in a loving home. I hate that he hasn't seen his Mom and sister in years and know that he must miss them terribly. His ex did more than just break his heart—she drove a wedge between him and his family. But, had she not been so selfish and deceitful, I never would have met Eamon.

Chapter Twenty-Two

Eamon

I'm on top of the world, sitting on the dock of the best local pizza joint in Wilmington with my beautiful girl nestled next to me and friends across from me. After we left the practice field, we decided to make our way to the River Walk for dinner. We've been sitting here for a couple of hours, talking about anything and everything, while the water lapping against the dock provides ambiance. Teagan has spent the majority of the evening flirting with Layla, making her blush any chance he can, and this amuses Norah to no end. I could get drunk on her laugh. It's music to my ears and I've determined that I'll do anything to make her laugh more.

I also can't keep my hands to myself. If I'm not brushing hair behind her ears, lacing our fingers together, or putting my arm around her, I'm brushing a kiss to her temple or trailing my fingers along her shoulder. I'm well and truly addicted to this girl. I wouldn't mind if we found ourselves alone soon so that I could kiss her properly. The need to feel her hands in my hair and her lush body pressed up against mine is overwhelming. My cock twitches and I squirm in my chair to hide the evidence of what she does to me. She doesn't help matters when she absentmindedly rests her hand on my upper thigh. She's unconsciously torturing me. I wonder how I can call this night to an end without being obvious.

As if reading my mind, Norah announces, "I hate to end the fun, but I have a full day of classes tomorrow, starting bright and early."

Teagan nods and pushes back from the table. "Aye, we have practice before the sun is even awake, so we probably better head back too." He stretches his arms above his head, then exclaims, "Oh, shite. My car's still at the field."

"Do you need a ride?" Layla asks him, trying and failing to sound nonchalant.

"You wouldn't mind?" he asks with a grin.

"It's on my way, and I'm guessing these two want some *alone* time," Layla nods towards Norah and me.

"You're right. We would," I say quickly. God bless Layla. "Teag, you have your key?"

"Aye. I won't wait up." He winks at me and gestures for Layla to lead the way. "Shall we, lovely?"

Norah gives her friend a quick hug and tells her to text when she gets home. I hear her whisper, "Have fun." in Layla's ear before turning back to me.

"Ready?" I ask, snagging her hand in mine.

She nods, intertwining our fingers. "Tonight was fun. I'm glad we did this, and I'm glad Layla and Teagan came too. It looked like they were enjoying themselves, don't you think?"

I chuckle and release her hand to wrap my arm around her waist. "He'll be courtin' her by the end of the week, I'm sure."

"Courting?" Norah asks dubiously. "That sounds pretty old-fashioned."

I chuckle again. "It's what we call dating in Ireland. Didn't you have anyone trying to court you on your trip?"

I don't know why I asked. The thought of her even talking to another guy makes me feel like a possessive arsehole.

"Ha!" She laughs. "No, definitely not. Flirting, yes, but nothing more than that."

I don't believe that for a second, so I tell her, "Chances are, if they were flirting, they were trying to court you."

"Well, I did have one proposition, but *courting* was *not* what they were asking of me." She tenses under my arm.

"Norah, did someone try to—" I can barely get the words out.

"No," she quickly assures me. "We had been chatting in Temple Bar, flirting. He simply asked if I wanted to head to his place. I declined, and he left it at that. No harm done."

I breathe a sigh of relief. "Smart bloke."

When we reach the car, Norah turns to lean against the passenger door, crossing her arms over her chest. I don't let my eyes linger too long on the V of her shirt.

"Don't worry, Kennedy. No Irishman tickled my fancy while I was there."

"That's because you were in the wrong part of the country," I tease. "All the good-looking ones, or just the one actually, lived away from Dublin. Had you met him, chances are your fancies would *absolutely* have been tickled."

To reiterate my point, I suddenly grab her waist and tickle her. She squeals and tries to twist away, but I band my arms around her, holding her firmly in place. Her laugh fills the parking lot. God, I love that sound. I keep tickling her until she cries out, "I surrender! No more! Please!"

Chuckling, I still my fingers but refuse to relinquish my hold on her. I keep one arm wrapped around her while I trail my free hand up her arm to her neck. "Sorry, I couldn't help it. You set yourself up for that one, love."

"Hmm. I suppose I did," she muses, eyes sparkling as she looks up at me.

She unfolds her arms to slowly snake her palms up my chest to my shoulders, then down to my biceps. Her caress leaves a trail of fire in its wake. My grip tightens on her waist as I press into her, leaving no space between our bodies. I wind my fingers into the hair at the base of her head, tilting her head to the side to pepper her neck with slow, feather-light kisses. She arches into me, letting out a soft moan that drowns out the noises around us and has me positively feral. I skim the tip of my nose from her shoulder to her earlobe, then flick my tongue just under it. Norah whimpers and moves her hands back to my chest, clutching my shirt in her fists.

"Eamon," she gasps.

"Hmm?" I hum, moving to kiss and nip along her jaw.

A small voice in my head warns me to stop. We are in a public parking lot for God's sake. And more importantly, I promised her that she was in control. But I can't get enough of her touch and those noises she's making.

"People are staring," she whispers, gently pushing at my chest.

I let out a low growl, reluctantly removing my lips from her skin, and turn my head to the left to see a group of teenage boys openly staring and not so subtly adjusting themselves. I glare and take a step in their direction, just to scare them off. It works because they turn and flee.

"Little fuckers," I say, turning back to Norah. "I can't believe I stopped for a group of teenage wankers. This is the most action they'll see for the rest of the year."

Norah snorts in amusement, then erupts into a full laugh. Rubbing her hands over her face, she says, "Oh my god. I'm not sure if I should be embarrassed or angry. You probably ruined their fun."

"Doubtful," I grumble. "They'll probably use that to get off later."

Norah bursts into another fit of giggles. I don't love the idea of them wanking off to an image of Norah, but maybe they can use this as their first lesson in how to properly love on a woman.

"I could have gone my entire life without the mental image of a bunch of teenage boys masturbating to the thought of you kissing me." She laughs.

"Ach, it's not *me* they're going to be thinking about. It will be you and those little noises you make," I tease, enjoying the tinge of blush spreading across her cheeks. Grinning, I lean in to kiss her forehead. "Come on, love. Let's get you home."

Norah

"I'd like to walk you to your door," Eamon says, pulling my hand to his lips to kiss my knuckles, "but I'm afraid I'd be sorely tempted to continue what we started in the parking lot."

"Oh," I breathe out then suck my bottom lip between my teeth, trying to conceal how disappointed I am.

Eamon's hungry eyes zero in on my mouth. He exhales heavily, his breath brushing over my face. "So, I'm going to kiss you goodnight and watch you walk into your house. Then you're going to text me once you're safely inside with the doors locked."

"Do I get a say in the matter?" I ask softly.

"Not tonight, love. I have to be up for practice sooner than I'd like, and you have an early class," he reminds me. "And time with you, like that, is not something I want to rush."

A rush of heat through my core has me pressing my thighs together. Had it not been for the snickering teenagers in the parking lot drawing my attention away from the feel of Eamon's hot breath on my skin, I would have let him carry on for far longer than what's acceptable in a public place. When I arched into him, I could feel his erection growing against my stomach. I expected it to trigger my fight-or-flight response, but all it did was turn me on. I wanted his mouth all over me, to feel his skin under my hands and my tongue. I've seen him without a shirt, but touching the masterpiece that is his body will be so much better than simply worshiping him with my eyes.

"Well," I stammer, "when you put it that way."

"What time do you get done with classes?"

"Four o'clock," I tell him, "but I have a meeting with the theater department from five until seven."

Eamon's lips turn down in displeasure. "Damn. I'm done at three, but I have mountains of homework to do. Some red-headed lass keeps distracting me."

I snort in amusement, rolling my eyes at him. "What happened to that

159

excellent focus you were talking about?"

"Oh, it's still there. Just directed at other things." He winks at me.

"You're incorrigible, Eamon Kennedy," I quip, shaking my head.

"Absolutely. Now, let me kiss you goodnight, Norah."

Before I can even respond, his mouth descends on mine in a firm but tender kiss. He brushes his tongue over the seam of my lips, and I gladly grant him access, twining my tongue with his in a gloriously slow rhythm. All too soon, he breaks the kiss and rests his forehead against mine.

"Go inside, love," he says in a pained whisper. "I'll call you tomorrow."

"Goodnight, Eamon," I whisper back, dipping my head to kiss him quickly one more time before climbing out of the car and up the steps to my door. I unlock it, then turn to wave at him before walking inside. Once the door is securely shut and locked, I send him the text he requested.

Norah: *Safely inside, doors locked. Be safe driving home.*

Eamon: *Always. Sweet dreams, Norah.*

I peek out of the window, watching him drive away, and have no doubt that my dreams will be very sweet tonight.

* * *

Tuesday morning is here too soon and I hit the snooze on my alarm about five times before dragging myself out of bed. Seriously considering playing hooky, I trudge into the kitchen to start a pot of coffee before taking a shower. Since I'm late getting up, I skip washing my hair and just throw it up into a messy bun. I desperately want to don my sweats and favorite hoodie, but I need to be somewhat put together for the meeting later. With the production only weeks away, we need to iron out the details.

Thirty minutes later, I'm dressed in a long emerald tunic-style top over black leggings and gray knee-high boots. I put on enough makeup to hide the dark circles under my eyes but don't overdo it. I hear my phone chirp an alert for a text message and reach for it. It's from Eamon. My heart flips in my chest, and a grin spreads across my face.

Eamon: *Good morning, beautiful. I dreamed of you all night.*

160

CHAPTER TWENTY-TWO

My cheeks heat as I text him back.

Norah: *Good morning, yourself. Oh yeah? All perfectly appropriate, I'm sure.*

Eamon: *I'll never tell. ;)*

Norah: *Cheeky. I guess that means I'll keep my dreams to myself then.*

Eamon: *I take it back. Trade a dream for a dream?*

Norah: *Haha! Nice try, Kennedy. A lady never dirty-dreams and tells. ;)*

I'm thoroughly enjoying the banter when a loud knock sounds at the door. Startled, I shriek and almost drop my phone. I quickly compose myself and hurry to the door, fully expecting Layla, though I don't know why she's knocking when she has a key. I open the door, and standing there in all his deliciousness, arm propped on the door frame above his head, is the subject of my dreams.

"What are you doing here?" I ask in shock.

"You can't just expect me to stay put while you tease me with words like 'dirty dreams,'" Eamon says, smirking devilishly at me.

"But you—when did you—" I sputter.

Eamon laughs and steps inside. "My first class isn't until nine, and I remembered yours is at eight. I wanted to give you a ride."

Grinning like an idiot, I watch as his eyes slowly move from my face, down my body, and back up. He lets out a low whistle and steps towards me.

"You look breathtaking." He leans in to kiss me before adding, "This color is perfect on you."

"Thank you," I reply. "You don't look too bad yourself."

That's an understatement. I'm practically drooling at the sight of him in a navy blue V-neck sweater, sleeves pushed up to his elbows, exposing his corded forearms. He's paired it with light-wash jeans and black motorcycle boots.

"Want a ride?"

I raise a brow, smirking at him.

"To class." He feigns shock. "Get your mind out of the gutter, Grady."

Laughing, I grab my bag and sling it over my shoulder. "Yes, I'd love a ride...to class. Thank you."

I stretch onto my toes and kiss his cheek before heading out the door.

* * *

We've been cuddled up on the couch, watching a movie until I make the mistake of kissing Eamon. One thing leads to another and I'm on my back with my legs wrapped around his waist as he sucks on my neck. He rocks into me, his cock hard and pressing the seam of my jeans into my clit. I moan in response, angling my hips to add more pressure. Taking that as the encouragement it's meant to be, he slips a warm hand over my exposed stomach towards my breasts, and as soon as he cups one of them, I freeze. He immediately senses the switch and crawls off of me.

Growling in frustration, I bury my face in my hands. My stupid, traitorous body and its trauma responses ruin everything. I want this man. I want to touch him and for him to touch me. But the moment his hands are on me, my body locks up and that familiar panic starts to set in. I know beyond a shadow of a doubt that he won't hurt me, so why can't my mind and body get on the same page?

"I'm sorry, Eamon," I mutter, ashamed of myself.

"Norah, look at me."

Peeking through my fingers, I see him sitting across from me on the coffee table, elbows resting on his knees and hands clasped together. He's so beautiful. Even after all of that, I still want nothing more than to touch him. With measured movements, he lifts his hands and gently grasps my wrists, prying my fingers from my face.

"You don't need to apologize, love. I know this is hard for you. I'm not in a hurry," he says softly.

"But I want this with you." My eyes prick with tears so I squeeze them tight.

"We have all the time in the world. I'm not going anywhere," he tells me softly.

The sad part is that I'm the one that's in a hurry. I'm the one who's ready to have a fully physical relationship with Eamon.

"Can we just...try that again?" I ask, slipping my hands into his. "But slower? Like glacially slow? Maybe if my mind and body have time to adjust together, I won't freeze up."

Eamon inhales deeply as his eyes search mine. What does he see in them? Is it fear? Desperation for intimacy? Or maybe he sees how badly I want to heal. Finally, he nods and stands, pulling me to my feet with him.

"Come on. I have an idea," he says, leading me toward the front door.

"Where are we going?"

I'm not sure if he remembers what we were doing before I panicked, but it wasn't appropriate anywhere but behind closed doors.

Ushering me onto the front porch, he all but drags me to his car. I climb into the front seat when he opens the door for me and watch as he lopes around to the driver's side. Once he's in, he turns the ignition and backs out of the drive.

"Eamon, where are we going?" I ask again, completely confused.

"You said you wanted to go glacially slow, so we're going dancing."

Dancing? What does he mean we're going dancing? And how the hell is that supposed to help?

"Um. Explain please."

"The whole point of us taking things slow is so you're used to my touch, aye?" He glances over at me with questioning eyes.

"Yes?"

"Dancing requires close proximity and touch, but we'll be in a public place. All the times you've started to panic, it's because we've been secluded. Nobody else was around. My thoughts are that after your attack, being alone with a man is what triggers your fight or flight response."

Huh. He's right. I've never shied away from his touch when we're at Paddy's or with our friends. How have I never considered that? A knot forms in my throat at how thoughtful and observant he is. Then I remember I can't dance.

"There's just one problem though," I say.

"What's that love?"

"I don't dance. No, I can't dance." I admit, my face flaming in humiliation.

163

"Good," he says with a grin.

"Good? Why on earth is that good?" Eamon has lost his mind.

"Neither can I, so we can learn together." He reaches out and laces our fingers together.

"Where exactly do you plan on dancing?" I question.

"There are ballroom dancing lessons at the student rec center tonight." He shrugs nonchalantly. "We'll be a few minutes late, but I'm sure we can slip in the back."

My jaw drops as I stare at the side of his head. "How do you know this?"

"Don't you read the newsletters they send out every week?"

"No. What newsletter?"

He just laughs as he pulls into the parking lot outside of the rec center and parks the car a few rows away from the entrance. He turns to me and asks expectantly, "Shall we?"

Nervous energy washes over me and I fidget with the hem of my shirt. I don't think I'm even dressed properly for this, but when we walk into the back of the room, the instructor waves us in. Salsa just happens to be the style being taught, so there is no chance we won't be touching.

Eamon was right. He cannot dance. We've spent more time stepping on each others' feet than actually dancing, but his hands are on me at all times. Forgetting that I'm supposed to take a step back when he steps forward, our bodies are constantly colliding, making my breath hitch and my pulse skyrocket when our hips meet with each seductive swivel. My body doesn't freeze once. If anything, it's overheating. By the time the lesson ends, I'm ready to take our practicing back to my place.

"Come inside," I whisper against Eamon's mouth as he kisses me good-night on my front porch.

"Norah," he groans, wrapping his arms around my waist and pulling me into him. "I don't think that's a good idea."

"Why not?" I whine.

"Glacially slow, remember?" He pulls back to look at me. "Salsa dancing felt like hitting the fast-forward button."

Raising a brow at him, I say, "I don't see the problem here, Kennedy."

"We're not rushing this," he says with finality and a quick peck to my lips. "Being with you isn't a conquest to be made by a certain date. When we reach that point, I don't want there to be any doubt or fear for either of us."

God, is he real? I don't think he realizes that his words make me burn for him even more.

Chapter Twenty-Three

Eamon

The next handful of weeks fly by in a blur as I complete the last season of my college football career with thirteen total goals, five of them being game-winners. The MLS SuperDraft is in January, and I'm trying to decide if I want to try out with Ro and Teagan. Unfortunately, Mac is also going, but I have a hard time believing that he'll actually be picked up by any pro teams. He has talent, sure, but the dosser cares more about partying and chasing women.

Normally, I'd spend every moment of the off-season training, but my class load is heavier with final exams coming. Plus, I have Norah now. We don't get to spend nearly as much time together as I would like, but there's nothing to be done about it since she has finals and the play. When we do see each other, it's usually at her house while she's putting together costumes in her sewing room or sitting next to me on the couch studying. Occasionally, I'm lucky enough to help her study for her history class. My favorite part is rewarding her correct answers with a kiss. Kissing Norah is addictive, and so is touching her. I love every single one of her curves. We pump the brakes every time it starts to get too heated, though. I want her more than my next breath, but it's not the right time yet. We've made it to a couple of other dance lessons that seem to be helping, but I just don't want to risk setting her back because of my inability to keep my hands to myself.

"What do you have left to do for the costumes?" I ask her, flopping onto the couch.

It's Friday night, and we just got back to Norah's after getting a quick pint at Paddy's and checking in with him. It's become sort of a ritual for us. Even with our packed schedules, we still make it a point to go once a week.

Norah sits down next to me, stretches her arms above her head, and groans. "I think I finished the last dress today, actually. I'll have to go back and reinspect it, but the hard parts are done. Anything from here on out will just be touch-ups or small alterations."

I try and fail to keep my eyes off of the exposed skin of her stomach.

She clears her throat. "Eyes up here, Kennedy."

"How can you expect me to not admire God's handiwork when it's right in front of me?" I ask innocently.

Norah rolls her eyes and readjusts her shirt. "You're ridiculous."

"And you need to learn to accept a compliment, love."

She sticks her tongue out at me, and that's all it takes for me to lunge for her. I grip her hips and pull her into my lap. She squeals in alarm but doesn't protest once she's straddling me.

She pushes her hair out of her face and playfully glares at me. "Is there a reason you pulled me over here?"

"Aye. There is. When I compliment you, I mean it," I tell her seriously, cupping her cheek with one hand and brushing her stomach with my fingertips.

Norah shivers at the touch and slides her arms around my neck. "I know you do."

My brow furrows as I ask, "Then why am I ridiculous?"

She shrugs. "You're not. I just have a hard time seeing what you see, I guess."

"There's not one thing about you that I don't find beautiful, Norah," I tell her, cupping the back of her neck and pulling her towards me. I lightly kiss the sensitive spot just below her ear.

"Eamon," she breathes.

"Yes, love?" I murmur while pressing soft kisses down her neck and back up again. When I reach her earlobe, I nip it gently with my teeth.

She sucks in a breath and curls her fingers in my hair. "Show me," Norah whispers.

I freeze, then pull back slowly to look into her eyes. Her cheeks are flushed, and she doesn't show a single sign of hesitation.

"What?" I ask stupidly.

She trails a hand down my chest to my stomach and continues lower still. She stops at the waistband of my jeans, her fingers are slightly trembling, and her breathing is heavier. She lifts her eyes to mine. "I want you to show me what you see. I want...I want *you*."

I'm pretty sure my heart stops beating for a second. Did she just say what I think she said?

"Norah, are you—do you—" I stammer.

She nods slowly, biting her bottom lip then grabs the hem of her shirt and pulls it over her head before tossing it on the ground.

Holy. Fuck.

She's perfect. A goddess in jeans and a black lacy bra is straddling me right now, telling me she wants me. I've died and gone to heaven. Mouth gaping like a fish out of water, I struggle to speak. Finally, I clear my throat and manage to tear my gaze from her chest and back to her eyes.

My hands tighten slightly on her hips. "Are you sure?"

"Yes," she breathes, leaning in and pressing herself against my chest. "I'm one hundred percent sure. I want this. I want you."

Then she kisses me. Gently at first, but as my hands skim from her waist to her ribs, the kiss deepens, our tongues colliding and winding around each other. Her hands knot in my hair as my palms glide over her back. I'm not making any move to unhook her bra. Yet. I'm savoring every moment while making sure she's still in control.

When she starts to slowly rock her hips back and forth over me, my brain short circuits and I make a guttural noise in the back of my throat as I feel her heat through our clothes. This must encourage her, because her hands leave my hair and snake down to my waistband, never breaking the kiss. I'm vibrating in my skin as she hesitantly grips the bottom of my shirt and begins to slowly pull it up my torso. I drag my mouth from hers long enough to yank it all the way off before crushing her to me again in a searing kiss, my hands splayed across her back. The feel of her skin on mine is euphoric. It's better than I ever expected. Tearing away again, I pepper her with kisses from her neck to her shoulder and lick a path back up, repeating on the other side because fair is fair.

"Eamon," Norah gasps, her hands roaming all over my chest and stomach. I freeze when they go lower suddenly remembering I don't have any condoms with me.

"Wait," I say, grabbing her wrists to halt her creeping fingers. "Protection? I didn't bring…"

"I'm on the pill," she cuts me off. "And I haven't been with anyone since…"

Swallowing down the rage that the mention of Norah's assault brings, I brush a tendril of her auburn curls from her face. "I'm clean. It's been nearly a year since my last time."

Norah narrows her eyes at me before grabbing both sides of my face and devouring my mouth, sucking my tongue between her teeth and nipping my bottom lip. Growling, I stand up, hands cupping her round arse as she wraps her legs around me tightly. I stalk towards her bedroom and, once inside, I gently slide her down my body until her feet touch the floor. I pull back to gauge her mental state, not wanting to push this any further if she's not ready. But what I see there isn't fear. It's passion and trust. She's trusting me with her body, and I plan to worship it like she deserves.

Norah

I'm panting as my body burns for the man standing in front of me. Something about his words broke down the last of my defenses, and I want to show him exactly how I feel. So I move a hand behind my back, unhook my bra, and let it slip from my arms to the floor.

"Christ Almighty," Eamon breathes reverently.

He lifts a slightly trembling hand to trail his fingers from my collarbone down to the swell of my right breast before gently cupping it. When he brushes the calloused pad of his thumb over my nipple, goosebumps break out over my skin as molten lava descends to the apex of my thighs. I moan in response and my body arches into the touch rather than freezing in fear.

He closes what little space is between us. "We'll go slow," he whispers against my mouth. "And if at any point you want to stop, just tell me and I will."

My heart is pounding so hard that I can barely hear myself think, but I know beyond a shadow of a doubt that he means every word he just said. I loop my arms around his neck and nod before saying, "Now stop talking and kiss me."

Eamon doesn't waste a second claiming my mouth again. His hands skim down my sides, over my hips, then grip the back of my thighs before scooping me up again and carrying me to the bed. Laying me down gently, his lips roam from my mouth to my neck, kissing and nipping as he makes his way lower. He takes my nipple into his mouth and rolls it gently between his teeth before tracing it with his tongue.

"Oh God…" I gasp, spearing my fingers into his hair.

Laughing softly against my skin, he moves to the other nipple, repeating the same motions. My body is writhing beneath his, and when he sinks further down my torso, my breath hitches in my throat.

Eamon lifts his head at the sound, "Do you want me to stop?"

I huff a laugh. "Don't you fucking dare." He sits back on his legs, and I

170

whine, propping myself up on my elbows, "I said *not* to stop. What are you doing?"

Raising a brow, he slides his hand down the valley between my breasts and lower until he reaches the waistband of my jeans. His beautiful mouth tilts into a smirk as he pops the button and tugs the zipper down.

"Oh," I breathe out.

Slowly, almost tortuously, he peels my jeans off and tosses them on the floor. His gaze pores over every inch of me like a blind man seeing light for the first time, and he bites his lower lip before finding my eyes with his.

"You are the most beautiful thing I've ever laid eyes on," he whispers longingly before dipping back down to kiss my stomach.

Lazily, he travels farther and farther south. The closer he gets to my core, the more I squirm. I'm overwhelmed by the sensation of the scruff of his beard on my body, but that's nothing compared to the way his tongue traces the skin just above my panties. My hips buck slightly at the contact, and I whimper for more.

"I'm taking these off now, love," he says, raising his eyes to mine before hooking his fingers through the sides and pulling.

When they reach my knees, he stands to slide them all the way off, then grabs my left foot and begins planting kisses from my ankle to my inner thigh, my heart thundering as he inches closer and closer to my center. He's almost where I want him most when he stops and switches to the other foot. I groan in frustration.

"You're killing me here," I whine, never taking my eyes off him. The way his muscles bunch with every movement is mesmerizing.

Grinning, he says, "Good things come to those who wait, lass." Then he runs a hand over my hip bone, towards my chest, pressing gently. "Now lay back and let me show you."

Is it possible to combust just by listening to his deep brogue? Everything about this man drives me crazy in the best ways. I always thought the first time I slept with someone, consensually, I'd be terrified and have a panic attack, but there's no room for fear while Eamon is touching me. I am, however, feeling quite impatient as his breath fans over me. I run my fingers into his dark hair to direct him where I need him, but I don't get the chance.

"Oh my—*fuck*," I cry out when his tongue finally tastes me.

My hands fist tightly in his hair, making him grunt, but he doesn't stop. If anything, he goes deeper. Reaching under me to lift my hips, he brings me closer to his mouth than I thought possible. Each stroke of his tongue is deliberate as if he's savoring me. When he flicks my clit with the tip of his tongue before latching on and sucking gently, the sound that comes out of me is more animal than human. I'm hanging on the precipice of release when I feel him ease a finger inside me, then another, carefully stretching my inner walls. He plunges them in and out in a steady rhythm, bringing me closer and closer until I'm moaning louder and louder. Rotating his wrist, he curls a finger forward, brushing that elusive spot, and I shatter. Mind-blowing pleasure courses through me, unlike anything I've ever experienced. He doesn't stop while I ride out my high and drift back to earth.

When my body stops shaking, he kisses and licks his way back up to my throat, where he presses his lips gently. I grip his face and bring his mouth to mine in a slow kiss that conveys all of the emotions I can't put into words. My hand drifts down his chest, wedging between us to unbutton his jeans and he pulls back to look at me, silently asking, once again, if this is what I want. I answer by sliding my hand into his boxers and wrapping my hand around his cock. He jerks and lets out a husky laugh that makes me preen with satisfaction. Before I can do more, he's moving off me to stand at the foot of the bed.

Propping myself up on my elbows, I watch him remove the rest of his clothing, appreciating every curve and ridge of his muscular body. My gaze stops briefly on the tattoo inked into his left pec. It's a complicated design of Celtic knots and what looks to be a family crest. I'll have to ask him about that later. *Much later.* Right now, I'm gawking at what's below the waist. He felt huge in my hand, but actually seeing it…well, I expected to be scared, but all I feel is pure lust at seeing him in all of his glory.

He climbs onto the bed and crawls over my body, nudging my thighs apart with his knees. With one arm braced on the left side of my head, he

172

cups my cheek with the opposite hand before dipping his head to kiss me again. Just like before, it morphs from a small spark to an all-encompassing fire. His hand falls from my face, fingers dancing down my body until his thumb finds my still-sensitive clit, making me whimper with need. His length presses against me and my hips roll instinctively.

"Please," I beg against his mouth.

Palming his cock, he positions himself against my entrance. His breath coming fast, he raises his head to look into my eyes. "Last chance to stop, darlin.'"

I shake my head. "I don't want to stop. Please, Eamon."

Crushing his mouth to mine, he plunges his tongue past my lips as he pushes himself inside of me, inch by inch. A muffled groan sounds from my throat, and I tighten my arms around him. Slowly, he begins to rock into me until I'm filled by him.

"Fuck, Norah," he growls. "You feel so good."

The sensation is foreign, but my body quickly adjusts to him as we find our rhythm. I can't keep my hands from roaming all over his body, relishing in the feel of his skin on mine. He's hard *everywhere*. The more we touch, the more fervent our movements become. As if sensing that I'm getting closer to another release, Eamon thrusts deeper, eliciting small mewls of pleasure from me. He circles my clit with his thumb and dips his mouth to my nipple, sucking hard. That's my undoing. I cry out as another orgasm rips through me. Eamon's breathing becomes ragged, and he thrusts a few more times before finding his own release. With a deep groan, he stills as he comes, then collapses on me, burying his face in my neck.

We lay there panting, our bodies damp with sweat, as I lazily rake my fingers through his hair with one hand while cradling his head to me with the other. My heart is racing, but I feel peaceful. There's not a hint of regret or anxiety, just an overwhelming sense of rightness. He shifts as if to move, and I hold onto him tightly.

"I'm probably crushing you," he says, kissing my neck.

I smile and shake my head. "You're not. Promise. You're like the world's best weighted blanket."

Eamon laughs, softly at first, then his shoulders shake as his laugh deepens. "Of all the things I expected you to say, love, that was *not* it."

I can't stop the giggle that bursts from my mouth. "Now I'm curious as to what you expected me to say."

"Something along the lines of, 'Oh, Eamon, you've completely ruined me for other men. I'll never take another lover for as long as I live!'" His voice pitches higher in mock falsetto.

I'm laughing harder now. "How inconsiderate of me. Please allow me to rephrase that." I clear my throat dramatically and say, "Eamon Kennedy, I thank you for the mind-altering orgasm. I shall never, for the rest of my days, ever be satisfied by another man."

"You're damn right, you won't, Norah Grady," he says playfully at first, but then sobers quickly. "At least, I hope you won't."

I touch my fingertips to his jaw and say, "No, I don't think I will."

Chapter Twenty-Four

Eamon

There's a gorgeous, naked woman asleep in my arms, her back tucked into my chest, and legs entangled with my own. The curtains are parted enough to let the sun bathe her in its warm light and her hair is a flaming mess of curls fanned over my arm. I'm completely mesmerized by Norah.

Last night was everything I had hoped for and more. We spent hours wrapped around each other, sometimes talking, but mostly touching and kissing, resulting in me being buried inside her once again. She was so responsive to every caress of my hands and mouth, never shying away but meeting every moment with anticipation. I'm aching for her again at the thought.

Unable to keep my hands to myself any longer, I trail my fingers over her ribs and up through the valley between her breasts then back down again before lightly brushing under each one. I graze a thumb over her nipple, watching it stiffen immediately. I shower the other side with the same affection then cruise down to her stomach. I splay my hand over her belly and drag it over her hip, then down the outside of her thigh. God, I love her curves. Norah stirs but doesn't wake. A soft *mmmm* sounds from her throat and her backside instinctively presses into my already hard cock.

I drop a kiss on her shoulder before wrapping my arm around her waist to pull her even closer. Without thinking, I start singing softly into her hair. The first time I sang to her, it was in an attempt to get her to share a drink with me. Now the lyrics to Ringsend Rose hold more weight.

"In Dublin Town there lived a girl - Fairer than the flower I'm wearin'. Rose Donoghue—all fresh and new. And I love her past all carin'."

My heart squeezes in my chest when I finally admit that I *love her past all carin'.*

Norah

I've been residing somewhere between asleep and awake, but am hyper-aware of Eamon's hand leaving a blazing trail on my skin and the feel of him hardening behind me. I'm also blissfully aware of the soreness between my legs and the tingle of desire that stirs inside of me...again. I imperceptibly shift my hips back and into his body. He grazes my shoulder with his lips and wraps a strong arm around me before he begins to sing and I recognize the song instantly. It was romantic at Paddy's, but hearing it now, after last night? It feels different. Tears prick behind my eyelids when I feel his arm tighten around me as he sings the words, *And I love her past all carin'.*

I stay motionless for a couple of minutes, soaking it all in, before slowly rolling to face him. When I do, I inhale deeply. His mussed hair and hooded eyes mixed with his naked body *in my bed* just do something to me.

"Good morning, handsome."

"Mornin', love," he murmurs, tucking my hair behind my ear. "Sleep okay?"

"Like a rock," I say, sliding my hands up his chest to his shoulders. "What about you?"

He leans in to nuzzle my neck. "Aye, I slept great. But I'm wide awake now," he says, sliding his hand down to cup my ass and pulling my pelvis against his.

"Mmmm," I purr, nipping his ear. "I can tell."

A low growl emits from his throat as he rolls me to my back and settles between my thighs. "You keep doing that and we're never leaving this bed."

"Don't threaten me with a good time, Kennedy." I chide, thrusting my hips up to grind against him.

"Oh, you think that's a threat? You doubt my follow through?" he teases before ducking his head and sucking a pert nipple into his mouth.

"Eamon!" I gasp, throwing my head back into the pillow.

He chuckles then licks his way to my other nipple. I grab his face and pull his mouth back to mine, kissing him hungrily. As the kiss deepens, I hitch a leg over his hip and roll us until I'm on top. I sit up and marvel at how powerful I feel in this position. Bracing my hands on his chest, I lift my hips and then plunge myself onto his length.

"Fuck," Eamon moans as I cry out.

I ride him slow and easy, but it's not long before he's bruising my hips with his grip and rocking me back and forth, up and down over him. I'm addicted to the grunts and pants coming from him. Knowing that he's as wild for me as I am for him brings me to the edge.

"I'm going to come," I gasp.

"Me too," he grinds out between clenched teeth as he vibrates his thumb against my clit.

We careen over the edge together, crying out our release. I collapse onto his chest, breathing heavily and he slowly rolls us to our sides.

Tracing my fingertips over the intricate curls of his tattoo, I say quietly, "Tell me about this."

"I got it on my eighteenth birthday in honor of my Da. This," he says, circling a finger around the shield and lions, "is the Kennedy family crest. The rest is the Dara Celtic Knot. It's a symbol of the oak tree and its roots.

It represents inner strength and is supposed to help the wearer find wisdom in challenging situations."

"I love that," I tell him, leaning forward to press a kiss to the center of it.

"My Da always told me that being physically strong is all well and good, but if a man can't find strength within and trust himself to make a tough decision, then he's a weak man despite all the muscle."

"Lucky for you," I say, winding my fingers into the hair at the nape of his neck, "you have both."

Chuckling, he kisses me, while rubbing soothing circles on my back. I'm half tempted to show him just how much I appreciate all of those muscles until my stomach growls loudly, making us both laugh.

"As tempting as it is to stay here all day if I don't eat something, I won't be able to do *anything* later," I warn him.

"That won't do," he admits, kissing the top of my head. "Food is fuel."

I press a kiss to his lips and crawl out of bed feeling like a new woman.

* * *

Eamon left after breakfast, but not before a very lengthy and heated goodbye kiss that nearly led us back to my bed. With the play only a couple of weeks away, I need to buckle down and go through everything with a fine-toothed comb, and he needs to finish a paper without wanting to, as he put it, *score the face off* me. I love Irish slang.

I'm sitting in my sewing room inspecting the last of the costumes when I hear my front door open and a voice call out, "Hey Norie!"

Rounding the corner, I see Amelia setting her keys and phone down on the counter.

"Hey, Amie," I greet her with a hug. "I wasn't expecting you. Everything okay?"

"What?" She asks. "Can't a girl just want to visit one of her besties? Why do you just assume something is wrong?"

I curl up on the couch and raise my eyebrows at her. "Amelia..."

"Ugh, fine," the vivacious blonde groans, throwing her hands in the air.

"It's Myra. She's so upset."

"*She's* upset?" I ask in disbelief. "Last I checked, she's the one that was being a royal bitch."

"I know, I know," Amelia says, sitting next to me. "She's upset with herself and feels awful for what she said. And she doesn't know what to do to make things right."

"So, what? She sent you here to fix it?" I cross my arms over my chest, feeling like a petulant child.

"No, she didn't send me here. I came on my own to talk. I love you both and it feels wrong having you two at odds."

I sigh heavily and run my hands over my face. "Listen. I hate fighting with her and would love for things to go back to normal, but what she said was really hurtful. This is the second time now that she's crossed the line since getting together with Mac. Eamon says he's bad news and I'm starting to believe it."

"I don't disagree," Amelia confesses, twirling a lock of her long blonde hair around her fingers. "And I think she's starting to realize that too. She didn't even go out last night."

I roll my eyes in annoyance. "She's just so overcome with guilt that she can't even go out. Boo friggin' hoo."

Amelia's jaw drops and her eyes widen at my response. "Someone is feeling salty today. What's got you all fired up?"

I try to suppress the grin that's blooming, but I can't. When a deep blush paints my cheeks, I look away. "I don't know what you're talking about..."

"Norah!" Amelia gasps and grabs my arm. "Did something happen with Eamon? Did you two finally..." she wags her eyebrows.

I make a high-pitched *eek* noise and bury my face in my hands. I'm not ashamed of sleeping with Eamon, but this is a big deal for me, and I know my friends will want to know every little detail, no matter how intimate.

"You did! Oh my god! Norie! This is huge! Tell me everything!" Amelia demands.

I finally look at her and give her the cliff notes version, with enough detail to satisfy her without being too explicit. Some things are meant to be kept between Eamon and me anyway.

Amelia is practically convulsing with excitement. "Have you told anyone else?"

"No, you're the first person I've seen, let alone talked to today, besides Eamon." I shrug.

"Are you *going* to tell the others?" Amelia questions.

"I assumed I would, but maybe not with as much detail," I say, winking at her.

"Damn. I need to get me an Irish guy. Are the other two single?"

"Well," I say with a laugh. "Teagan and Layla have been hanging out a little and apparently Ro has it bad for Alicia. But maybe one of them has a cousin."

We sit and talk for a little while longer before Amelia has to leave, deciding to have a girls' night so I can fill everyone in at once. I even agreed to let Myra come just to appease Amelia, but I'm not going to let her off the hook so easily.

I send out a group text inviting them over tonight. It's a long shot that they'll all be able to make it, but I'm hopeful.

Amelia: *You KNOW I'm in! I'll bring beer!*

Charlie: *Yeah girl, I'm down. I'll bring chips and dip!*

Layla: *Holy shit, I'm actually free tonight!*

Amelia: *Myra, cancel whatever plans you have going on and make it a point to be here! I WILL drag your ass here if I have to!*

Myra: *Okay, okay, calm your tits. I'll be there.*

I grin at the exchange between my girlfriends. We all live such different lives, but we each have unique qualities that complement the other. I can't imagine my life without them. They're more than just my best friends. They're my family. The sisters I never had growing up.

* * *

It's late, but we're all sitting on my living room floor, furniture pushed out of the way to make room for all of us. In the center of our circle is a spread of snacks and alcohol that we've been digging into like a bunch of teenagers at a sleepover. I just finished confessing how Eamon and I took the next step in our relationship, and they're all beside themselves. They beg me for all of the dirty details, gush over Eamon singing to me when he thought I was asleep, and told me countless times how much of a *lucky bitch* I am for snagging such a sexy man. I laugh until my sides hurt, enjoying the buzz of the alcohol and estrogen-fueled girl talk.

"Our little Norah is all grown up now!" Charlie fake cries as she drains her glass of wine.

"Shut up," I shove her shoulder playfully. "I'm still me!"

"Of course you are, honey," Amelia cuts in. "But now you have a fine piece of man warming your bed!"

"Where is the man in question, tonight?" Layla asks around a mouth full of chips.

"He had a paper to finish, so I'm assuming he's at his place. With *Teagan.*" I say pointedly, tossing a grape at her.

Layla blushes furiously and glares in my direction.

"Wait, what's going on with Teagan?" Amelia blurts, shooting a wink at Norah. "Are you two a thing?"

"No!" Layla yells just as I sing, "Yes!"

"Norah Grady, I hate you with the fire of a million suns! *Nothing* is going on between me and Teagan!"

"Not yet, anyway!" I laugh. "But it's only a matter of time. You can cut that sexual tension with a knife!"

We stay up way too late, giggling and teasing each other. When the fun starts to die down and my friends are dropping like flies on my couch or the floor, I notice Myra sneaking out to the sewing room. I follow her out to find her sitting on one of the patio chairs, legs pulled up, and her arms wrapped around her legs.

"My…" I whisper, trying not to startle her. "What are you doing?"

She whips her head around and hurriedly wipes at her cheeks. "Hey. I was just getting some air. What are you doing?"

I sigh, folding myself into the chair across from her. "Checking on you.

You've been quiet tonight."

"Yeah," she starts. "I didn't want to kill the mood. And I didn't feel like I had the right to celebrate your big news after the way I've been treating you." Her breath hitches and she wipes at her eyes again.

"I won't pretend that it's okay because it's not, but you're one of my best friends and I love you no matter what," I tell her, honestly. "Can you just talk to me? What's going on with you?"

Myra's bottom lip quivers for a moment before she bursts into tears. "I'm pregnant!"

I freeze. "Oh...my god. Myra, I...what? When? Wait...is it Mac's?"

Myra only nods, crying harder. I hurry to her side and wrap my arms around her, stroking her hair. "Shhh. It's okay. We'll figure this out. How far along are you?"

"Eight weeks," she mumbles into my shoulder.

"Does he know?" I ask hesitantly.

She shakes her head violently. "I can't tell him. He'll freak out. We weren't even supposed to be anything serious. Neither of us wants a commitment."

I blow out a breath and grab her shoulders. "Look at me. You need to tell him. Even if you two aren't in a relationship, he needs to know. And who knows? Maybe he'll surprise you."

I wince as I say the words. I don't believe there's a chance in hell that Mac will put aside his playboy ways and step up to the responsibility of a baby.

Myra barks out a humorless laugh. "Nice try, Norie. You don't even believe that. But now you know why I haven't been myself. It's no excuse for treating you like dirt, I know. I'm so sorry. I fucked everything up."

I hug her again. "I forgive you, My. Thank you for telling me. Who else knows?"

"Just you," she says. "I can't bring myself to tell anyone."

"That's okay. The first thing you need to do is make an appointment. Do you want me to go with you?"

"Would you do that? Really?" Myra's eyes start watering again.

"Of course! I'll support you every step of the way. Whatever you need, I'm here."

"Thank you, Norie. I'd feel so much better if you were there," she confesses.

"Consider it done. You don't have to do this alone. Promise."

Even after all the drama, the last thing I'm going to do is let my friend go through this pregnancy alone.

Chapter Twenty-Five

Eamon

"Hello? Earth to Kennedy," Teagan waves his hand in front of my face, effectively bringing me back to earth.

"What? Sorry, mate. I was miles away." I confess, glancing his way.

"I'd say. What's got your head in the clouds?"

I can't help the grin that spreads across my face. I thought heading to my place would help me focus on the paper that's due tomorrow, but I can't stop thinking about Norah.

"Oh," Teagan says with a knowing look. "You and Norah finally consummate the relationship, then?"

He wags his eyebrows before slapping me on the back. I shove him away, the grin still firmly plastered on his face.

"Fuck off. A gentleman doesn't kiss and tell."

"What about shag and tell? And I know for a fact you're no gentleman," he jokes.

"I'll tell you what," I concede. "When you and Layla finally seal the deal, we can swap stories over wine like a group of lasses at a hen party."

"Ooh, can we do each other's nails too? I quite fancy a new mani," Teagan quips.

I'm glad Teagan agreed to be flatmates. He's tidy and quiet but knows how to have a good time. We're constantly slagging one another, but we're also able to have serious conversations when the time calls for it.

"Yeah, alright. Manis it is, but no waxing. I'm adopting a more natural look these days." I chuckle and ask, "What *is* the deal with you and Layla? Have you seen her lately?"

He shakes his head and rubs the back of his neck. "I don't want to scare her off. I'm trying to let her know that I'm into her without coming on too strong, yeah?"

"You know she's nervous, right?" I ask. "Norah said she hasn't had a serious relationship before and doesn't sleep around, so she's probably completely out of her comfort zone. You may have to be more assertive."

"Aye, I figured that was the case. I'm fine with taking it slow. I'd like to build a friendship with her so she knows I'm not going to muck about with her. I'm not Ro." he laughs.

"Thank God for that. The world can only handle so much."

We spend the next couple of hours finishing homework in silence. I finish my paper and decide to reward myself by texting Norah. I'm itching to not only see her again but to touch her and kiss her breathless.

Eamon: *Fancy some company?*

Norah: *He IS alive! I was beginning to wonder if you were still around.*

Eamon: *Can't get rid of me that easily, lass. I'm afraid you're stuck with me.*

Norah: *I could think of worse things. Finish your paper?*

Eamon: *Aye. Took a while to get my mind focused. Can't stop thinking about you.*

Norah: *The feeling is mutual. What are you going to do about it?*

Eamon: *Are you home?*

185

Norah: *Yes...all by myself...*

Eamon: *Don't move. See you in twenty.*

I all but jump up and run to the shower, cleaning myself in record time. I throw on a UNCW hoodie and a pair of sweats before tossing Teagan a wave and a cheeky, "Don't wait up for me!"

The drive to Norah's feels like an eternity, but in reality, it's only about ten minutes. I fly out of my car and bound up the steps, rapping my knuckles on the door. Too busy glancing down at my shoes when the door opens, the first thing I see is a pair of dainty, bare feet connected to shapely legs swathed in a tiny pair of silk shorts with lace edges. My eyes continue their ascent over Norah's body, drinking in the sight of her in a strappy tank top. She's not wearing a bra and I practically weep with thanks. Her nipples are peaked under the thin fabric, just waiting for my mouth. That wavy, auburn hair of hers hangs loosely over her shoulder. She rests a hip against the door frame and smirks.

"Hi," she says in a sultry voice.

"Hello, beautiful." I grin. "You look mouthwatering."

Her cheeks turn pink, but she steps aside, letting me enter. The door isn't even closed before I grab her and tangle one hand in her hair while the other latches onto her waist. My mouth descends on her in a hungry kiss that has her whimpering. Walking her backward into the living room, I never take my mouth from her skin. My lips, tongue, and teeth travel over her jaw, down her neck, and back up to that sensitive spot behind her ear. She moans and shoves her hands under my hoodie, exploring the lines of my stomach and chest. I pause long enough to tear the offending hoodie off and toss it somewhere on the floor. Norah places her hands on my chest and gently pushes me away, taking a small step back. Her eyes roam over me until she stops briefly on the low-hanging waistband of my sweatpants before openly staring at my growing erection. She bites her lower lip and then looks me in the eyes as she drops to her knees.

My brain malfunctions at the sight of my fire sprite kneeling before me. She grabs my waistband, but I stop her and choke out, "Norah, love, you don't have to do that."

"Shhh," she whispers demurely, still holding my gaze. "I want to. Please let me?"

How can I say no to that? I can't and don't want to, so I brush my thumb over her lips and nod.

Norah slowly pulls my sweats and boxers down my legs, eyes widening once she sees how hard I am for her. Cautiously wrapping a hand around the base of my cock, she leans in and brings her eyes back to mine. When she parts those pretty lips and takes me into her mouth, swirling her tongue around the tip, it's all I can do to keep from finishing this before it's even started. She takes me further, sucking like a goddamn pro. I'm sweating as my fingers tangle into her hair, guiding her carefully. She doesn't resist. If anything, she becomes more enthusiastic. Increasing her pace, she works her hand in time with her mouth. I'm not going to last much longer, so I cup her cheek and gently pull back.

She looks at me questioningly, "Did I do something wrong?"

I chuckle as I help her to her feet. "Quite the opposite, lass. You were a little too good."

Norah's eyes light up with pride. "Then why did you stop me?" Her fingers trail down my stomach, making my cock twitch against her torso.

Cupping her backside with both hands, I pull her against me and lower my mouth to her ear before growling out, "Because I need to make you come at least twice first."

She shudders and says breathlessly, "Well when you put it that way..."

I don't let her finish that thought before scooping her up and hauling her to the bedroom. She huffs out a laugh when I toss her on the bed then props herself up on her elbows. I just stand there for a moment, enjoying the sight of her mussed hair and swollen lips. *God, she's stunning.*

"What are you waiting for, Kennedy? You said something about making me come twice?" Norah questions, tilting her head to the side.

Oh, I like it when she gets mouthy. "You keep that up and I'll have to teach that pretty mouth of yours a lesson."

Her throaty laugh travels down my spine and straight to my cock. I grab her ankles and yank her to the edge of the bed, earning a squeal. Wasting no time ridding her of those little shorts, I'm pleasantly surprised to see she didn't bother with underwear. Before she can catch her breath, my mouth is on her and I devour her like she's my last meal. Her thighs clench like a vice around my head, and when I thrust my tongue deep into her, she screams out, "Eamon! Oh god, oh god, oh god..."

I can tell she's getting close, so I attach my mouth to her clit and suck. *Hard.* She goes off like a fucking firework, mumbling unintelligible words. I turn and bite her thigh, causing her to convulse once more. The taste of her on my tongue is an addiction I don't think I'll ever want to quit.

Norah

I'm spread out on my bed, gasping for air as Eamon moves up my body, caressing and kissing me all over. Sliding my shirt up and over my head, he palms my breasts, sucking and licking them in turn. I writhe against him, needing him as close as possible. When he finally makes it to my mouth, he kisses me slowly and deeply. I told Layla people don't fall in love this fast, but I'm beginning to think that what I feel for Eamon goes beyond lust. Undeniably happy, I can envision a future with him. I *want* a future with him.

His traveling fingers bring me back to the present, skimming down my body until he reaches my thigh. Gripping it, he hikes it over his hip and sinks into me in one smooth motion. The angle makes him go impossibly deeper and we both moan as we fall into a steady rhythm, our breath mingling with every gasp and pant. He keeps his word and makes me come a second time before he finds his own release. We lay there with our foreheads pressed together, catching our breath for a long moment.

"Well," I eventually say, "that was the best greeting I've ever had."

Eamon chuckles and buries his face in my neck. "Aye. I might have missed you a bit."

"Mmmm. I missed you, too." I purr as I trail my fingers up and down his spine. I'm not sure if I'll ever get used to the feel of his body under my hands, but I'm willing to spend as much time as possible finding out.

He rolls to the side, draping an arm over my stomach, and asks, "How was your day, love?"

Turning to face him, I lay my hands on his chest. "Uneventful. The girls and I got together last night for an old-fashioned slumber party, so this morning was for sleeping and nursing hangovers."

"Please don't tell me you painted your nails and swapped sex stories..." his eyes widen in alarm, making me laugh.

"Alright, I won't tell you that."

Eamon groans loudly. "I'll never be able to look your friends in the eye again, will I?"

This makes me laugh harder. "Sure, you can. They won't be looking at your face anyway."

His mouth falls open and he *actually blushes*.

"Are you blushing, Kennedy?" I giggle.

He rolls to his back, groaning again, and scrubs a hand over his face. I'm enjoying his discomfort far more than I should.

"Relax," I say soothingly. "Do you really think I gave them all the dirty details?"

"I don't think you would do it willingly, but that lot is pretty demanding. They could have tortured it out of you for all I know," he says with a grimace.

"You're not too far off, actually..." I concede.

"Ach! I knew it!" Eamon snatches my hand and rolls us back over, trapping me beneath him.

He pins my hand above my head and leans in to nibble my neck. I love this playful side of him as much as his serious side.

I lift my head enough to kiss him quickly. "I'm not the only one that spilled secrets last night. I probably shouldn't tell you this, but I know I can trust you not to blab to the world."

He furrows his brow and says seriously, "Anything you tell me in secret will stay that way, love."

"Well," I begin, "Myra was here."

"Is that right? I hope she apologized for her nasty behavior the other night."

"She did, but there's a reason she's been acting out of sorts." I hesitate before saying, "She's pregnant."

Eamon's eyes are as wide as saucers, shock written all over his face. "No. You're not serious."

"It's true. It's still early, but she's definitely pregnant."

"Who's the father?" he asks, the puzzle pieces not fitting in place yet. I raise an eyebrow at him and wait.

"Fuck. It's Mac's, isn't it?"

I nod in confirmation. "She's panicking. I don't blame her. I wouldn't want to be carrying Mac's baby."

Eamon's features darken as he growls. "I'd rather you didn't bring up carrying another man's child while we're naked in your bed if it's all the same with you. The thought of another man even touching you has me feeling rather murderous."

I shouldn't be turned on by his possessive, caveman behavior, but it gets me seriously hot and bothered. I'm not ready for kids yet, but I don't hate the idea of having Eamon's babies someday.

"Has she told him yet?" he asks, clearly ready to move the conversation back to the topic at hand.

"No, she's not sure what she's going to do yet. I told her to make an initial appointment with an OB before she makes any decisions."

"Christ. This is huge. Mac can barely take care of himself. I can't imagine him being a father. Or even a supportive partner for her. On the one hand, if it were me, I'd want to know, but he's a selfish arsehole, so it might be better for him not to know." Eamon speculates.

Now I'm the one feeling murderous thinking about Myra, or anyone else for that matter, carrying Eamon's baby. I take a deep breath and push the thought out of my head.

"Just to play devil's advocate," I start, "what if this is what causes him to turn a new leaf? Makes him grow up and take responsibility?"

Eamon nods absently. "Aye, that's a good point. Is there anything more sobering than bringing a child into the world? It at least forces you to put things in perspective, doesn't it?"

"I would think so." I agree.

He tucks a strand of hair behind my ear. "It doesn't excuse her behavior, but it makes sense why she's been acting the maggot around ya."

I snort in amusement. "I think I need a book of Irish slang definitions if I'm ever going to keep up. What does that one mean?"

"Ach, I forgot you're a Yank." He teases, kissing my forehead. "*Acting the maggot* means a person is being a jerk."

"Yeah, that's accurate. I forgive her though."

"You're pure class, Norah Grady. You know that?"

"Whatever, Kennedy." I roll my eyes at him. "Now, what are we going to do the rest of the day?"

"I don't have that bleedin' paper hanging over my head anymore, so I'm content to stay right here, actually," Eamon mutters as he nuzzles my neck some more. "And I'm guessing the next two weeks you'll be tied up with the play. Not sure I can go that long without you, love."

"You make a very valid point," I agree. "I like your plan."

And that's exactly what we do.

Chapter Twenty-Six

Norah

It's the final showing of Beauty and the Beast, and I am utterly exhausted. The cast put on two performances a day for four straight days. It's been a massive success, and I have never been more proud of my work. Not only did my costumes catch the eye of critics around the state, but the actors went above and beyond portraying their characters. Dr. Andrews received no less than fifteen requests for interviews from local and national news outlets and he's been adamant that the entire cast and crew be present for all of them. I hate being in the spotlight, but I can't deny I'm excited about my designs being publicized. My own phone has been blowing up with calls and text messages begging me to create costumes for productions ranging from high school plays to accredited dance and theater academies statewide.

"Norah! Belle has a petal coming off!" I hear Macie yell from behind me.

I race over with my sewing kit and quickly begin stitching the petal overlay back to the bodice of Belle's dress. With as much as this gown has been worn over the last weeks, it's not too surprising that it's starting to show some wear and tear.

"All set, Leah," I say, smiling up at the actress playing Belle. "This should hold through the final curtain. You're doing amazing!"

"I still can't get over the garden scene," Macie says, coming to stand beside me. "You'd think I'd be sick of looking at people in flower dresses after dressing them for months, but no, it's still just as stunning as when you first showed us your designs."

"Thanks, Macie," I say, squeezing her arm. "I couldn't have done it without you and the rest of the team."

I mean every word. They all worked tirelessly to get proper measurements and help with alterations this week. Macie, especially, has been a godsend. Whenever I struggle with a design, Macie is the one that helps me figure it out. Plus, she's brilliant with headpieces.

"You know, I'd like to be humble, but we do make a pretty damn good team, don't we?" Macie gushes, propping her hands on her hips.

"We absolutely do," I agree wholeheartedly as I watch my team members hustle to and from the costume rack.

When the final curtain is called, all of the actors gather in the dressing areas to change their costumes. I'm hanging gowns up on the racks when I hear someone clear their throat behind me. Turning, I see a middle-aged woman with short, black hair and cat-eye glasses in a smart business suit standing a few feet away.

"Ms. Norah Grady?" the woman questions.

"Yes, I'm Norah Grady."

The woman walks closer and extends her hand. "Hello, Ms. Grady. My name is Melinda Sanchez. I'm with American Theatre Magazine."

My jaw drops in shock as I slowly grasp Melinda's hand. "Oh! Wow, Ms.

Sanchez, it's an honor!"

"Please, call me Melinda," she says, retracting her hand and placing it over her heart. "And the honor is all mine. I understand you're the mind behind the incredible costumes for this production?"

"I...uh...no. I mean, yes, but it wasn't just me," I stammer and fidget nervously. "There's an entire team devoted to these costumes."

Melinda chuckles. "Of that, I have no doubt, Ms. Grady. I won't take much of your time, but I was wondering if we could schedule an interview with you and your team soon. I've already spoken with Dr. Andrews, and he's given his blessing so to speak. Would you be available tomorrow morning? We can meet back here."

Holy shit. An interview with American Theatre Magazine is *huge*.

"Yes, of course! Let me just check with the team to make sure that works for all of them." I'm shaking with excitement.

"Sure, just gather whoever is available, and we'll do a small interview to start. Between you and me," Melinda lowers her voice conspiratorially, "after the holidays, ATM is exploring a television series dedicated to university theater departments across the country, and they've been eyeing UNCW as their primary focus."

Completely dumbfounded, I pinch the back of my hand to make sure I'm not dreaming. I've lost sleep over the last two weeks between the play and Eamon's insatiable needs, so this could all be a figment of my imagination.

"I don't even know what to say. What an incredible honor that would be!"

Melinda stretches out a hand and squeezes my arm gently. "Remember, mum's the word. See you tomorrow, Ms. Grady."

I stand there in shock for several minutes before I go in search of the team. Once everyone is gathered, I fill them in on the interview for tomorrow morning and am met with shrieks of excitement and just as many frozen faces. Macie produces a bottle of champagne, seemingly out of thin air, and pops the cork immediately.

"I was saving this for the after-party, but I think this is a big enough cause to celebrate!" Macie laughs as everyone cheers and surrounds her eagerly.

Standing on the outskirts of the group, I watch them proudly. They deserve to celebrate. I was invited to the after-party, but if I go, it won't be for long. I want nothing more than to snuggle with my Irishman and drink a bottle of wine. A hand touches my elbow, pulling me from my thoughts, and I turn to find Dr. Andrews smiling at me.

"You should be celebrating with them, Norah. It's because of you that we even have interviews with any media outlet."

I shake my head. "That's not true. Every aspect of the production was incredible, and you are the one who chose a modern retelling of Beauty and the Beast. We just embellished and brought it to life."

He laughs heartily. "Well, I guess there's some truth to that. But I'm convinced you could have turned any idea of mine into pure magic. You have a gift, Ms. Grady. I hope you'll consider staying on with the department after graduation. You'll always have a place here."

The relief I feel knowing that I have a job after graduation no matter what is overwhelming.

"Thank you, Dr. Andrews. You have no idea how much that means to me. Working with you and the department has been an absolute dream come true. I'm planning to spend the holiday break coming up with a game plan. If I stay in the area, I can't imagine working anywhere else." I tell him honestly.

Most seniors know what they want to do at the start of the Fall Semester, but I haven't given it much thought past getting my business degree. I love what I do, and I love living in Wilmington.

"I'm glad to hear that. Go celebrate. I'll see you bright and early for the interview," he says before sauntering off.

It's nearly ten o'clock before I leave the theater, and I'm dead on my feet. I'm anxious to see Eamon and tell him about the interview. He was at the performance tonight, but I never had a chance to do more than wave at him. He messaged me earlier saying that he would pick me up and take me for a celebratory drink at Paddy's. I haven't seen Paddy and Alicia in ages, and I miss them, but I don't think I'll make it through a pint without falling asleep in it.

I step outside, thankful I had the foresight to bring a thicker jacket with me, as there's a chill breeze blowing through the parking lot. Eamon is leaning against his car, holding up a single yellow rose and looking absolutely mouthwatering all dressed up in gray slacks and a black button-up.

"Well, don't you look handsome," I tell him, walking directly into his waiting arms.

"Aye, it's a special occasion," he says, caressing my cheek with the soft rose petals. "That was incredible, love. I've never been much into plays, but I can honestly say that was pure quality. I'm so proud of you."

"Thank you," I say, mouth curving into a grin. "You'll never believe what happened after the final curtain!"

"Tell me on the way to Paddy's. I know it's late and you're exhausted, but humor me." He winks and kisses me quickly.

Before he can pull away, I bury my fingers in his hair and deepen the kiss. He grunts in surprise but doesn't put up much of a fight. The hand he had on my waist is now squeezing my ass.

"Can we just go home?" I murmur against his mouth.

Eamon groans in frustration as I press my hips into him. "You're killing me, Norah."

"There's an easy solution. Take me home, Eamon. We can go to Paddy's tomorrow night," I beg him, trailing my hands down to his waistband.

He circles both of my wrists with one hand. "No, love, we can't. I promised to deliver you to Paddy's as soon as you left the theater."

My eyes narrow in suspicion. "Promised who? And why?"

"Please do me a favor and cooperate. I'll make it up to you later. With gusto," he promises with a wink.

I scrunch my nose at him. "Ugh. Fine. This better be good, Kennedy."

We climb into Eamon's SUV and head towards Paddy's. As we're driving, I turn in my seat to tell him about my conversation with Miranda Sanchez.

"And then she told me they're thinking about doing a TV series and featuring UNCW! I don't even know what all that would entail, but it could be huge for the department!"

"You're kidding!" Eamon exclaims, glancing over at me. "Ah, Acushla, that's incredible!"

I look at him curiously. "Acushla. What does that mean? Paddy has called me that a time or two."

He reaches for my hand, bringing it up to kiss my knuckles. "It's Irish Gaelic for *my darling*. Is it too much?"

My darling. Swoon.

"No! I think it's lovely. I'll have to find a term of endearment for you now," I tease him.

Eamon chuckles. "You can always go with *Eamon, the incredibly handsome and most amazing lover*. I'd respond well to that."

I throw my head back in laughter. If he isn't wooing me with sweet words like *Acushla*, then he has me in stitches. "Oh yes, I can see how that will flow smoothly in conversation. And definitely won't make your ego swell at all."

"*Something* will be swelling, that's for sure."

I laugh again. "Oh my god, stop! You're ridiculous. Maybe I'll just call you *boo bear*."

Eamon makes a noise of disgust. "*Boo bear*? You're slagging me. Please say you're slagging me."

"I don't know. It has a nice ring to it, don't you think? Especially while cheering you on at a game!"

We park the car, and he turns to scowl at me. "If you think for one minute that I'm going to let you call me *boo bear* or anything remotely close, you're banjaxed."

I giggle and lean over the console to kiss him. "Fine. No *boo bear*, but I will find something."

"I don't see what's wrong with my first suggestion," he grumbles as we get out of the car. "Now, remember. I'm going to make this up to you."

I narrow my eyes at him. Whatever is going on, he knows I won't love it. That can only mean the girls are behind this.

"Just tell me now who I'll be killing later."

Chuckling, Eamon intertwines our fingers and leads me to the entrance of Paddy's. He ushers me inside, and as soon we pass the threshold, a loud cheer rings out. All of my friends and their collective partners are standing and applauding. Eamon nudges me forward. I can feel my cheeks flushing and tears filling my eyes.

"You guys… What is this?" I choke out.

Charlie steps forward and hugs me tightly. "We're so proud of you!"

I'm so touched and honored to call these people my friends and spend the next couple of hours accepting hugs and congratulations while sipping a glass of wine. When we arrived, I had expected just a round of drinks, much like we do every week, but the girls somehow talked Paddy into letting them reserve the entire pub for the occasion. As I walk around, I realize that each table has a frame in the middle of it and that every single frame contains a picture of one of the costumes from the play. On the bar sits a thick album filled with pictures of all the pieces I've created since moving to Wilmington. Every ballet recital, Halloween, and theater costume. I'm overcome with emotion as I flip through the pages. I don't know how they managed to find all of these, but I'm floored.

"You've a gift, lass."

Looking up, I find Paddy peering at me over the bar with those grandfatherly eyes I've come to love. He took me under his wing from the moment we met, and since I've never met my father's parents and my Mom's parents passed away when I was a toddler, he's the closest thing to a grandparent I've ever had. I wouldn't trade him for the world.

"Thank you, Pat. You know you're my anchor, right?" I tell him.

His cheeks turn pink, and his eyes are glassy with unshed tears. "Ach, nonsense. You're a strong young woman with a good head on your shoulders. You've never needed me."

I reach over and grasp his fingers, squeezing gently. "I'm serious. You're family. Before Charlie moved here, you were the only one I had."

Paddy's bottom lip quivers for a moment before he sucks in a deep breath.

"Alright, Pat?" Eamon's deep voice sounds from over my shoulder, his forehead creased with concern.

"Aye, just dust from the vents getting in my eyes." He harrumphs. "Didn't you clean those this week? What am I paying you for anyway?"

"Right, knew I forgot something. Apologies, Paddy. Won't happen again," Eamon says in mock seriousness.

My heart warms while listening to the two of them. The way Eamon goes out of his way to protect Paddy's pride is endearing and makes me feel all kinds of ooey gooey feelings.

"Oi! Kennedy!" a raucous voice suddenly bellows from the entrance and Ro saunters in, followed closely by Teagan.

"Ro. Teag. Glad you could make it," Eamon greets them with a handshake that leads to a one-armed hug.

"Yeah, mate. Wouldn't miss it," Teagan says before shifting his gaze to me. "Congrats, Norah. I'm not a costume expert, but even I can tell your work is savage."

"Righto, love! Absolutely bang on!" Ro cajoles.

I grin at them. "Thank you! Ro, I'm surprised you even saw the play."

I can't help but tease him. Teagan came to the play with Layla on opening night.

Ro snorts loudly. "Oh, god no! You won't catch me at a play. But I've heard yer fella here wax poetic about you and yer frocks, so I can only assume they're quality!"

"For fuck's sake, Ro," Teagan murmurs. "I saw it, and I'm not ashamed to say it was one of the best I've seen."

Ro rolls his eyes dramatically and fake whispers, "Lickarse."

"So, uh, who all is here tonight?" Teagan asks, craning his neck to look around the pub with hopeful eyes.

Eamon and I give each other a knowing glance.

"If you're looking for Layla, she's over in the corner booth with Charlie and Amelia." I wink at him.

"Yeah?" His eyes light up like a Christmas tree.

"You're bloody away in the head, aren't you?" Ro exclaims. "Pining after her like some sort of lost puppy."

"Who has a lost puppy?" Alicia asks as she comes bouncing out of the kitchen with a bucket of ice.

Her long black hair is pulled back in two French braids, and her lips are painted bright red. She's wearing a cropped black V-neck sweater with skin-tight leather leggings.

"Hey, Norie!" She says, setting the bucket on top of the bar. "I didn't get a chance to tell you how much I loved Beauty and the Beast! I saw it on opening night. I can't get over Belle's gown!"

"Thank you!" I gush. "You look amazing, by the way!"

"I'd say," Ro lets out a low whistle. "But she's always a fine thing, am I right? Hiya, Alicia."

"Rowan," she greets him coldly before turning on her heel towards the kitchen. "I'm going to get back to work, but let's do lunch next week, Norie! Congrats again!"

We all turn to stare at Ro with wide eyes.

"What did you do?" Eamon glares at his friend.

"Why do you assume I did something?" he cries indignantly.

Even I scoff at that. I don't know him that well, but I know him well enough to know that he's a troublemaker.

"Because you *always* do something, you buck eejit. You're always mucking about with her, but clearly, you've done something to set her off."

Ro runs a hand through his ginger locks and frowns. "Listen, I'd rather not get into it here, okay? We're supposed to be celebrating the lovely Norah anyway. Catch me tomorrow, and I'll fill you in, alright?"

Eamon nods. "Fine. But don't try to get out of it."

"Yeah, grand," he agrees before following Teagan toward the corner booth.

"Well, that was interesting," I mutter, turning to Eamon.

"It was, yeah," he agrees. "I hope he didn't do anything that warrants a kick to the bollox. Though I'm sure Alicia would have handled that on her own."

I step into him, wrapping my arms around his torso. "You're right about that. Now, can we go home? It's late, and I do believe you said something about making this up to me...with gusto?"

A low growl rumbles through his chest before he leans down and nips my earlobe. I shiver in anticipation of what's to come.

"I did, didn't I?" he whispers against my neck. The feel of his lips brushing my skin sends sparks straight through me. "Go say your goodbyes, Acushla."

Chapter Twenty-Seven

Norah

"I can't believe I'm going to be in a magazine. How did this even happen?"

I came home from the interview bouncing with excitement. The whole situation is so surreal. I arrived before the rest of the team, so Melinda pulled me aside for a personal interview. It wasn't anything too in-depth, just basics like: How long have you been designing and making costumes? What inspired you to pursue this particular avenue? What are you hoping to do with your skills after graduation?

I never thought that watching my Mom sew curtains and pillowcases would lead me to making my own Halloween costumes which led to where I'm at today. The first costume I ever made, all on my own, was a parrot costume. I had been talking about being a parrot for Halloween for months. When my Mom couldn't find a store-bought one, she made an offhand comment about making one myself or picking a new costume. I sat down that day and designed every part of it. When I showed the sketch to my Mom, she gaped at it for a long moment before loading me up in the car and heading to the fabric store. Other than a few suggestions and instructions here and there, she just sat back and watched me make it. I ended up winning first place in our third-grade costume contest.

"How did this happen?" Eamon asks me incredulously, sliding onto the bar stool at the kitchen island. "Because you're bloody brilliant, that's how! I'm not surprised in the slightest that the media is flocking to you right now. I know fuck all about designing and sewing, but even I can see how incredible your work is. Don't sell yourself short, love."

I beam at him over my coffee mug. "Thank you, *schnookums*."

"No. Definitely not."

"What?" I laugh. "Not feeling it?"

"You better just stick with costume design." Eamon cringes.

Laughing harder, I level him with a playful glare. "So you're saying I should leave *Official Boyfriend Pet Name Giver* off of my resume after graduation?"

"Absolutely." He deadpans.

"So, I was thinking. Thanksgiving is next week. I know you don't celebrate it in Ireland, but how would you feel about hosting with me for our friends?"

Eamon takes a sip from his coffee before placing it back on the table. "Grand. Let's do it. Ro and Teag would love it. Teag especially, if Layla is there."

"I'm confident she will be. Her family lives in Texas, so we're usually together anyway. What about Alicia and Ro? I always invite her, but given her behavior towards Ro, I'm not sure if that spells a recipe for disaster or not."

"Aye, I'm meeting with him in a bit," Eamon tells me. "I'll let you know. But don't let Ro keep you from inviting Alicia. I'd suggest inviting Paddy, but he's spending the day with his sons and their significant others. Time to meet the parents and all that."

My breath catches in my throat, and my heart constricts painfully. Eamon notices and stretches his hand across the island to brush the back of mine with his knuckles.

"What's wrong, love? What happened there?"

I give him a small smile. "Just thinking about how much my Mom would have liked you. I'd love nothing more than to have the opportunity to drag you back to my hometown to meet her."

"Ach, Acushla, I'm so sorry. I wasn't thinking," he starts.

"No, it's okay. Really. I usually do okay during the holidays, but sometimes the smallest thing will trigger memories of her. I'm sure you understand that since losing your dad."

"I do, yeah." He nods.

Our eyes meet in silent understanding, and I lace my fingers with his.

"How much time do we have before you have to leave?" I ask with a sly grin.

His dark eyebrows shoot up. "Depends on what you had in mind."

"I might like a repeat of last night, handsome."

"We have time," he says, standing abruptly, coffee forgotten as he stalks around the island. "And if you keep calling me that, I'm putty in your hands," he tells me before scooping me up and tossing me over his shoulder before racing for my room.

Eamon

"You don't think they...you know," Teagan hedges with a grimace.

We've been sitting at the small round table in our flat discussing what Ro could have possibly done to piss off Alicia for the last hour while we wait for him to show up.

"Christ, he better not have pulled his normal shite," I groan, scrubbing a hand over my beard. "Surely he wouldn't shag and bail on *Alicia*. Not just because she's pure gold, but she'd murder him."

"I swear to god, if we have to find a new pub, I'll rip his bollocks off and shove them so far up his arse they'll hang out of his nose."

I let out a sharp laugh. It's not often Teagan is graphic or violent, but when he is, it's usually regarding Ro.

The man in question sneaks in the door at that moment. "What'd I miss, mates?"

"Just our plans to disfigure you if we have to find a new pub." Teagan glares at him.

Flinging himself into one of the chairs, Ro props his feet on the table. "Why the feck would we have to find a new pub? What did you wankers get up to?"

"Not us, you gobshite," I bark while pushing Ro's feet off the table. "Keep those boats of yours on the floor, will ya? Now, tell us what you did to Alicia."

He spears his fingers through his hair and groans. "It's not what you're thinking. In fact, it's quite the opposite."

Teagan and I exchange disbelieving glances.

"Alright, so Alicia and I bumped into each other last week at a club. We'd both been drinking, obviously, and dancing. Next thing I know, we're in the jacks snogging. It was getting heated, but I put on the brakes. Alicia's not just some random wagon, is she? Snogging is one thing, but shagging her is a different story altogether. If I'm going to shag her, it's not going to be while we're hammered in the jacks of some manky club. I have more respect for her than that. So anyway, she was raging and ran out of there before I could even explain myself. It's been frigid ever since."

The room is silent. Teag and I sit there speechless. Ro is rarely serious, especially when it comes to women. We've known he's had a thing for Alicia but never thought he really *liked* her.

"Stall the ball," Teagan finally says. "You're saying that *Alicia* wanted to hook up and you turned her down?"

"Not because I didn't want her! God knows how much I'd love to sink my—"

204

"Stop," I interrupt. "We don't need the details."

"Right. So anyway. That's the story. Every time I try to talk to her, she goes all ice queen on me." Ro shrugs.

"Well, Rowan, for once, I can actually say you did the right thing, but you're going to have to find a way to explain it to her," Teagan cautions.

"And how do you suppose I do that when she barely acknowledges me?"

We sit there thinking for a few moments before an idea comes to me.

"Norah and I are hosting Thanksgiving at hers next week. For all of our mates. She always invites Alicia. If I can make sure she's there, you can corner her at some point. We can orchestrate something."

Rowan rubs his jaw then finally nods. "Alright, that could work. You and the fire sprite are getting serious, yeah?"

"Yeah." I blow out a breath and prop my elbows on the table. "She's amazing."

Teagan stares at me thoughtfully. "You love her, don't you, mate?"

"Without a doubt," I answer immediately.

Norah

Friendsgiving went off without a hitch. It was so much fun that we decided to make it an annual event. I saw Rowan follow Alicia back to my sewing room at one point but never found out what happened after that. Teagan and Layla made eyes at each other from across the table the entire time. Myra and Amelia were there as well, making us laugh with their antics.

Once the last of the company left for the night, Eamon and I were finally alone. The subtle touches and heated glances he kept giving me throughout the day had stoked a fire in my core. More than once, I had to talk myself out of dragging him into another room. But not the sewing room. We had concocted a plan for Alicia to go out and grab something for our dinner, then sent Ro in after her, hoping she'd give him a chance to talk to her about their *misunderstanding*.

Eamon is sitting on the couch, legs stretched out in front of him. He grabs my hand to tug me down beside him.

"Come here to me," he orders. "Put your feet up. You've got to be spent."

He drapes an arm around my shoulders, circling it across my chest and pulling me into him.

"Thank you," I murmur, turning my head up towards him. "For being here and helping."

He kisses the top of my head. "I enjoyed celebrating the holiday with you and the gang. My first Thanksgiving in the States was spent drinking too much and eating takeout with Ro and Teagan in my flat. This was a vast improvement."

I smile at the thought of the three of them together. I can just hear all of the drunken banter. I face him and place a hand on his chest. His beautiful eyes search my face.

I open my mouth, then look away when nerves start to take root.

"What is it, Norah?" he asks, lightly cupping my cheek to turn my face back to his.

I take a deep breath and lock my eyes with his. "I just want you to know how much you mean to me. How thankful I am to be here with you."

He beams at me and says, "I feel the same way. There's no one else I'd rather be spending this day with than you."

I trace my fingers along his scruff-covered jaw to his lips, brushing my thumb across the bottom one. I'm about to lay my heart on the line. I've completely fallen for this dark-haired, blue-eyed Irishman, and I can't contain it any longer.

"Eamon," I whisper. "I…I love you."

He sucks in a sharp breath and I watch his eyes widen, then soften before he says, "I love you too, Norah. More than words can say."

My heart swells to the point I think it might explode. It's not that I thought he didn't love me back, but to hear the words come out of his mouth revives a part of me that's been long dormant. I love my friends, and they love me, but *this* love is all-consuming.

Eamon winds a hand through my hair to grip the back of my neck, pulling my face to his to kiss me gently, reverently, emphasizing the words we just professed. As the kiss deepens, I crawl into his lap to straddle him. Pressing me closer to him, he erases any space left between us. Breaking the kiss, my fingers move to the buttons of his shirt, slowly loosening each one. I lean in to lick a path up the column of his neck while slipping the shirt over his broad shoulders. Eamon's hands creep under my sweater, palms skimming my sides before unhooking my bra. I raise my arms above my head, a silent invitation for him to undress me. He holds my gaze while he draws the top off, tosses it aside, and slides the straps off of my shoulders. His calloused fingers brush the sides of my breasts. When I lean in to kiss him again, he pinches my nipples and I bite his bottom lip in return, making him grunt.

"I don't recommend doing that when another part of you is in my mouth," I say against his lips.

"Noted," he mumbles, then dips his head down to suck one of my firm peaks between his teeth.

Moaning when he bites down gently, he braces his hands between my shoulder blades, arching me into him and holding me firmly in place while he continues to suck and nip at me. I'm desperate to feel him inside me, so the moment his mouth leaves me, I shimmy off of his lap.

He looks at me questioningly. "Too much, lass?"

Shaking my head, I begin peeling my leggings and panties from my body. My feet are barely free before he lunges from the couch and drops to his knees before me, hands gripping the sides of my thighs. Giving me a devilish wink, he tosses a leg over his shoulder and devours me. Squeaking out his name, I dig my fingers into his shoulders for balance, but he holds me steady while I writhe against his magical mouth. When he plunges a finger into me and finds my G-spot, I orgasm so hard that I see stars. Eamon doesn't relent until he's wrung every last ounce of pleasure from me and I collapse into his arms. Lowering me gently to the floor, he kisses a path from my navel to my collarbone.

"God, you're gorgeous when you come all over my mouth," he mutters into my neck, before quickly stripping the rest of his clothes and settling between my legs.

He slowly pushes himself in as far as he can, and holds still for a moment, before pulling out and repeating the movement over and over. Wrapping my legs around his waist, I pull his mouth to mine, tongue mimicking the motion of his body. He grinds against me with every thrust, placing pressure right on my clit.

"Eamon," I pant. "Keep doing that. Don't stop."

"I can't hold back any longer," he grinds out.

"Come with me," I gasp.

It's the last thing we both need as we go careening over the edge together, crying out.

We cling to each other in the aftermath, our hearts racing and sweat coating our bodies. After a long moment, Eamon props himself up and smiles softly.

"You're beautiful," he whispers.

"You make me feel beautiful," I whisper back. "And confident. And incredibly safe."

"There's nothing I wouldn't do to keep you safe. You're precious to me. I think I've loved you from the first moment I saw you."

My heart trips over itself at his words and my eyes pool with tears. Eamon brushes away the one that escaped with his thumb.

"How is that possible?" I sniff. "You didn't even know me."

"My Mam told me once that true love is filled not just with romantic moments, but fun, laughter, and a sense of peace when you're with that person. She said, 'Eamon, my boy when you meet the love of your life, you'll feel the world tip on its axis.' That night at Paddy's, when you challenged me to that drinking contest, my world shifted."

I think his Mom was right. Looking back on that fateful night, I was so enamored by him, even before we spoke. I saw him across the pub and couldn't take my eyes off of him.

"You probably thought I was a special kind of idiot." I laugh. "I can't believe I did that."

Chuckling, he rolls us so we're on our sides, facing each other. He drapes an arm over my hip and walks his fingers up my spine. When he reaches the base of my neck, he grabs my hair and pulls slightly so that I'm looking at him.

"Definitely not an eejit," he says. "I wouldn't be here right now if not for that temper of yours."

"Rude." I feign offense and kiss the tip of his nose.

"I love you, Acushla."

I snuggle closer, sighing contentedly. "I love you too, handsome."

Chapter Twenty-Eight

Norah

The last week of the Fall Semester has finally arrived, and luckily for me, I only have two finals, and they're both later this week. I've spent the last two days studying, but today, I'm taking a break to have lunch with Alicia. After Thanksgiving, we didn't really have a chance to talk about whatever happened between her and Ro, so when the opportunity became available, we took advantage.

"So, are you going to tell me what happened between you and Ro, or am I going to have to beat it out of you?" I ask, folding my arms on the table.

Alicia groans and hangs her head. "Ugh, Norie, do we have to talk about this?"

"If you really don't want to, then I respect that, but you might feel better if you get it off your chest."

"You're right, I guess. It's just…it's kind of embarrassing," she confesses.

Eamon relayed Ro's side of the story to me already, but I need to hear it from Alicia.

I place my hand over my heart and vow, "I won't laugh or make fun of you. I promise."

She hesitates, then points a finger at me. "Fine. But this goes nowhere, understand? I don't want Pat to know. I'd never hear the end of it."

Alicia divulges the story of running into Rowan at a club. They participated in their regular banter, but as their alcohol levels increased, the banter turned more suggestive. Alicia begged Rowan to dance with her, so between the booze and the physical proximity, one thing led to another, and they found themselves locked in the bathroom.

"I was fully aware that this was going to be a one-time hookup. I know Ro. He doesn't do relationships, and I know better than to expect more," she tells me. "I just wanted to live in the moment, you know? How often do you get to hook up with a sexy Irish soccer player?"

I shrug and say, "Well, I don't know about you, but I…"

"Okay, well we can't all be Norah Grady, and I doubt that you want to share."

I laugh and say, "No, I really don't. But I can speak from experience that one time will never satisfy that craving."

God, isn't that the truth? Just thinking about Eamon has me feeling hot and bothered.

Alicia gapes at me, "That's not helpful. Especially since he stopped us before anything happened."

She scowls while stabbing the food on her plate with a fork. Note to self, Rowan denying her makes her stabby.

Acting like I don't know anything, I gasp incredulously, "You're joking! Rowan Gallagher *stopped* a hookup?"

"Yes," she whines but continues, "he said it wasn't right and that we'd had too much to drink. Which is true, but I knew what I was doing. He wouldn't believe me when I told him that. I was so embarrassed and pissed off that I stormed out of there, and I haven't spoken to him since. He's tried to talk to me a few times at the pub. I try to ignore him, but I'd love nothing more than to throw a beer in his face."

"It's hard to believe that Ro has a gallant bone in his body, but it sounds like he was trying to keep from taking advantage of you. I'd say that's a sign of respect, which we all know is not something he's known for," I say soothingly.

"Did you know he cornered me at your place on Thanksgiving?" Alicia asks, setting her fork down.

"Yeah." I nod. "I saw him follow you back there, but that's all."

"He basically said the same thing. That he respected me too much to make me one of his casual hookups. I'm not sure if I believe him. He'll sleep with anything that has a vagina, but not me. Clearly, there's something wrong with me if even Rowan Gallagher won't touch me," Alicia says, picking her fork back up and spearing her food as if it were Ro's face.

"Hey," I say softly, stretching my hand out to stop her from breaking the plate. "I can guarantee you that there is *nothing* wrong with you." She rolls her eyes in answer, and I hesitate before asking, "What if I told you that he talked to Eamon and Teagan about that night?"

Her head pops up, and the fork clatters against her plate. "You already knew?"

I nod and tell her, "I did, but I wanted to know your side since Ro is known for his tall tales. I'm sorry if that feels like trickery."

Alicia lets out a long sigh. "No, it's fine. I guess if anyone had to know, I'm glad it was you. So…what exactly did Ro say?"

I can't tell her all of the details because they need to come from Rowan.

"All that I'll say is that he definitely *doesn't* think there's anything wrong with you. The rest you'll have to ask him about."

We spend the rest of our time catching up on everything but O'Nelly's and Irish soccer players.

After lunch, I head home to go over my study guides again, but as I settle on the couch, books and note cards spread out on the coffee table before me, when my phone rings. I don't recognize the number, but the area code is from back home, and a sense of foreboding washes over me.

"Hello?" I answer cautiously.

"Hello, this is Detective Morrow from the Ozark Police Department. Is this Norah Grady?" a deep and matter-of-fact voice asks.

I'm stunned momentarily but slowly say, "Yes, this is Norah Grady."

"I'm sorry to bother you, ma'am, but I understand you went to high school with an Ashton Kirk. Is that correct?"

My blood runs cold, and my hands start shaking. I feel like I'm going to throw up.

"Um," I start, my voice shaking, "Yes, I did. I'm sorry, what is this about?"

"We've recently launched an investigation into some allegations made against him, and your name was given to us by another one of your former classmates who prefers to remain anonymous. She's accusing Mr. Kirk of assault and gave us a list of some of his possible past victims. Ms. Grady, I realize this is probably very uncomfortable for you to hear, but I'd greatly appreciate any information you may have," Detective Morrow states professionally.

"Um..." I say again, "Did this person say how she found out about that?"

My mind is reeling. The only person I told in that town was Charlie.

"Our source said that she found a notebook in Mr. Kirk's home listing his victims," he tells me.

My stomach rolls, but I take a deep breath. If this other person can be brave enough to tell her story, then I can be brave enough to tell mine.

"Yes, Detective Morrow. Ashton Kirk raped me when I was seventeen."

"I'm sorry to hear that, Ms. Grady. May I ask why the incident wasn't reported at the time?" he asks, honest curiosity in his voice.

"Honestly? I was terrified and convinced that no one would believe me. He was the golden boy of our town. In hindsight, I realize how stupid it was of me to not tell someone, but I was seventeen and naive," I say, then add, "I'd never been intimate with anyone before."

"I understand, Ms. Grady. Times have certainly changed regarding sexual assault and victims reporting it. I'll be frank with you. According to this list, Mr. Kirk raped or assaulted fourteen girls and young women between the year you graduated and now. I know this will be difficult, but would you be willing to come to the station to give your statement?" he asks.

I choke on a sob, completely devastated by the number of women who endured the same abuse at Ashton's hands.

"Is it possible to do this remotely, Detective?" I ask. "I live in North Carolina now, and I'm in the middle of final exams."

"Yes, Ms. Grady," he says, "I can take a verbal statement over the phone, then you can type it up and send it via email. However, when the case goes to trial, you'll likely be called upon to testify in court."

My stomach revolts again, but I tell him, "I understand, Detective. I'll do all that I can to help."

After giving my verbal testimony and reliving the horror of the attack, I hang up the phone. As soon as I do, I break down, sobbing uncontrollably. I can feel myself starting to sink into a panic attack, but I can't get a handle on it. I never thought I'd hear Ashton's name again, let alone *see* him. I moved forward with my life. I live in a wonderful city, have an amazing job, and incredible friends, and I found Eamon. I'm trying to focus on these things, but my throat is tightening and my heart is pounding out of my chest. I'm gasping for breath when there's a quick knock on the door and Eamon walks in.

He's immediately on his knees before me, cupping my face in both of his large warm hands.

"Norah! Christ, what's wrong?"

I can't answer him.

"Norah, look at me. Focus on my face," he commands. "That's it. Now take a deep breath. In and out. Breathe with me, love. There's a good lass. In. And out."

He keeps a firm grip on my face, eyes locked with mine, breathing deeply with me. Finally, my eyes begin to clear and the sobbing subsides. I'm still shaking slightly, but he rubs his thumbs soothingly over my cheekbones until it stops.

When I'm able to speak, I ask, "How did you know to do that?"

He brushes away the tear that slips out. "My sister. She had panic attacks for a while after my Da died. I was the only one who could calm her down. Now, can you tell me what triggered this?"

My eyes fill with tears again as I relay the conversation with Detective Morrow. I focus on his face, his eyes tethering me to the here and now.

"He told me I'll have to testify in court," I say. "Obviously, I'll do whatever they need me to, but I don't think I'm strong enough to be in the same room as him."

Still kneeling in front of me, he grips my hands in his. "Listen to me, Acushla. You are not only strong enough, but you're brave enough to do this. And you won't be alone. There's no way in hell I'll let you be anywhere near him without me present. I'll be with you through it all. If we have to travel back to Missouri a hundred times, so be it. I, personally, won't rest until this fucker is in prison."

"Thank you," I whisper.

"I'm not going anywhere, love," he says, kissing my forehead and stroking my hair comfortingly. "Do you want to go to Paddy's for a distraction? It's been a while, and I know he always makes you smile."

"He does make me smile, but I'm not exactly ready," I gesture to my sweatpants.

"So go get ready. You look good enough to eat to me," he winks, "but if it makes you feel better, do it. I'll ring the crew and have them meet us there."

I love this man. Not only does he soothe my panic attacks, but he knows just what to say to bring me back to myself.

"Okay, deal."

I have the immense satisfaction of watching Eamon's eyes widen and jaw drop when I walk out of the bathroom in a black cable-knit sweater dress that sits mid-thigh and knee-high black boots. My hair is twisted up into a sleek ballerina bun at the top of my head, showcasing a pair of diamond studs that belonged to my Mom.

Clearing his throat, he slides off the bar stool and slowly stalks towards me.

"I take it back," he says roughly. "We don't need to go anywhere tonight. I have better ideas involving you and these boots."

I giggle as he grips my hips and pulls me to him.

"I didn't put on a full face of makeup just to stay home, Kennedy. But don't forget that idea for later." I pat his chest with a hand.

"I don't think forgetting will be an issue while you're wearing this, Acushla," he growls in my ear. "I feel underdressed now."

"You're definitely not. You look ridiculously sexy. In fact, if you wanted to wear this leather jacket all the time, I wouldn't complain," I tease.

I hadn't noticed what he was wearing until just now. His black leather jacket covered up a light blue shirt that looks like it's plastered to his toned body. It makes his eyes pop.

"Yeah? I'll wear it on the pitch then too?"

I cock my head to the side and purse my lips in mock consideration. "Maybe not while you're playing, but when we go out, I demand it."

"Your wish is my command," he chuckles as he presses a kiss to my forehead. "Shall we go?"

"We shall," I answer.

Eamon

"Norah, lass! It does my soul good to see you this fine evening!" Paddy exclaims, embracing her warmly. "You look lovely as ever."

"Thanks, Pat. I've missed you," Norah says, hugging him back.

He looks over his shoulder at me then. "Hello, lad! I wondered when I'd be seeing your ugly mug again. I've a list a mile long of things for you to do once you're on holiday break."

"'Course you do," I say, rolling my eyes before pulling him in for a hug. "How ya gettin' on, Pat?"

"Ach, grand!" he says, practically dancing a jig. "My oldest boy is coming home for Christmas, and I couldn't be happier!"

"That's wonderful!" Norah tells him. "You'll have such a great time!"

"Aye, I will! Now, tell me, love, is our Eamon here taking good care of

216

you? If not, you just let me know and I'll set him straight."

I roll my eyes again and pull Norah closer to me. As if I'd do anything *but* take care of her.

Norah giggles and says, "He's taking great care of me, Pat. Nothing to worry about there."

Pat nods his head knowingly but says no more, as Norah is suddenly whisked away by Charlie and Layla, leaving me feeling bereft in her absence. She's still in the same room as me, but I have the overwhelming urge to keep her tucked into my side all night. After witnessing her panic attack earlier and hearing the reason for it, I want her to feel safe.

He turns back to me, clapping a hand on my shoulder, and says, "She looks happier than I've ever seen her, that one. You must not be mucking things up too terribly, eh?"

I rub a hand over the back of my neck. "Ach, go on with you. Doing my best not to."

"Whatever you're doing, keep it up, boyo."

"She's amazing, Pat," I tell him as I look towards where she's chatting with her friends. I can't take my eyes off of her. She's laughing at something Layla said and my heart flip flops in my chest. "I love her."

"'Course you do," he says. "It's clear as day. Have you told her as much?"

I nod. "Aye. And by some miracle, she loves me too."

When I don't get a response from Pat, I tear my eyes away from my girl and look at him. His eyes are pooling with tears, and he's grinning widely.

"What?" I demand.

"Ah, my boy. You've found your Ellie. Don't let her go."

"I don't intend to," I vow.

Norah

I just finished telling Charlie and Layla about the phone call with Detective Morrow and, remarkably, didn't fall apart again. Being surrounded by the most important people in my life bolstered my courage.

"Fourteen?" Charlie gasps in shock.

"That's what he said," I confirm. "It's heartbreaking."

"What are you going to do?" Layla asks.

"I'll do whatever they need. If it helps other victims and gets him put in prison, then I have to, right?"

"You're so brave, Norie. I hope you know we'll be with you throughout the whole thing," Charlie says, squeezing my hand.

"I know. I'd be lost without you both."

I take a drink of my beer and glance around the pub. "I know Amelia's working, but is Myra coming? Have any of you talked to her lately?"

Shrugging, Charlie says, "I asked her if she was coming out tonight, but she said she wasn't feeling well. I think she needs to see a doctor. She's been battling something for a while now."

I don't want to give away Myra's secret, so I say, "She's been working more than usual at the boutique, so maybe she's just really tired."

I glance at Layla to gauge her reaction, but she's thoroughly distracted. Teagan just walked into the pub with Ro. I watch as he clasps hands with Pat and pulls him in for a quick hug. His eyes start wandering around the room, obviously looking for someone. When his gaze settles on Layla, his entire face lights up. He's adorable.

"Alright, Lay. What's the tea on Teag?" Charlie demands.

Her cheeks turn pink, and she looks away, tucking her dark hair behind her ears. "What are you talking about? We're just friends."

"For now..." I mutter, elbowing her in the ribs.

Eamon, Teagan, and Ro are making their way over to the table, drinks in hand. Teagan, to absolutely no one's surprise, takes the seat next to Layla, slinging his arm over the back of her chair.

"Evenin'," he croons. "You're looking lovely, Layla."

CHAPTER TWENTY-EIGHT

"Thanks," she murmurs, face reddening even more.

Ro grabs a chair from a neighboring table, turns it around, and straddles it, arms propped up on the back. "Hello, ladies. What's the craic?"

We've spent enough time around the Irish trio to understand most of their colloquialisms by now that we know *craic* means "fun." Their accents, however, never grow old. Even the non-single ladies sit in rapt attention when they speak

We're sitting around chatting and drinking, the conversation never stalling. Mostly because Ro is a master storyteller. He's so animated that we're laughing and rolling our eyes the entire time he's talking. If a story isn't made up, he's embellished it so much that there's barely any truth left to it. He's in the middle of such a story when there's a loud commotion at the entrance of the pub. We all look up to see Mac and a few of the other players from the team stumble inside, clearly intoxicated. Mac is worse off than the others. Looking at Eamon, we exchange a silent conversation. Did Myra finally tell him about the baby? I grab my phone to send her a quick text to find out.

Norah: *Hey, we're all at Paddy's, and Mac just came in completely trashed. More so than normal. Did you tell him?*

Myra: *OMG. Of course he is. Yes, I told him a few hours ago. He handled it about as well as I thought he would. Looks like this is how he's coping.*

Norah: *I'm so sorry. Are you okay? Do you need me?*

Myra: *I'm okay. You stay. Amelia is coming over when she gets off work. Make sure he doesn't kill himself with alcohol poisoning. Idiot.*

Norah: *Will do. Let me know if you change your mind.*

Norah: *About coming over. Not letting him kill himself. ;)*

Myra: *LOL well... kidding. Kind of.*

I angle the screen towards Eamon, who snorts at the last part.

"Should I bring him over here?" he asks.

I shrug, feeling at a complete loss. "I'm not sure. He needs some water or something."

"Ro," Eamon says, catching his friend's attention, "Go get that arsehole and have him come sit. Get him some water too, will ya?"

Ro looks at Eamon like he's grown an extra head. "Will I, yeah? It's not my fault he's in ribbons."

"Aye, true enough, but you're the only one he'll respond to without being a complete tool," Eamon answers.

Ro rolls his eyes but gets up anyway. We watch him saunter up to Mac and toss an arm over his shoulder. He says something that makes the blonde laugh while mouthing *water* to Paddy. After filling a couple of glasses, Ro leads Mac and the rest of the guys to our corner. Eamon and Teagan pull another table and some chairs over to connect them. When Mac collapses into the seat, he looks around suspiciously at us.

"Did you hear the news?" he slurs, looking pointedly at me. "I'm going to be—"

"Completely wrecked tomorrow?" Eamon interrupts him.

Mac pauses to glare at his teammate, then his eyes go wide. "*You* knew? Before me? Of fucking course you did. Not sure why I'm surprised when you're fucking one of her friends."

"Easy, Mac," Eamon warns. "You don't want to go there."

"What did I miss?" Ro pipes up, eyes alight with excitement at being in the middle of drama.

"You mean you don't know? I thought for sure all of you were in on it!" Mac bellows belligerently. "What you missed is that I knocked up Myra. Surprise! I'm going to be a dad!"

Charlie and Layla gasp loudly while Ro and Teagan sit there stunned, jaws dropped.

I cover my face with my hands. Myra is going to be livid.

"Mac," Eamon commands, getting his attention, "not the time or place, mate."

"Fuck off, Irish. It's my kid, I can tell the whole world if I want!"

Leaning forward, I stretch a hand across the table and place it on his forearm.

"Mac," I say softly, "I'm the only one Myra told. Eamon only knows because of me."

I'm vaguely aware of Charlie and Layla whipping their heads in my direction.

Mac narrows his eyes at me, then heaves a long sigh. "She hates me," he says, crestfallen.

I shake my head. "No, she doesn't hate you. She's scared. Aren't you?"

He drops his head into his hands, nodding, as he whispers, "I don't know what to do."

"Mate, the best thing you can do is sober up and sleep on it. Don't do anything until your head's clear," Eamon says compassionately.

"Yeah," he groans, "that's probably a good idea."

"I'll call you guys an Uber," Charlie offers. "You can't drive, and none of us are sober enough to drive you."

While we wait for Mac's ride, we make him drink more water and eat some fries to help soak up the alcohol. He doesn't say anything as he sits there, only nodding or shaking his head when someone asks him a question. I actually feel sorry for him. Becoming a parent isn't what he or Myra wants at this point in their lives, so it makes sense that they're terrified. He could have handled it better, but this *is* Mac we're talking about. I send Myra another text.

Norah: *I have good news and bad news. Which do you want first?*

Myra: *Shit. Give me the good news.*

Norah: *We have Mac sobering up and called him an Uber.*

Myra: *And the bad news...?*

Norah: *He announced to pretty much the entire pub that he knocked you up. *insert grimace here**

Myra: *...he did not...*

Norah: *I wish I was lying.*

Myra: *Fucking fantastic. I'm going to kill him. Who all is there?*

Norah: *Eamon and me, Charlie, Layla, Teagan, Ro, and a few others from the team.*

Myra: *What else did he say?*

I type out a shortened version of the incident, telling her I'm hopeful he'll have a better response once he's sober. Myra replies that she won't hold her breath but appreciates the sentiment. Once we have Mac and the others tucked safely into their Uber, I prepare for the onslaught of questions.

"I can't believe you didn't tell me!" Charlie whines playfully. "How far along is she?"

"It wasn't my story to share," I say. "I think she's around four months now. Or at least getting close to it."

"She's always so safe. I can't believe it," Layla comments.

"Mac as a father. Now that's something I can't believe," Ro exclaims. "That wanker can't even take care of himself!"

Teagan barks out a laugh. "True enough. I hope Myra is prepared to raise the kid without him."

"You never know," Layla says, turning to him with a shrug. "Maybe he'll wake up tomorrow a new man."

"Also true, love." He winks and brushes her dark hair off of her shoulder. "I'll swing by and check in on him in the morning."

The smile she gives him is blinding. I wish I could take a picture of this moment. I'd label it as *The Moment Layla Fell For Teagan.*

"Text me after," she suggests. "I was thinking about going to Airlie Gardens. I might want some company."

Then she stands up, hugs Charlie and me goodbye, and leaves.

Teagan's gaze follows her all the way out of the pub. When he turns back to the table, all of us are watching with wide eyes.

"What?" he asks sheepishly.

"If you don't text her, you're an idiot," Charlie states with a shrug.

"Course I'm going to text her!" he says, lifting his beer to his lips. "I'm not about to look a gift horse in the mouth."

"That was definitely out of her comfort zone," I tell him. "Whatever you're doing, keep it up. It's fun watching her come out of her shell."

Teagan grins in triumph. "Aye, I'm on a mission."

Chapter Twenty-Nine

Eamon

Finals week is over, and the relief is palpable. I handed in my last paper for the semester and joyfully walked from the building. Late last night I had an idea come to me that I can't wait to run by Norah. Since neither of us has family obligations, I was hoping to convince her to take a short holiday with me. Nothing far away or too grand, just a few days on the Outer Banks. It's a short drive and the thought of waking up next to her with the sound of the ocean just outside sounds like heaven.

Norah is in the middle of a class, so I decide to grab a cup of coffee from the campus cafe and wait in the library. I was an avid reader growing up but rarely have the time to sit and enjoy a novel anymore. Maybe I'll check one out to read over the holiday. I can't spend the entire time in bed with Norah, as tempting as that sounds. As I walk through the rows of books, I think about the future. Before Norah, I hadn't been looking for a relationship of any kind, but now that I have her, I'm not about to let her go. Even though I have no desire to go back to Ireland, I can't wait to introduce her to my Mam. We haven't been together long, but I'm certain I want her around for the long haul and I think Mam will love her almost as much as I do.

My phone buzzes, alerting me to a text from Norah.

Norah: *All done! Where are you?*

Eamon: *In the library. I'll meet you outside. I have an idea to run by you.*

Norah: *Sounds intriguing. See you soon. xoxo*

I'm leaning against the side of the building when I see Norah scurrying up the sidewalk. It's colder out today than it has been recently, so I open my arms as soon as she approaches and gather her close to me. Her cheeks and nose are rosy from the biting wind, making her face glow. I kiss her softly.

"Hello, you," I purr.

"Hi," she breathes.

"Let's get you out of here and warmed up," I say suggestively.

She giggles, pushing up on her toes to kiss my jawline before saying, "I support this decision. And I want to know more about this idea you were talking about."

"Right. Did you have any big plans for the holiday break?" I ask tentatively.

She cants her head to the side. "No, not really. I thought I'd get a jump start on designing costumes for the spring play, but I can take a sketchbook and pencil with me anywhere. What did you have in mind?"

"Well," I say, turning our bodies towards my car, "I was thinking maybe you and I could rent a place on the Outer Banks and have ourselves a proper holiday together. What do you think?"

Norah beams at me, her eyes lighting up with excitement. "Eamon! That sounds perfect. I'd love that."

"Alright, it's settled. Let's head back to your place, get you warmed up, then we can plan our getaway."

CHAPTER TWENTY-NINE

Norah

We're barely through the door when Eamon lifts me and slams my back against the wall. I'm wild with desire, kissing him like my life depends on it. He's holding me up with one hand, while the other kneads my breast through my clothes. I moan loudly when he pinches my nipple. Unwrapping my legs from around his waist, I drop my feet to the floor, shoving his jacket off of his broad shoulders and tugging his shirt over his head. He makes easy work of my hoodie and bra, practically tearing them from me. He presses himself against me roughly, trapping me between the wall and his solid body. When he grinds his hips into mine, I turn feral and spin us around. He starts to protest, but I place my hand firmly against his chest, holding him still. With his back against the wall, I sink to my knees, unbuckle his jeans, and shove them, along with his boxers, to his ankles. I grip his cock with one hand and take him into my mouth as deep as possible. He groans loudly as I suck and swirl my tongue around him then digs his fingers into my hair, holding my head still while he fucks my mouth frantically. It's the hottest thing I've ever seen, even as I gag around him. He finally comes, a string of unintelligible words flowing from his mouth. I swallow everything with pride, knowing that I'm the one making him feel this good. Panting heavily, he looks down at me, and I smile demurely.

"I've been wanting to do that for a while," I admit.

Pulling me to my feet, he kisses me brutally before spinning me around, my back to his chest. He nips his way down my neck to my shoulder and back while cupping my breasts in his hands. He walks us forward until we reach the couch, then splays a hand on my back, bending me forward.

"Put your hands on the back of the sofa, Acushla. And don't let go."

I whimper with need but do as I'm told. My senses are on overload as he runs his tongue up my spine and cups my center, rubbing the heel of his hand against my clit. I writhe against him.

"Eamon," I beg, "please."

225

Eamon

I don't make her wait long before I'm plunging into her, buried to the hilt. Pulling back enough to drive deeply into her again, I continue thrusting harder and faster. She's gasping and moaning—so close to coming. I press the pad of my middle finger to her clit and begin circling quickly. That's all it takes for her to cry out her release. When I feel her inner walls contracting around me, I come again with a growl. Dragging us to the floor, I wrap my arms around her while we regain our breath, properly warmed up now.

"Wow…" Norah eventually murmurs. "That was intense."

"You won't find any complaints from me," I respond.

"Mmmm," she hums in agreement. "So. What about that trip?"

I kiss the top of her head, happy to spend all day every day like this if I could. The feel of her naked skin, covered in our sweat, pressed against mine is an aphrodisiac of its own.

"Right. Where do you want to go? And how long can you be away?"

"Can we do a week? Is that too long?" she asks.

"No, not at all," I tell her. "Have you been to Avon? It's a quiet place, very few people."

"I haven't been," Norah answers. "Sounds perfect though. Let's make it happen, Kennedy."

We spend the rest of the evening planning our holiday and eating take-out. Once the rental is booked and the leftover food put away, Norah leads me to the bedroom. We love each other slowly, kissing, caressing, and tasting leisurely. We come simultaneously, foreheads pressed together, and eventually, drift off to sleep, limbs tangled together and blissfully sated.

I'm dreaming about being buried deep in Norah on the beach when my phone starts ringing. I reach for it intending to send the caller to voicemail so I can go back to my dream, but I pause when I see that it's my Mam calling. It's half past four in the morning. She knows the time difference and never calls at this time. My pulse starts to skyrocket.

226

"Mam," I answer immediately, voice thick with sleep, "is everything okay?"

She's crying frantically, and I think my heart stops. "What is it? What's happened?"

I untangle myself from a sleeping Norah, careful not to wake her, and pad into the living room.

"Eamon," my Mam cries, "it's your sister."

Fear grips me as I sink to the couch. "What's happened to Caitlin?"

"They found her a few hours ago, barely breathing," she tells me through sobs.

"Is she…alive?" I whisper, the words barely able to leave my mouth.

"They have her hooked up to so many machines, Eamon. She's unconscious, and her blood tests show high levels of heroin. They're worried about brain damage."

"Fuck," I mutter. "Was anyone with her?"

Sniffling, she says, "No, she was found behind one of the shops. The fella that found her thought she was…dead. I'm afraid that if he'd found her later, it would have been a reality."

She breaks down sobbing again. *God, Caity.* My emotions are all over the place. I'm scared of losing my sister but angry at her for putting herself in this position to begin with. I'm also ashamed of ever loaning her money and overwhelmed with worry for my mother.

"I don't know what to do," she says, interrupting my thoughts. "I wish your Da were here. He'd know what to do."

I rub a hand over my face, sighing heavily. I already know what I'm going to do, but I say, "Tell me what the doctors are saying."

"Right now, it's a waiting game," she tells me. "They're going to do all sorts of scans to see the extent of the brain damage, but they're also concerned about organ failure. Given the amount of heroin in her body, it will be a miracle if she comes out of this unscathed. Oh, Eamon. Where did I go wrong with her?"

"Shhh, Ma," I comfort her. "You didn't do anything wrong with Caity. She knows what's right and wrong. Her behavior doesn't reflect the type of mother you are."

"Do you suppose it's because she had fewer years with your da? You were older and had more time with him. She was such a wee wan when he left us," she cries.

My eyes prickle. I think of my Da often, but hearing Mam talk about him is painful.

"I don't know, Ma. That could be part of it, but I think a lot of it has to do with the tossers she's been hangin' with over the years. They dug their claws in pretty deep."

A hand lands gently on my shoulder and I turn with a start. Norah's eyes are filled with concern as she rounds the couch. Before she can sit, I grip her waist and pull her into my lap, burying my head against her chest. She strokes her fingers through my hair, providing me with a sense of peace in all of the chaos. I let Ma go on about Caity's friends and how she should have known those girls were no good. How she should have sent her to boarding school, or at least a Catholic school.

"I don't think sending her to either of those would have helped, honestly. She would have rebelled even more. I guess you could have locked her in the cellar," I say in jest.

"Ach, Eamon Kennedy!" she chastises but then huffs a laugh. "You're a good lad, my boy. I miss the devil out of you."

"I know, Ma. I miss you too," I pause, looking into Norah's deep blue eyes. She's looking at me with such compassion and steadfastness that it bolsters me to make my decision. Releasing a shaky breath and never breaking eye contact, I say, "Sit tight, Mam. I'm coming home."

"You're what?" she screeches from the other end of the line, loud enough for Norah to hear. "Oh, Eamon! I won't lie and say that isn't the best thing I've heard in the last five years, but are you sure, lad?"

I look back to Norah who cups the side of my face and nods.

"Yeah, I'll grab the first flight I can find and let you know the details," I say, then add, "Oh, and Ma?"

"What is it, my love?"

"I'm bringing someone with me."

228

Chapter Thirty

Eamon

The sun is just beginning to rise by the time I finish telling Norah about my sister. Naturally, she has so many questions since I've only briefly mentioned Caity before in our conversations about family. I'd spoken more of my Mam, but even that was minimal.

"Oh my god, Eamon," she says quietly. "I'm so sorry. This is awful. I bet your Mom is beside herself."

I nod solemnly. "I knew I'd have to go back to Ireland at some point, I just wasn't planning on it for a while, and certainly not for this reason. But I can't leave her alone to deal with Caity."

Although that's exactly what I did when I left, wasn't it? The thought chokes me with guilt.

"You're a good man, Eamon Kennedy," Norah says, brushing a strand of hair from my forehead, making the guilt fester even more. I don't feel like a good man right now. "I imagine your Mom feels so relieved to know you're going to be there."

"*We* are going to be there, Acushla," I correct her. "I'm sorry we have to cancel our getaway though. Maybe we can reschedule it soon."

"Are you kidding?" She scoffs. "You're taking me to Ireland with you. I know it's not for fun, but I get to be with you in *Ireland*."

She's trying so hard to be reserved for me, but I can see the absolute delight shining through her eyes and I never want to see it dull.

Pulling her into the crook of my arm, I kiss her temple and say, "A trip to my hometown to take care of my Ma and drug addict sister is not nearly as enticing as spending a week alone with you on the beach. Especially when I envisioned you naked or mostly naked for the week."

She lets out a snort of amusement. "Do I need to remind you that even though it's a beach, it is *December*? I'm not sure how often I'd be in a bikini."

"Ah, but the rental has a hot tub, remember? The things I want to do with you in any body of water…," I trail off.

She leans in to kiss me before saying, "Surely there's a body of water *somewhere* in Ireland that you could make good on your threats."

"December in Ireland is much colder than December in North Carolina, love. I wouldn't be able to do anything with you because my cock would shrivel up and die from the freezing water," I pout at her. "Surely you wouldn't wish that on me?"

"Hmm. Good point. Well, you'll have to find a way to make it up to me then," she says, then gets up and heads to the coffee pot.

I watch her for a minute. "Acushla?"

She looks over her shoulder at me. "Yeah?"

"I love you."

A small smile forms on her lips, "I love you too."

"Thank you for coming with me. I don't think I could go without you. For a multitude of reasons," I say earnestly.

She starts the coffee pot before padding back to the couch and sitting on my lap again.

"You don't need to thank me, Eamon. You aren't letting me face my demons alone, so why would I let you do the same?"

"You're so perfect," I say thickly. "How did I get so lucky?"

"Well, you *are* Irish…" she begins, but I quickly silence her with my mouth.

"I'm not a fucking leprechaun, you cheeky fire sprite," I growl against her lips.

Laughing, she pushes me away and climbs off of my lap. "Why don't you book our flight and I'll make us breakfast?"

I slap her arse playfully as she walks away, earning a shriek, then get to work booking our flight. I also need to cancel our reservation for the beach rental, but a thought occurs to me. I quickly send an email to the owner, explaining the situation and requesting to put the reservation in Teagan's name. As I'm typing out the email, my phone buzzes with an incoming text message on the table next to my laptop. I cringe when I see not only the name of the sender but the number of messages they've already sent. Of course, she'd know about Caity already.

Small towns don't have secrets.

Norah

The soonest, and cheapest, flight Eamon could find is a red eye leaving Raleigh at nine o'clock tonight with a three-hour layover at London Heathrow. I'm not complaining though. The flight to Dublin takes roughly eight hours, and we're already exhausted from our late night and early morning wake-up call. Sleeping on the flight should help with the jet lag. By the time we reach Eamon's hometown, it will be early afternoon.

"How are you feeling?" I ask him while sitting at the gate waiting to board. He's been understandably quiet since arriving at the airport.

"Other than completely bushed? I'm not sure," he admits with a grimace. "I'm anxious but excited to see my ma, though."

I bring our intertwined hands to my lips and kiss his knuckles. "She's going to be so happy. I'm proud of you for doing this."

231

Eamon's mouth tips up in a small smile, then falters.

"What's wrong?"

He sighs deeply. "There's a good chance that we'll run into my ex. Are you prepared for that?"

"Are you? I'm not worried about her." I shrug. "She made her choice, and you're mine now."

"Aye, that I am, Acushla," he agrees, pressing a kiss to my temple. "I'm not worried. Just apprehensive. I think it will be harder seeing Declan, to be honest."

I nod though I don't really know. I can't even imagine how I'd feel about being around an ex who cheated on me with my best friend, but I'd like to think if I was in another committed relationship with someone that I loved, I wouldn't care.

"Do you think they'll try to see you while you're home?"

Eamon leans his head back onto the chair. "It's hard to say. Since they live next door, it will be pretty hard to avoid them."

A voice calls out over the PA system before I can respond, announcing that our flight is now boarding. Once we've stowed our bags, we settle into our seats and mindlessly watch the flight attendant instruct us what to do in case of an emergency as the plane is taxiing towards the runway. It's not long before we're in the sky, jetting towards the Green Isle. I should be trying to sleep, but I'm jittery with excitement. I can't wait to be in Ireland again, even if the circumstances are horrid. For me, a bad day in Ireland beats a good day anywhere else.

Eamon places a hand on my knee, squeezing gently. "You're about to fidget out of your seat. Are you nervous?"

"No." I laugh. "I'm excited. I realize that sounds pretty awful considering the reason for going, but I can't help it. I've been waiting so long to go back. I know you don't love it like I do, so I'll try to contain my excitement."

"Norah," he says, angling his body towards mine as much as the small seats will allow. "It's fine. Really. I may not appreciate it the same as you, but I *do* love Ireland. It's my home. What I love most though is that I get to take you with me. When we were doing dishes at Paddy's that night and you were going on about your trip, I could picture you there, and all I wanted at that moment was to experience it with you. To watch your face as you immerse yourself in my world. It's not a real holiday, what with Caity and all, but I promise I will make time for us to explore properly."

He said once that I was perfect, but he's wrong. It's not me. It's him. Eamon is everything good in the world. The way he loves me is unlike anything I've ever experienced. "As much as I want that," I say, laying my hand on top of his, "you need to focus on your Mom and sister. I'll be there to help out in whatever way you need. I knew this wasn't going to be a vacation."

"How about this," he bargains. "We'll just take one day at a time, yeah? Today, or tonight rather, let's try to rest. Tomorrow is going to be a very long day."

"Deal," I agree with a smile before resting my head on his shoulder.

By some miracle, we both managed to sleep a good portion of the flight. When the plane lands in Dublin, it's chilly, but the sun is shining brightly. Eamon is quiet as we navigate the airport and go through customs. His shoulders are tense, and his anxiety is radiating off of him, but he seems to be handling it well as long as he has a task to focus on. It's similar to watching him on the soccer field. The pressure motivates him and keeps him grounded.

We gather our luggage and head towards the rental car area. His Mom offered to pick us up, but he insisted on getting a separate car. I think part of him just doesn't want the first reunion with his mother in four years to be in an airport. Once we have the key to the rental, Eamon loads our suitcases in the back and we climb in. It takes him a minute to reacquaint himself with driving a European car, but as he tells me, it's like riding a bike. Once you learn, you don't unlearn it.

"Alright, love," he says. "Mam said she would be at home for a shower by the time we reach Kilkenny, so we'll head there after our first stop— breakfast."

"Yes, please," I yawn. "And coffee. Lots of coffee."

"Yer in Ireland now, Acushla. It's tea you'll be having." His accent seems to be thicker now that he's back on his home turf, and it's sexy as hell.

"Listen, Kennedy. I don't care what country I'm in. Coffee will always come first," I say, glaring playfully at him. "And I know for a fact that I can get coffee in Ireland."

Eamon gapes at me in mock horror. "That's sacrilege right there. You better not let my mam hear you talk like that."

I roll my eyes as I reach up to tighten my ponytail. "Just keep your eyes on the road, mister."

He laughs loudly. "Are you nervous, Norah? Worried I'll drive us right off the M50?"

"Oh, c'mon. You can't tell me that this isn't completely insane compared to the States! I'm on the verge of having a panic attack. Are there even any traffic laws here?"

"Alright, I'll admit it's a little more...complex than back in North Carolina, but there is a method to the madness," he says soothingly.

"And that method is what? Try not to die?"

Eamon laughs again and reaches to grab my hand. I snatch it away from him. "Oh no, both hands on the wheel."

"Calm down, Grady. I'm not going to get us killed. Why would I drag you all the way across the Atlantic just to end us as soon as we land?" he asks, purposefully grabbing my hand and not letting go. "Trust me, Norah."

I hesitate before taking a deep breath. "Okay, you're right. I'm sorry. I do trust you."

"Good. Now, just relax and take in the sights."

So that's what I did. Rather than watching the highway fill with speeding cars, I soak in my surroundings. The excitement I felt earlier floods back in, overshadowing the anxiety I was feeling over our *impending doom.* I'm in Ireland again, and it's just as beautiful as I remember. Everything is so *green.* So alive. The architecture of the buildings never ceases to amaze me and the brightly colored doors of the dwellings lining the streets make the smile on my face grow. I think I'll paint my front door when we get home.

Occasionally, Eamon points out something that was a part of his childhood. A football field where he played regular tournaments during his school days. A restaurant his family loved. A historical site that the history teacher in him just has to share, recounting all of the stories that have circulated through the ages. I learn a little more about him with each memory he relives for me. It's a surprisingly intimate experience. My first time in Ireland was incredible, but being here with Eamon, knowing how much I love him, makes it all the sweeter.

I think back to my first conversation with Paddy after discovering O'Nelly's. "I'm going to find my husband in Ireland," I'd told him. I'm sure I sounded both ignorant and arrogant. But now, I turn to look at Eamon, admiring his profile, and wonder if maybe that dream will become a reality.

Eventually, we turn down a narrow street lined with a variety of shops and cafes. Eamon pulls into the small parking lot of a quaint place called *Sealed With A Quiche*.

"That's clever," I remark, pointing at the name.

"Aye, and if I remember correctly, their quiche is quite good. Shall we?" he asks, turning to face me.

Stepping out of the car, we make our way to the door. Eamon holds it open for me and ushers me in with a hand on the small of my back. The inside of the cafe is just as cute as the name with antique quiche pans lining the pale yellow walls, painted in a rainbow of colors. There's an array of eclectic cafe tables scattered around the room in no particular pattern. Each one is adorned with a small teapot filled with flowers, a sugar bowl, and a milk carafe all nestled on a tray in the center.

"Mornin', loves!" a tall older woman calls as she walks through a swinging door carrying a tray of baked goods. "Grab yourselves a table. I'll be right over."

I turn to Eamon. "This place is adorable! Have you been here often?"

"Only a few times when I had a match up here," he says, leading me to a table near the front window.

I sit on the edge of my seat and lean in. "Thank you for bringing me here."

His mouth tips up on one side in response.

"Alright, yous, thanks a million for waitin' on me," the lady from behind the counter interrupts as she walks towards our table. "I'm Moira. Can I start ya a cuppa?"

"Aye, grand," Eamon answers. "And a coffee for you, Acushla?"

"Yes, please," I say with a smile.

"Ach, an American!" Moira says knowingly. "Is it your first time visiting, love?"

"No, I've been one other time, but it's been several years."

"Just couldn't stay away, could ya?" Moira asks with a wink.

"Definitely not. It's lovely here. This place is amazing, by the way," I gush. "I love the decor."

She beams. "That's kind of ya. Now, how do you take your coffee, love? Milk and sugar?"

"That would be great, thank you."

"Be back in a tick!" Moira promises, turning back towards the swinging door.

I turn my attention back to Eamon, finding him watching me with a bemused expression. "What?"

"Ireland suits you," he says with a shrug, picking up a menu.

I pick up my own menu and ask, "You can tell that just in the short time we've been here?"

"Aye."

I wait for him to continue, but he's looking back at the menu. "That's it? No explanation?"

Eamon strokes his chin in mock contemplation. "For starters, your whole face has been lit up like a firework since we got here. You're practically glowing."

"I'm not sure if that's a good thing or not, considering the circumstances. Maybe I should tone it down a bit," I say apologetically, biting my bottom lip.

Eamon's eyes zero in on my mouth. "No. I love seeing this side of you. You're always beautiful, but seeing you here in my home country? Breathtaking. And quit biting that lip. It's giving me impure thoughts."

I gasp. "Eamon Kennedy, behave. We're in public!"

He chuckles, leaning closer. "I didn't say I was going to act on those thoughts...yet."

Moira comes bustling back to our table, placing a saucer in front of each of us. She puts a French Press full of dark coffee and pours cream into the milk carafe in front of me before setting a pot of hot tea in front of Eamon.

"Here you are, loves. Have you decided on food, or do you need a minute?"

Eamon looks at me expectantly. "After you."

"I can't decide. It all sounds wonderful," I say. "What's your favorite, Moira?"

"Nobody's ever asked me that!" She taps her ink pen on her chin. "The smoked bacon and leek quiche is my go-to. With a side of breakfast mushrooms, of course."

"I'll have that, please! With a brown scone," I add quickly. There's no way my first meal in Ireland isn't going to include a brown scone.

"Good, lass. And for you, lad?"

"Full breakfast for me, Moira. I'll have a scone as well. It's been a while."

"You're Irish, young fella, how long could it have been?" Moira raises a brow.

"Ah, this is my first time back in several years. I've been in the States going to university and playing football," he tells her.

She nods towards me. "That where you met this one?"

"Aye, she challenged me to a drinking contest," he says, winking at me. "The black stuff too."

"Catch yourself on!" Moira laughs, looking at me with wide eyes. "And did you win, lass?"

I chuckle in response. "The pub owner interrupted before we could finish, but I didn't feel like a winner the next morning. Though I'd say Eamon was a pretty good prize."

"Ach, too right! Well, welcome back, both of you. I'll go get yer food," Moira says, turning and heading back to the kitchen.

"I'm a prize, am I?" Eamon asks, grinning slyly.

I study him for a long minute before responding, just to mess with him. Finally, I nod slowly. "Definitely."

We eat our breakfast and say goodbye to Moira before climbing back in the rental to head towards Kilkenny. The majority of the drive is spent in companionable silence, observing the landscape with the occasional remark on something that catches my eye.

"I promise I'll take you on the longer, more scenic, route before we head back to the States. I'm anxious to see my Mam. I knew I missed her, but now that we're so close, I just want to get there," he says longingly.

Reaching across the console for his hand, I wind our fingers together. "You don't have to explain, Eamon. If my Mom were still alive, I'd be the same way."

"Will it be hard for you? Being around me and Ma?"

"I don't think so," I admit. "I think, if anything, I'll probably fall more in love with you seeing the two of you together."

Eamon glances at me curiously. "No complaints here. I'm always open to finding more ways to win your heart."

In an attempt to infuse a little laughter into the day, I say, "If you keep being sweet like this, we're going to have to pull this car over and christen it, Kennedy."

He turns his head so sharply that the car swerves into the other lane. I shriek and grab the handle above the window. "Christ, Norah," Eamon barks out. "You can't say that to a man while he's driving!"

I giggle and wag my eyebrows at him. "Why do you think I waited until there were no other cars around before teasing you?"

"You're trouble, woman," he says, reaching over and squeezing my thigh roughly.

"Gah! Stop!" I squeak as he laughs. "I surrender! I surrender!"

"That's what I thought." He shakes his head and says, "Thank you for that. I needed the laugh today."

Chapter Thirty-One

Norah

Kilkenny is beautiful and just as magical as all of the pictures showed. There are light displays and Christmas decorations stationed all over the city. Street lamps are wrapped in lights and hold decorative wreaths while door frames are lined with garlands or bows. I had forgotten about the holiday in the midst of getting ready for the trip. This time of year always makes me a little melancholy. Even though my friends welcome me into their homes, it just isn't the same without my Mom.

"Do you think we'll still be here for Christmas?" I ask Eamon.

He releases a breath before answering, "I don't honestly know, love. If we are, I'm sorry."

"What on earth are you sorry for?"

"Well," he begins, "we didn't talk about it, but don't you have traditions or plans you don't want to miss out on?"

"Not really. I usually just go to Charlie's." I shrug. "I'm excited to be spending Christmas with you. And your Mom. And hopefully your sister." Eamon doesn't respond right away, so I reach across the console for his hand. "Hey, you okay?"

He laces our fingers together and squeezes my hand. "Aye. Sorry. I was just thinking about the last Christmas I spent with Mam. Caity was actually home and sober for that one. It was one of the more pleasant holidays since losing Da."

"Hopefully this time will be just as good," I offer.

"It will be," he says, turning his head and smiling at me. "You're here. I can't imagine anything better than spending it with you and my family."

Eamon navigates through his hometown with ease, remembering every road like he never left. Eventually, he turns onto a quiet street lined with quaint houses, all similar in size and style. They're each two stories high with brown brick covering the lower level of the house and white siding on the upper level. The second-floor exterior boasts twin windows with queen post gables crowning them. Each home has a small yard in the front, some landscaped with precision while others are littered with children's toys or bicycles. We reach the end of the cul-de-sac and pull into the driveway of the second house on the right. The yard is tidy, and there are flower boxes nestled below the bay windows flanking the front door, which has a simple Christmas wreath hanging from a hook.

After putting the car in park, Eamon turns off the ignition but doesn't move. When I look over, his hands are gripping the steering wheel tightly while he hangs his head, eyes closed. My heart aches for him, so I reach over and stroke the back of his head.

"Hey," I say softly. "Babe, talk to me."

"I'm okay, love," he whispers. "I just need a minute."

"I know. This is big. But I'm here. You're not doing this alone," I promise him.

"Thank you," he says hoarsely before leaning across the console to place a gentle kiss on my lips. "I love you."

"I love you, too," I answer, resting my forehead against his. "Are you ready to go in now?"

"Aye," he nods. "Let's do this. I'm surprised Mam hasn't come tearing out the door already."

I glance towards the front of the house, nerves fluttering in my stomach. This trip isn't even remotely about me, but I'm meeting his Mom for the first time. This is big.

"She'll love you, Acushla. Don't worry," Eamon assures me, sensing my hesitation. "C'mon, we're in this together now."

We step out of the car and Eamon rounds the front to grasp my hand, squeezing my fingers reassuringly. Before we hit the front steps, the door flies open and a curvy middle-aged woman with curly copper hair rushes out. She freezes on the top step, a hand immediately going to her chest, while tears fill her eyes and her bottom lip quivers.

"Eamon, my boy..." is all she manages to get out before breaking into a sob and lunging for him. She throws her arms around his neck, holding him tightly as she openly weeps.

Wrapping his arms around her waist, he pulls her close and whispers, "Hiya, Mam."

Tears escape my eyes watching the man I love reunite with the woman who brought him into this world. The tender way he holds her and lets her cry all over him is endearing, to say the least, and a small part of my heart cracks, missing my own mother. What I wouldn't give to hug her again.

When they finally pull apart, his Mom cups his tear-streaked face and absorbs every detail. "Ach, son, you've grown even more handsome. I didn't think that was possible. You look so much like your Da."

Her lip quivers again, and Eamon's brow furrows in sadness. He lets out a ragged breath and glances at me, drawing his Mom's attention. She pulls back, wiping her eyes, and fixates on me.

"Oh!" she exclaims. "You must be Norah!"

I smile and step forward, extending my hand. "It's an honor to meet you, Mrs. Kennedy. I'm so sorry it's not under better circumstances."

Mrs. Kennedy grabs my hand, abruptly pulling me into a hug. "Please, call me Rosie. And thank you, love."

I'm stunned for a moment, absorbing the motherly affection that I've gone so long without. I've had numerous hugs from friends and Eamon, but there's nothing like a mother's hug. The way their arms are gentle but full of strength, love, and security. I almost let loose a sob of my own at the contact.

I lean back, looking into eyes so similar to Eamon's it's shocking. "Thank me? What for?"

"For making my boy so happy and bringing him home to me for a short while. You'll never know how much that means to me."

"I can't take credit for bringing him home, but I'm happy to be here with him," I tell her.

Rosie cups my cheek and studies my face before saying, "Aye, I doubt he would have been so willing to come if you weren't with him. He wasn't stretching the truth when he said you were beautiful. It's no wonder he doesn't want to leave your side."

I blush, in response to the compliment and look to Eamon. Winking at me, he steps towards us and slides an arm around my waist. When he kisses my temple, I can't help but melt into him a little bit.

"Yer not completely wrong, Mam," he interjects. "I would have come regardless, but having Norah with me feels right."

His mother presses her fingers to her mouth as her eyes fill with tears again. "Ach, enough of my blubbering. Come inside. I'll make us a cuppa."

We follow Rosie through the door, stepping into a small entryway connected to a staircase leading to the second floor. To my right is a dining room outfitted with a simple rectangular table and four matching chairs, a small buffet up against the far wall with a painting of a seaside above it. To my left is a small sitting room that is the epitome of cozy with a loveseat sitting in front of the bay window and facing an oval coffee table and two recliners. An old wood-burning fireplace takes up the adjacent wall, and the mantle is adorned with a garland, long tapered candles, and various picture frames.

"Are you hungry, Eamon, love? Norah? Shall I make you a bite to eat?"

CHAPTER THIRTY-ONE

Rosie asks.

Eamon looks at me, and I shake my head. "No, Ma," he says, "we're grand. We ate in Dublin before we set off."

"Did ye get enough? It would be no trouble at all," she offers.

I place a hand on her elbow. "Really, Mrs. Kennedy. We're fine. There's no need to do any extra work."

She playfully shakes a finger at me. "What did I tell ya about calling me Rosie? There will be no *Mrs. Kennedy* as long as you're taking good care of my boy."

"Sorry. *Rosie*," I say pointedly, grinning at her. "Just tea would be lovely."

"Grand! I'll be right back. Eamon, would you give Norah the tour? I've set your room up with fresh sheets and all…" She hesitates. "I don't mean to be sticking my nose where it doesn't belong, but I assumed you'd be sharing a room. I can make up Caity's if need be…"

"One room is fine, Mam," Eamon says, clearing his throat nervously, his cheeks coloring slightly.

Rosie's cheeks turn a darker shade of red. "Right, I'll just go wet the tea." She scurries down the hall towards what I assume is the kitchen.

"Well," I begin, eyeing Eamon, "that wasn't awkward at all. If she's uncomfortable with us sharing, I don't mind moving to a separate room."

"No," he says quickly. "That doesn't bother her. She and Da weren't married before they…uh…right. It's just a topic that can be a bit tricky talking about with your Mam while your girlfriend is standing there."

I nod in understanding. "It's awkward being the girlfriend while your boyfriend discusses sleeping arrangements with his mother. I don't want her to think I'm some sort of hussy!"

Eamon rolls his eyes and grabs my hand. "C'mon, Acushla. Let's go check out the den of iniquity."

Leading me up the staircase, we turn left at the landing. It's a short hallway with two doors on either side. The walls are covered in a subtle, floral wallpaper and various paintings and photographs.

"Right, so, this first door," he says, pointing to the right, "is the jacks. Shower, all that. Across from it is Caity's room. My room is the last on the left, and across from that is the office. Mam's room is back on the other side of the stairs."

I follow him to the last door on the left, suddenly feeling butterflies in my stomach. We've shared much more than a bed, but something about being in the room he grew up in, in his mother's house, makes me feel like a teenager sneaking into a boy's room.

He stops in front of the door and crosses his arms. "There are a few rules you must know before entering this room, Grady."

I raise an eyebrow at him. "Is that right, Kennedy?"

"Aye," he begins with a quick nod of his head. "First, thou shalt not laugh at anything that may or may not still be hanging on the walls or sitting on the shelves. I told her to turn this into a guest room, but she refuses to change anything about it. Second, thou shalt not rummage through the closets and drawers, for fear of being subjected to twenty-plus-year-old jumpers that should have been tossed in the bin ages ago. And last…" He steps closer and leans down to kiss the space between my neck and shoulder before murmuring in my ear, "Thou shalt not wear any clothing when in my bed."

I shiver and croak out, "Why not?"

"Because I've been fantasizing about having you naked in this bed since I knew we were staying here," he says, nibbling my earlobe.

"That's a little weird," I breathe out, pressing my body closer to his.

Eamon chuckles and slips his hands under my sweater, gripping my waist. "I want you in every part of my life. I can't go back in time and make you a part of my past, but we can pretend we're teenagers, and I can fuck you in my bed."

"Hmm, I didn't know that being back in Ireland would bring out the dirty talk. I'm not sad about it." I hook my fingers through the belt loops of his jeans and pull him closer.

"Eamon, love, the tea is ready!" Rosie calls up the stairs, effectively putting an end to our heated moment.

He growls in frustration, resting his forehead on my shoulder.

"What?" I giggle. "Did you really think making tea would take that long?"

244

He pinches my side, causing me to squeak in protest. "No, but a man can dream, can't he? This isn't over, Acushla."

I kiss his cheek before saying, "I'd be disappointed if it was. Now, come on. You've kept your mother waiting for years. Let's not make her wait any longer."

We lumber down the stairs and back into the sitting room where Rosie is perched in an armchair, pouring steaming tea into mugs.

"Thanks, Mam," Eamon mutters, pressing a kiss to her cheek before taking a seat on the sofa next to me. After doctoring our mugs and getting settled, he turns his attention to his Mom. "How's Caity?"

Rosie lets out a heavy sigh, her eyes flooding with tears. "She's stable but still comatose. They talked about waking her up soon if the swelling in her brain goes down."

He nods absently. "Has the prognosis changed at all, then? Are her chances of going without brain damage any better?"

She shakes her head in defeat. "It's anyone's guess at this point. Oh, Eamon. Where did I go wrong with her?"

"Mam, stop," he urges. "I already told ya; you didn't do anything wrong. Caity has been difficult most of her life, and it only got worse after Da passed. She always hung with the wrong crowd, and there's not a thing you could have done to stop her, short of sending her off to a nunnery. I doubt even that would have helped. She would have taken it as a personal challenge to see how much shite she could stir up."

"Does that not reflect on how she was brought up, then?"

"Course not. Did you raise me any differently than you raised her?" Eamon challenges.

Rosie shrugs and wipes at her eyes. "I like to think your Da and I showed you both the same love and support and discipline."

"You did, Ma. That's what I'm saying. Caity has always been headstrong, and there's not a soul in this world that can make her do what she doesn't want to do. That's just her personality. She knows right from wrong though."

"He's right, Rosie," I interject. "Anyone can see what an amazing mother you are. Eamon is testimony to that. He's thoughtful and caring and selfless, but he's also the human being he is because he makes the choice every day to be that way. Some behaviors are just a part of who we are, and we have to make the conscious decision to rise above them and do good."

Rosie gives me a watery smile. "Ach, you're right. Of course, you are. All I ever wanted for her was a good life. It's just so hard as a mother to see your child struggle and suffer. You'll understand one day."

Eamon and I glance at each other. Crimson creeps over his cheeks and his eyes sparkle. I'm not ready for kids yet, but for a split second, I see a flash of what our future could be and the idea is thrilling.

"Heavens! What was I thinking? I am so sorry, to the two of ya. Nobody likes a Mam that starts harping about grandchildren. I wasn't insinuating that you two…"

"It's grand, Ma," Eamon reassures her. "No harm done. Right, Acushla?" He winks at me, and I grin back.

"Right," I confirm. "I wasn't under that impression at all."

Rosie glances back and forth between us, then starts crying again. "Ach. I'm a weepy mess this morning, aren't I? Your Da called me that before we were married."

"He did? I had no idea," he murmurs, grief clouding his eyes. I reach for his hand and give it a small squeeze.

"Aye. And your Grandda called your granny that as well," she says, studying my hand on Eamon's. "It suits you, dear."

I smile shyly, but inside, I'm beaming.

Chapter Thirty-Two

Eamon

The hospital is quiet when we arrive. After checking in at the nurses' station, Mam leads us down the corridor to the last room on our left, a sense of dread flooding my mind. As if reading my thoughts, she turns and fixes her eyes on me.

"She won't look how you last saw her. She's barely more than skin and bones. And the bruising on her arms..." Mam shudders.

I take a deep breath, steeling myself to see my baby sister. Norah squeezes my hand, giving me a small reassuring smile. Words cannot express how thankful I am that she's here. As long as she's by my side, I feel like I can be strong enough to face whatever comes our way. Her constant encouragement strengthens my resolve and I square my shoulders before following my Mam into the room.

The lights are low, but the curtains are pulled back, letting in the morning sunlight. Mam hurries to Caity's bedside, taking her hand and kissing her forehead. I'm barely through the door, and I can see how frail she is from here.

"Caity, love," she whispers. "You'll never guess who's here to see you. Your brother, Eamon, has come home at last. And he's brought a lass with him."

I slowly approach my sister, sucking in a sharp breath once I see her fully. Her face is gaunt with dark circles under her closed eyes, and her dark hair, the same color as mine and our Da's, is brittle and lifeless. She looks ages older than her meager twenty-one years. Her arms are thin and scattered with bruises and track marks, and there's dirt caked under her fingernails. A wave of sorrow washes over me, and I can't stop the tears that stream silently down my face. I round the end of the bed to sit on the opposite side. Like our mother, I press a kiss to her forehead.

"Ach, Caity Bug. What did you get yourself into?" I mutter.

Guilt floods me. I should have never left Ireland. I should have been strong enough to stay here for my family. I could have ignored Rhiannan and Declan and moved to my own flat if I couldn't handle being next door. Instead, I fled to the States like a coward, thinking only about myself, not once considering how it could hurt those I left behind. I look over at my Mam, whose eyes are glued to my sister.

"Mam," I choke out, furiously blinking away the tears. "I'm so sorry. I should have stayed here. I could have helped watch after Caity. I could have been here for you. *I should have stayed.*"

"Eamon, love, no," she rushes out, reaching across the bed to grip my arm. "You're not to blame for this. You had to do what was right for you. Make a life for yourself. You followed your heart, and that's an honorable thing."

I scoff. "No, I was a selfish eejit that couldn't stomach the idea of being around my cheating girlfriend and best mate. I ran away."

Standing abruptly, I lace my fingers behind my head and stare out the window. All I see is my shame. Norah sidles up next to me, and when she places a calming hand on my arm, I shrug it off, disgusted with myself. Maybe that's cold of me, but I don't deserve any sort of comfort right now.

"Ach, don't be daft," my mother chastises me. "Were you not just telling me that Caity made her own decisions and there's nothing I could have done about it? You being here wouldn't have changed a thing for her."

I release a heavy breath and hang my head. "Aye, that may be, but you shouldn't have been dealing with it alone, Mam. I failed you."

She stands and strides around the bed to meet me by the window. I don't resist when she places her hands on either side of my face, forcing me to look at her.

"Oh, my lovely boy. You've not failed me. And I haven't been alone. You're not the only strapping young lad in Kilkenny, you know."

One corner of my mouth lifts in a humorless smile. "That's not the point. With Da gone, I'm *supposed* to be the *strapping young lad* that takes care of you."

"Hush," she orders. "I'll not hear another word about it. You understand me?"

I close my eyes and pinch the bridge of my nose. Before I can argue further, there's a quiet knock at the door. We all turn to see a tall, thin man with snow-white hair walk in.

"Hello there, Mrs. Kennedy," the older gentleman greets my mother warmly.

To my surprise and utter confusion, her cheeks flush and she becomes absolutely flustered.

"Oh, Dr. Colm, good morning," she says nervously. "This is my son, Eamon, and his lass, Norah. They've come from the States to visit Caity."

Dr. Colm extends a hand in my direction and I grip it, shaking firmly.

"Nice to meet you, young man. It's good of you to make the journey. I'm sure it brings your mother comfort," he says.

"Aye, hello, Doctor Colm," I say, then gesture a hand to Norah. "This is my lass, as Mam said. Norah Grady."

She smiles, but her posture is stiff and hesitant. I know my reaction earlier is responsible for that and I silently vow to make it up to her as soon as possible.

"Hi, Dr. Colm," Norah says politely, shaking his hand quickly.

249

"Pleasure, Miss Grady. I can see why the lad was drawn to America," he says with a wink.

"Oh," she giggles. "Thank you, but I can't take credit for that. Eamon has been in the States for a while. We only just met a few months ago."

"Remember," Mam states, "Eamon went to the States on a football scholarship."

"Oh yes, that's right. Your mother told me all about that just the other day. How was the season for you?"

As much as I'd love to give this man my entire life story, that's not why I'm here. I want to know about my sister's condition. At the risk of sounding like a major wanker, I hold up a hand.

"It was grand, thanks. But, if you don't mind, Dr. Colm, could you please update me on Caity? Mam filled me in, but I'd like to hear from you."

The doctor looks taken aback but recovers with patience I'm sure he's earned over the years dealing with anxious family members.

"Of course, lad," he says apologetically. "That is, after all, why I'm here. I just got the results from her latest scan. Due to restricted oxygen from her overdose, she has what we call hypoxic brain damage. The good news is that this is the less severe form of brain damage caused by drug overdose. There isn't any sign of stroke or bleeding, but she does still have some swelling. Her recovery will depend on that swelling going down. The most rapid recovery is usually within the first six months, but we won't know the long-term outcome until about a year. That being said, right now, we are going to work on reducing that swelling with a respirator and IV treatments. I'm hopeful that because the damage isn't as severe as we first thought, she'll respond positively. I know that you're all anxious to have her awake and alert, but we'll be keeping her in a medically induced coma to help reduce that swelling as well."

"Excuse me, Dr. Colm?" Norah interjects. "But can you tell me how the induced coma will help? I think I understand, but I'd like to know how the process works. If you don't mind."

He smiles kindly at her. "Not at all, Miss Grady. Think of it as a vehicle that's overheating. If you keep the motor running, it's just going to make the condition worse and, ultimately, kill the engine. The brain is similar. If we were to wake Caity up and try to force her to interact, it would essentially send her brain into overdrive, exacerbating the swelling and injury. Placing her in a comatose state allows the brain to rest and *charge* if you will. Does that help?"

"Yes, thank you," she says with a nod.

I sit down on the edge of Caity's bed, mind reeling. The medical world has never really interested me before, but I won't deny how fascinating it is to learn about the brain.

"So," I say, resting my elbows on my knees, "let's say that you're able to reduce the swelling. What does her prognosis look like?"

"It's difficult to say at this time," he says, folding his arms across his chest. "Ideally, when the swelling goes down, we can slowly bring her out of the comatose state. Then we'll be able to further assess her condition. We will, of course, be doing regular scans to check the status and to determine if there is any underlying damage not showing up currently. Let's say that over the course of a couple of weeks, the swelling has reduced enough to wake Caity up, she would be looking at extensive physical and occupational therapy. It's possible that she could have some amnesia, either short-term or long-term, I can't say. Best case scenario, in six months, she'll be well on her way to a mostly full recovery. Worst case scenario, she is severely disabled, requiring full-time aid. Or she could fall somewhere in between—mentally stable, but years spent recovering her motor skills."

My mother places a trembling hand over her mouth, squeezing her eyes shut. "My poor, sweet Caity Bug."

I blow out a deep breath and ask, "So, it's a waiting game for right now, correct?"

Dr. Colm nods, "That's correct, lad. I wish I could give you a definite outcome, but unfortunately, the human brain is quite complex. Is there anything else I can do for you or any other questions I can answer?"

"I have one more," Norah says quietly. "Is it helpful to talk to her while she's in the coma? I've heard stories about loved ones reading or talking to them frequently, but I'm not sure if those are accurate. I guess I just wonder if talking would cause the brain to be more active or if would it be soothing. I'm not sure if that even makes sense."

"That's a very insightful question, lass," he tells her. "I don't think it would be harmful to her to have someone sit and read or talk to her a couple of times a day. I wouldn't recommend round the clock, of course, but a couple of hours a day would be just fine."

Mam gives Norah a small smile of gratitude. "I hadn't even thought of that. Thank the good Lord for you, love."

Dr. Colm smiles at my Mam and places a comforting hand on her arm. "If there's anything you need, please don't hesitate to reach out. I'm on call for the next few days, so I'll be here. You have my mobile number, so just give us a ring if you think of something. If I don't answer, just leave a message and I'll ring you back."

She blushes deeply and says, "Thanks a million, Dr. Colm."

I look back and forth between them. She's acting odd, and he's borderline unprofessional. I make a mental note to discuss this with her later.

"You're free to stay and visit as long as you like. The nursing staff will be making their rounds frequently, and I'll pop back in this evening," Dr. Colm says before leaving the room.

"Ach, he's just the nicest man. I'm so thankful that our Caity has such good care here," Mam says absently.

"He does seem very kind," Norah says, standing up from the chair she's been in. "I think I'm going to go get a cup of coffee. Rosie, can I get you anything?"

"Bless you. No, I'm fine for the moment."

"Eamon, what about you?" she asks cautiously like she's afraid I'll snap again. I could kick myself for being such an arse to her a moment ago.

"No, I'm okay," I say. "I'll come with you."

She holds up her hand to stop me. "No, it's fine. Stay here with your Mom. I'm sure you have some things to discuss without me lurking around."

"Acushla…" I protest.

"Really." She forces a smile at me. "I don't mind. It will do me good to stretch my legs. I'll be fine. I have my phone on me, so if either of you

252

change your mind or think of something you need, let me know."

Norah walks past me, and I reach out to grab her hand, giving it a squeeze in apology. When she looks up at me, I see pain and wariness in her eyes, and I hate myself a little more.

Norah

I take my time finding the cafeteria. I'm a little ashamed to admit that Eamon's behavior earlier rattled me, but I chastise myself for being so selfish. This is a stressful situation and he's clearly fighting an internal battle. I'll give him space for today, stay quiet, and blend into the surroundings. I'll be the errand girl, doing whatever I can to make life easier for him and Rosie. Maybe I'll persuade both of them to get out tomorrow for some fresh air. Having spent so much time with my Mom during her chemo and radiation treatments, I know all too well what it feels like to be cooped up in a cold, stale hospital room for hours upon hours.

I'm just passing the reception area where a girl around my age is standing at the desk. I don't mean to eavesdrop, but when I hear her mention Caity's name, I halt my steps.

"Hi, I'm here to visit Caity Kennedy. She's in the intensive care unit," the girl states. "I'm a friend of the family."

"As I mentioned yesterday, lass…" the kind-looking older lady begins and a niggling in my brain urges me to step forward.

"I'm so sorry to interrupt and for eavesdropping, but I just came from Caity Kennedy's room. Her mother and brother are still up there now."

The girl whirls around, long black hair swishing with the movement. "Eamon is here?"

"Yes, we just arrived earlier this morning. I'm Norah, his girlfriend," I say, extending my hand in greeting, but she doesn't reciprocate.

She does, however, look me up and down, eyes skeptical. "His girlfriend?" she asks in disbelief. "You're American."

"Last time I checked," I say with a bemused expression. I have a sneaking suspicion I know exactly who this is, but I ask, "I'm sorry, what did you say your name was?"

The girl straightens and sneers, "I didn't. I'm Rhiannan. Eamon and I have...*history.*"

Knew it.

It takes all of my self-control to keep from scoffing at her. Instead, I narrow my eyes slightly before saying, "Oh, I know all about your *history.* He's told me *so much* about you. Is Declan with you or at home with your kiddo?"

Rhiannan physically jerks her head back in shock. "That's not really any of your business. I came to visit Caity, but now that I know Eamon is here, I think it'll be nice to catch up with him."

The nerve of this bitch. Channeling my inner Myra, I say, "Oh, I'm sorry. Eamon and Rosie requested no more visitors today. But I'll be sure to tell them you stopped by. It was a *pleasure* meeting you."

Rhiannan clenches her fists at her side and glares at me before turning and storming through the sliding doors leading to the parking lot. I blow out a shaky breath and decide that I don't want coffee after all.

"Miss," the lady at the desk says softly, startling me.

I'd forgotten she was there. I smile sheepishly. "I'm sorry. I didn't mean to cause a scene."

The lady, Orla, according to her name tag, laughs, "Quite the opposite actually. You handled that well. This isn't the first time that young lady has come in trying to see Miss Kennedy. As she isn't family, we can't allow her up there without a family member escorting her. She didn't react in a friendly manner the last time either, so thank you for taking the brunt of it."

My brow furrows in confusion. "She still came back even though she knows she can't go up? Why?"

"I think she's hoping she'll find someone different at the desk and try to talk her way up. Silly lass. I've worked at this desk for the last twenty years. It's unlikely anyone but myself will be present," Orla says, rolling her eyes.

"That's ridiculous," I reply. "I'm sorry you've had to endure that. I feel

254

like I might have overstepped a little, but I can't imagine Eamon would be happy to have her waltz up there unannounced."

"Between you and me, you're much prettier anyway," Orla winks. "'Course, when I was a young wan, my hair was the same red as yours, so I might be a wee bit biased."

I grin at the silver-haired woman and say, "Well then I have something to look forward to in the future! Hopefully, my hair looks like yours!"

"Ach, you flatter me," she coos, waving a hand. "Have that fella of yours stop at the desk on his way out so I can see the young man that snagged such a catch. I imagine he's quite the looker."

I nod my head vigorously in agreement. "He is definitely that! I'll make sure to stop by with him when we leave."

Saying goodbye to Orla, I make my way back to Caity's room hoping Rosie and Eamon won't be upset at me for turning Rhiannan away. I was mostly looking out for them, but selfishly, I don't think I could have handled being in the same room as the two of them right now. With Eamon's behavior earlier and Rhiannan's beauty, I'm already feeling insecure. It's hard not to when you're standing next to the woman your boyfriend had planned on marrying and she looks like a supermodel. I'm still mulling it over when I walk back into the room.

"Did you not find any coffee?" Eamon's deep voice asks, shaking me from my thoughts.

"What? Oh, I didn't make it that far," I pause before continuing. "I, uh, ran into Rhiannan at the reception desk in the lobby..."

Eamon goes wholly still. "She was here? Did you talk to her?"

"I overheard her asking to visit Caity. Thinking she might have been a friend, I introduced myself."

I tell them everything in full, feeling slightly embarrassed. "I'm sorry if that was out of line. I should have called up here first."

Rosie laughs delightedly. "No, love. You did the right thing. Had it been just me up here, I probably would have allowed it, but with Eamon here, I doubt that would have been a pleasant visit. The day she and Declan moved to a new neighborhood was a day I'll always cherish."

Eamon's head whips towards his mother. "They moved out? When?"

Rosie waves a hand, "Ach, it was a couple of years ago. I didn't bring it up because I didn't think you'd want to hear anything about them."

Eamon just nods, then clears his throat nervously, "I suppose I'll have to have a conversation with her at some point while I'm here."

"Why?" I ask incredulously. "If you don't want to see her, you're not obligated to talk to her."

He sighs heavily and rakes his fingers through his hair, refusing to meet my eyes. Rosie, sensing the tension in the air, decides that she'd like some tea after all. Once the door closes behind her, he leans back in the chair, extending his legs out in front of him.

"I know you won't like it," he says, "but now that she knows I'm here, she's just going to keep coming around until I talk to her. I'd like to get it over with sooner rather than later."

I shake my head angrily and plant my hands on my hips. "It's not about me liking it or not, Eamon. How do you know she'll keep coming around? And why do you have to talk to her?"

"I just know how she is. After we ended things, she kept trying to get me to take her back. She didn't relent until I moved. And then…" He hesitates, not meeting my eyes.

"And then what?" I demand, fearing I'm not going to like the answer.

"It's not a big deal. I didn't say anything to you because I didn't want you to worry," he starts.

I feel a sinking sensation in my stomach. "Worry about what?"

"After Caity was found, Rhiannan started texting me under the guise of concern. I rarely responded unless it was a direct question about Mam needing anything," Eamon says calmly.

My eyes pool with tears. I'm probably overreacting, but the fact that he kept this from me hurts.

"Why wouldn't you tell me that? And why did she act like she didn't know you were in a relationship?"

"It never came up." He shrugs. "And it's none of her business. This is why I didn't tell you. I knew it would upset you."

"Eamon, you could have—*should have*—told me from the beginning. I would have understood. But now it just seems like you're hiding things from me. And maybe telling her you were seeing someone would have kept her from messaging you more. Or you could have told her it wasn't appropriate," I say, throwing my hands in the air.

He stands and stalks towards me, grasping my hands gently. "Acushla, stop. I don't want to fight with you. I was just trying to shelter you from the unpleasantness that is Rhiannan, but I can see now that was a mistake. I'm so sorry. I'm not hiding anything from you. She's nothing to me and never will be."

I wilt at his admission. Sliding his hands up my arms and over my shoulders to cup my face, he whispers, "It's just you for me, love."

Wrapping my hands around his wrists, I close my eyes and inhale deeply to keep any more tears from falling.

"I'm sorry," I whisper. "I overreacted. Meeting her like that rattled me. You have more important things to worry about than my petty jealousy."

He leans in to kiss an escaped tear away. "You've nothing to be jealous of, I swear it. She doesn't hold a candle to you."

I snort indelicately, "You sound like Orla downstairs."

Eamon furrows his brow in confusion. "Who the feck is Orla?"

"She's the lady that was at the desk when I met Rhiannan. We became friends. She told me she thought I was prettier because of my hair and that she was a redhead in her younger years. She also wants to meet you."

"Why does she want to meet me?" He chuckles.

"We might have talked about how handsome you are." I shrug.

"Well, we better not let Orla down. I'd hate for her to miss out on seeing this face," he teases. "But she's right. You're much more beautiful than Rhiannan."

He wraps his arms around my waist and pulls me close, kissing the crown of my head. I bury my face in his chest and breathe him in, feeling more peaceful knowing that we can effectively communicate without things getting too heated. Speaking of communication...

"Are *you* okay?" I ask. "You seemed a little off earlier."

257

He rubs his hands up and down my back soothingly. "Aye, I'm alright. I'm sorry for brushing you off like I did."

"It's okay," I mutter. "I know you have a lot on your mind. Just remember that I'm here to help, so please let me. If you need space, then tell me. I can't read your mind, and my first instinct is to comfort you when you're struggling. I promise you won't hurt my feelings if you need some time to yourself."

He doesn't say a word, just tightens his arms around me and presses another kiss to my head. The gesture isn't as reassuring as it should be.

Chapter Thirty-Three

Norah

We spend the day in Caity's hospital room, talking quietly or reading. Occasionally, I drift off—jet lag is no joke. I did eventually get that cup of coffee, but it wasn't enough to clear the fog in my brain. Deciding that I need some fresh air, I look over at Eamon to ask if he wants to walk with me but find that he dozed off at some point. I don't have the heart to wake him. He's exhausted, physically and emotionally.

"He still looks like my little boy when he sleeps," Rosie whispers from her seat next to Caity's bed. "When he was just a wee lad, he'd curl up in my lap and beg for a story. We'd end up reading a few different books, but by the end of the last one, he'd be asleep. I can remember staring at his sweet face for what felt like hours. So peaceful. Not a care in the world. But when he was awake, he was a problem solver. If he couldn't fix something, he felt like he had failed." Her features go from happily reminiscent to sorrowful as she closes her eyes and sighs. "I fear that's what's going through his head now."

I nod in agreement. "I think you're right. I wish I knew how to help him."

"Ach, you *are* helping him just by being here. Sometimes, all a person needs is to know that they have someone in their corner when the hard times come. His Da and I always worked better as a team than individually. Lord, how I miss that man," she says in a tremulous voice.

"I'm so sorry, Rosie. I understand loss and how lonely it can be. After my Mom passed away, I felt like I was just drifting through the days, doing the absolute minimum to get by. I can't even begin to imagine grieving with children."

Rosie smiles sadly before turning to me. "It was harder and easier, in a way. Carrying the weight of two young wan's grief while also drowning in your own is nearly impossible. But they also proved to be a sweet distraction. Children can only focus on one thing for so long before they're off on the next adventure. I remember this one time, several days after Seamus passed, Eamon and Caity were out in the garden bickering about who knows what. Caity comes running in, wailing like a banshee and covered in mud. 'Mam! Eamon threw mud at me!' And here comes Eamon, with a shite-eating grin on his face." She shakes her head, huffing a laugh.

"'Eamon Kennedy, what have you to say for yourself?' I asked, sternly. He looked me right in the eye and said, 'Aye, I did it. But she kept poking me in the arse with a stick!' It took everything in me not to bust up laughing. So I said, 'Eamon, don't say *arse*. That's a grown-up word.' He looked at me like I was daft. 'But Da said the only words I can't say are the ones I don't know what they mean. Like *fuck* and *gobshite*. I hear those all the time, but I don't know what they mean.' At that moment, I wanted to throttle Seamus. I always told him that he was too grown up with them. Teaching them things they were too young to be learning."

I can't help but laugh picturing little Eamon. "What did you end up doing?"

"Ach, what any good mother would do. I told him that the next time

I heard him using that type of language, and I didn't care if he knew the meaning or not, I'd be taking a wooden spoon to him, I would."

"What about Caity?"

"That girl." She rolls her eyes. "She was always pestering her brother just to get a rise out of him. She got a talking-to as well. I told her if she kept poking him with that stick, I'd let him dunk her in an entire puddle of mud! She, of course, was enraged, but you would have thought Eamon had won the World Cup."

"What about the World Cup?" a groggy Eamon says, sitting up in his chair.

Rosie and I grin at each other.

"Nice of you to join us, then," his Mom teases.

"You're not telling stories about me, are you? It's not fair to do that while a man's sleeping," he grumbles as he stretches his arms over his head.

"Listen to you, going on," Rosie says. "I haven't even *begun* to tell Norah all the stories about you she needs to hear."

"I think I'll be the judge of that, Ma," He stands then turns to me and asks, "Did you sleep any?"

I shake my head. "Not really. I dozed off a few times, but I have a hard time sleeping in hospitals."

He caresses my cheek with the back of his fingers. "Want me to take you back to the house? I could use a shower anyway. I feel like a kip and a half."

"It's up to you and your Mom. I'll do whatever you need me to. If the two of you want to head back, I can stay with Caity for a bit."

"Don't be silly," Rosie interrupts. "Go on, you two. I'm fine here. Shower and get some sleep. There's plenty of food in the fridge and pantry. Or I can order in something for you two."

"You sure, Mam?" Eamon asks, bending to hug her and kiss her cheek.

"Aye, 'course I am. I'll call you if I need you, love. Go on."

We say our goodbyes and leave the hospital. The sun is just setting, painting the sky in vibrant pinks and oranges on our drive to the house. Once we arrive, I send Eamon up to shower while I make us something to eat. It's awkward rooting around in someone else's kitchen, but I eventually find all of the ingredients for sandwiches. I'll make something more substantial later, but right now, we need sustenance and rest. When I finish assembling the sandwiches, I place them on plates with chips, or rather *crisps*, as they're called in Europe.

I'm so lost in thought that I don't hear Eamon come down the stairs. When a pair of large warm hands envelop my waist, I shriek, nearly dropping the glasses I had just pulled out of the cabinet.

"Eamon! You scared the shit out of me!" I yell, turning to glare at him until I see what he's wearing. Which is nothing but a pair of gray sweatpants that are hanging deliciously low on his hips.

"Sorry, Acushla," he chuckles, sliding his arms around me. "Did you not hear me?"

I place my hands on his chest and begin tracing the Dara knot of his tattoo before looking up at him. His hair is damp, with loose tendrils hanging over his forehead, and his beard is thicker than normal.

"Obviously not, or I wouldn't have shattered the windows screaming. Warn a girl next time, sheesh."

He kisses my forehead and asks, "What were you thinking about so deeply that you didn't hear me thundering down the stairs?"

"Nothing really," I say with a shrug. "Just trying to clear my brain out. Are you hungry?"

I slide a hand up to his shoulder and run my fingers through the hair at the nape of his neck. He steps forward and buries his face in the dip between neck and shoulder, pressing me back into the counter.

"Mmmm," he murmurs, hands creeping under the hem of my shirt. "Aye, I can think of something I'd like to eat right now."

I shiver as heat pools between my thighs. I arch into him, tipping my head back to give him better access to my throat. He takes the bait, kissing and nibbling his way to my earlobe, gently taking it between his teeth.

"I really need a shower first," I mumble distractedly. It's hard to focus on anything other than his mouth and hands on me.

"Me too," he purrs against my skin.

I release a breathy laugh. "You just got out of the shower."

"I need another one," he says, kissing under my ear. "With you." Another kiss to my jaw. "Right now." A kiss to the corner of my mouth.

"Okay," I pant into his ear. "I probably need your help anyway."

"Good lass," he growls, bending to grip my thighs and lifting me. I gasp, instinctively wrapping my legs around his hips and arms around his neck. He lifts his head enough to kiss me quickly before turning and bounding up the stairs, food forgotten.

Once we're in the bathroom, Eamon sits me on the vanity, leaving me only to turn on the shower and adjust the temperature. I never grow tired of watching his body move. The way the muscles in his back and broad shoulders bunch make my hands itch to touch him. When he steps back between my thighs, I lay my hands on his chest and drag them down the defined planes of his stomach. His eyes burn with desire as he slowly lifts my arms to pull my sweater over my head. I reach behind my back, unhooking my bra and letting the straps slide down my arms before casting it in the direction of my sweater. Eamon's face almost looks pained as he takes me in. Ever so gently, he brushes the pads of his thumbs over my nipples and watches as they tighten for him. The contact is almost too much with how turned on I am.

"Eamon…" I whine, steam from the shower billowing around us.

He smirks playfully at me before pulling me off of the vanity, his hands immediately moving to the waistband of my leggings. Sinking to his knees, he kisses my stomach and strips me bare. My heart races in anticipation. Even after all of the times we've been together, my body still reacts like it's the first time. Rising to his feet, he quickly discards his own clothing and walks me backward into the shower. Once I'm under the spray, I tip my head back and close my eyes, letting the warm water cascade over me. Eamon runs his fingers gently through my hair, brushing stray strands over my shoulder. When I open my eyes, his are dark with yearning. Gazing back at him, I wrap my hands around his wrists and pull him flush against me, the feel of his body against mine sending sparks from my head to my toes. A feeling of urgency courses through me and I fuse our mouths together. Grunting in surprise, he backs me up against the shower wall. Our kiss turns frantic and sloppy as our hands slide over wet skin. He grips me by the back of my thighs again, lifting me like he did in the kitchen, and as soon as my legs are wrapped around him, he slams into me. I cry out loudly at the sensation of him filling me. My head falls back onto the tiles and I dig my fingers into his shoulders, probably leaving marks, as he continues driving himself into me in slow, deep thrusts.

"Eamon, I'm close…" I pant in his ear. "Don't stop. Please."

"Not likely, love. I've got you," he breathes heavily into my neck.

His words send me over the edge. My mouth opens in a silent scream as my orgasm shoots from my core to my fingertips, making me dizzy from the rush. Eamon thrusts into me one more time and stills. A low growl emanates from his chest as he rides out his own release.

"Norah," he whispers roughly, face still buried in my neck and our chests heaving. "God, I love you."

"I love you, too."

Eamon

Norah's legs unwind from around me, and she sets her feet on the shower floor, but I don't release my hold on her for long moments. Eventually, I relinquish her to help wash her hair and that glorious body. It's the most sensuous experience of my life. If we could just stay here and forget the world around us, I wouldn't complain.

After seeing Caity and knowing that Rhiannan came by, my mind fell into a dark place. It sent me back to the weeks after discovering Declan and Rhi in bed together. The days spent drinking too much, numbing the pain at home or in the pubs, but never getting so pissed that I became belligerent or violent, just despondent and taciturn. When I moved to the States I thought I'd rid myself of those demons, but being back here brought them all to the surface. I felt so out of control that once Norah and I were finally alone, I needed her desperately. I needed to lose myself in her, to feel anchored to the life I made for myself in the States. And while I do feel reconnected to her, I can't shake the shame of leaving my Mam behind in the hospital to handle it all on her own.

My mood doesn't improve over the next couple of days. While the swelling in Caity's brain doesn't increase, it doesn't decrease either. Each time Dr. Colm comes in to deliver the news that nothing has changed, I see the hope in Mam's eyes diminish. The weight of the world is sitting on her shoulders, and I'm laden with guilt. What if Caity doesn't make it? How could I ever go back to the States then? I'd be leaving her completely alone. A widow and bereaved mother.

I'm still absorbed in those thoughts when a hand touches my shoulder. Norah is looking at me with a worried expression. "I've been calling your name. You okay?"

"Yeah," I grunt, rubbing my hands over my beard. I should probably trim it soon. It's beginning to get a little out of control. "Sorry. Just off in my own world. What did you need?"

"I just got a text from Myra," she says, the hint of a smile on her lips. "She found out the sex of the baby. I thought you might like to know."

I frown. That was the very last thing I was expecting her to say. "Oh, yeah, of course."

"It's a girl." Norah's eyes are shining with absolute delight. "She said Mac went with her to the appointment and started crying when he found out. Maybe there's hope for him after all."

I still can't wrap my mind around Mac becoming a father, let alone a father to a little girl.

"Let's hope so. Tell Myra I said congratulations," I say, giving her a forced smile.

"This is the closest I'll get to being an aunt. I can't wait to spoil this baby girl!" she squeals, then gasps. "Oh my gosh, I'm going to make her an entire little baby wardrobe!"

Norah prattles on and on about baby showers, clothes, nurseries, and a slew of other things I assume are baby-related. I smile again, but it doesn't reach my eyes. I can't focus on anything but the guilt that consumes me.

There's a war waging in my mind over what I need to do. There are two choices, and one just might kill me.

Chapter Thirty-Four

Norah

"What's going on in that head of yours, Eamon Kennedy?" I ask quietly. "You've been miles away."

After spending a few days at the hospital without a hint of improvement in Caity's condition, we're now sitting at a table on the patio in the backyard. Eamon has been quiet and brooding all day. He heaves a sigh before turning to look at me, his eyes filled with pain and regret and I get a bad feeling in the pit of my stomach, my anxiety skyrocketing. It doesn't get any better when Eamon reaches for my hands. He grips both of them in his and stares into my eyes.

"Norah, love," he starts, releasing a shuddering breath, "I'm going to stay."

My brow furrows in confusion. "Stay? What do you mean?"

"I mean I'm staying here with Mam. She needs me."

Nodding, I say, "I know. That's why we're here."

"I don't mean a short stay. I'm going to stay indefinitely," he mutters, looking down at our hands.

I open my mouth to object, but I can't form words. What is he saying? My eyes well with tears, and I begin nodding my head. "Okay, so I'll stay too."

He shakes his head, then whispers, "No, Acushla. You need to go home. You have too much there to give up. And I won't be—"

"Stop!" I cry out. "Don't you dare do what I think you're trying to do, Eamon Kennedy. You have a life there too. *We* have a life there."

"Norah, please," he pleads, "don't make this any harder than it already is. My family is here."

"But *you* are my family," I choke out. "How can you just tell me to go back? Do these last months mean nothing to you?"

Eamon raises his head, eyes wide as he grips my fingers tighter and says, "'Course they mean something to me. They mean *everything* to me, but I can't just abandon my family in their time of need for a lass."

I recoil as if he'd physically slapped me.

"For a *lass*," I hiss through my teeth. "Is that all I am to you? Obviously what we've had doesn't mean *everything* to you if you can refer to me as *just a lass*. I gave you everything, Eamon. Every part of me. My heart, my body, everything. And you can just dismiss it so easily?"

"Norah, that's not what I meant," he growls in frustration, jabbing his fingers into his hair. "Did you not drop everything for your Mam when she was sick?"

"That's different. And you know it," I seethe. "We had no one! Not one single family member or friend could come and help. All we had was each other. I can't believe you can sit there and compare them."

I rise from my chair to stalk back towards the house. I can't sit here and listen to this anymore. I can't believe that he's honestly trying to end us when we've only just begun.

"Norah, wait!" Eamon follows after me and grabs my arm, turning me towards him.

I gasp at the contact, then glare at him. "Let go of me, Eamon. Right now."

"No, we need to talk about this," his grip tightens and I flinch, the contact triggering my fight-or-flight instinct. He releases my arm immediately, shock shuddering over his face, then quickly turning to regret.

"Norah, I'm so sorry," he whispers. "I didn't mean to hurt you."

Tears stream down my face as I wrap my arms around my torso. I know he didn't mean to hurt me, but the aggressiveness of his actions brought all of the fears I thought I'd banished rushing back.

"Why are you doing this, Eamon? Why are you pushing me away? You said you love me."

He slowly reaches towards my face to brush a loose strand of my auburn hair behind my ear. "Aye, I do. Which is why I can't ask you to give up your life in the States. I don't plan on going back. Even if Caity comes out of this, she'll most likely need extra care. I can't leave Mam to do that on her own. I just can't."

"Let me help you," I beg. "Please. I want to be here with you, *for you*. I love you," I choke out between sobs.

He pulls me into his chest, wrapping me in a firm embrace, then kisses the top of my head. The gesture is so gentle that it breaks me further.

"I don't want you here to help. That's not fair to you. You're almost done with school. I won't let you throw that away," he mutters into my hair.

"So, then I'll go back when the semester starts, and come back here after graduation. I can take my degree and skills anywhere. You know this."

Eamon puts me at arm's length, his face set into hard lines, and says callously, "No, Norah. I don't want you to come back here."

I jerk my head back, stunned. None of this makes sense. Not his words, not his actions, and especially not the tone in which he just spoke to me.

"Why?" I whisper through trembling lips. "I don't understand why you're doing this. Please explain it to me, Eamon. How can you go from telling me how much you love me one day, to telling me you don't want me the next?"

"I do love you," he says, red-rimmed eyes refusing to meet mine. "But I can't love you the way you'd want *here*. In Ireland. You'll just be a distraction I can't afford right now and I don't want that."

A distraction? Pain and anger flood my veins so hard, that my knees start to buckle.

"I didn't realize I was such a burden to you." I spit at him, jerking my arms from his grasp.

I hear him calling after me as I flee towards the house. Rushing up the staircase, I storm into his bedroom and grab my suitcase. In a fury, I start throwing my clothes in, not even bothering to fold them. Once everything is packed, I pull out my phone to search for a taxi service. I can't handle another minute here and asking him to take me back to the Dublin Airport is out of the question. The drive alone would be torture. After securing my taxi, I search for the cheapest flight I can find back to the States and purchase it. Quickly and quietly, I trudge down the stairs and out of the front door to wait on the curb. Being inside the house is suffocating. The fact that he hasn't come inside looking for me is both a relief and heart-shattering.

Five minutes later, I'm in the cab, instructing the driver to take me to the nearest train station. It will be faster and cheaper than taking a taxi the entire way. I consider it a blessing that the driver isn't chatty. The last thing I want to do is to make idle chit-chat when I'm dying inside. I do send a text to Charlie though.

Norah: *I'm coming back. My flight lands in Raleigh tomorrow a little after 8:00 am. Could you please pick me up?*

Charlie: *What? Why?*

Norah: *It's a long story, but I'm coming back alone.*

Charlie: *Norie, what happened?*

Norah: *He broke up with me.*

Charlie: *HE DID WHAT?! OMG! Tell me what's going on.*

Norah: *I'll call you when I get to the airport, okay? I'm in a cab right now headed for the train station.*

Charlie: *Okay babe. I'll keep my phone right beside me so I won't miss you. Love you!*

Norah: *Love you.*

It takes every ounce of self-control I have to keep from sobbing in the back of the taxi. The driver only looks in the rear-view mirror once, but quickly averts his gaze when he sees the tears falling over my cheeks. On the way to the station, I look up the train schedule and purchase a ticket to Dublin. Once we arrive, I pay the driver, tipping him a little extra for leaving me to my thoughts. Making my way inside the station, I find a quiet corner and wait for my departure. A text message alert sounds on my phone.

Charlie: *Don't be mad, but I told the girls. You're going to need us when you get back and we're here for you.*

Amelia: *Yeah, Norie. We love you and are here to be whatever you need.*

Layla: *Love you!*

Myra: *I'll supply the booze! Of course, I can't drink it, but more for you!*

I sniff back a fresh wave of tears. My friends really are the best. I think about the prospect of staying in Ireland and leaving them behind. My heart throbs painfully. Would I have given it up for Eamon? It would have been difficult, but yes. I would have. But now? I need my friends. I need the love and support they always offer, even when we're bickering.

Once I'm settled on the train and it pulls away from the station, I pull out my phone to send a text to Eamon, letting him know that I'm headed home. Just as a courtesy. He beat me to it. I have two missed calls and a text message from him.

Eamon: *Norah, where are you?*

Norah: *I'm on my way to Dublin. I'm flying back home, just like you asked. Please tell your Mom I'm sorry I didn't say goodbye.*

Eamon: *Stop wherever you are. I'm coming to get you. You don't need to travel by yourself.*

Norah: *No, Eamon. I'm on a train. And I'm quite capable of taking care of myself. This isn't the first time I've traveled through Ireland alone. Stay with your Mom. She needs you more than I do.*

Eamon: *Don't do that. How could you leave without telling me?*

Norah: *Goodbye, Eamon. Please don't contact me again. I can't bear it.*

I shut my phone off and stuff it in my purse. Tilting my head back to rest on the seat, I close my eyes and take a shuddering breath. The small bandage I put over the crack in my heart is in danger of falling off and I refuse to have a breakdown on the train. I just need to make it home and into the safety of my house, then I can fall apart. The steady hum and movement of the train begins lulling me to sleep and all I can think is that I really wish my Mom was still here.

Eamon

"Fuck!" I yell, throwing my phone across the room.

I can't believe Norah just up and left without saying anything. I would have taken her to the airport if she was so set on going. I don't even know where she's at right now, but I'm sure she's headed for Dublin. Sitting on the edge of my bed, I pull at my hair and swear again. I was an absolute arsehole to her. It killed me to be so cruel, but it had to be done. I'm not going to let her waste her life here. She has so much waiting for her back home. Sticking by my side while I take care of my mother and sister is not what I want for her. She deserves so much better.

My phone lights up on the floor and I lunge for it. "Norah? Norah, where are you?"

"It's Teagan, mate. What the fuck is going on? I just had a text from Layla that you broke up with Norah and she's on her way back to the States. Please tell me this is some sort of sick joke."

I groan into the phone, "It's a long story."

"You fecking eejit," my mate snarls through the phone."What on earth possessed you to make such a dick move? I thought you were in love with her?"

"I was. I am," I tell him. "It's complicated, Teag. My Mam and sister need me here. Caity is doing poorly and Mam shouldn't have to do this alone. I need to be here for my family."

"I get that, but how does ending things with Norah factor into this?" Teagan demands. "Surely she'd give up everything to be there with you. Everyone can see she's head over heels for you."

"I can't do that to her. She has a life in Wilmington and I won't ask her to

272

give it all up just so I can selfishly keep her by my side. I love her too much to tie her down."

Teagan lets out a humorless laugh. "You're a thick gobshite, aren't you, Kennedy? Did you even think to ask her what she wanted? Because it sounds like you made the decision for her."

I stop short. I *didn't* ask her.

"No, I didn't, but..."

"But nothing. This isn't the Middle Ages, mate. Women don't need men making the decisions for 'em," he barks out.

"Fuck off," I growl, flinging myself onto my bed. "That's not what I was doing. I was trying to save her from a miserable life. She might be willing now, but what happens when the years drag on and she starts resenting me? Better to end it now after a few months than years."

Even as I say the words, I don't really believe them. I know deep down that Norah wouldn't resent me or my family. She'd fit right in, bringing light to the darkness. That's just who she is.

As if reading my mind, Teagan says, "You don't believe that."

"I can't take it back," I mutter, pinching the bridge of my nose. "She's already on her way to Dublin. I don't even know which train she took. She just...left without telling me. I would have driven her."

"You think she really wanted to spend all that time in a car with you after you basically sent her packing? And then to say goodbye at the airport?" he asks in disbelief.

I hadn't thought of that. I was so upset over her traveling alone that I never even considered how difficult that would be for her. For me as well. Could I have really let her get on a plane and fly across the ocean?

"Fuck. I've bolloxed everything, haven't I?"

"Yeah, mate. You really have," Teagan agrees, not showing a hint of sympathy. "So what are you going to do about it?"

Chapter Thirty-Five

Norah

I've been home for three days and have rarely left my bed. If not for my friends, I likely would have forgotten to eat and shower. The moment I stepped off the plane in North Carolina, I was greeted by Charlie and Layla. I managed to maintain my composure the entire flight from Ireland, but as soon as they enveloped me in their arms, I broke. My knees hit the ground and I wept openly. It felt like my heart had been ripped out of my chest, shattered, then shoved back in haphazardly, piece by piece. It hurt to even breathe. Charlie and Layla didn't bat an eye. They sank to the ground and wrapped their arms around me, not saying a word. They didn't ask for details or slander Eamon's name. They got me in the car, took me home, made me shower and eat, then sent me straight to bed. They took my phone away and unplugged any electronic devices in my room before curling up on either side of me and going to sleep.

I've finally had enough of my own moping and crawl out of bed. I force myself to shower, willing myself to not think about the shower with Eamon. It feels like a losing battle, so I turn the water all the way cold and screech when the icy water hits my skin. It's enough to clear the haze of unwanted memories. After showering, I forego the sweats and pajamas I've been living in and don jeans and a hoodie. When I step into the living room, I find Charlie and Layla perched on the bar stools around the island, and Amelia and Myra curled up on the couch. Charlie hops from her perch to pour me a cup of coffee. She doctors it just the way I like it and hands it to me with a kiss on my cheek.

"Thanks," I murmur, then look around the space. "What are you all doing here?"

"What do you think we're doing here?" Myra asks softly, folding her hands over her growing belly. "We're here for *you*."

My eyes brim with tears. Before they can overflow, I shake my head and blink rapidly.

"I'm not going to cry anymore," I whine, waving my hands in front of my face in an attempt to dry the tears. "I'm really happy to see all of you."

One by one, they all come to hug me. When it's Myra's turn, I can't hold it back any longer. "Just kidding. I'm definitely going to cry. My, you're having a baby girl! I'm getting a new niece!"

Myra laughs, wiping the tears from her face. "I know. I can't even believe it. I thought I'd feel terrified, but I'm so freaking excited!"

Placing my hands on her slightly rounded belly, I tell her, "You're going to be one of those pregnant women who looks like she just swallowed a basketball. The rest of you will still be perfect."

"Ugh, I don't know about that. I feel like I'm already swelling," she groans.

"No," I say, shaking my head. "You're perfect. When I found out you were having a girl, I told Eam…"

I suck in a sharp breath that feels like swallowing glass.

"Do you want to talk about it, Norie?" Layla asks tentatively.

No. I don't want to talk about it. I don't want to relive the moment he broke my heart, the moment he told me he didn't want me anymore. But that's why they're all here. I move to the couch and snuggle in next to Amelia, who drapes an arm around my shoulders.

"Might as well get this over with," I mutter "The sooner I get it all out, the sooner I can move forward, right?"

Charlie and Layla exchange a doubtful look with each other. I start to question it when Amelia says, "Norah, there's no rush. No timeline. You can take as much time as you need. This was a blow you didn't see coming. Hell, none of us did."

Nodding, I say, "I know. I just don't want to stay stuck here for too long. I went through all of the stages of grief after my Mom died. I know this isn't a death, but I can already feel myself becoming that shell of a person. I'm not going to waste my life pining for someone who doesn't want me around."

So I tell them the entire story, from the moment we got the call from Eamon's Mom to the moment my flight landed and Charlie and Layla met me at the airport. I told them, without going into too much detail, about making love in the shower and how intimate it was. How we'd professed our love for each other and I just knew that he was my future.

"What the hell is he thinking?" Myra demands once I've finished the recounting, outrage etched all over her face.

"It sounds like he's got a lot of guilt about leaving his Mom," Layla offers, causing everyone to stare at her like she's just committed treason.

"Lay, you're not supposed to be defending him," Amelia scoffs, crossing her arms over her chest.

"I'm not! He's absolutely in the wrong here, but I can kind of understand *why* he felt like he needed to stay," she defends.

"You're not wrong," I admit. "I completely understand why he wants to stay, but what I don't understand is why he doesn't want me with him. Why does he feel like he needs to make that decision for me?"

"Exactly what I'm trying to say," Layla clarifies. "He shouldn't be making that decision, but it also sounds like he's trying to put your needs first, knowing everything you'd be leaving if you stayed there with him. He doesn't want you to give up anything for him."

"Again," Charlie interjects, holding up a finger, "Not his call to make."

"I didn't even say goodbye to his Mom," I groan. "She must think I'm so self-centered."

"Have you called her or messaged her?" Layla questions.

"No," I say, hanging my head. "But I probably should. As painful as it is, I adore Rosie."

"Maybe she can talk some sense into him," Amelia suggests with a one-shouldered shrug. "Make him realize his mistake."

"Even if she did, Norie isn't going to take him back. He had his chance," Myra scoffs. "Right, Nor?"

All eyes turn to me and I hesitate. "Honestly? I don't know. I still love him and want to be with him, but even if he wanted me back, I'm not sure how we'd make a relationship work on two separate continents." Blowing out a frustrated breath, I rub my forehead with my fingertips. "This is all hypothetical anyway."

We spend the next few hours talking about everything but Eamon. Most of the conversation revolves around Myra and the baby. We talk about names, baby shower planning, and Mac's sweet reaction to finding out he was going to have a daughter. I don't miss how distracted Layla has been. Her eyes and fingers racing across the screen of her phone. Is she texting Teagan? Surely he's talked to Eamon by now. I'm desperate to ask, but can't seem to muster up the courage to do so. I'm too scared of the answer.

Later, after everyone but Layla leaves, I'm exhausted. The mental and emotional unloading was overwhelming and I just want to crawl back into the oblivion of sleep.

"Are you staying tonight, Lay?" I ask while pouring the last dregs of wine from a bottle down the drain.

"I had planned on it," she hedges. "Unless you want me to give you some space. It won't hurt my feelings either way."

"You can stay. I may head to bed soon, though. I want to get up early tomorrow and start designs for the spring production," I tell her with a shrug.

"Okay," she says, the corner of her mouth tipping up in a sympathetic smile.

We sit at the island in companionable silence for a few minutes before I just can't take it anymore.

"How are things with Teagan?" I ask suddenly.

Layla's eyes shoot to mine in alarm. "What?"

"Oh, come on. There's obviously something going on there, and you guys seem to talk all the time," I nod towards the phone in her hands.

"I was hoping you didn't notice that," she says with a grimace.

"It's okay," I tell her honestly. "You can talk to me about him. If you want. I still want to know what's going on with you."

She pulls her dark hair over her shoulder and starts braiding it absently. "Well...did you know that Eamon told Teagan to take the reservation for the rental in OBX?"

My head snaps up, and I gape at her. When had he done that? And why didn't he tell me? "What? No, I had no idea."

"Yeah," Layla continues, wringing her hands together. "Teagan invited me to join him, so I did. One thing led to another, and we... Yeah."

There's a stretch of silence while my brain processes this. When the information all clicks into place, I gasp loudly and grab Layla's arm.

"You slept together!"

Layla blushes deeply and looks away. When she finally brings her eyes back to mine, she's fighting a grin. She loses the battle and says, "Yeah, we did."

"Layla, this is amazing! I'm so happy for you! So, you're official now?" I ask, genuinely happy for her.

An ache fills my chest at the thought of not being able to double date with them, but I shove it aside to focus on Layla.

"Yeah, I guess we are," she says, exhaling heavily. "It seems surreal, you know? I keep waiting for the other shoe to drop. I keep waiting for him to realize that I'm not anything like his ex and that he doesn't want me anymore."

"Not likely! Eamon said—" I stop short. Saying his name feels like being stabbed with a serrated knife.

Layla winces and reaches forward to grab my hand. "Hey, it's okay. Let's not talk about this anymore."

I nod, slipping off of the bar stool to give Layla a hug. "Yeah, I'm going to go to bed. Night."

I pad into my bedroom, each step feeling heavier than the last. Crawling into bed, I pull the covers over my head, and let the tears flow freely. How is it possible to feel so much for someone over the course of a few months? Eamon Kennedy embedded himself into my heart and soul so deeply, and I miss him. I miss talking and laughing with him. I miss having him in my bed, with his strong arms wrapped around me. I miss the weight of him and the feel of his lips on my skin. Burying my face into my pillow, I realize it still smells like him, and the ache in my heart intensifies, threatening to suffocate me. I throw the pillow across the room. I'll strip the sheets in the morning. Tomorrow, I'm determined to stop wallowing and move forward.

Eamon

"We got the results from Caity's latest scan, and we're pleased to see that the swelling in her brain has reduced significantly. So much so that we would like to start bringing her out of her coma tomorrow," Dr. Colm says, smiling at us.

Mam bursts into tears, and I release a huge sigh of relief. It's the first time I've felt something other than regret since Norah left.

"Oh, do you mean it?" Mam cries. "Will we finally be able to talk to her?"

"Well," Dr. Colm hesitates, "that would be the ideal situation. However, there's no guarantee that she'll be responsive. It could take anywhere from several hours to even a couple of days for her to fully wake. We don't want to rush her into consciousness, so we'll be gradually reducing the medications."

"'Course." She sniffles. "I should have known better."

"Mam, it's okay. We're all anxious to see Caity awake," I tell her soothingly, wrapping an arm around her.

"No worries at all," Dr. Colm assures her. "We'll begin weaning her off the medication tomorrow morning around seven. I would recommend waiting a couple of hours before coming to visit. She will be under close and constant observation, and those first hours are critical. Of course, you're welcome to wait in the lobby if you decide to come in first thing."

"Thank you, Doctor. I'd like to be here just in case anything happens. Is that alright, Eamon?" she asks me.

"'Course it is. We'll come whenever you want." It's not like I have anywhere else to be.

"Do you have any other questions for me, Rosie?" Dr. Colm asks, giving her elbow a lingering squeeze.

"Not that I can think of," she says with a shake of her head. "I'm just ready to see my Caity Bug's eyes open again."

"Absolutely. That's our goal," he says. "I'll see you in the morning, then."

"Thanks a million," she says, her eyes filled with hope. It's the brightest I've seen them in years.

After the doctor leaves the room, she turns her watery gaze towards me. She hasn't said much to me since learning that Norah left. When I told her what happened, she fully embraced her Irish Mam status and gave me a tongue-lashing like I hadn't experienced since I was a boy. I didn't realize that I could feel worse than I already did, but knowing how disappointed she is, guts me.

"Eamon," she chokes out, "do you think she'll come back to us, our Caity?"

I pull her in for a hug, resting my chin on the top of her head. "I don't know, Ma. I'd like to say she will without a doubt, but I honestly haven't any idea what to expect."

Taking a deep breath, she returns my embrace but says, "I'm glad you're here, son. Even if you are an eejit for letting that sweet girl walk away like that."

"*Jaysus*, Mam," I groan out. "I know I messed up. I wasn't thinking straight. If I could go back and change it, I would."

She pulls back, eyeing me sternly. "Eamon Seamus Kennedy. You listen to me. I want you to go back to the States. I love you for wanting to stay and take care of me, but I don't *need* you to stay here."

When I furrow my brow at her, she takes a deep breath before saying, "I've debated on telling you this, but I suppose it's time. We could have avoided all of this turmoil had I told you sooner. John—Dr. Colm—and I have been seeing each other for a while now. I didn't want to tell you because I was afraid you'd think I was dishonoring your father's memory. We've made no real plans, but things have become quite serious recently."

My jaw drops, leaving me gaping in shock. I thought something was going on between the two of them, but I just figured it was harmless flirting. To find out they've been seeing each other? I'm completely flabbergasted. And more than a little irritated.

"You're joking," I deadpan.

"No, love, I'm not," she says gently, squeezing my forearms. "We've been courting for about six months now, just enjoying each other's company. We didn't intend on getting serious, but as time has gone on, we've grown closer. He's a good man, Eamon. He'll never replace your Da, no one can, but he makes me happy and he treats me well."

"I can't believe you didn't tell me sooner," I mumble, rubbing my hands over my face. "I wouldn't begrudge you finding someone that makes you happy. Did Caity know?"

"No, she didn't. She was hardly ever around, and when she was, she barely talked to me."

I heave a sigh, looking over at my sister. I'm sleep deprived, feeling like an arse for what I did to Norah, and now I'm stunned by my mother's confession. I need a drink. "I'm not sure if I should be offended or not right now, Mam," I say, smiling wryly at her. She raises a brow at me in question. "My own mother basically told me to get the fuck out of here and leave the country," I tease her.

"Ach, you wee shite," she exclaims, playfully slapping my bicep. "That's not what I meant, and you know it. I'd be overjoyed to have you back in Ireland for good, but your heart isn't here, love. It flew to the States, and you need to get it back. If someday you and Norah decide to live here and give me grandchildren, I'd be the happiest woman in the world, but you belong with her."

There's a crushing sensation in my chest at the thought of raising a family with Norah in Ireland.

"I want to be with her," I say earnestly. "More than anything I've ever wanted before."

"I know, love. That's why you need to go back."

My mind is racing. I'm ready to hop on a plane right now, but I know I'm still needed here. "I will, but not until we know what's going on with Caity. That's non-negotiable."

She rests a hand on my cheek, smiling warmly. "There's a good lad."

"I want to ask you something though," I say nervously.

"Anything, my boy."

Chapter Thirty-Six

Norah

I'm in my sewing room, so fully engrossed in sketches that I don't even realize my phone is ringing. Once the chiming registers, I fumble for it, eyes never leaving my sketchbook, and answer the call.

"Hello?" I answer absently.

"Norah, it's Teagan."

I drop the pencil and sit up straight, heart pounding in my chest. Teagan never calls me, never even texts me.

"Hi, Teag. Is everything okay?" I ask hesitantly.

"Aye, it is." The relief in his voice is palpable, and I breathe easier. "I thought you'd want to know that Caity came out of her coma."

"Oh my god," I say, smiling through the tears flooding my eyes. "That's wonderful news. How is she? How's…everyone else?" I can't bring myself to say Eamon's name out loud.

"It *is* good news," he agrees. "They started weaning her off the medicine on Tuesday, and she opened her eyes yesterday. She hasn't said much, but she's shown signs that she knows who she is and recognizes her family. They're still monitoring her of course, but so far, all signs are looking good. They imagine she'll have to go through quite a bit of physical and occupational therapy and possibly speech therapy."

"Oh, thank god. I'm sure Rosie is just beside herself with joy. If you talk to them," I say, swallowing thickly, "will you please tell them how glad I am?"

"Aye, 'course I will," he says genuinely. "Listen, I won't keep you, but I wanted to relay the information and see if you'd like to meet us at O'Nelly's tomorrow night. I know Friday nights are crazy, but Layla and the girls will be there. And Paddy's been asking about you."

I flinch. I miss Paddy like crazy, but I've been avoiding anything and anyone that reminds me of Eamon. O'Nelly's being the biggest.

"I don't know, Teag. I'll think about it, okay?"

"Sure. I understand," he says compassionately, "but, Norah, lass? I really think you ought to join us. It will do you good."

I'm not used to Teagan being so forthright, especially with me. He's always kept things lighthearted. "Uh...okay. I'll stop by for a bit. Just long enough to say hi to everyone," I concede.

"Atta girl! You'll make Paddy's night! The old codger has been downright cranky lately."

I chuckle, picturing Paddy as anything but jovial. "Well, that's unacceptable. Can't have him grumpy."

"Too right," Teagan says. "Alright, I'll talk to you later, Norah."

I end the call, feeling confused about the whole conversation. I text Layla.

Norah: *Hey, Teagan just called me with an update on Caity. She's awake. He also said you're all getting together at O'Nelly's tomorrow night?*

Layla: *Oh, thank God! How is she doing? Yes, just a few drinks at the pub. Nothing big. We miss you.*

Norah: *I didn't get a lot of details, but her memory seems to be okay. Which is huge. I told him I'd be there for a bit, but I don't know if I'll keep my word or not. I miss you girls and Paddy, but I'm not sure if I'm ready to go back there yet.*

Layla: *I get it. But just...try? For me?*

Norah: *I'll try.*

I sit, staring out the window for a long time, debating on if I should reach out to Eamon. Just to see how Caity is doing. But even bringing his name up in a blank message has my heart cracking. I eventually decide against it. Hopefully, Teagan will have more information tomorrow.

* * *

Friday arrives with dark skies and steady rain. My mood matches the weather. I spent a couple of hours working on sketches and compiling a list of supplies for the spring production. Once I'm satisfied that I'm off to a good start, I set my sketchpad aside and reach for my coffee. Curling up in my chair, I stare out the window and watch the rain pour down, wrap both hands around my mug, and wage war with my thoughts. I told Teagan and Layla I'd be at O'Nelly's tonight, but I just don't think I can do it. The thought of getting dressed and interacting with everyone exhausts me down to my bones. I want nothing more than to hide in my house and do nothing. Decision made, I text the group.

Norah: *Hey, girls, I'm not feeling up to coming out tonight. I'm sorry. Rain check?*

Amelia: *What?! No way! Just come for a little bit! One drink!*

Myra: *Norie, I'm all for a good pity party, but you NEED to join us!*

Norah: *Girls, you know I love you, but I don't think I can do it.*

Myra: *If you don't come willingly, I will drag my pregnant ass to your house and get you.*

Amelia: *Same! Just not the pregnant part!*

Norah: *You two are impossible. Can we do it another time? Please?*

I don't get a response after that, which doesn't bode well. If they are serious about coming to get me, I'm just going to have to put my foot down. I'm not going out tonight, and that's final. Feeling proud of my resolve, I reward myself with a long, hot bath followed by an Outlander marathon.

The rain finally lets up, and I'm in the middle of watching Claire and Jamie's wedding when my front door bursts open, and a pregnant Myra and not-pregnant Amelia saunter in.

"Get up! Get dressed! You're coming with us!"

I groan and throw the blanket I was snuggled under over my head. Clearly, my prayers of my friends *not* coming for me are going unanswered. "Go away," I mutter.

"Nope. We're not leaving without you," Amelia says, ripping the blanket away.

"Gah!" I yell, hands reaching for the blanket. "Give it back! I'm serious. I don't want to go to Paddy's tonight. You can't make me!"

* * *

Soon, I'm sulking in the backseat of the car while Amelia drives us to O'Nelly's. She and Myra are singing loudly to Beyoncé's *Single Ladies*, completely ignoring my pleas and the insults I'm hurling at them. I'm still not sure how I ended up here. One minute, I was in my favorite pajamas on the couch, and now I'm dressed in light-wash skinny jeans and a taupe sweater with my curls tamed and hanging free around my face. I even have a little bit of makeup on.

"You do know that I hate you both, right?" I glare at the back of their heads.

Amelia laughs, and Myra turns in her seat to blow me a kiss before saying, "No, you don't. We're your favorites."

I roll my eyes and flip them off, which makes them both howl with laughter. *I need new friends.*

Paddy's is absolutely packed when we walk in. It's usually busy on Friday nights, but there's hardly any room to move. Alicia is behind the bar slinging drinks with Paddy, and I smile despite my mood.

Paddy turns his head towards the door when the chilly air from outside rushes in his direction. He grins widely, eyes sparkling with delight.

"Norah!" he bellows in greeting.

Alicia's head snaps up, and she beams at me before whispering something to Paddy. He nods and walks out from behind the bar, weaving through the crowd, shaking hands and patting backs as he passes. When he reaches me, he envelops me in a bear hug, and I laugh, hugging him back. I didn't realize how much I needed this. Maybe I don't hate my friends.

"Hey, Paddy," I say, placing a quick kiss on his cheek.

"It's good to see you, lass!" he exclaims, holding me at arm's length and looking at me carefully. "You alright, then?"

"Yeah, Paddy. I'm alright. How are you?" I ask, forcing myself to smile and act like I'm not about to have a meltdown.

He studies my face, clearly not buying the lies. "Have a pint of the black stuff on the house, aye?"

I swallow the lump in my throat, nodding, and follow him to the bar.

"Norie!" Alicia greets me while filling pint glasses with beer. "It's so good to see you!"

"Looking good, Li. Loving the outfit tonight," I wink, admiring the black leather vest she's wearing over a deep purple tank top. Her full sleeve of colorful tattoos runs up her left arm, making her look even more badass. It's warm enough in the pub that she can get away with it.

"Thanks, girl!" Alicia says, handing me a perfectly stacked Guinness.

I thank her and start towards our group's usual spot, Ro's shock of red hair catching my attention first. I shouldn't be surprised by his presence, but seeing Ro and Teagan without Eamon feels wrong. I shake it off, determined to not dwell on him, and take the open seat next to Layla.

"I'm so glad you made it!" she says, hugging me.

"I didn't have much of a choice." I roll my eyes and nod towards Amelia and Myra. "Those two don't take no for an answer. Remind me why I'm friends with them again?"

Layla laughs. "Because you love them and life would be significantly more boring without them?"

"I like boring. Boring I can work with. I'm happy with boring." I shrug, glaring playfully at the two in question.

I glance around the table while sipping on my beer. Mac and Myra are cozied up together, heads bent in hushed conversation. Mac's hand is rubbing soft circles over Myra's baby bump. It's such a sweet gesture that I have to look away. My eyes fall on Rowan. The normally boisterous Irishman is hunched over his drink, forearms resting on the table, looking desolate. He must sense me watching him because he glances up and plasters a fake smile on his face.

"Everything okay, Ro?" I ask cautiously.

"Aye, right as rain, love!" he says a little too brightly. "Good to see you out and about. Wasn't sure if we'd have the pleasure of seeing you tonight."

I shrug. "I was brought against my will. I'm just having one drink and then heading back home."

"Suppose I'll have to try and change your mind, then. We're playing some songs in a bit. You have to stay for that at least," he says with a wink.

"If it's the soccer team, forget about it." I grimace. "I'd rather not lose my sense of hearing, thanks."

He barks out a short laugh. "Just us Irishmen tonight, so your ears will survive."

It takes everything in me not to flinch in pain. As much as I love listening to them, it brings back more than one memory of Eamon singing to me.

"We'll see," I tell him. "No promises though."

He gives me a look I can't decipher before standing and rapping his knuckles on the table. "Be right back. Think I need another drink. You want one?"

"No, thanks." I shake my head and hold up a finger. "Just the one, remember?"

He winks and walks away.

"What's going on with Ro?" I mutter to Layla.

"Oh, right!" She turns to face me fully. "I forgot to tell you about that. Teagan said he got into it with Alicia and has been off ever since."

Thinking back to my lunch date with Alicia, I wonder if Ro's current mood has anything to do with that or if something happened while I was gone.

"Yikes," I reply unenthusiastically before saying, "I'm going to the bathroom; I'll be right back."

Winding through the pub's patrons, I slip into the bathroom, locking the door behind me. I need just a moment. While I'm glad I came, I feel so overwhelmed. I finish using the restroom and am washing my hands when I hear Paddy over the PA system.

"Good evenin', lads and lasses! Thanks so much for coming out tonight! I've a special treat for you! I've been missing me home country something fierce, so I asked our favorite Irish footballers to play a few ditties for us tonight!"

The crowd goes crazy—applauding, whistling, and hollering. Maybe I can sneak out before they start playing. It's packed, so I can easily get lost in the throngs of people. I step out of the bathroom and make a beeline for the bar to let Alicia know I'm leaving, refusing to look at the stage. I open my mouth to say goodbye when I hear a familiar guitar cord being strummed. I squeeze my eyes shut and take a steadying breath. If this is Ro's idea of a joke, I'll murder him. When I open my eyes, Alicia is staring at me with tear-filled eyes, her fingers pressed against her mouth.

Then I hear a deep, familiar brogue say, "This one's for my Ringsend Rose."

Chapter Thirty-Seven

Norah

Whirling around, I see Eamon standing on stage, guitar strapped over his shoulder, eyes locked on me. I can't breathe. It's only been days since I've seen him, but I drink in every detail like a woman dying of thirst. He looks tired, with dark circles under his eyes and his hair is disheveled. The sleeves of his black Henley are pushed up to his elbows, exposing his strong forearms, the muscles flexing with each strum of the guitar. His eyes stay fixed on me as he begins singing.

"In Dublin Town there lived a girl
Fairer than the flower I'm wearin'
Rose Donoghue—all fresh and new
And I love her past all carin'
And there she goes my Ringsend Rose

In God's Garden there's none rarer
And there she goes my Ringsend Rose
Dublin Town has seen none fairer."

I stand frozen to the spot through the entirety of the song, tears spilling down my face. His gaze is full of unspoken apologies. As the song concludes, he mumbles a quick thank you to the crowd before pulling the guitar strap over his head and setting the instrument on its stand before stepping off the stage and stalking straight for me. The audience follows his every move. When he stops inches from me, the pub goes silent, but Rowan comes to the rescue and starts playing a jaunty tune.

"Alright, who's ready for a lively version of The Last Shanty? You all know the words!" he declares.

The crowd cheers loudly and turns back to the stage, forgetting about us. Eamon reaches for my hand and leads me through the pub entrance. As soon as we're outside, he cups my face.

"Norah," he starts, eyes watching me earnestly. "I'm so sorry. I was the biggest arse thinking I was doing what I thought was best for you without even talking to you about it. I was wrong, so wrong. My head was all fucked up, Acushla. I don't think there are words to convey how truly sorry I am."

"Eamon," I begin, wrapping my fingers around his wrists and pulling them from my face. It's hard to think while he's touching me. "I understand why you felt the way you did. Honestly, I do. I just don't understand why you felt you couldn't talk to me about it."

He laces his fingers through mine and says, "Because I'm a fucking eejit is why. I felt so guilty about not being there for my Mam, that it clouded my better judgment. And because you're the selfless person you are, I knew you'd give up anything to stay, and I didn't want you to give up your life. You were so excited about Myra's baby. How could I ask you to leave all of that?"

"Simple," I say, looking him in the eyes. "You just *ask*. Would it be easy to leave this behind and move across the ocean? No, but, Eamon, *you* were as much a part of my life as they are. We could have figured something out if you just would have asked."

291

He pulls me close to him, resting his forehead against mine. "I know, love. I know. Will you please let me fix this?"

I breathe him in, reeling over the fact that he's actually here right now, and choke out, "You said you didn't want me. You said I was a burden."

Eamon cups my face again and whispers, "I lied. Of course I want you. I need you. I need you like I need air to breathe. You *are* the air I breathe. I never thought I'd move on from Rhiannon. I didn't *want* to. Then I met this gorgeous fire sprite that challenged me to a drinking contest, and my world turned on its head. I love you, Norah. So much so that I want to be by your side for the rest of our lives."

He doesn't give me a chance to respond before he drops to one knee before me. The air leaves my lungs when he holds up a delicate gold band of Celtic knots surrounding a small, round emerald.

"Eamon," I gasp. "What are you doing?"

He takes my left hand, squeezing my fingers gently. "This is my mother's ring. My Da gave it to her three months after meeting her. He told her he knew there would never be another woman for him and wanted to marry her right then and there. She felt the same about him. Before I left, I told her that you were it for me. My beginning, middle, and end. She gave the ring to me, saying it would look perfect on you. No matter where life takes us, I don't want to do it without you. I love you, Norah. So this is me *just asking* like you said to do. Will you marry me?"

I'm crying hard, unable to harness the emotions soaring through me. Our relationship has been a whirlwind from day one. Proposing after only three months is insanity, but nothing has ever felt so right. Eamon stirred something in me from the moment I laid eyes on him, but I never dreamed that I'd be standing here before my kneeling Irishman who's asking me to spend the rest of my life with him. And I want that. I want it all with him.

He's staring at me expectantly, so I grin widely and whisper, "Yes, Eamon. Yes."

Beaming and eyes shining with unshed tears, Eamon slips the ring on my finger before springing from the ground and kissing me, winding his fingers through my hair to tilt my head and deepen the kiss. He parts my lips, plunging his tongue into my mouth, claiming me, body and soul. This isn't just a celebratory kiss, it's an apology and a promise. This kiss says everything words cannot and I revel in it. I have a fistful of his shirt in one hand as I cup his scruff-covered jaw with the other. A muscled arm winds around my back, arching me closer to his hard body. I pull away, gasping for breath. We're grinning like fools, oblivious to the world around us.

"I love you, Acushla," Eamon whispers.

"I love you, too," I say breathlessly. "Can we get out of here?"

"Aye, let's go," he laughs, starting to pull me away from the pub.

"Wait, I need to let the girls know I'm leaving."

He turns to smirk at me, showing off that dimple I love. "Oh, they know. How do you think I got you here tonight?"

I gawk at him. "They knew? How? When?"

"I called Teagan. Who told Layla. She employed Myra and Amelia as backup in case you tried to back out of coming tonight," he winks at me.

"Traitors," I mumble.

He pulls me back to his chest and kisses me softly. "I would have come to you no matter where you were, love."

"Take me home," I whisper against his lips.

Eamon

On the short drive from O'Nelly's to Norah's house, I tell her about Caity waking up from the coma. Once she was fully weaned from the medicine, it took a while for her to come to, but when she did, she immediately recognized me and our Mam. She wasn't sure of the date and had no memory of what she did the night that landed her in the hospital. When Dr. Colm and Mam explained what happened, Caity cried silently and didn't speak to anyone for a long while. Eventually, after everyone else left the room, she finally spoke.

"Are you home for good, Eam?" she whispered.

I studied her face before replying, "No, Caity Bug. I'm not."

"Oh," is all she said.

"I, uh, I have a lass waiting for me back in the States."

Her eyes widened slightly at the admission. "Tell me about her."

So I did. I told her everything. She laughed at our drinking contest and told me I was a fecking eejit when I told her how I sent Norah home.

"Aye, I am. But I'm going to fix it. I'm going to ask her to marry me," I said sheepishly.

"No kidding?" Caity asked, her jaw dropping in surprise. "I didn't think you'd even throw around the idea of marriage after Rhiannan and Declan. I'm proud of you, big brother."

"Thanks, wee sister. I can't wait for you to meet her. I'll bring her back to meet you," I promised.

"Aye, you better. She sounds lovely. And if she's willing to take your sorry arse back, then she must be one hell of a woman. What does Mam think of her?"

"Ach, she loves her. She thinks I'm a fecking eejit too. Which I am," I laughed. "But let's talk about you, Caity. This was a pretty scary ordeal."

She hung her head, sniffling back tears. "I know. I just…I don't know how to get over losing Da. I know I was young, but Christ, I loved that man. But I didn't know how to grieve, you know? So I did everything I could to numb the pain or forget about it entirely. I made every bad decision in the book."

I reached for her hand and gave it a gentle squeeze. "I wish you would have talked to me more about it. Hell, I probably should have forced you to."

Caity barked out a laugh. "I would have fought you tooth and nail. The last thing I wanted was my big brother to call me on my shite. But in hindsight, I probably wouldn't be in this mess if I'd just swallowed my pride."

"You know I'm always here for you, right?" I asked. "From now on, promise me that when you're feeling lost, you'll call me. You're not alone in your grief, Caity Bug."

Tears filled her eyes. "You always seem so sound, Eamon. Like nothing

294

can hurt you."

"That's because I'm an eejit that buries his feelings deep down in his gut and does stupid shite, like sending the love of his life packing," I chuckled but sobered quickly. "I wish I could show you the mess my head was in when Mam called to tell me you were in the hospital. I was an absolute wreck. I know we haven't been close over the last years, but Christ, Caity. You're my wee, baby sister and I love you. Always have, always will."

"I love you too, big brother," she sniffled.

* * *

I pull into Norah's driveway, putting the car in park, and turning to face her.

"We spent the rest of the day catching up. It was like we built a bridge over the gap that's been between us for so long. I'm so proud of her Norah. Not only is she determined to put her all into occupational and physical therapy, but she's found a counselor and is talking about going to rehab."

"That's amazing!" Norah grins. "I'm excited to hear about her progress. Sometimes it takes a significant setback to propel us forward towards a better future."

I reach across the console to take her hand. The hand with my ring on it. Mam was right. It looks perfect on her. I run my thumb over the emerald before bringing her hand to my lips.

"Aye. No more setbacks for us, Acushla," I tell her. "I'm ready for that better future with you."

"Me too," she agrees. "Now let's go inside so I can welcome you home properly."

We race from the car to the door, struggling to get the key in the lock. It doesn't help that I'm gripping her waist and banding her neck with open-mouthed kisses. The door barely clicks shut before I whirl her around and back her up against it. I press my chest into hers and trail a finger down between her breasts to hook a finger through her belt loop and yank her hips forward. She grabs the hem of my shirt, breaking the kiss long enough to rip it over my head and toss it on the floor. Her hands roam over my shoulders and coast down my chest to the top of my jeans. She manages to unbutton them, but I grab her hands and pin them above her head.

"Not yet, beautiful," I growl against her mouth. "I haven't had a chance to take anything off of you yet."

"Then hurry up, Kennedy. I'm not getting any younger," she challenges, eyes bright with need.

I release her hands immediately and don't waste another second ridding her of her sweater and bra. I cup her breasts firmly and graze my thumbs over her nipples, making her groan.

"God, I've missed you. I'm never letting you go again," I murmur against her shoulder.

"Eamon, please," she begs, fumbling with the button on my jeans again.

I bite down on her neck hard enough to elicit another loud groan from her before ducking down to lave her breasts with my tongue. I give each one an equal amount of attention while I pop the button on her jeans and push them over her luscious hips. Dropping to my knees, I grovel by gripping her thighs, trailing kisses over her stomach, and swirling my tongue around her belly button. She's panting and digging her fingers into my hair, urging me lower. I willingly oblige, hooking my fingers around the edge of her underwear and sliding them down to her ankles. I nudge her legs further apart, so I can kiss my way up her inner thigh. She growls in frustration when I skip over where she wants me in favor of her other leg.

"I'm dying here," Norah whines. "I need you inside me."

I chuckle before seizing her hips and burying my face between her legs. I flatten my tongue and lick her slowly, applying extra pressure.

"Oh god," she groans. "Keep doing that."

I don't stop as she writhes against my mouth, legs quivering around my head. I keep a steady pace until she cries out my name, coming all over my mouth. Rising swiftly, I kiss her hard, swirling my tongue inside her mouth so she can taste how delicious she is. She whimpers as I scoop her into my arms, carrying her to the bedroom where I lay her gently out on the bed.

"I'll never get tired of hearing you call out my name like that. I'll never get tired of loving you like this," I say softly, hovering over her, arms braced on either side of her head.

Norah gazes up at me, "I love you."

I dip my mouth to hers once again, kissing her like I did at O'Nelly's. Claiming her forever. She wraps her legs around my waist, tightening them to force me closer, so without breaking our kiss, I position my cock at her entrance and slowly push inside, groaning at the sensation. I begin rocking into her, pulling out most of the way before plunging deeply back in, burying myself to the hilt. I planned on loving her slowly, savoring every second of our reunion, but the noises coming from her mouth snap my control. I fuck her harder and faster until I feel her clamp around me. That's all it takes and we're both careening over the edge together, crying out incoherent words. As we lay there panting, wrapped in each other's arms, Norah runs her fingers through my hair, scraping her nails over my scalp, trailing them down my spine and back up again. I rest my forehead against hers and kiss her softly.

"Thank you," I whisper.

Norah huffs a laugh, "For what? An orgasm?"

"No, smart arse," I tease, pinching her side playfully, which only makes her laugh harder. "Though I'm thankful for that too. Thank you for taking me back."

She quiets and looks up at me, "I don't think I ever really let go if I'm being honest. I told myself I was going to move on, but it was a lie. I don't want anyone else but you."

"Good. Because I'm here to stay, love. There's no getting rid of me now," I tell her, rolling to my back and pulling her to my chest.

Norah

I sigh contentedly, running my left hand over the planes of his stomach and onto his chest. I follow the lines of his tattoo, observing the Kennedy crest. My future last name. I grin at the ring on my finger, holding my hand up to admire it. *Norah Kennedy.* I could get used to that.

"Are we really getting married?" I ask.

"That was the plan," Eamon says sleepily. "Not getting cold feet already are you?"

I slap his chest. "Never. Just trying to wrap my mind around it. I don't even know where to begin with planning a wedding."

"I'd think the first, and most important, thing would be deciding when. We can wait as long as you want, but I'd marry you right this second if there was someone to officiate," he says seriously, intertwining our fingers.

"Naked and in bed?"

"It would make the consummation quicker," he deadpans.

I snort loudly at that. "You're ridiculous."

"Alright, fine. Not naked and in bed," he grumbles. "How long do you need to plan?"

I prop myself onto my elbow and gaze down at my *fiance*, getting momentarily lost in the depths of his blue eyes.

"When I was little, I always imagined a huge, lavish wedding complete with twelve bridesmaids. I would, of course, make all of the dresses. And we would release doves at the end of the ceremony."

Eamon raises an eyebrow at me, "Doves? You're joking."

"Looking back, that does seem a little excessive," I laugh. "But I would like to at least make my own dress. As far as everything else, I don't have a clue. We could get married in Ireland and come back and do a reception at Paddy's for all I care. I don't need anything extravagant."

He turns his head to me abruptly. "Really? You'd get married in Ireland? What about our friends? I'm pretty sure a few of yours would be quite unhappy about that."

"It's not their wedding," I shrug. "Though they could always come too. The girls and I had talked a while back about going together someday, so it's not too far-fetched. I'm sure Teag and Ro wouldn't mind going back home for a visit. Maybe we could even get Paddy to go."

"Ach, Paddy would love that," Eamon grins. "I bet he'd even give you away if you wanted him to."

I inhale sharply and feel tears start to well in my eyes. Eamon immediately wraps his arms around me, pulling my head to his shoulder. "Shite, I'm sorry, love. That was stupid of me."

"No, it's okay." I sniffle. "I wasn't even thinking about not having parents at my wedding. I mean, I knew there wouldn't be a dad, but my Mom…"

"I know, Acushla. I'm so sorry. We can elope if you want…" he offers.

I shake my head. "Mom wouldn't want that. She'd want me to do what makes my heart happy. Even though she's not here anymore, it would feel like an insult to her memory. But I do love the idea of Paddy giving me away. He's the one responsible for us being together anyway."

"Aye, I suppose that's true. Though I always give credit to that pint of black stuff you were choking on that night."

I snort again. "I'll never live that down, will I?"

"Not a chance, fire sprite."

Chapter Thirty-Eight

Norah

"You can't get married!" Myra cries, slapping a hand on the table.

I'm sitting at our usual table at Paddy's with all of the girls and just finished telling them about making up with Eamon and his proposal, flashing my ring as proof.

"Myra," Amelia chides. "What the hell are you talking about? She's a grown-ass woman."

Myra growls in frustration. "Sorry, that's not what I meant. Of course you can get married, but you can't get married until after the baby gets here and I've lost the baby weight! I refuse to wear a bridesmaid's dress until I'm back to normal."

I roll my eyes at her. "What if I told you we're going to Ireland to elope?"

"What?" they all screech in unison. It's comical really.

"Norie, you *have* to have a wedding! A big one!" Myra continues to whine. "This is like a fairy-tale love story. You need the princess dress to go with your Prince Charming."

"Are you really thinking about eloping?" Charlie asks.

I shrug in response. "Kind of. We both love the idea of getting married and honeymooning in Ireland then having a small reception here at O'Nelly's after. But…"

"But what?" Layla asks, tilting her head to the side.

"Well, we'd like for you all to come with us."

Myra gasps loudly. "Well, now you really can't get married until this baby is born!"

"Wait, are you being serious? You want us to come to Ireland for your wedding?" Amelia asks disbelievingly.

"I know that's asking a lot of you all, so there's no pressure, but yeah, we would love that," I confess. "We're also thinking of his sister. With her recovery, travel may not be an option for her, which means his Mom may not be able to come either. After everything they've been through, I know how important it is for Eamon to share this with his family."

"Fine," Myra pouts dramatically. "I *guess* you can get married whenever you want. But I want to be able to drink at the reception."

We all agree that it's a fair compromise before diving into wedding and reception details. I may not have biological sisters, but these girls are my sisters in the only way that matters. If there was ever a group of friends that loved so completely, it's this group. They've been with me through the highs and the lows, showing up day in and day out.

"Where is your *fiance* tonight?" Charlie asks, emphasizing his new title. I like it.

"He's with Ro and Teagan, I think. Is that right, Layla?" I wink at her from across the table.

The others turn to her and she glares at me. I just smile in response.

"Yes," she says slowly. "They're all together. I think Teagan said there was a pick-up game tonight."

Myra and Amelia pounce, spouting off question after question without waiting for a response.

"Wait, are you two together now? When did this happen? What's he like...*you know?*"

Layla groans and starts fidgeting with her hair. She's spunky, but reserved, so all of this attention is probably the last thing she wants. I should feel bad, but I don't. If Teagan is half as amazing as Eamon is, then she's going to be a very happy girl.

* * *

Weeks after Eamon's return, we're back into the throes of school. This new semester has started with a vengeance. On top of classes, Eamon's busy student teaching, while I'm completely engulfed in plans for the Spring play. I'm having a blast designing the costumes though. Especially since Eamon, Ro, and Teagan lost a bet and are now my own personal mannequins for fittings.

We had all been together, celebrating our engagement at Paddy's when Ro suggested a drinking game. I swore I'd never do that again, but I was blissfully happy and up for anything. After a few rounds, we were all well and truly drunk. During one turn, Teagan and I were facing off, and I was determined to win.

"Alright O'Brien," I slurred. "I challenge you to a tequila shot contest."

He groaned loudly. "Ach, tequila? I fucking hate tequila."

"Well, if you don't take the challenge, you automatically lose."

"What happens if I lose, Grady?" he smirked.

Grinning mischievously, I said, "If you lose, or don't accept the challenge, you, Eamon, and Ro have to be my models for costume fittings for the Drag show."

Eamon cursed under his breath. "Don't do it, mate."

"What kind of costumes?" Ro asked with a raised brow.

At that, I burst into a fit of giggles. "Wellllll..." I sang. "It *is* a drag show.

CHAPTER THIRTY-EIGHT

And I *am* the costume designer, so you do the math."

"No fucking way, Grady!" Teagan roared.

"You must really think I'll beat you then." I teased.

He glared at me for a moment then gave a terse nod. "Alright. If you outdrink me, then we'll agree to play dress-up."

Eamon and Ro gawked at him in disbelief.

"But," he began. "If I outdrink *you*, then you and Layla have to come up with *and perform* a cheer at our next match. In front of the whole crowd."

My face paled at the idea of doing anything in front of a crowd. I glanced at Layla who was shooting daggers at him.

"Absolutely no fucking way, Teagan," Layla sneered.

He grinned at her in response, threw an arm around her shoulders, and kissed her on the cheek.

"What's the matter, Norah?" he crooned. "You look a little scared. Afraid I'll beat you?"

"Norah, don't you dare agree to this," Layla threatened.

After a tense moment of glaring at Teagan, I nodded. "Alright. Deal."

"What?" Layla yelled. "Shit. You better win or we're not friends anymore."

We made our way to the bar where Amelia informed Alicia of the contest. She smirked knowingly and started lining up shot glasses and filling them. The only reason we were getting away with this was because Paddy had taken the night off.

Eamon wrapped an arm around my waist, drawing me back to his chest, and whispered in my ear, "Acushla, if he loses, you're going to get it when we get home."

I shivered in anticipation. I failed to inform them that before I became a Guinness girl, tequila was my drink of choice. I turned to face Eamon, pressing my mouth to his, and muttered, "I look forward to my punishment then."

Ro was rubbing Teagan's shoulders like a boxer getting ready to enter the ring.

"Alright, Teags. Our fate is in your hands. Don't fuck this up."

I laughed loudly. "Oh Ro. I have a denim thong with your name on it."

When Alicia broke into a fit of giggles, he actually growled at her. "That will be enough out of you, lass. I bet you'd enjoy seeing me in that, wouldn't you?"

She snorted. "I'd pluck my eyes out with these bar tongs if I saw your ass in a denim thong."

"Let's do this, Grady," Teagan interrupted. "I hope you and Layla enjoy coming up with your cheer."

I saluted him and said, "Bring it, Irish."

Twenty minutes later, I was roaring my victory while Teagan was curled up in the fetal position on the floor. Eamon and Ro were groaning loudly and calling their friend every name in the book and some that weren't found in any book at all. My friends were surrounding me, singing a drunken version of "We Are The Champions". I squatted down and patted Teagan on the head, who lifted his eyes to glare at me.

"Don't worry, O'Brien. I'll make sure your costume is a flattering color. With a matching boa."

"Fuck me," he moaned. "How are you even standing? This whole pub is spinning right now."

I giggled at him. "It's okay, Teag. There's no shame in being a lightweight. Some of us can just hold our liquor better than others."

When I stood up, strong arms wrapped around me from behind. Turning my head, I met Eamon's heated eyes and couldn't help but tease him as well. "I'll let you wear your costume while you punish me."

He rolled his eyes at me and said, "Neither one of you will remember this in the morning. I think we're safe from playing dress up."

"We'll see," I smirked.

When the next morning rolled around, I was certainly hungover, but I remembered every part of the bet I'd won. Once I had a few cups of coffee in me, I got to work on designing the costumes for the Irish trio. I flipped back to the sketch I had done earlier in the year of Eamon dressed in drag and he, of course, chose that moment to look over my shoulder at the sketches.

"Is that me? What the fuck am I wearing?" he demanded.

I broke into a fit of laughter and tried to close the notebook. He easily

304

plucked it from my hands and turned back to the offending page.

Attempting to calm my giggles, I shrugged and said, "I told you I was going to design costumes for you and the boys."

He narrowed his eyes at me. "You dated this picture, love. It's before we even started really talking. Try again."

"Damn. You weren't supposed to look that close," I grinned up at him.

"Not that close? You've drawn me in a fecking wet suit and cat ears. Is this a secret fantasy of yours, Grady?"

I threw my head back and laughed so hard that tears streamed down my face. "Oh my god, Eamon, stop. I can't even with you. No, I don't fantasize about you in drag. I was a little obsessed with you then and started sketching you from memory. I was fantasizing about you on the soccer field, running around all sweaty and gorgeous, then I started picturing the entire team, and next thing I knew, you're all in drag."

"First, I'd like to address the fact that you said you were a little obsessed with me *then*. Are you saying you're no longer obsessed with me?" he teased.

I rolled my eyes. "Hush. I said I was a *little* obsessed with you then. Now I'm *really* obsessed with you."

"I will allow it. Now, let's discuss how you just used the word *soccer* when referring to football. Then we can talk more about how gorgeous you think I am," he said with a wink.

I snorted in amusement. "Soccer, football, same difference. And I meant to say sweaty and smelly. Not gorgeous."

"Liar," he growled, tossing the sketchbook on the floor. "Liars get punished."

"Promises, promises, Kennedy. You said you were going to punish me last night too and that didn't happen," I goaded, eyeing him appreciatively.

His eyes darkened and he caged me in with a hand on each armrest. Leaning in, he whispered against the shell of my ear, "You keep saying things like that and I'll have to bend you over my knee, love."

I shivered violently. "Don't tease me, handsome."

Eamon nipped my earlobe before kissing the sensitive spot under it. "Oh, I'm not teasing."

I turned my face towards his, our lips barely a whisper apart, and breathed out, "Prove it".

His mouth crashed into mine, tongue plunging in and laying claim to me. A surprised squeak escaped me as I knotted my fingers in his hair and held on for dear life. Eamon scooped me up from the chair and stalked toward the bedroom. Kicking the door closed behind him, he let my feet hit the ground before turning me around and walking us to the foot of the bed. When my knees hit the edge, he placed a hand on my upper back, gently bending me forward.

"Place your hands flat on the bed and don't move. Understand?" he growled.

My heart was thundering, my arousal at an all-time high. This wasn't an area I ever thought I wanted to experience, but the anticipation was killing me. I nodded.

"Say it, Acushla."

"I understand," I breathed, flattening my hands against the mattress.

"Good lass," he praised me, officially unlocking a kink I didn't know I had. His hands slid lazily down my back and over my hips before making the trail back up to push my shirt up and over my head. I felt his fingers lightly brush down my spine, followed by his lips. Goosebumps covered my skin while heat coiled in my core. His hands migrated back to my hips where he started pulling my leggings and underwear down slowly. He left them pooled around my ankles as he ran his tongue up the back of my right thigh, switching to the left to give it the same attention. I couldn't stop the moan that spilled from my mouth.

"You're so beautiful like this," he murmured when he rose to his feet again. He ran his hands over my ass, kneading his fingers into my skin. I felt a hand leave my body and return half a moment later as he spanked me hard enough to make me cry out.

"You actually spanked me," I panted, words laced with shock and a hint of arousal.

"I told you I wasn't teasing," he reminded me as he rubbed away the sting of his punishment.

In the same breath, he lifted his other hand to deliver the same treatment to my other side. This time when I cried out, it wasn't in shock. My body was vibrating with need.

"Have you learned your lesson, Acushla?" he murmured.

I looked at him over my shoulder and said defiantly, "No."

His eyebrows rose in surprise before he grinned devilishly at me. "Thought not, fire sprite," he said, then proceeded to spank me twice more, soothing the pain away each time.

"Eamon, I need you. Now." I demanded.

"Aye," he said simply.

The sound of his sweatpants dropping to the floor only intensified the pulsing heat between my legs. He kicked them off and placed a hand flat on my lower back then rubbed the tip of his cock along my entrance, teasing me.

"Please," I managed to whimper just as he drove into me. We both moaned loudly, stilling once he was fully seated inside. My leggings were still wrapped around my ankles, binding my legs together and creating more friction.

"I don't think I can be gentle right now, Norah," Eamon confessed in a strained voice.

"I don't want you to be."

"Thank fuck," he bit out before pulling out and slamming back into me. His hands dug into my hips with a bruising grip, holding me in place while he thrust hard and deep, over and over. He was relentless, and I loved every second of it. When my release came, he followed close behind, growling my name.

Chapter Thirty-Nine

Eamon

After Norah and I collapsed onto her bed in a sweaty heap, I wrapped my arms around her and we drifted off into a state of utter bliss. Obviously, I enjoy sex, but sex with Norah is like an out-of-body experience. Every time. She took me completely by surprise when she played along with her punishment. My fantasies don't usually include spanking, but when I saw her naked body bent over the bed, mixed with that sassy mouth of hers, the idea of leaving my handprint on her arse turned me on in a way I wasn't expecting.

A loud chiming brings me out of my slumber and Norah groans as she untangles herself from me. When she rolls over to snatch her phone from the bedside table, I roll with her, unwilling to break contact and hoping she doesn't answer so I can keep her in bed longer.

"Oh no," she whispers, her voice laced with worry.

I prop myself up on an elbow and pull her close, tucking my chin over her shoulder to glance at the screen. It's a number I don't recognize.

"Who is it, love?" I ask, pressing a kiss to the nape of her neck.

"I think it's the detective from back home," she mutters before answering and putting it on speaker.

"Hello?"

"Hello, this is Detective Morrow from the Ozark Police Department. Is this Norah Grady?" a man's voice says.

"Hello Detective," she answers. "Yes, this is Norah. What can I do for you?"

Her body begins trembling slightly, so I tighten my hold on her.

"I just wanted to let you know that we won't be requiring your testimony against Ashton Kirk. He was found deceased last night."

She sucks in a sharp breath. "Oh my god. I don't even know what to say to that. What...happened?"

"The investigation is still ongoing, but right now it looks like Mr. Kirk committed suicide," he says gravely.

"Wow...that's...," she starts. "I'm sorry. I should say that's awful, but I can't seem to find any remorse over this after what he did to me and all of those other women."

"Between you and me, Miss Grady, the world is a better place with one less rapist using up oxygen. That's off the record, of course. Do you have any questions for me?"

I've imagined more than once finding that piece of trash and beating the shite out of him, so I agree with Norah and the detective.

"No, Detective Morrow," she mutters. "Thank you so much for calling."

"It was my pleasure, Miss Grady. Take care now."

The call ends and Norah bursts into tears, sobs racking her shoulders. She cries so hard it feels like she's breaking. I can't do anything but hold her closer, murmuring words of comfort into her hair.

"Shhh, Acushla. It's okay. I've got you," I promise her.

She turns in my arms and buries her face against my chest. Eventually her sobs quiet to the occasional sniffle, but I continue to soothe her with words and gentle touches, rubbing my hand lightly up and down her spine. I hate feeling so helpless, but this isn't something I can just kiss away. It's not some dragon I can vanquish. But I can, *I will,* be by her side every step of the way as she processes and heals from this part of her life. It doesn't escape me how incredibly lucky I am to be the man she chose to move forward from this with. And soon she'll be my wife.

Norah lifts her head, looking at me with red-rimmed eyes, and says, "I'm sorry. I didn't mean to turn into a sobbing mess."

I brush a strand of hair off of her brow. "You don't need to apologize for a thing. That was big news. I'm sure a lot is going on in that head of yours now. I'm here if you want to talk about it."

"I don't even really know how to feel or think," she says. "I always hate to hear that someone felt so lost they thought suicide was the only answer, but after everything...I just feel a huge sense of relief. Relief knowing that that chapter of my life is closed. Relief that I won't have to testify and see his face. Relief that he can't hurt anyone again. Does that make me a horrible person?"

"No, Acushla. You're not a horrible person," I assure her. "You're a victim of a horrible crime and, although not ideal, justice has been served."

Norah nods once then tucks her head under my chin. "I'm glad you were here, Eamon."

"Always. I'm not going anywhere."

Norah

"No. Absolutely no fecking way am I wearing that. Forget it, Grady," Teagan growls, tossing my sketchbook across the table at me.

"Don't be such a baby, O'Brien," I laugh at him. "Yours isn't even that bad! Ro's is the worst, and even that isn't horrible."

Teagan glowers at me over the rim of his pint glass. "Eamon, please talk some sense into your mot. Bets done while pissed don't count."

CHAPTER THIRTY-NINE

"Sorry, mate. I tried to talk you both out of it." Eamon smirks.

"Besides," I say, pointing a finger at him. "If you had won, you *know* you wouldn't let Layla and me out of doing our cheer. It's not like you're performing on stage. You're just modeling the costumes for the actors."

"Oh, is that all?" he scoffs. "Just my arse exposed and in fucking high heels? I could break my ankle and never be able to play football again!"

I wince. "Okay, no high heels. Just the rest of it! And the makeup will mask your face, so no one will even really know it's you."

Eamon groans loudly, "Fuck, I forgot about the makeup. Teagan, you arsehole."

"Yeah, you arsehole," Ro agrees, sitting down next to Teagan. "Why are you an arsehole this time?"

Teagan grabs the sketch pad, flips a page, and slides it over to Ro. "This. This right here is what Eamon's *fiance* has created for you to wear. And somehow I'm the arsehole?"

Rowan studies the page, his eyes widening before looking up to glare at me. "You're joking. Right? This is all one big gag, isn't it?"

"Hey," I say, raising my hands in defense. "I told you I was going to make you a denim thong originally. Just be thankful I changed it to a pair of denim boy shorts instead."

Ro looks to Eamon with pleading eyes. "Kennedy, do something about this."

"I'm not excited about this either, but a bet's a bet," he says with a shrug.

Ro flips back a couple of pages to Eamon's sketch, which shows him in a black leather bodysuit, black combat boots, and dark makeup.

"Ach! No wonder you're not as pissed about that. Yours is actually decent! You're hardly showing anything!" Ro exclaims in outrage. "More like a sexy Batman!"

"Catman. See the ears?" Eamon corrects, pointing to the cat ear headband I've drawn on.

"Well, I can't have everyone staring at my fiance's half-naked body, now can I?" I tease. "Besides, he has the whole dark and mysterious thing going for him, so it fits."

"How much can I pay you to forget all about this?" Ro asks, reaching for his wallet.

"Not a dime, Gallagher," I say, tipping my glass in salute. "Suck it up."

Ro looks like he's about to rip me a new one when Alicia saunters up to the table with a pitcher of water. She stops beside him, looking amused.

"What are you bitching about now, Rowan?"

He whips his head in her direction and straightens in his chair. He's drinking her in, eyes roaming from the top of her midnight Dutch braid down to her red combat boots. She pretends not to notice, but her cheeks flush slightly.

"Hello there, love. Norah here is being unnecessarily cruel. Try to make her see some sense, would ya?"

Alicia just laughs. "Norie, cruel? How much have you had to drink?"

"Not a fecking thing! I only just got here!" he cries indignantly. "Look at this and tell me it's not cruel. The fire sprite expects me to wear *this* in front of people!"

He holds the drawing in front of her and a bubble of laughter escapes her. She tries to cover it with a cough, but it's not fooling anyone.

"What's the matter, Ro?" Alicia coos, placing a hand on his shoulder that has him stiffening in response. "I thought you were confident with your body? This seems right up your alley."

He stares at her in disbelief for a moment before blurting out, "What the feck is that supposed to mean? Aye, I may know that my body is in pristine condition, but that doesn't mean I want to go flaunting it in front of Jesus, Mary, Joseph, and the entire drama department!"

"Welcome to the world of women, where we're expected to look a certain way and dress accordingly to please the male species," Alicia says with an eye-roll. "But God forbid something happens to us in those clothes. Then it's clearly our fault for dressing provocatively."

The table goes silent, everyone's eyes widening.

"Sorry," she mumbles. "Sensitive subject. Anyway. The point is, don't be such a baby. Embrace the opportunity and give it your all like you do on the pitch."

Spinning on her heel, she stalks back to the bar. Layla and I share a look and rise from the table in pursuit of Alicia. We find her drying glasses behind the bar, staring pointedly at the floor.

"Hey," Layla says, getting her attention. "Is everything okay, Li?"

She looks up, quickly quelling the tears threatening to escape. "Yeah, I'm good. It's just been a long day."

"Do you want to talk about it?" I ask softly. If anyone can understand what it's like to be objectified and taken advantage of by a man, it's me.

"Nah," she says, picking up another glass. "Really, I'm okay. Thanks for checking though."

"Okay, but if you change your mind, you know we're here for you, right?" Layla reminds her.

"Yeah, I know. Love you girls," she says, then grins devilishly. "Now, tell me what else I can do to torment Ro."

I chuckle at the gleam in her eyes. "I think challenging him to own it like he does while he plays will go a long way. If he thinks it's something he can win at, I bet he'll jump in full force."

Alicia smiles and then casts a glance over my shoulder. "Incoming..." she warns.

The Irishman in question sidles up next to me, resting his corded forearms on the bar. Glancing at me and Layla, he says, "Eamon and Teagan are asking for ya, ladies."

Taking the hint, we wave at Alicia and head back to the table. Eamon pulls me down next to him, wrapping an arm around my shoulders.

"Everything okay?" he mutters.

"She says she's fine, but I don't buy it. I'm going to try to catch her alone and see if she'll open up."

"She looked like she was about to cry," Layla interjects.

"Shite," Teagan breathes. "She's one of the toughest lasses I know. Something big must have happened if she was that upset. Here's hoping Gallagher can get her to spill."

"Only if she wants to," I say pointedly. "Whatever is going on, she doesn't seem comfortable sharing it. And if it has anything to do with her outburst,

I can understand that. I just hope I'm wrong."

"Fuck, if something happened to her, Ro will commit murder," Eamon says.

We sit in silence for a few minutes, each of us pondering what could have possibly happened to rile our favorite bartender. My phone buzzes on the table, pulling us from our thoughts.

Myra: *Hey, we're going to skip out tonight. My feet are swollen and killing me. The idea of walking even across the room, let alone putting on shoes, makes me want to cry. And Mac has offered to rub my feet. ;)*

Norah: *You can't really turn that down. You'll be missed, but I understand. Hope you're able to get some rest. Tell that baby Auntie Norie loves her!*

Myra: *Will do! xoxo*

"Myra and Mac aren't coming tonight. She has some swelling and wants to take it easy," I tell everyone.

"I still can't believe they're having a baby. And *happy together*," Layla says in mock astonishment.

"Aye," Teagan agrees as he toys with the braid hanging over Layla's shoulder. "It's scary how much Mac has changed. He's almost tolerable now."

"Almost," Eamon says with a grimace. "I still think he's a wanker."

"Stop it," I chastise, playfully smacking his chest with the back of my hand.

He catches it and brings my knuckles to his lips. "Sorry love. He'll never be my favorite person. Not after all the things he said about you."

I roll my eyes at him. "Eamon, that ship has sailed. I'm over it, so should you be."

"Not until he officially apologizes to you," Eamon says decidedly. "Even if he was just joking, it's not okay to talk about any woman that way."

"He's right," Teagan agrees. "He has a daughter on the way, so the sooner he learns to control that mouth of his, the better."

We all hum in agreement.

Chapter Forty

Norah

It's the week before the spring play. Dr. Andrews wrote the entire production himself and titled it "BeDRAGgled." When I originally told him about having the Irish trio model the costumes for the cast, he laughed to the point of tears. He loved all of my designs for the characters but thought the one Rowan modeled was genius. I had successfully turned him into a cowboy drag queen.

"Fecking hell, Norah," Rowan grouses. "These chaps are heavy."

I chuckle as I secure the last buckle on his fringed chaps. "You look great, Ro. And you're a good sport. You've complained the least out of the three of you."

"Ach, well if we *have* to do this, we might as well give it our all! Plus," he says, turning the lower half of his body to look in the mirror, "these knickers really make my arse look good."

"I'm going to hurl," Teagan mumbles into the trash can between his knees. "If I puke, do I still have to do this?"

"Teag," I scold, "you play on stage at Paddy's, and you play on the field in front of tons of people all the time. How is this any different?"

He lifts his head long enough to scowl at me. "I usually have my arse covered during both of those, thank you very much."

I shake my head and motion for him to rise. "Stand up. Let me make sure everything is still in place."

"There's not much here to *be* in place," he grumbles but complies anyway. His costume consists of a red cheeky leotard covered in shiny beading, black fishnet stockings, red platform ankle boots, and a devil-horned headdress.

After begging her and promising to cook her dinner for a week, Layla agreed to help with the makeup on the guys. She transformed Teagan's face from the handsome and rugged Irishman into a smirking devil with hooded eyes. I can't wait to see what she did with Eamon.

"Where the hell is Kennedy?" Ro calls from the other side of the room where he's still posing in front of the floor-length mirror, running his hands over the glittery denim bustier while admiring his ass in the matching cheeky boy shorts. The tasseled chaps, cowboy boots, and cowboy hat complete the look. We put him in a curly red wig, that matches his beard perfectly, and ridiculously long fake lashes covered in glitter. He doesn't seem to mind them in the least.

"That's a good question," I muse, looking around backstage. "I'll go check on him. Teagan, you're good. Go over there with Ro and let him boost your confidence." I meander out of the general dressing area to the private dressing rooms and knock on the door to the room Eamon was getting ready in. "Eamon? You in there?"

"No," he grumbles.

I swallow the laugh getting ready to burst from my mouth at his sullen tone and ask, "Can I come in?"

There's a pause, then a loud, exasperated sigh. "If you must," he finally says.

Cautiously cracking the door open, I slip inside, closing it behind me. Then I stop, and my jaw hits the floor. Eamon is standing there in his skintight black faux leather bodysuit that covers him from neck to ankles. I designed it without sleeves to showcase his muscular biceps. I've seen him in the bodysuit before, but seeing him in it with hair and make-up leaves me stunned. Layla outdid herself, and I make a mental note to thank her with a bottle of wine. He's wearing a straight waist-length wig and cat ears on top. There's a long black tail hanging limply from the back of the suit. Layla painted on a black eye mask and gave him blood-red lips. He looks hot as hell.

"What?" he asks, fidgeting.

I clear my throat and rake my eyes slowly up and down his body again. "How is it that you're sexy as sin in your sweats *and as a cat woman?* Life is so unfair."

"Ach. Stop. You're having a laugh at me, and I feel ridiculous." He pouts.

"I'm not!" I promise, closing the distance between us. "If you didn't have to be out there modeling in thirty minutes, I'd jump your bones."

He snorts and gestures down his torso. "This bodysuit was practically painted on."

"Uh huh…" I say, ogling the way the bodysuit clings to him below the waist.

"Acushla."

"Hmmm?"

"Eyes up here," he deadpans.

"Sorry," I say, though I'm not sorry at all. "I didn't realize just how distracting you'd be."

Eamon rolls his eyes and crosses his arms over his chest, which does nothing for my current state of arousal.

"Okay, but on a serious note," I say, clearing my throat again. "Does anything need to be adjusted or altered? Can you walk towards me, turn, and walk away?"

"You just want to check out my arse, don't you?" he accuses, narrowing his eyes at me.

I huff out a laugh. "I won't deny it, but I really do need to make sure everything is where it should be."

"I can assure you that my cock is *not* where it should be right now."

"Stop." I giggle. "I'm serious."

"So am I, love," he growls, stalking towards me.

"No, you have to walk like you will out there." I throw a thumb over my shoulder towards the direction of the stage. "I need the swagger."

"You're killing me," he grinds out. "But fine. Don't you dare laugh at me."

"Never," I promise with a wink.

Eamon takes a deep breath, lifts his eyes to the ceiling as if saying a prayer, and then starts sashaying towards me with the grace of a lion. *Of course he does.*

He comes within half a foot of me, then suddenly spins on his heel, tossing his long wig in my face, and traipses away, swinging his hips. I can't stop staring at his ass. What can I say? I'm a weak woman.

"Alright, kitty," I say roughly. "It definitely looks good on my end. Anything you need me to check? Besides your cock?"

He lifts his eyebrows in surprise. "I don't think I've ever heard anything so filthy come out of that sweet mouth of yours. I like it."

I pin him with a glare.

"Alright, alright. No, nothing seems out of place. You've done quality work, love."

I grin at the praise, then say, "Now, come on out. Teagan is about to throw up his lunch, and Rowan might be considering a career in cross-dressing."

Eamon chuckles. "'Course he is."

We walk into the dressing area, and Rowan lets out a loud whistle. "Fecking hell, Kennedy. You make one sexy cat woman. Can I borrow that for Halloween?"

I laugh loudly while Eamon replies, "Sure thing, Ro. But only if you let me borrow yours. Especially the chaps."

Rowan grins broadly. "Aye, alright. It's a deal, mate."

"Where's Teagan?" Eamon asks, looking around the room. I do the same, but don't see him anywhere.

Ro stops taking selfies long enough to say, "He's in the jacks. Bet you a pint he's got a bad dose of it."

"I'll go check on him," Eamon sighs, sauntering towards the bathrooms.

Eamon

"Teagan, mate? You in here?" I call out as soon as I walk into the bathroom. There are a couple of stalls parallel to the urinals, but only one has the door closed and a pair of fishnet-covered legs kneeling on the floor.

"I can't do this, Eam," Teagan groans. "I'm fucking losing it. I've never felt so nervous in all my life." The toilet flushes, and he emerges, clutching his devil tail.

"Shite. Looks like Ro was right. You *do* look like you've had a bad dose of it." I smirk at him.

"Fuck off. That's not helping."

"Sorry, mate. I'm just messing with you. But, seriously, your costume is fierce. Have you actually looked in the mirror?" I ask, gesturing towards the mirrors over the sinks.

Teagan shakes his head. "No. I'm afraid I'll hurl what's left of my guts up if I look at myself."

"Why? What's got you so up to high doh?" I ask, tilting my head to the side.

"You're not?" Teagan asks in disbelief.

"Aye," I nod. "'Course I am, but not to the point of being sick."

"Your arse isn't hanging out either," he says pointedly.

"Not hanging out, no, but this thing is so tight you can make out every hair on my arse along with the outline of my cock." I gesture towards my groin.

Teagan's eyes widen as he takes in my costume. "Fecking hell. You're not kidding. How'd you even get into that?"

"It wasn't easy." I grimace. "I thought about greasing myself up but didn't want to be sliding around inside this wetsuit. You can at least move somewhat freely in that. Your skin can breathe."

"Aye, that's true." Teag snorts in agreement. "I guess it's just the setting. A small stage at the pub or being on the pitch isn't nearly as terrifying as being on an actual performing stage with the lights and being expected to walk in a way I'm not used to all while *actual* drag queens critique me."

I nod in understanding. "Look at it this way, Teag. You're in costume. No one will even recognize you this way. We don't even have to say anything. Just march our arses onto that stage, model Norah's designs, then we're done."

Blowing out a deep breath, he says, "You're right."

"Plus," I add cheerfully. "Ro has fully embraced this and is already begging to use my costume at Halloween. He has enough confidence for all of us. And he's going out first, so he can pave the way."

Inhaling another breath and releasing it, Teagan rolls his shoulders, straightens his spine, and nods. "Alright. Let's do this."

Norah

It's time for the guys to make their way to the stage, and Rowan has convinced them they're the sexiest cross-dressers in the state of North Carolina. They're huddled up like they do before games, chanting encouraging words at each other. It's hilarious. I break up their huddle to usher them to stage right, where they're going to strut out from. I remind them to smile, bat their fake lashes, and exaggerate their hip swaying.

Rowan rolls his eyes at me, then prances onto the stage with enthusiasm. He's blowing kisses at the actors in the audience and gyrating his hips like it's his job; circling the lasso over his head while thrusting provocatively. The cast is laughing and cheering loudly, begging for more.

I send Teagan out next. He takes a deep breath, then saunters onto the stage, swinging his devil tail for all he's worth, all while holding his head high and grinning wickedly. I look over at Layla, who's laughing so hard I think she might fall over.

Finally, it's Eamon's turn. Before he steps out, he grabs my face and plants a quick but hard kiss on my mouth, winks at me, and then swaggers toward his friends. He twirls his cat tail in one hand while clawing the air with the other. Next thing I know, he's dropped into a low squat and rolled his body back up, smacking a hand on his ass. The audience eats it up, and I might actually die from laughing. He's not only completed the task set before him, but gone above the bar to excel at it.

At the end of the costume reveal, the Irishmen take a bow to a standing ovation and loud cheering. When they make their way back to the dressing rooms, Eamon sneaks up behind me, wrapping his arms around my torso and swinging me in a circle. I screech loudly until he sets me down. Wheeling around, I throw my arms around his neck, grinning wildly. "Oh my god, Eamon, that was amazing!"

Chuckling, he presses a kiss to my temple. "That was more fun than I thought it would be."

I pull back, wagging my eyebrows at him. "Fun enough to be a regular costume model for me?"

"Fuck no." He laughs. "I can't breathe in this thing, and the makeup is making me itch."

"Speak for yourself, Kennedy!" Rowan yells over his shoulder. "I'm going to make a killing doing this! Who needs business school?"

"You're on your own, mate," Teagan chimes in. "My thighs are chafing, and my eyes won't stop watering with all this stuff on my face."

Laughing, I rest my head on Eamon's chest.

"Are we allowed to change now, Acushla?" he mutters against my hair. "My balls need air."

Rowan and Teagan howl with laughter, which earns them a middle finger from Eamon. I step out of his embrace and twine our fingers together. "Yes, you're free to change and wash the make-up off. I'll help you."

"Ach, I bet you'll help him, fire sprite!" Rowan winks.

"Be nice, or I'll have Layla use super glue on those lashes instead of the remover," I threaten.

321

He puts his hands up in surrender. "No need to get scary, Grady."

I glare at Ro playfully before following Eamon back to the dressing room, where I definitely do more than just help him out of his costume.

* * *

Eamon and I are curled up on the couch, having just hung up from the call to his Mom and sister to tell them about our engagement and desire to marry in Ireland. Rosie and Caity both squealed with delight and Rosie immediately started listing all of the venues, florists, and bakeries. We tried to tell her that we just wanted something simple and affordable, but she scoffed at us, insisting that she would pay for everything. We playfully argued for a while before convincing her that, if she really wanted to contribute, she could pay for the photographer since we cared more about preserving the memories from the day than the frills. Then I chatted with Caity for a few minutes about her recovery and therapy. She told me that everything has been going surprisingly well and she's already able to walk with just the help of a cane. Her motor skills are still a little delayed, but overall, she's thriving. We've yet to talk face-to-face, but I can already sense a bond forming. I feel like I've known her for years.

After saying our goodbyes, I set my phone on the coffee table then turn to Eamon. I open my mouth to say something when he suddenly cups my face in his hands and kisses me passionately, stealing my breath.

"What was that for?" I gasp.

He shrugs and kisses me again. "You're amazing, and I love you. I love that my Mam and sister love you almost as much as I do. I love that you're mine and I'm yours."

I crawl over him, straddling his lap. He rests his hands on my waist while I link my arms around his neck. Pressing a soft kiss to his lips, I say, "I love you too. And I love that I'm yours and you're mine."

He flashes a grin at me as his hands drift over my hips and down to my thighs, skimming his fingers under the hem of my sleep shorts. When I lean in to kiss him again, I slowly rock my hips over him. He growls against my mouth, slipping his fingers higher until he reaches my already damp panties.

"Already wet for me, Acushla?" he asks, pressing his thumb through the fabric against my clit.

"Yes," I gasp. "Always."

Kissing his way along my jaw, he flicks his tongue against the sensitive spot behind my ear. I hum my approval, arching my back as he nips and sucks on my neck. Wrenching away from him, I tear my tank top over my head, my hair a wild halo framing my face.

Eamon raises his other hand to slide his knuckles between my breasts. "God, you're beautiful," he says reverently.

In response, I grip the bottom of his shirt, lift it over his head, and toss it behind me. Slowly, I trail my hands over his chest, scraping my nails over his nipples. His stomach tenses in anticipation as I run my fingers down his abs to his sweatpants. Hooking a finger over the edge, I pull the elastic waistband out, then release it, letting it snap against his skin and making him grunt. Untangling myself, I sink to my knees in front of him.

"Take these off," I order him, pulling on the fabric of his pants.

Eamon raises his hips to pull his sweats down to his knees, and I remove them the rest of the way, then quickly lean forward to run my tongue up the line separating his abs before kissing my way back down to his cock. I wrap a hand around the base and lick the underside of him slowly, preening at the growl coming from his throat. Catching his gaze, I take him into my mouth as far as I can before sucking my way back to the tip. His hands fist in my hair, and he starts slowly pumping into my mouth. The tip of my tongue massages the ridge around the head of his cock, causing his hips to buck. His moans grow louder and louder until he thrusts one last time and stills, spilling himself down my throat. I swallow it all, then give one last lazy lick up his shaft.

"Fucking hell. You're way too good at that," he pants in praise.

I'm practically purring as I shuck my shorts and panties and clamber back onto his lap, sinking down onto him in one smooth motion. He curses under his breath and grips my ass firmly with both hands, rocking me gently. But I don't want gentle.

So I lean in and whisper against the shell of his ear, "Harder. I want you to fuck me harder, handsome."

With another growl, he lifts me slightly slamming me back down. I cry out each time our bodies collide, and just as I'm getting close, he flips us and pins me down on the couch. Lifting one of my legs over his shoulder, he thrusts harder and faster. Bending over me, he lightly grazes my nipple with his teeth. My body arches at the contact, and I gasp loudly when he bites down harder. He's fucking me so hard, I have to brace my hands on the arm of the couch above my head. I've never felt so alive, so feral, and. I can't get enough of him.

"Eamon," I rasp, "I'm going to...Oh god. Don't stop!"

Within a matter of seconds, I'm coming so hard that I see stars. As I clamp down around him, he barks out my name and comes again. Before I can recover, he's vibrating his thumb over my clit.

"You're going to come for me again," he orders in a low, husky voice.

"I can't...I don't think...Fuck...Oh god, oh god, oh god!" I scream, thrashing my head from side to side as another orgasm shatters through me.

I'm completely spent, and my limbs feel boneless. It's several minutes before either of us moves. We just lay there, holding each other and breathing heavily.

Eamon is nuzzling his face into my neck when Rowan interrupts my flashback. "Fire sprite! What do you say we have ourselves another drinking contest? See if you can beat Kennedy this time!"

I shake my head to dispel the lingering lust and laugh at Ro. "No thanks. Beating Teagan last time was enough for me. I think I've proven that I can hold my own."

"Aye, but not the black stuff. But then again, you probably wouldn't beat him anyway," he taunts me.

"Don't let him bait you, Acushla," Eamon mutters into my hair.

I turn to give him an accusatory glare. "Are you afraid you'll lose, Kennedy?"

He pecks my lips quickly before saying, "No, not at all. Just would hate to see you wound your pride like last time. I'm looking out for you, love."

I hold his gaze for a moment, then say, "Line 'em up, Alicia."

Epilogue

Norah

Graduation came and went in a blur. It was bittersweet walking across that stage to shake the Dean's hand and accept my diploma. I missed my Mom so much and would have given anything to have her there, but I wasn't without family. When my name was called, cheers rang out so loudly that every head in the auditorium turned. My girls were on their feet, holding up hand-painted signs while three Irishmen in their own caps and gowns were standing and making just as much noise. At that moment, everything around me faded as my gaze snagged on Eamon's brilliant blue eyes. A grin spread across his face and he mouthed, "I love you". Smiling through the tears forming, I blew him a kiss. My heart was overflowing with love and gratitude as I made my way back to my seat.

Dr. Andrews and UNCW offered me a full-time position as Head Designer of the Costume Department after the spring play. They also offered Layla a position with the Makeup Department after seeing her work on the drag show, and she was more than ecstatic to turn in her notice at the grocery store. It's an added bonus that we'll be able to commute to work together.

Eamon was scouted by a couple of MLS teams but decided in the end that he'd rather use his skills to teach high school kids and accepted a joint position at a local high school as a history teacher and soccer coach. As much as he loves the sport, he didn't want to spend the majority of his time traveling, especially since moving in with me after the spring play. We've thoroughly enjoyed our engagement.

Rowan was drafted by the Charlotte Football Club. His primary residence will be in Wilmington, though he'll be traveling quite a bit. This suits him perfectly, as he's always up for a new adventure. Teagan was offered a position as the Director of Communications for the North Carolina Independent Colleges and Universities nonprofit organization. Like Eamon, the idea of being constantly on the road didn't appeal to him since his goal was to take his business degree and use it to help underprivileged communities. He's always been against large corporations taking over local establishments, so he hopes to be an advocate for them.

Now we're at Paddy's after the ceremony to celebrate. When Eamon and I arrive, Paddy pulls us both in for a crushing hug. "Ach, I can't tell ya how proud I am of the two of ya. It's been an absolute privilege to watch ya both work so hard and end up here."

"Thanks, Paddy," I say, kissing him on the cheek. Then fighting back tears, I add, "I couldn't have done it without you. You'll never know how much your love and support means to me. Which is why I want to ask a favor of you."

Paddy's brows furrow. "Aye? What's that, Norah love?"

I take his weathered hand in mine and ask, "Would you do me the honor of giving me away at our wedding?"

His bottom lip quivers before he pulls me back into his arms, engulfing me in a bear hug. "Ach, of course I will! It would be *my* honor!" He steps back to place one hand on my shoulder and the other on Eamon's. "I couldn't have parted with either of you for anyone else. I wouldn't trust my Norah's care to anyone other than Eamon, and I wouldn't have trusted Eamon's heart with anyone but my Norah. The two of ya make me so proud."

"Thanks a million, Paddy," Eamon says. "Love you, aul fella."

"Now don't go getting all sappy on me, lad," Pat says with a wink. "So, when is the big day?"

I look to Eamon before saying, "Well, that depends on when you can take time off to come to Ireland with us."

Pat's eyes widen, and his jaw drops. "You're joking!"

Eamon wraps an arm around my waist, pulling me closer. "Not a joke. We want to get married in Ireland if possible. Will you come with us?"

"Aye," he says, tears filling his eyes, "I'd love to. It's been too long since I've visited my sweet Ellie's resting place."

After another round of hugs and tears, we make our way to the table surrounded by our friends where we spend several hours talking and reminiscing about the last eight months. I soak it all in, not wanting to forget a single moment of this night. The warmth of Eamon's arm around my shoulders. The sound of Myra and Amelia laughing at whatever story Mac is telling them. The blush that fans Layla's cheeks as Teagan leans in to whisper in her ear. The way Rowan lightly grasps Alicia's wrist when she places a pitcher of water on the table, and the look they share thinking no one is watching.

Looking around the pub, I think back to the night I met Eamon. What started as the most embarrassing moment of my life ended up leading to the happiest moments of my life. I snuggle into Eamon's side and share a look with Charlie across the table from me. My best friend of nearly twenty years, who can read me like a book, who sees the joy in my eyes, winks at me. This is my family. In a handful of months, I'll be married. Now that Paddy has agreed to walk me down the aisle, we can finally set a date.

Eamon

Four Months Later

"Stop fidgeting, mate," Teagan whispers, clapping a hand on my shoulder.

I inhale deeply through my nose and then release through my mouth, steeling my mind. I'm not exactly nervous, just impatient. Soon, Norah will be walking down this short aisle with Paddy at her side. I'm still amazed that we're here. After everything we've been through, before and after we met, we're exactly where we're meant to be.

We arrived in Ireland a week ago, spending nearly every waking hour planning this wedding with our family and friends who came over for the event, including my Mom and sister. We've managed to sneak away once or twice for some more *private excursions,* but today is our day. Today, we promise to have and to hold in good times and bad, in sickness and health, as long as we both shall live. Today is the start of our forever.

Exactly one year ago, I saw a beautiful girl with auburn curls in a Kelly green shirt across the pub. I'd just finished a set with Teagan and Ro, and we were headed for a pint. I pretended not to notice her as we approached the bar, but every nerve ending was hyper-aware of the fire sprite just a couple of feet away. I could feel her staring at me, so I turned to smile at her, and she…choked on her Guinness. Her face turned an alarming shade of red, and I reached over on instinct to thump her back. Then, like the eejit I am, I made a comment about her not being able to hold her Guinness which led to an epic drinking contest. And here we are.

The room at the Butler House in Kilkenny is small and decorated simply with white chairs, red and peach roses, and lanterns. Less than twenty people are present to witness and celebrate our union. Teagan and Ro are standing with me at the front of the room. We're all dressed in simple charcoal gray suits adorned with a single rose on our lapels. My Mam gives me a tearful smile from the front row, where she's sitting next to Dr. Colm.

Peering out at our friends who made the journey from the States to Ireland, I feel so fucking fortunate. Charlie and my sister, Caity, stand across from me and the groomsmen in their rose-colored bridesmaids' dresses. Mac and Myra are snuggled up beside each other in the second row, staring blissfully at their sleeping baby girl, Scarlett. Amelia and Alicia are sitting next to Myra, while Layla and Charlie's husband, Mark, both sit across the aisle behind Mam. In front of Amelia sits Ro's cousin, Luke. He was in the area, and Ro, being Ro, invited him to attend a wedding that was not his own. But I don't care. The room could have been full of elephants, and it wouldn't have phased me. All that matters is that I'm marrying Norah.

After another glance at my Ma, a recording of a soft, acoustic version of Ringsend Rose starts playing. The French doors at the back of the room open, and everyone stands. In steps Pat O'Nelly with the most beautiful woman in the world on his arm. My breath catches in my throat, and I swallow thickly. Norah is radiant; she looks otherworldly in the ivory lace dress that she designed and made herself. The sweetheart bodice is covered in a sheer lace boat neck overlay that extends to full-length sleeves and the delicate lace runs over the A-line frame of the dress into a small train. Her curls are up in an intricate braid around her head, with soft tendrils framing her face. Her makeup is understated, leaving her skin looking soft and glowing and she's wearing the small diamond earrings I gave her the night before. She beams at me, eyes shimmering with unshed tears, and I grin back at her, fighting my own tears.

Norah floats towards me confidently. When she's close enough to touch, Paddy turns to her and places a soft kiss on her cheek, then brushes it tenderly with a knuckle before facing me. We clasp hands, and he pulls me in for a firm embrace.

"Take good care of her, lad," he whispers in my ear.

"With everything I have," I whisper back.

He takes Norah's hand and places it in mine before returning to sit next to my mother and Dr. Colm, who has made my Mam happier than she's been in years.

Norah takes a step closer and tips her face up to meet my eyes. "Hi, handsome," she whispers.

"You're gorgeous," I say in reply.

The ceremony is short and sweet. We recite handwritten vows, have our hands wrapped in the traditional Celtic knot, and then exchange rings. When the officiant announces we're finally wed, I pull Norah close with one arm around her waist and the other on her cheek and kiss her as I've never kissed her before to the cheers of our closest friends and family. *My wife.* She's my wife. When we break the kiss, her stormy blue eyes meet mine, and I see my future there. Our future.

"I love you," Norah says softly.

"I love you more, Acushla."

The End

Bonus Content

What happens next?

Norah and Eamon have set off on their happily ever after, but what about the rest of the crew? Find out with Layla and Teagan in *His Spanish Rose*, coming soon! Keep reading for a sneak peek!

Teagan

"Where the hell is Kennedy going?" Rowan asks.

As soon as the final buzzer sounded, declaring the Seahawks' victory, Eamon Kennedy untangled himself from the pile of teammates and took off across the pitch toward his new mot, Norah. They recently started dating and he's already head over heels for her.

"Isn't it obvious, Ro? Norah's here." I shrug.

I'll be honest. I'm a little jealous. My last relationship ended out of the blue at the end of last semester. I'd been with Ashley for over a year and thought I loved her. She was a beautiful blonde bombshell with an infectious laugh. The lass didn't know a stranger either. Everywhere we went she knew someone or made friends with whoever just happened to be nearby. I loved that about her. We met towards the end of our sophomore year at UNCW and instantly connected. She loved that I'm Irish, but said she loved me for so much more. Until one day she didn't anymore.

"I'm sorry, Teags. I just can't do this anymore. I should have called it months ago, but I hated the idea of hurting you. I still want to be friends though," she said flippantly in the small kitchen of my apartment.

Laughing, I reached for her. "What are you talking about? Are you slagging me? Very funny, you."

Ashley stepped away from my grasp and crossed her arms over her chest.

"I'm not kidding. We've been drifting apart for a while now. Haven't you noticed?"

I was completely flummoxed. I thought we'd been happy together. Yeah, we were always busy with school, jobs, and life in general, but I always made it a point to see her nearly every day.

"No, Ash, I haven't. I thought everything was fine. We've been up to ninety with finals, but I've done my best to connect with you."

"It's not that," she said hesitantly, running her hand through her golden tresses. "Our spark is gone."

"Our spark is gone? What the feck does that mean?" I asked incredulously. "Am I not pleasing ya in the bedroom, then? That was one area where I thought we excelled, love. Now yer tellin' me that my cock isn't keeping ya happy?"

My Irish accent tends to thicken when I'm frustrated or drunk.

"God, Teagan, that's not what I'm talking about. That's all our relationship had going for it. And I want more. I don't think..." she paused, pressing her lips together in a thin line.

"You don't think what, Ashley?" This is so out of left field, so I'm going to make her spell it out for me.

She took a deep breath and squared her shoulders before looking me in the eyes and saying, "I don't love you anymore. I haven't for a while now."

It felt like I'd just taken a hit on the pitch. She didn't love me? Hadn't loved me. I sank onto the bar stool behind me.

"I'm sorry," she continued softly. "I don't want to hurt you. I care about you, but I'm not in love with you. I can't keep dragging you along like this. It's not fair to either of us."

I just stared at her in utter disbelief for a moment before whispering, "When?"

"When what?" Ashley questioned.

"When did you stop loving me?"

"Teagan..." she started.

"No," I shrug again, "You at least owe me that much, love. I've devoted myself to you and thought I was giving you everything, but at some point, it wasn't enough. I'd like to know when."

She wrung her hands in front of her and muttered, "Since February."

My head shot up, eyes narrowing, "February? You haven't loved me since fucking February? Why didn't you say anything to me? I would have done anything to help fix this!"

"What was I supposed to say, 'Teagan, I'm feeling like I don't love you anymore?'" she said, throwing her hands in the air.

"Yes!" I bellowed, rising out of my chair and walking around the kitchen island. "You could have told me anything! Even a simple, 'something doesn't feel right' and then I would have explored that with you! I've always been open and honest with you, since the very beginning."

I stopped in my tracks, a thought coming to me. "Wait…" I said, "February. That's when you did that internship in Texas."

Ashley's cheeks started to flush and she refused to look at me.

"Is there…did you…meet someone else?"

"Teagan…" she pleaded. "Can we just leave it? Please?"

My arms dropped to my sides in defeat. She cheated on me. I should have known. Every time I called her while she was away, she either kept the conversation short or didn't answer. She would text me later, claiming that she had been in meetings all day and was exhausted. I wanted her to stay focused and be successful while she was there, so I never pressed the issue.

"Who is he?"

"Don't, Teag. All you need to know is that I'm moving to San Antonio this summer and finishing my degree there," she told me, shame lacing her every word.

I blew out a rough breath and raked my fingers through my brown hair. "You're moving? You must really love him then. I guess there's nothing left to say, is there? You didn't talk to me because you'd already made up your mind, didn't you?"

Ashley timidly closed the space between us, placing a kiss on my cheek. "I'm sorry. I really am. I never wanted to hurt you."

Then she walked out of my apartment and out of my life.

* * *

"Oy! Earth to O'Brien!" Rowan yells, pulling me from my thoughts.

"Right, sorry, mate. Yeah, I'll go get him."

I take off in a jog across the pitch to where my friend and teammate is kissing his girl passionately. It's pretty impressive actually. I'm about to make some smart-arse comment when I hear someone clear their throat. Turning, my gaze lands on the most luscious woman I've ever seen. Her long black hair hangs to the middle of her back in loose waves. The setting sun is gilding her tawny skin and lighting up the brightest pair of brown eyes I've ever had the pleasure of staring into.

"I didn't think they were going to come up for air, did you, lass?" I ask, peering up at the dark beauty from the sideline.

She giggles and shakes her head. Her cheeks darken with blush and it makes me want to preen like a damned peacock.

"Oy! Kennedy! You can snog your girl later! Coach wants us in the locker room like five minutes ago!" Ro yells from across the field, clearly not trusting me to do my job.

All three of us are Irish, having transferred overseas at the same time. We didn't know each other at all until meeting on the field, but we bonded immediately and are usually referred to as *The Irish Trio*. Eamon and I have similar personalities, both more reserved. Rowan Gallagher, however, is anything but reserved. I'm convinced it's due to the ginger hair.

While Eamon says goodbye to Norah, I keep my eyes on her friend. She has that voluptuous hourglass figure that makes me want to bite my knuckles and groan. She's an absolute smoke show and I'm not leaving until I know her name.

"It's true," the girl says, with a faint accent, remarking on something Norah just said. "She's an amazing baker too! I can blame every single one of these curves on her!"

"You say that like it's a problem," I say, climbing over the barrier to stand by Eamon. I eye her appreciatively, which makes her blush again. Sticking a hand in her direction, I drawl, "Name's Teagan O'Brien. You are?"

"Uh…um. Layla. Layla Diaz," she says nervously, placing her soft hand in mine.

"Pleasure, love. Now, excuse me while I take Romeo here before Coach blows a gasket." I wink at her. "See you around, Layla."

A grin spreads across my face as we jog back across the pitch and enter the locker rooms.

By the time I get home, I'm completely spent, having been up early to study for a test and then in class until about an hour before I had to be at the pitch. I used that hour to eat a late lunch and call my mum. I try to call her once every couple of weeks. After visiting for a few minutes and ascertaining that all is well back in Ireland, I made my way to the pitch to do warm-ups with the team. The game had gone spectacularly. We beat our rivals from Duke University, mostly thanks to Eamon's hat trick, but I'm pretty proud of the shots I blocked from entering the net. As the Seahawks' goalie, I make it my mission to defend that goal like a warrior defending a fortress.

I walk into my apartment complex and stop to check the mail. Unlocking the box, I open it to find a couple of bills, junk mail, and a letter from the landlord. Christ, I hope the rent isn't going up. I'm doing okay financially, but I've been saving for a trip back home to see my family. I slide a finger under the flap of the envelope while walking up the stairs to my second-floor flat. I always choose the stairs over the elevator. Small, closed-in spaces give me the willies. I've just reached the landing when I get to the point of the letter.

Attention Tenants:

I regret to inform you that the building will be under new management as of two weeks from today's date. The new management will be completely renovating the complex, requiring all current tenants to relocate indefinitely. If interested in keeping residence here, please visit the website listed below to fill out the inquiry form. Unfortunately, they will not be offering the completed units to current tenants before listing them to the public. It is strictly on a first come first served basis. Due to these circumstances, I will be refunding everyone's original deposits and this month's rent. I will refer anyone to a new complex should they decide to pursue that route.

I apologize for any inconvenience this causes.

Sincerely,

Allen Roper

Rosewood Apartments Management

What the actual fuck? Is this a joke?

"Got your letter, I see," says a withered voice behind me.

I turn to find my elderly neighbor, Mrs. Bailey, standing in her doorway, leaning against her walker.

"Aye," I tell her with a nod hello. "I'm hoping this is some sort of prank."

"I wish it were. Roper came to my door not two hours ago to tell me in person," she says with disdain.

"How can he do this? Is this even legal?" I ask dumbfounded.

"It's not him doing it. He didn't have a say in the matter. He's not the owner, just management. They're just making him do all the dirty work. The poor man was just sick over the whole thing." Mrs. Bailey explains.

"How do they expect us all to not only pack up and move out, but to also find a new place to live?"

She wheezes a sardonic laugh. "They don't give two shits about us. Why would they when they know the new units will be bringing in three times what we're paying now?"

I gape at her. "Three times?! That's absolute bollocks is what that is! Something needs to be done to stop this."

Shaking her head, she turns to go back inside her apartment. "Too late, sonny boy. It's already done."

Entering my own flat, I kick the door closed behind me and drop my backpack and sports bag on the floor. Raking my fingers through my hair in frustration, I stalk towards the kitchen. What am I supposed to do? Two weeks isn't feasible at all. I yank a beer out of the fridge and twist the cap off. Taking a deep pull from the bottle, I make my way to the living area and sink onto the sofa, resting my head on the back of it. I stare at the ceiling as

I process all of this new information.

When I enrolled at UNCW, I knew I wanted to pursue a degree that would allow me to work with nonprofit organizations, so I could do my part in making the world a better place. Receiving this bogus eviction notice only fuels that desire. I hate giant corporations that prey on small or local businesses. They don't care who they hurt, as long as those zeros keep getting added to the end of their paycheck. Something needs to change. But for now, I need to figure out what the hell I'm going to do about finding a new place to live.

Acknowledgments

Wow…I don't even know where to begin. This book has been a labor of love. I started it several years ago but put it on the back burner when my second baby was born. In the chaos of having two kids, and life in general, it went unnoticed for far too long. I actually thought I'd lost the story until I found a lone USB flash drive hiding in the back of my desk drawer. There she was. As I started reading what I had so far, I fully expected to cringe and trash the whole thing. However, Norah and Eamon's story jumped right out at me and I knew I needed to tell it in its entirety.

I have a huge list of people that deserve recognition and gooey words of praise. Starting with my husband, my soul mate, my better half. I wouldn't be half the person I am without you. Even though you're not into "romance", you've encouraged me every step of the way, always picking up my slack when I ignored housework in favor of writing, and being the best dad our girls could ever have. You're the real MVP. I love you.

To my two amazing daughters - the sun and moon in my sky. I hope that when I was busy writing, you didn't think I was ignoring you. I hope that you saw your mommy stepping out of her comfort zone and working towards a dream. I hope that you always know how incredible you both are. You are brilliant, beautiful little woman who will change this world for the better. Don't let anyone tell you that you can't do something just because you're "a girl". You're whatever you want to be and I'll always have your backs. I'll always love you with all that I am.

To Jordan, my little sister, the inspiration for Layla. You've listened to me prattle on about my book for years now, giving me insight, or just nodding your head in agreement with whatever I said. You'll always be my person. Love you to the moon and back.

To Andi - you've taught me so much and have helped me be a better-informed human. You've listened to me and encouraged me. And you make my sister happy. Love you!

To Whittney, McKenzie, and Morgan - the driving forces behind Charlie, Amelia, and Myra. I love you bitches. More than words can say. Even when you're trying to convince me country music is enjoyable. I won't be swayed. Thank you for reading along as I wrote this book, and for giving me feedback and tips on writing spicy scenes. Thanks for all of the "research". Oh, and extra thanks to McKenzie for coming up with the name of the series as a whole. It's perfect.

To M.K. Franklin - my favorite writing buddy. I'm not sure if I can express just how much our Wednesdays mean to me. You're the friend I didn't know I was missing until you brought your Kindle out that one day during our kids' dance class. Now you're stuck with me.

To Allie - thank you for taking a chance on my book and scrutinizing it so closely! Honestly, you made His Ringsend Rose so much better and I'm not sure if I can ever really thank you enough. Your talents are beyond compare! Also, thank you for making me laugh! Your brand of humor is my favorite!

To Rachel - the best hype person to ever live. Your "sandwiches" are the best and I wish everyone was as patient and supportive as you. The world would be a far better place. Thank you for being another set of eyes and understanding my characters so well.

To my Alpha readers (and Eamon's Fan Club) - the first ones I shared my words with. It was the scariest thing I've ever done, letting you into this part of me. You gave me the encouragement and motivation to keep writing, even when I doubted my abilities.

To my Beta and ARC readers - my last line of defense. You made sure this book went out into the world in the best possible shape it could be in. Thank you, thank you, thank you!

To my mom and mother-in-law - thank you for telling me you can't wait to read my book even though we all know you probably won't because it's spicy. And I'm okay with that! But in all seriousness, where would any of us be without the love and support of a good mom? Thank you for all that you do and have done for us over the years. We love you.

To coffee - my lifeblood. Without you, nothing is possible.

www.ingramcontent.com/pod-product-compliance
Lightning Source LLC
Chambersburg PA
CBHW022033120726
47899CB00001BB/157